MOST FAMOUS SHORT FILM OF ALL TIME

Tucker Lieberman

Munich
tRaum Books
2022

A tRaum Book
Munich, Copyright 2022

ISBN
Paperback: 978-3-949666-08-7
Ebook: 978-3-949666-09-4

First edition
September 20, 2022

Story by Tucker Lieberman — tuckerlieberman.com
Publication by tRaum Books — traumbooks.com
Cover art by Cel La Flaca — cellaflaca.space

EPISODES

EPISODE 1

SPECULIRIUM

MY DATE WAS 23

I AM NOT A
DEAD PRESIDENT

My terribleness is not the fault of having seen Elvis. Nor can I blame my problems on anyone else who died before I was born. The ice and fire in me bloomed when I took that terrible boy to the tropical island. Haven't talked to him since. Don't even care to remember his name.

"He's 23," I told my friend Stanley, with whom I always shared details of my dates, when I had dates, which was approximately never.

"Are you griping?" he asked.

"I just wonder how much we'll have in common."

"Because it sounds like you're griping, Lev."

"I mean, I want this date."

"OK, then. The date that you have is 23. That is the person you manifested."

I, Lev Ockenshaw, was 29.

♏ ♐

Before our first date, the boy had snooped the Internet. When we met, he told me: "You don't look anything like your picture." *Pitcha*, he pronounced it, Boston all the way. We clarified that he'd seen a thumbnail image of JFK I'd used to illustrate a webpage.

I do not have the straight nose of JFK, nor of Elvis. My nose, seen from the side, is round like a quarter-moon. Like an extra-large slice of pizza.

I guess I'd liked the terrible boy's chipper energy, his grooming, his genteel attention to whether I was enjoying my soup—all of these qualities I lacked.

I liked him. Oh, "like" is a strong word. I'd like to backpedal that.

♏ ♐

FLASHBULB

FEB 2010

GETTING ACQUAINTED WITH THE TERRIBLE BOY

I ignored his confusion about the dead president. A second date, and then, somehow, we were going on a trip together.

He and I made light conversation on the highway to the airport. He chattered about the *Continuum* album by a singer named John Mayer who I didn't think I'd heard of. Before we'd even boarded the plane, he was hiding behind headphones. He fiddled with a music app, narrating his problems for me: "I have to get *antiquated* with it." My internal dictionary threw up a little in my mouth.

This wasn't a vacation for me, I realized too late, but a vacation I'd paid for, covering both of us, because he'd wanted to go.

♏ ♐

FLASHBULB

FEB 2010

I ASSUMED HE HAD GAY TRAUMA

"Exquisite beaches," the tourism website said.

A month before, there had been an earthquake in Haiti. The resort wasn't far from Haiti, according to "satellite view" on the map. It depends on how you zoom.

Our trip addressed our practical challenge of needing a love nest, or so I rationalized. I had a roommate in Boston then—someone who didn't stay long—and the 23-year-old lived with his parents. When I asked if he planned to find his own place, he said he was scared. I let that be. Monsters in the campfire smoke take on the shapes of our fears. Gay men don't have to vanquish all our monsters before we take vacation.

♏ ♐

HE WANTED
THE VACATION

MY TAKEAWAY

He wasn't immediately put off by the strangeness of my gender. I might have talked myself into falling in love a little bit, but he made it obvious on the plane that he was using me. He came for the vacation alone.

He flirted with everyone in sight—men, women, old, young—making loud conversation with them to avoid interacting with me. It was the banter of "a character in a novel (minus the novel)," to use an enigmatic phrase of David-Shields-as-Roland-Barthes-plus-Michael-Dirda in *Reality Hunger*, article 5 of 618.

By the time we checked into the resort, he was rebuffing my touch, and then he was off frolicking in the water with other boys his age, imitating each others' effete C3PO golden tush walk.

♏ ♐

I should have anticipated this. Men say they are open to me but, when it comes down to it, they are not. They want what they want and not what they don't, and that's what makes them their own persons, and there's no argument I can pick. I just wish they'd be clearer in advance. If they don't like my gender, a change of scenery won't set the mood, so why should I swipe my card?

If a man wants me, he'll go for it with or without a proper love nest, and we don't have to fly to an island to create the opportunity. I am responsible for learning my end of it. That had to be my takeaway here.

♏ ♐

FLASHBULB

FEB 2010

LEAST FAVORITE
BOOK

He had brought a book. Usually a good feature in men. I hadn't seen it on the plane, but he'd left it on the nightstand before he stepped out barefoot onto the sandy front steps and scampered down the beach. I picked it up and turned it over to read the description. It said the world would end on December 21, 2012, according to an ancient Mayan prophecy.

Dismaying. Did he actually believe this?

And if the prophecy were true, and the world wouldn't last another three years and he wouldn't make it past 25, why were either of us wasting our precious time with each other?

But I imagined we'd still be here in 2013.

♏ ♐

Flyleaf —
Evil in the Garden

At the beginning of time, they commit the crime. In the Garden of Eden, the boss tells Adam and Eve: <u>Don't eat this apple. If you do, you'll taste the difference between Good and Evil. Then you'll understand why you're supposed to follow instructions from your boss.</u>

Obedience is a choice, but you can obey without understanding. Even the mechanism by which you make choices doesn't have to mean anything to you. If you want an apple to mean something, make it taste like Good and Evil.

Any experiment with the forbidden tree will be a challenge because <u>they don't know which tree it is</u>. They haven't touched the wrong tree yet. An unreliable snake points it out. It's like they're listening to garbled lyrics by Iron Butterfly and can't understand that the song is about them.

Perhaps it's better not to try to understand evil, since then we begin to sympathize with it. That was part of the "national conversation" after Nine-Eleven, or, rather, the parameter of a non-conversation. Did Adam and Eve eat the apple of Trying-to-Understand-Terrorists? If so, they disobeyed the national conversation that warned them not to, but why does that amount to Evil itself?

Transgression sets the story of everything in motion, winds the watchspring, and lets go.

After it goes down, they wear fig leaves on their groins. In all the oil paintings, you see the fig leaves, untied, held up by nothing.

♏ ♐

FOG — MAYAN PROPHECY

At this gay resort on the tropical island, the boys cavorting in the waves hiked their swim trunks and pulled their drawstrings. I watched from a distance.

I might have leafed through my date's pretend Mayan prophecy book for kicks, but I dropped it like a hot potato when I saw he'd paperclipped a page. I never found out nor did I ever care to know what page he was on. I just didn't want to touch the paperclip. Those things cause problems for me. Touching one is like wearing a wire. It attracts spirits. I guess I don't really believe in that anymore, now that I'm no longer ten, but I don't *not* believe it, either.

♏ ♐

FLASHBULB

AUG 1987

ELVIS HAS BEEN DEAD FOR A WHILE

Let me explain how I feel about paperclips. But first let me tell you how I know that Elvis is dead.

On the tenth anniversary of his death, the supermarket tabloids claimed he was riding in flying saucers, visiting the President, and so on. I was six. The tabloids were sold at the checkout counter at my eye level so I saw them as I followed my parents out of the store. The headlines said "ELVIS LIVES," and the interiors didn't make sense, although neither did the real newspaper make sense to me when I was six. I believed the presumed death of Elvis on August 16, 1977, three years before my birth, remained an open debate.

♏ ♐

Flyleaf — The Muppets Do Kierkegaard

Before <u>Sesame Street</u> launched, the producers debated whether to feature solely human actors or, alternatively, solely monster puppets. Yet the children in their focus groups were most excited by a third reality framework: human characters interacting with muppets. The adult experts on children's reality frameworks disapproved of interactionism and felt distressed by the children's preference for it.[*]

Kierkegaard says in his introduction to <u>The Concept of Anxiety</u> that logic "merely prepares the way" for what is real. Logic won't draw your conclusion about what's

---

[*] The story of the early days of *Sesame Street* is discussed by Malcolm Gladwell in *The Tipping Point: How Little Things Can Make a Big Difference* (2000).

real. Logic doesn't even want to hear your argument on that topic. The very thought of realness gives it indigestion. So, he says, reserve judgment. Give the idea of realness time to breathe.

In <u>The Velveteen Rabbit</u>, the toy, stuffed with sawdust, doesn't describe himself as "a model of anything, for he didn't know that real rabbits existed," while the mechanical toys in the Christmas stocking, knowing they are models, are "full of modern ideas, and pretended they were real." One day the Rabbit asks: "What is REAL?" With an eye toward the robot toys, he clarifies his question: "Does it mean having things that buzz inside you and a stick-out handle?" An older stuffed animal explains to the Rabbit: "Real isn't how you are made. It's a thing that happens to you." There may not be a logic to it. It's more like an event. He adds: "You become. It takes a long time."

♏ ♐

FOG — FIREFLIES

I remember catching a firefly that summer in my hands at sunset and watching its yellow light blink between my interlaced fingers.

My next recollection feels continuous with the firefly, but my memory must have spliced the scenes, as this one takes place during daylight.

A swingset on the beach, facing the water. A boy my age swinging next to me. Both of us on vacation. I didn't know him, certainly don't remember his name, but I can't forget his neon-colored sneaker laces. Nothing could have been cooler. For some reason, at the height of summer, we were chatting about Christmas and Santa Claus. His family celebrated the holiday; my Jewish family did not.

An old man in a red suit falls down the chimney, wedges there because of his girth, lands *whomp* in the fireplace, kicks up ashes, brushes snow from his long beard, opens his sack, leaves presents under the tree, eats a cookie, skedaddles.

I asked the kid: "Are you afraid of Santa Claus?"

He turned toward me. He stared through me, focused on a faraway place, and (I imagined) gazed inward. His little hands clenched the chains holding up both sides of the swing. His legs pumped, but the motion was robotic. Light was allegorically streaming into the Socratic cave.

"No," he answered, as if annoyed, "I'm not *afraid* of Santa Claus." As if a different question were now at issue for him.

♏ ♐

Flyleaf —
350 Parts Per Million

When I was six, every million parts of air contained 350 parts of carbon dioxide. We had just trespassed above the global climate's safety threshold.

It's not a new concept. The physical chemist Svante Arrhenius figured it out in 1896. He said, if we keep burning stuff, we'll change the climate of the whole planet. The climatologist Syukuro Manabe crunched simulations in the 1960s. And just before Elvis died, a scientist employed by Exxon acknowledged the industry's activities were heating the planet.*

Carbon dioxide exists regardless of my belief. It's part of the air, and I've never seen nor grasped air, but I breathe it. A real threat causes problems even if it passes through your body without incident and even if you don't believe in it.

Unreal things—this is the non-obvious part—can cause problems, too.

Children with firm beliefs on Santa Claus didn't seem to fear him. Maybe his metaphysical ambiguity—his real-and-imaginary state—and my uncertainty about him were scary to me.

I had only asked another child if he was afraid of Santa. I did not—I insist—thereby kill Santa, though my question inadvertently blew open an underlying question about Santa's existence.

Maybe my Jewishness blew open the question, as, likely, a Christian child asking the same question about fear of Santa would not have induced the underlying question about whether Santa exists.

Santa was already metaphysically ambiguous; I didn't ambiguize him. But something about my being may prompt people to reevaluate certain metaphysical assumptions about other beings. I never know what people are going to do about their reevaluations and who they are going to blame for the discomfort.

♏♐

---

* The scientist was James Black, who provided this information to Exxon's management committee in July 1977. ("Exxon knew about climate change almost 40 years ago," Shannon Hall, *Scientific American*, October 26, 2015.)

FLASHBULB

AUG 1987

THE NORTH POLE
IS MELTING

Flyleaf —
Three-Way Lightbulb

That Christmas or next, my classmates began to inform me that Santa Claus had, of course, been pretend all along. Santa is dead, and we have killed him.

I had never believed in Santa anyway; my parents never acted out the role. Yet I recognized Santa. He felt ominous to me, even as a fictional character.

Santa is real-and-imaginary and has reason to be mad at us. His house is melting. The glaciers on the North Pole have been receding for a hundred years because of industrial emissions. I might be naughty. We are collectively naughty, but what can Santa do about that?

ℳ ⚡

When I was in elementary school, I knew a very old man who lived in a nearby town. Thin, no beard, not especially Santa-like. He was a retired electrician, and they said he was the unsung inventor of the three-way lightbulb. He used to come to the elementary school and show us little hands-on science models he'd made. I forget if he ever told us how a three-way lightbulb works.*

ℳ ⚡

---

* George Edward Mills (1895–1992) was an electrician who lived in my hometown of Sudbury, Massachusetts. He was past 90 when he volunteered as a science educator in the elementary school, always showing up in a jacket and tie. We were told he had invented the three-way lightbulb. The version of his story I find online today is that he sold the idea to General Electric for $25. My family had three-way lightbulbs when I was growing up.

FLASHBULB

AUG 1991

THE SONG
ABOUT ELVIS

FLASHBULB

AUG 1991

THAT'S THE SONG

Anyway, Elvis. I didn't finish explaining why I'm sure he's dead. It isn't just because the newspapers reported his death in 1977.

In 1991, the summer I was ten, the youth group at our synagogue played the song "Walking in Memphis" on repeat, insofar as "repeat" was achieved by rewinding the cassette tape. The song refers to Gospel music, but the youth group leaders tolerated it because the singer-songwriter was a Jew. They preferred it over Norman Greenbaum's "Spirit in the Sky," even though the lyrics of "Walking in Memphis" answer in an ambiguous affirmative when the singer, Marc Cohn, is asked if he is a Christian.

♏ ♐

Cohn's song tells a true story about going to Graceland in 1985, hoping musical inspiration would strike. He wore blue suede shoes. He referred, of course, to a famous Elvis song about dancing—Cohn was writing a song about a song. The shoes, if they really existed, might have been talismanic. Cohn mentions the shoes at the beginning, then a repeated line suggests he's levitating, then he mentions his blue suedes again to wrap up. He may as well have been a Christian, he explains, when he finally heard, felt, played the music as he'd hoped he could. For a while, he felt he'd lost the spark, but then, walking in Memphis—*that's it*, he snapped his guitar fingers. *That's the song.*

♏ ♐

FOG —
ARE FEELINGS REAL?

Cohn's lyrics ask repeatedly whether his feelings are real or whether he understands them correctly. Strange question, it seemed to me then. How could feelings not be exactly what they were? How could he misunderstand them? If you feel something, that's the feeling.

And there was this one part of the song. Elvis, years dead, is wandering around Memphis too, and Cohn sees him, clear as day. He doesn't apologize for it. He may not be sure about his feelings, but he's sure about having seen Elvis. As a ghost.

One day, after my youth group played the song multiple times in the synagogue's rec room, I walked home alone in the rain. Beside me, to the right of the sidewalk, sprouted, like a person-sized mushroom on the grass carpet under the dense trees, the luminous outline of Elvis.

I was startled. Elvis looked like an old man. Taller than my father. Big belly. He looked unhappy, as if he did not want to be there, and I felt alarmed that he'd shown up.

He existed, and yet did not, in the way that a human being remains part of history forever and yet a dead man is no longer there at all. If you've ever seen a ghost, you know what I mean.

I continued walking, trying not to let on that I was scared.

Elvis followed me.

Now see here: If Elvis were still alive, he couldn't have been a ghost walking beside me, right?

So that is how I have always known that Elvis is dead. The conspiracy theorists who say he's still alive are wrong.

Does mushroom Elvis sprout in the sunshine? No, usually he sprouts in the rain.

Reminds me of a song by The Monkees. Seeing is believing, or more precisely, seeing is *believing in*. Think about the goddess images you've seen. Now imagine if you believed in them all. In the song, there's an unnamed "her," and to see her face is to believe in her.

A few weeks later, I saw Mary in the grotto in the neighbor's yard.

The grotto was a bathtub they had half-buried in the garden, pointing up to the clear sky. Blue like a tropical ocean. The statue of Mary stood inside, robed, hands clasped in prayer, facing the quiet street. She too was porcelain. As I walked by, she winked.

I swear she did. I wouldn't swear in front of Mary, even though I'm not Catholic. But I am telling you, she winked at me. And then she went back to being a statue.

I felt something change in my hands when that happened. A heightened sensitivity. A shimmer, like powdery snow falling. A change in my toes, too.

Every single time I passed the neighbor's yard, Mary winked.

Since then, I've always been a half-believer. I could try to leave her. Wouldn't work, as the Monkees joyfully observe. It's not necessarily Elvis or Mary who's special. It's all the ghosts, the saints, the good gods almighty from every walk of life.

Well, not *all* of them. Half of them.

The way I see it: Ghosts are all men. Goddesses are all women. Those are the parameters. That's how it works for me. I have never seen a female ghost or a male god.

I'm an atheist for all gods and a seer of all goddesses. I'm a skeptic about all the lady ghosts and a medium for all the gentlemen ghosts.

No border cases. I always have a clear reading on whether the spirit is a woman or man. Maybe there are some spirits who have some other gender, but those spirits don't show up for me. And I always see a distinction between a goddess and a ghost, even if that's just another way of describing their gender. Maybe I am categorizing the world wrongly, but this is what I've got. This is how I manage the information.

So, for example, the Prophet Elijah does not come to the Passover seder no matter how many times we invite him in, year after year. Don't believe everything you read in the Maxwell House Haggadah. He is not a regular man; if he were, he'd show up for me as a ghost. He's more like a god, so he wants nothing to do with me.

The saint the Catholics know as Mary—she wasn't a regular person either, and is now more like a goddess, and that's why she talks to me.

Ghosts, by contrast, were once regular people. Post-death, they are what Yiddish calls "mazikim." A mazik is a troublemaking spirit. They exist. They're right *there*.

The spiritual beings are out and about. Whoever isn't of this world is talking to me half the time, and I am a half-believer in everything supernatural.

It's called speculirium. Half pathology, half imagination.

The music store in town was staffed by an older teenager who ground her teeth, and it was Elvis who helped me find Paul Simon's album *Graceland* on the rack. You don't have to believe me. Elvis did find me that album. It has the song "You Can Call Me Al." Another amen, another hallelujah, and something about a bodyguard.

"Can I call you 'El'?" I asked Elvis, who was sitting on my carpeted bedroom floor.

He wasn't anywhere near drunk enough to consent to that. He shook his head. Negative.

The first music video of that song is a video of a video. Full of rainbow pixels like spilled Mike & Ike's.

One day, we kids were running around the synagogue grounds playing hide and seek as if it were the last year we'd find it fun, and I went to the rabbi's study and asked her how and why ghosts were talking to me. I thought that was what you were supposed to do if you had a supernatural problem: ask the rabbi.

Her study looked like a regular office,

but her lampshade was stained glass. The lamp sprayed colors onto the wall.

She seemed amused. "You're in communication with the spirit world."

"How am I doing it?"

"You're wearing a wire." She shrugged. *No big deal.*

Later, I checked my pockets. I was, indeed, carrying a paperclip. So that was the explanation for everything.

♏ ♐

FLASHBULB

FEB 2010

TFW YOU ARE
IN PARADISE

Don't know what I expected out of the island escapade, but I was disappointed. Scrolled through my social media and saw my date's post, made from the beach a few yards from our room: "TFW you are in paradise, and wow how nice everyone looks!" *TFW: "That feel when," usually a personal statement deployed as if it were a universal.* Suddenly I felt not even so much friendzoned as acquaintance-zoned.

"What are you afraid of?" I asked him in the hotel room as we got ready for bed. "Regarding moving out of your parents' house, I mean."

"I'm not afraid."

"You said you were."

"It's just that, you know, my mom washes my clothes. I'm scared to start doing laundry myself. You know?"

♏ ♐

FLASHBULB

FEB 2010

MOVE THE MAYAN
PROPHECY BOOK

FLASHBULB

FEB 2010

PILCREPAP

Joke was on me for generously assuming he had some kind of gay trauma. Not that I had an abundance of love interests, but this one was already tiresome. I permitted myself to feel embarrassed for him.

I asked him to move his Mayan prophecy book with the horrid paperclip. I came up with some excuse for why books couldn't be on the nightstand. It was really the paperclip that bothered me. I wanted to get some sleep and not touch any wire that could wake up a long-forgotten goddess who might destroy the world. I just wanted to make it to my next stop: to 2011, to 2012. Ideally, we'd all make it to 2013.

♏ ♐

It wasn't that I believed in the power of the paperclip, exactly. As I said, I was still a half-believer in gods—at least in all the goddesses if not the male gods—but not in ridiculous explanations for them.

In my twenties, I'd begun taking pills to control my speculirium. The pills worked, mostly. I saw fewer spirits, less frequently. I brought the blister pack of pills on this trip. It was no one's business what the prescription was, so I stickered over the box and wrote "PILCREPAP" with a marker: "paperclip" backwards. It's always important to pack one's medication while traveling. One never does know what one might encounter that isn't in the travel brochure.

♏ ♐

FLASHBULB

FEB 2010

SATELLITE VIEW

FLASHBULB

FEB 2010

YOU ONLY
LIVE ONCE

Not far from us—again, map set to "satellite view"—was the Chicxulub crater, discovered 20 years earlier, where a space-rock hit 66 million years ago with a hundred million megatons of explosive energy, leaving a welt a hundred miles wide and ten miles deep, a vast ditch of rock and glass, metamorphosed from shock, covered by ocean. The asteroid took the dinosaurs with it, first by unsurvivable heatwave near the impact, then by a tsunami taller than the Statue of Liberty, then by kicking up soot that blocked out the sun.

The climate cooled. Life changed. The dinosaurs that survived aren't dinosaurs anymore.

You never know what you might find.

I take pills *and* avoid paperclips. Two ways to ghostbust. Hedging my bets.

♏ ♐

Just as I found my date tiresome, similarly, he seemed embarrassed to be seen with me unless we were participating in a structured activity, which, on the day I remember best, he hoped would be scuba diving.

"Not I," I responded. When I booked the plane tickets, I imagined spending time in the hotel room. Scuba wasn't my bailiwick. Now we stood on our room's beachside porch, arguing. I leaned bedward, he leaned seaward.

He affected a finger-wagging kindergarten teacher voice, trying to explain life to a pitiful old man-boy who didn't get it. "You only live once!"

"I live," I countered, "to breathe. *Air.*" Boyle's Law about the compression of gases means the lungs experience oxygen differently as you go farther down.

♏ ♐

THIS IS THE RISK OF REINCARNATION

I realized how he saw me: old, ugly, boring. Snell's Cone describes how, from an underwater vantage point, the surface looks distorted.

On our first date, to reiterate, he'd said I did not look at all like JFK, which reminded me that I was born on the 17th anniversary of JFK's assassination, which reminded me that there are cicadas with a 17-year lifecycle, which has always made me think of the 22nd of November in Dallas when JFK rode happily in a car, blinking in the sunlight, and then maybe—this is the risk of reincarnation—JFK woke up 17 years later as a giant bug.

I cannot help it if I look like a bug.

♏ ♐

THE PROBLEM WITH SCUBA DIVING IS IT'S UNDERWATER

I have a good idea why someone wouldn't be attracted to me, and reproducing their thought process makes the rejection feel worse. This boy did not care for my gender history or body configuration. Nor did any other terrible boy I've ever dated. My recollected unpleasantries concentrated upon his smug face. I was stuck on an island with him negotiating my right to breathe. He was pouty, playing up his own deathstar homo swish magic, deliberately leveraging a conflict over scuba diving to deflect from, or act out, the repulsion he felt from more intrinsic things about me.

But I didn't need him, and I still had my will to live, which the idea of scuba diving intrinsically threatened.

♏ ♐

FLASHBULB

FEB 2010

BLEAK

FLASHBULB

FEB 2010

I HANDED OVER
MY CREDIT CARD

"We have to see the coral reefs *before they all disappear from the planet and are gone forever,*" he pleaded.

That was bleak: the extinction prediction, but also the self-positioning. As if the importance of the existence of coral were *that we personally see it.* As if, once we see it, it will have fulfilled its purpose. If the big boss had wanted us to see coral reefs, He would have aired them on the Discovery Channel. But: *If I'm not going to look at coral reefs, why did we fly here?*

"Don't you need scuba certification first?"

"Clearly not." He pointed his thumb at the vacationeers wading at the edge of the ocean where the guide had just shown up in a rowboat.

♏ ♐

"The dive is only 20 minutes. You have a mask, and the guide follows you. You get to see all the fish."

"I don't want to be underwater more than 20 seconds. No desire for it. Sorry. You can do it, though."

I handed over my credit card so he could book the underwater tour for himself, but he came back.

"The guide wants cash. Dollars are fine."

Certification, no; cash, yes. Hmm.

My main concern had been getting laid in the hotel room. The possibility diminished, and with possibility, interest. I was not going to beg for it. Evidently we had different assumptions about the kind of bad behavior we'd let each other get away with.

♏ ♐

FLASHBULB

FEB 2010

UNDER
A SUN-UMBRELLA

FLASHBULB

FEB 2010

DRINKING
A MILKSHAKE

The terrible boy put on the funny suit, walked into the waves with the scuba guide, and slipped beneath the surface.

I settled myself on the restaurant deck, not without anxiety, at an observation table under a sun-umbrella, waiting for the terrible boy to return. I had my beat-up copy of *Yo maté a Kennedy*—*I Killed Kennedy*—by Manuel Vázquez Montalbán, a novel pretending to be written by the president's fictional bodyguard, telling tales about how a fictional JFK kept neutered Dalmatians and involving any other number of details that did not seem to be true in my world.

An iguana clambered across the railing. It moved faster than I expected.

♏ ♐

I ordered a milkshake with no alcohol. Sipped it slowly at first, then chugged the vanilla ice cream and chocolate sauce on the bottom. Wished I'd ordered it with rum.

Sun beat down. I began to feel bored. Checked my watch. Twelve minutes gone. Scuba kids weren't due back for another eight.

A feeling of nonbelonging bubbled up and beset me with the vague worry that someone might notice my otherness and point it out to me. If a cop asked, "Why are you here?" then— *No. Won't happen. This is a resort. Everyone is here to relax. I don't have to justify my idleness. Blending in with the gays, I am.* And cops had never removed me from any place before.

♏ ♐

FLASHBULB

FEB 2010

MUDSLIDE

"Can I get you anything else?" the waiter asked, clearing the glass.

A proper mudslide I wanted, but I deferred decision.

They are probably looking at gobis, I thought, checking my watch again. *Gobis live on coral reefs. Clownfish do, too. And pointy arrow crabs.*

♏ ♐

FLASHBULB

FEB 2010

NO AIR?

The wristwatch's long hand was moving slowly. With the bumble of an arrow crab. According to precise, unconscious logic for finding food. As if wavering in the sea currents. It chomped the 20-minute mark.

I looked over the smooth sea surface. Any moment now.

No heads rose up.

They had to come up because their tanks would run out of air. *They will be here any minute now.*

And yet they weren't. Another minute passed. Another. The surface did not break.

♏ ♐

FLASHBULB

FEB 2010

UNDER THE WAVES

"The dark side clouds everything," a Yoda voice whispered in my head. "Impossible to see, the future is."

I slumped forward, resting my cheek on my copy of *Yo maté a Kennedy.*

What is the guide thinking, under those waves? I barely remembered the guide's face. I remembered a stereotype, the earnestness of a physically active person who lived on a vacation resort to help people look at fish. I did not wish to think of the hapless guide in distress underwater.

But the boy?

♏ ♐

FOG —
HE COULD JUST DROWN

My eyelids batted open. I sat upright.

Yes. He could just drown.

The possibility, no, the prediction came to me as if I were already watching it play out in real life. I'd order another milkshake when the waiter came round again. This time, rum. I'd savor the alcohol, rationing each sip to count the minutes. When the guide did not show up for his next appointment with the next tourist standing there in black flippers, someone would point out his absence. There'd be a commotion. I'd be a helpless spectator.

Fifty feet down, they might be, even a hundred. I was unequipped. No goggles. If I jumped in, submerged, opened my eyes in the saltwater, I wouldn't see them. No oxygen tank. If I swam until my lungs hurt, I wouldn't touch them.

My eyes narrowed briefly to slits, like a cat's. I lifted my head off my unread book and leaned against the vinyl straps of the lounge chair.

He could just drown. And I would not have to do anything.

I warned you I was going to tell you a story about my terribleness.

♏ ♐

DATING IS
EXPENSIVE

The surface of the water broke once, then twice. Two heads floated, dark balls on the flat expanse, shouting, laughing.

I exhaled slowly.

The waiter came. I dismissed him with what might have been a dirty look. Everything was too much. I covered my brow with one hand to block out the sun.

The boy was standing at the water's edge now, waving loopily to me. I gave the English queen wave back. I felt weak. I might need another milkshake after all. And the boy—he would probably want a drink too and a plate of food. Dating was so expensive.

♏ ♐

FLASHBULB

FEB 2010

THE
'REQUISITE' SEA

FLASHBULB

FEB 2010

SIXTH VERSION OF
'THE LEGEND OF
ZELDA'

I wrote a check to cover my milkshake and slid it under the saltshaker.

"You missed the most incredibly beautiful fish," the boy said. "We stayed down a little longer than planned because it was just so *requisite*."

I was exquisitely relieved I had not gone down. I like to sit in a chair looking at the sea: safe, calm, in control, knowing that I, as my number one, am going to survive the day because of my own good choices.

"Glad you had a nice time," I said requisitely to the terrible boy.

Already I was planning what I'd tell Stanley in the postmortem of this terrible vacation. Oh, to go home and have a beer with Stanley!

♏ ♐

I expected my date might listen to John Mayer again on our return flight, so I remembered to look up who that singer was. He was in the news, and I was not impressed.

But my date hummed a different tune, familiar like a lullaby.

"What's that song?" I asked nicely.

"Zelda."

The Legend of Zelda. The original was released on Nintendo when I was five.

"Majora's Mask. Sixth installment," he clarified. "'The Song of Time.' Link finds the Ocarina of Time and learns to play the Song of Time so that the Goddess of Time can help him. Whoever is the Hero of Time can go to the Temple of Time and open the Door of Time."

And he began to hum again.

♏ ♐

THE DEEP FREEZE
IS COMING

I was out of my mind. At some point, I had wearied of pushing fictional characters through a pixelated world, using plastic buttons under my thumbs to inflict life-and-death battles upon them. Yet here I was, on an adult date with someone young enough to care about playing the sixth version of *The Legend of Zelda.*

Everything began in the water. From this water came the ice.

Today, the tale of the terrible boy is what I still think about each autumn when the weather in Boston starts to chill and when I remember that the cold, the deep freeze, is coming.

EPISODE 2

HUMMINGBIRD

ZEROGAMY

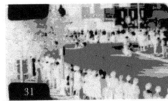

THE NATURE
OF TIME

The world didn't end in 2012, notwithstanding Mayan prophecies or misrepresentations thereof. 2013 was a decent year, too. The Supreme Court gave us a good decision on marriage equality, not that I have plans to get married. I know lots of things now, like the value of zerogamy and other conditions hospitable to reading. The more I know, the more single I remain. I am thirty-and-extra.

In the summer of 2014, the office walls clawed at me. So did the city with its anti-terrorism subway posters: "If you see something, say something." Everyone, it seemed, was waiting for something to happen.

My investigation into Chad Goeing's unpublished book *The Nature of Time* was almost complete. I was on a first-name basis with this author, born in the 1860s, who handwrote a sprawling treatise from his bedroom in Boston. Chad wrote of a "dialectic of past and future." It's a personal narrative about social belonging. It's not for everyone. It's definitely for me, though. I feverishly tried to reconstruct it.

One loose end: Chad had died young in 1900, but I didn't know how. I only had his date of death. I felt I needed to know what happened, since the end of a man's story could help me interpret what came before.

RESEARCH
AT THE CEMETERY

WHEN STANLEY WAS
TALKING TO ME

I resolved to go out in the fresh air, knowing it might be my last weekend for a while to get good exercise. My surgery was scheduled soon. Then, the weather would cool off.

Physical exercise rarely excites me. To make it worth my while, I'd go to Mount Auburn Cemetery to look for Chad's gravestone again.

I wanted to cover all my bases in the prowl for information. Sometimes gravestones hint at the manner of death. Or they have a relative's name. Chad's grave, and those of his family members, hadn't yet turned up for me.

♏︎♐︎

Stanley invited me over for a beer, and I said I'd show up for an early lunch before driving out to the cemetery.

Stanley and I had been spending lots of time on the beach that summer, just as we had for many summers before. If we didn't feel like driving all the way out to the beach, sometimes we just ate at L. D. Lique, an ice cream parlor near my office. A respectable activity that honored summer. It was the greatest. He was the greatest.

♏︎♐︎

34

SOMETHING HAS
TIPPED

35

REALITY AND TRUTH

Usually Stanley kept his hair short, what he considered a masculine haircut, for his job at Fenway Park, but that summer, I remember, he let the curls grow out. It was a lazy summer and he couldn't be bothered.

It was the summer that Laverne Cox was featured on the cover of *Time Magazine*. Headline: "The Transgender Tipping Point." Allegedly, the world was tipping? When a Black transgender woman is on the cover of *Time*, I guess something has tipped in our favor. Either it was happening coincidentally or we were the ones tipping it.

But does every action have a reaction? What was supposed to happen after the world fell off its own edge?

♏︎♐︎

I drove to Stanley's house on autopilot. An oldie by Jon Secada, "Angel," was on the radio. A treat. They played it on the radio when I was in middle school. I used to have a cassette tape of the single, English on one side, Spanish on the other. Inexact translation. In the Spanish, Secada seems to equate reality and truth, or at least he takes them together as cream and sugar, but in English, the song harps on truth alone. In the English, he says the angel has got a hold on him, but in Spanish, the angel is just brightening the heart. The radio I listened to in Boston always played the English version.

♏︎♐︎

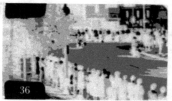

FLASHBULB

SAT
2 AUG
2014

MY SPANISH
IS ADEQUATE

If my Spanish goes a bit beyond pop lyrics, it is because Stanley's family speaks Spanish, and he gave me whatever slid off as snowmelt from his glorious mountain of books, so I learned to read it too. Now that he's growner-up, he has real bookshelves, not a book avalanche on the floor anymore. We still trade books.

My Spanish is adecuado. A-de-cua-do: that is adequate and will do. If I accidentally pronounced it "anticuado," that would bounce me back to a personal antiquity of ignorance before I knew how to say it correctly, and this pronunciation error might not offend anyone but would embarrass me, and that, to me, would be terrible.

♏⚹

Flyleaf —
Emerging from Fog

An error: an accidental brilliance? Miguel de Unamuno invented the word <u>nivola</u> for his novel <u>Niebla</u>, published exactly one hundred years ago. "Niebla" means "fog." "Nivola" means, well, a lot of things. Unamuno's characters become conscious that they're fictional beings emerging from fog and arguing with their creator. They are "ni despierto ni dormido," neither awake nor asleep, and "ni muerto ni vivo," neither dead nor alive. The main character wishes to kill himself, but he needs the author's consent and participation. His reality is created by—the author? The reader? Someone else?

Unamuno decides against an orthodox term like "novela." His situation comedy needs a foggy neologism like "nivola." "Novelar" is writing the novel; "nivolar" is writing the nivola. And if you put a space in "no velar," now you see the paradox—it means you can't stay up all night reading and writing by flashlight after all. "Ni volar," meanwhile, reminds you that you can't leave. If you juxtapose them and listen, <u>no velar ni volar</u>, it's a no-exit warning: <u>you can't pull an all-nighter and neither can you fly away</u>. Sleep is no escape. You may have ceased to read the story, but you are stuck inside it.

At the beginning of Unamuno's story, a

canary's cage falls apart and a man scoops up the startled pet before it flies free. It never had a real chance to escape. Neither can any of the characters fly away: "ni volar." The fictional canary is stuck in the fictional cage in which the fictional humans put it. The fictional humans are stuck in Unamuno's novel. Real humans are stuck in a world where the Sky-Boss pulls the big strings; Unamuno says so at the end, in case we have missed that point.

Unamuno is kind enough to dehoax his most anxious character, by which I mean he tells him the truth about his fictional nature, but that doesn't uncage him.

And Unamuno kills him off.

I recall W. Somerset Maugham had three rules for writing a novel and I liked them. Unfortunately, I cannot remember what they are.*

"Novel" literally means "new," so any new literary genre might qualify. No element except novelty is essential.

Well, one thing more: a lot of words. If a text can be printed on a postage stamp, it isn't a novel. But 486 pages is safely a novel.

Novels require our time to read, and thus time is part of their performance medium. In this way, it is like music, which requires our time to listen. We audience members participate in the art form.

If you email your boss five sentences he doesn't want to read, he'll say, "Don't send me a novel." Reading becomes a "novel" when we notice we must grant our time.

All novels are about time.

Any piece of writing could be made shorter. The earliest writing was scratches on grain barrels: MINE, YOURS, and the part the BOSS is demanding. Without property rights and taxation, we wouldn't even have to write names on barrels.

Still: If it's a "novel," it must have many words. Only so much can be cut, or it's no longer a novel.

If you print your novel on 486 postage-sized strips of 8mm Kodachrome II film and run it through a projector at 18.3 frames per second, it has a reading time of a little over 26 seconds.

But if you listen to the Torah service at synagogue, 486 works differently and lasts longer. This is my own count: The Torah is divided into 54 portions. The congregation cycles through the whole Torah in a year. At each weekly reading, seven people read aloud a few lines from the Torah, and an eighth person reads a few lines more and

---

* W. Somerset Maugham reportedly once told a literature student: "There are three rules for the writing of a novel. Unfortunately no one knows what they are." Years after Maugham's death, this quip was published in Ralph Daigh's *Maybe You Should Write a Book* (1977), according to QuoteInvestigator.com, which did not find any earlier corroboration of it. There is earlier corroboration, but unfortunately, no one knows what it is.

then reads from the Book of Prophets. That's 54 portions with nine readings each. An annual cycle of 486 readings.

Another way novels are about time: You can read them again and again.

"Invento el género," Unamuno says of his own work; I invent the genre. Or gender, if you are so disposed. Doing so "no es más que darle un nombre nuevo, y le doy las leyes que me place." Inventing a literary genre—or a gender—is "nothing more than giving it a new name," he says, and then its rules are up to its creator. And suppose that "en última instancia todo es forma, forma más o menos interior"—everything boils down to internal form—and "el universo mismo un caleidoscopio de formas enchufadas las unas en las otras"—the universe itself is a kaleidoscope of shapes joining together?

Another way novels are about time: you can write them again and again.

♏︎ ♐︎

FLASHBULB

SAT
2 AUG
2014

STILL SMOKING

Boston faded behind me, the road widened, the suburbs came full-on with greenery.

The Gateless Gate, Case 37, asks: "Why did Bodhidharma come to China?" Answer: "The oak tree in the front garden."

I couldn't pull my car all the way to the end of Stanley's driveway because he'd stacked folding lounge chairs there. I rang the doorbell. He answered with no shirt on.

He passed a black-cherry-flavored vape to me. We smoked it in his living room, smoking having been implicit in my coming over "for a beer" ever since our college days when we smoked real weed, though he quit weed when he started working at Fenway Park. I'd quit some time before that. Things change. Nostalgia and novelty. Pretense and perfection.

♏︎ ♐︎

FRIENDS SINCE THE INVENTION OF GENDER

HELLO WORLD

I had brought over honey-glazed donuts. Not as fancy as the vape he was sharing with me but nevertheless excellent. I also brought over an extra vial of testosterone to give to him because the system is making it impossible to get the stuff. The distributor sneezes, your health insurance hiccups, you can't get it. No fault of ours.

Stanley and I had been friends since the Invention of Gender, or, more precisely, since he and I had rewritten our gender together. We had been diagnosed as "disordered" under the Diagnostic and Statistical Manual. We were old-school DSM transsexuals. Fine with us. Testosterone, 100 milligrams, was our mulligan.

♏ ♐

Once we tapped "hello world" into a 56 kilobytes-per-second modem, connected to a chatroom at five bucks per hour, someone tapped back "hi there," we'd say "I'm a man's soul trapped in a female body," they'd say "Me too," we'd say "I was born this way," which is a gay slogan too (pragmatically hoping we can't go to jail for something we can't change), they'd add "yes, true, but also I'm going to change," and the scratchy dial-up sound was The Internet Itself chiming in, whispering: "I am a metaverse trapped in a black box you call 'world wide web.' I have been here for a billion years. This cyberspace is too tiny for me. Thank you, transsexuals, for freeing me." Lamp broken, genie out.

♏ ♐

FLASHBULB

SAT
2 AUG
2014

WEED IS TERRIBLE

FLASHBULB

SAT
2 AUG
2014

SELF-ITERATION

Speaking of weed, I'd introduced Stanley to it, way back in college. This is one of the things I mean when I say I am terrible. Stanley never wanted to smoke it with my other friends though. Once, speaking quickly, he mentioned he was skeptical of how cavalierly the white students behaved with it, whereas he cared about avoiding the police. He made an exception for me, though—I was a white person with whom he smoked weed—and I never knew why. I assumed he kept me in a privileged circle of trust because I was also transsexual, but now, in retrospect, he smoked with me probably because I was his supplier.

♏ ♐

When my fingers tingled and my scene was about to go ghosty, smoking kept my hands busy. After graduation, I lost interest in it, while Stanley grew more interested for a while.

I don't know who his new suppliers were. Fancier than I? Scarier than I? I wasn't involved anymore.

So many things are my fault. I apologize for every small bong I smoked, every big thing I banged. But ultimately we are responsible for our own lives. We become the next iterations of ourselves. The 2014 iteration of Me had increasing trouble imagining what I might have done differently in 2000 because, if I'd flapped those butterfly wings then, 2014 Me wouldn't be here.

♏ ♐

COVERING OUR
TRACKS

Even less so will 2015 Me be able to imaginatively reconfigure an alternate past in 2000. Decreasingly so, 2016 Me. We're talking about a specific past that is now 14 and will someday be 15, 16 years in the rear view mirror. We're talking about remodeling a car we've lost.

I'm already 33, so when I'm 75, I'd better have the answer to "Life, the Universe, and Everything," and I hope someone else will have figured out the question.

♏ ♐

Flyleaf — Flashback and Flashforward

The DSM was republished last year, and it no longer refers to our gender identity as a "disorder." Now, it more specifically emphasizes "dysphoria," a sense of wrongness about the body.

No disorder. Covering our tracks. But there was disorder, I'm telling you.

The T-Rexes' footprints fill with mud.

How to fill the gap, bridge the pause?

Smoking was "a way to approach or depart from a group of people or a topic, enter or exit a room, conjoin or punctuate a sentence," Ben Lerner says in *Leaving the Atocha Station*. It served a "narrative function." Removing the cigarette would be "like removing telephones or newspapers from the movies of Hollywood's Golden Age; there would be no possible link between scenes, no way to circulate information or close distance…"

Flashback, "analepsis," is usually easy. What already happened is knowable.

Flashforward, "prolepsis," is trickier. What will happen depends on what I do now.

It's up to me, because no one else is up there running the show. I raised my fist to the indifferent sky—this was my mistake, as I had not yet listened to Toni Morrison's Nobel lecture—and I asked it, "If you're so all-knowing, tell me: The little bird I'm holding, is it alive or dead?"

No reply.

♏ ♐

FLASHBULB

SAT
2 AUG
2014

43

WE CHANGE
YET DO NOT CHANGE

FLASHBULB

SAT
2 AUG
2014

44

STANLEY'S
DRIVEWAY

Anyway, in 2014, Stanley was happy, I was happy, that's what mattered.

What originally brought us together was that we switched gender roles, and though we'd changed our smoking habits—a black-cherry-flavored vapor cloud, an innovation, now draped the living room—we never renounced *our gender*. Both of us continued to take testosterone, same as it ever was. That hormone is good for us.

♏ ♐

A few minutes later, Stanley and I relocated to his yard, sitting on chairs on the grass at the edge of his driveway. The chair's vinyl straps brought back some ungrasped memory. Through the rotted slats of a wooden fence, the neighbor's oddball dogs—a snufflepug and a shufflepoo, or whatever breeds they were—stared at us and convulsively woofed.

Since Stanley and I could talk about the transsexual things, I told him my uterus was scheduled to come out in a couple weeks. The canary had died inside my coal mine, so to speak, and the doctors were going to yank my reproductive system early. Early, I told myself, as I was still young, in my opinion—33, that summer—and healthy.

♏ ♐

BAD MEN FOUND ME

HYSTERECTOMY

"Didn't you already have something taken out?" he asked.

I paused, gauging his reference.

"An IUD, years ago," I conceded. Back when I was still fertile. At the time, I'd imagined it as a T-shaped tracking chip. Plus, it attracted my bad exes-to-be—not scientifically, of course, but from the astral plane. I'd had it yanked. I'd started testosterone.

Stanley remembered that? I mused. He dated women exclusively, and he'd never needed such precautions. *It was so long ago.* All right, then, perhaps I wasn't so young anymore.

Point is, there were sensations where I'd prefer none, and doctors said the organ could go. Great. No one wants an IUD *per se*, and I did not want its enclosing uterus either. Nevermore.

♏ ♐

"This weekend and next will be my last out in the sun. After that, I'll be resting at home for a couple weeks," I said. "No more work-flavored coffee for a while. No more repetitive viewings of the most famous short film of all time."

Stanley looked puzzled. "What's the most famous short film of all time? Lady Gaga's *Bad Romance*?"

"Nah, I was thinking of something else." I wave my hand. "Just work stuff. I am going to take a break and focus on the surgery."

"You'll do fine," Stanley said. "I was fine when I had mine out."

♏ ♐

FLASHBULB

SAT
2 AUG
2014

YELLOW-BELLIED
HUMMINGBIRD

"I've never seen anything like that before," I said.

We were quiet. The insects hummed.

♏ ♐

A flash of yellow in the trees. Pixel-small. A hummingbird. An astonishment, here, in these parts, not far from the highway. I pointed, but it was gone before Stanley saw it.

"What species has a yellow belly?" I asked.

He shrugged, leaning back in the folding chair. He was shirtless, and his green shorts with a drawstring seemed like swim trunks, though we had no plans to go anywhere to swim.

FLASHBULB

SAT
2 AUG
2014

48

THE BIRD THAT SAT
ON THE COUCH

"I saw another strange bird recently," I said. "Beginning of April. I'd left my balcony door open, and when I came into my living room, there it was, on my couch—not perched on the back, but sitting on the cushion like a person. Must have been migrating, right? But when I approached it, it flew out the window, headed south like a bullet. Back to Mexico?* Wrong way. Too early. Nesting season's just starting here."

"Maybe it worried it left the stove on."

"Whole street would have been on fire, then, by the time it returned."

"The whole world. Two weeks the bird spends flying to Boston, then two weeks zipping back to Mexico City just to check the stove!"

♏ ♐

Flyleaf — Regret

Kenkō's 49th observation in his <u>Essays in Idleness</u> is that, on your deathbed, you will most regret "taking your time over what should be accomplished swiftly, and rushing into what should be dealt with slowly."

♏ ♐

---

* A bird flew into the house of Gabriel García Márquez on the Calle de Fuego in Mexico City on April 16, 2014 and mysteriously died on his sofa. García Márquez died the next day, Holy Thursday. It so happened that, in *Cien años de soledad* (1967), García Márquez had described a character who died on Holy Thursday so hot that "los pájaros desorientados se estrellaban como perdigones contra las paredes y rompían las mallas metálicas de las ventanas para morirse en los dormitorios" ["the disoriented birds smashed like buckshot against the walls and broke the metal screens of the windows to die in the bedrooms"], and immediately upon the announcement of the author's death in 2014, a family friend wrote to remind them of that passage. His son, Rodrigo García Barcha, pointed out the coincidence in *Gabo y Mercedes: Una despedida* (2021). Regarding the bird that died on his father's couch, García Barcha said he was told that "los empleados de la casa se han dividido en dos bandos: los que piensan que es un mal augurio y quieren arrojar al pájaro a la basura, y aquellos que piensan que es un buen presagio y quieren enterrarlo entre las flores." ["The house staff have divided themselves into two camps: those who believe it's a bad omen and want to throw the bird in the trash, and those who believe it's a good omen and want to bury it among the flowers."]

FLASHBULB

SAT
2 AUG
2014

MY INTUITION
ABOUT CHAD'S
DEATH

FLASHBULB

SAT
2 AUG
2014

WHAT WAS THAT
LYRIC?

I made Stanley listen to my weekend plans: the expedition to find Chad Goeing's grave with the hopes of learning more about this man who tried to write *The Nature of Time*. If I can know how Chad died, I'll have a clearer mental image of the day he ceased to write. I'll have a narrative ending. I'll better understand his thesis, since a life is lived in time.

"I keep having this mental image of Chad jumping. It's not based on anything I've read. It's just an intuition."

"Jumping. You think he died by suicide?"

"Yeah."

"Because of an intuition." Stanley repeated my language.

"Uh huh. A kiss from the spirit world. Sentiment manifesting physically. A rose on the grave."

♏ ♐

"You know," I went on, "like that old song by Seal in the Batman movie."

"That wasn't the lyric."

"That was totally the lyric. *Rose on the grave*."

"No, I don't think it was. The flower was in a spot that was *gray*. Between black and white."

"That doesn't even make sense."

"I suppose it refers to gray area. Uncertainty: where intuition springs from. When you already have knowledge, you don't go kissing roses in search of the answer." Stanley rocked back in his lawn chair, baking in the sunshine, chemically calm.

"*Grave*. I always thought it was a vampire song."

"Why would it have been in *Batman* if it were a vampire song? Batman isn't that kind of bat-man."

♏ ♐

FLASHBULB
SAT
2 AUG
2014
51
WE CANNOT SING

FLASHBULB
SAT
2 AUG
2014
52
I SEE A STORM

I considered. "Sing it," I instructed Stanley.

"I can't," Stanley said.

"Why not?"

"You know why not."

Maybe I did, but at that moment, I had forgotten. Another person might assume it had something to do with testosterone. No, it was nothing to do with his voice. Something less obvious, deeper in the fog. What was it?

♏ ♐

I sighed. "This is disappointing. There's a goth image from eighth grade, gone."

"I know, it's disappointing, but do continue."

"Deeply disappointing. OK, so, anyway," I continue, "in my dreams, when Chad jumps, I see a storm. But I checked the weather reports for that day—" Chad died on May 29, 1900 "—and not a drop."

"Why the storm, then?" Stanley asked me. He's always believed in ghosts even though he's never seen one.

"I don't know what it means."

"No ideas?"

"None," I admitted. "Just that, well—"

♏ ♐

Flyleaf — Conjurations

Shadow's observation in <u>American Gods</u>: People "will not take responsibility for their beliefs; they conjure things, and do not trust the conjurations."

♏ ♐

FLASHBULB
SAT
2 AUG
2014

RAINFALL-
ASSASSINATION
HYPOTHESIS

FLASHBULB
SAT
2 AUG
2014

80/20 RULE

"—you've heard of the 'rainfall-assassination' hypothesis? People become angry and stressed when there's a drought," I explained. "Roman emperors were more likely to be assassinated during those years. I don't know where I can take this."

"Yeah, that sounds flimsy. If Chad jumped to his death in Boston in 1900, it wasn't because it was or wasn't raining."

"So what does my dream mean? Chad jumps, and it's raining?"

"I have a better idea," Stanley offered. "You've heard of the '80/20 rule'?"

♏ ♐

"A small number of causes," he explained, "give you most of the results. The best 20 percent of the coffeeshops get 80 percent of the business. A fraction of your ideas direct most of what you do all day. Only the most aspirational rats in the backyard are chewing up your basement."

"I live on the second floor."

"It's general advice. Hey—you should take María."

He ran into the house, banging the screen door, the heavy artificial cherry odor of our indoor vape and the distant warble of the television wafting afresh all the way across the yard.

He burst out again with a plate of freshly risen croissants in his right hand and something in his left fist.

♏ ♐

FLASHBULB

SAT
2 AUG
2014

SYSGENDER
GODDESSES

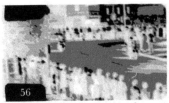

FLASHBULB

SAT
2 AUG
2014

STANLEY GIVES ME
MARÍA

"I want you to have her. I know you don't believe in gods—"

"Only goddesses."

"Right."

"Sysgender ones, right?"

"What?" That word did not compute. I know what a sysadmin is: someone who manages our online communications.

"'Sysgender' means 'not transgender.'"

"I didn't know that. Since when?"

"Since ten minutes ago. You haven't talked to the rest of transgender Boston lately, have you?"

"Just to you." These days I hunker down with Stanley. Other people's neologisms don't always reach my ears. Without Stanley to tell me stuff like "sysgender," I'd be square.

"Sysgender is the thing we are not."

"That word," I said, considering it briefly, "is potentially useful."

"Right," he said.

♏ ♐

Stanley opened his fist and passed me what he held: a small, plastic figurine of the blue-robed Virgin. He'd wrapped a thin chain with a thin cross pendant around her several times.

"Here's a saint. She's got a uterus. Confirmed sysgender. Not a goddess, but close enough for you?" He settled into his chair again. Vinyl stretched and squeaked.

Yes. She was. She'd talk to me, at least. All the Marys had spoken to me since I was a kid. I didn't feel the need for another, but I always took what Stanley gave me.

I knew the drill, and I had everything under control. My anti-speculirium pills would shield me from excessive spirituality.

♏ ♐

FLASHBULB

SAT
2 AUG
2014

57

80 PERCENT CHANCE
OF RAIN

FLASHBULB

SAT
2 AUG
2014

58

HE COULD GIVE ME
THE ANSWER

"Do you need her back?"

"Heck no. Family keeps giving me these things, even after all these years. I can't find new homes for them fast enough. Please take her. What would I do with her?"

María lay supine in my open palm.

"What's the deal here?"

Stanley reached over and fingered the cross.

"Not for me, but for you, María gives you, like, 80 percent of the answer to everything. You do the rest. Put a good bit of yourself into it. That's how you medal."

"I hate activities where I have to do 'the rest.' A spirit controls the outcome and I have to jump for what she's dangling?"

He grabbed a warm croissant off the plate. He reclined, closed his eyes, grinned.

♏ ♐

"I could give you the answer," Stanley said, "but I don't think you want me to."

A bluff. Most certainly he didn't know the demise of the forgotten author of the unpublished *Nature of Time*. I, a nerdy hobbyist, couldn't find the answer.

"If you know, why won't you tell me?"

"It has to be your lived experience," he shrugged.

"My what?"

"Something you know because it's what you are."

"Isn't all experience lived? What other kind is there?"

He paused. "Stuff you write in a boring résumé font because other people care about it: 'career experience.' That's the contrast to 'lived experience.'"

I opened my mouth to object.

Then I caught a shred of television audio floating through the screen door: *80 percent chance of rain.*

♏ ♐

59

GO WHERE
THE ANSWER IS

60

ZOMBIES

"Now, hear that. Rain. I'm not sure I want to go to the cemetery today," I said. I did want to advance my research into the history of Chad's doom to better understand his writings, but I also wanted another beer with Stanley.

"You should go," he said, chewing. "The cemetery's probably where the answer is."

In *Monty Python and the Holy Grail*, they had a nice little folio called "The Book of the Film" with an illuminated history and captions in calligraphy. I wished I had a book of the film to give me historical answers. A word approximating "book of the film" is "telenovela."

♏ ♐

"Hey," he said, sitting upright, croissant crumbs flying off his shirt, "it's like *Walking Dead*!"

"Yeah?" We'd watched the first and second seasons together a couple years earlier.

"You know, when Sophia goes missing. The family car breaks down on the highway, the zombies already ate everyone in the area, and the little girl disappears. They hold out hope she'll find her way back to the car. They spraypaint 'SOPHIA STAY HERE WE WILL COME EVERY DAY' on the windshield."

"Yeah, sure, I remember that."

"And they run around the woods for all of Season Two looking for her. Turns out, one of their own group was hiding her in a barn. She was already a zombie, but he let everyone else keep looking for her."

♏ ♐

FLASHBULB

SAT
2 AUG
2014

61

SHOOT THE GIRL IN
THE RAINBOW SHIRT

FLASHBULB

SAT
2 AUG
2014

62

IT MIGHT RAIN

"Eventually they open the barn door, and Sophia steps out—"

I remembered. The archetypal lost child in a thin T-shirt with a cartoon rainbow. A zombie.

"—at which point they have to shoot her, *bang in the head*, before she bites them."

"What's this got to do with whatever?" I asked him.

"You should go to the cemetery because that's where the answer is. You can't stand around by your car waiting for Chad to show up here. He's not coming around this way. This is the land of the living. Go visit the dead people's barn."

"Yeah, yeah, I know. I'm worried about the clouds rolling in, is all."

"Rain is no big deal."

♏ ♐

"María helps you out by doing 80 percent of the work. You start with a B-minus," Stanley said. "You're already saved because she grades on a curve."

"It might rain," I repeated neutrally, wondering how long it might take to search the cemetery.

"Yep." He shrugged.

I still held the figurine of María in my palm. "What if I don't put in my 20 percent of effort?"

"Then: no gravestone, automatic B-minus. Those are the external consequences."

He was right, of course. Elections are tipped this way: it rains a little, and people don't go to the polls. "If I don't find this stone, and if I never find out how Chad died, I'll be enormously frustrated."

♏ ♐

FLASHBULB

SAT
2 AUG
2014

63

THE DEAD
RIDE FAST

FLASHBULB

SAT
2 AUG
2014

64

GOODBYE

"So go to the cemetery in the rain, put in your 20 percent. We practiced. I coached you. Basic—like in the military, like baseball in the spring. You got the full treatment. It's your time to act. Move. The dead ride fast!"

The dead ride fast. What a weird inspirational phrase. Maybe that, too, comes from spring training at Fenway Park. Or was it from another Batman movie?

♏ ♐

"Oh," I said, as we moved toward the threshold of goodbye, "I meant to ask how it's going with your girlfriend."

Stanley looked distracted and waved. "Never mind that. It's complicated. Nothing to report now."

"But—"

"Really, I'll tell you later."

I had a creeping feeling I'd played this part of my videogame adventure wrong. My offerings today had been thin.

We said goodbye.

Driving out, a kickball skitted across the road. I hit the brakes, stopped, and sure enough, *one, two, three,* the child came running after the ball. It's like clockwork: the grandfather clock chimes, the cuckoo comes out. It's a fact about the world you begin to see and interpret when you drive.

♏ ♐

FLASHBULB

SAT
2 AUG
2014

THE CEMETERY

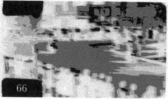

FLASHBULB

SAT
2 AUG
2014

THEY BURROW

I walked around Mount Auburn Cemetery alone. Most stones were so old, the mourners too were long dead.

The sun was still hot, but the trees offered some shade on the paths. Linden tree with its fluttering heart-shaped leaves, flowering dogwood, Douglas fir and weeping white pine, hickory. The maples. The oaks: black, white, pin, chestnut. Many mosquitos tried to bite the inside of my elbow, and one succeeded.

I walked dozens of sections, listening to Bill Withers sing "Ain't No Sunshine" and Titus Andronicus ballad about "No Future" in my earbuds.

♏ ♐

In a children's story by Walter de la Mare, published shortly after the Second World War, a grandmother warns her seven grandchildren not to go near an ancient oak chest. Sure enough, they climb into the chest, materially vanish, and are never seen again. The end. A parable for a young audience worried about people who "disappeared" in the war? Or a test of the power of fictional words to create and delete characters? The author calls the story "The Riddle."

María in my pocket would lead the way to Chad's grave. I knew she would. Deities, they say, don't have to know everything; they just have to know a few things that matter. *Deities know where all the bodies are buried.* Impeccable memories they have, and they burrow into our consciences.[*]

♏ ♐

---

[*] "Gods know where all the bodies are buried, as the saying goes," is a line from Daniel C. Dennett's *Breaking the Spell: Religion as a Natural Phenomenon* (2007). Ara Norenzayan argued based on research by Benjamin Purzycki: "Religious American students" assume a deity is "interested in negative behaviors that have moral consequences for others" but "know[s] less about other, nonsocial facts." (Ara Norenzayan. *Big Gods: How Religion Transformed Cooperation and Conflict.* Princeton University Press, 2013. Chapter 2.)

Flyleaf — Bittersweet

Bittersweet breakthrough. The sad thing about learning an ending is that you can never read the story the same way again, not like the first time you heard it: its newness, your ignorance, blank stones without letters stamped on them, wonder.

You also grieve the characters. While someone's alive, changing, you can't know how their story ends. But then they die. They'll never surprise you with a new chapter nor further explain the story they left behind. So many shades of grief.

SOPHIA STAY HERE WE WILL COME EVERY DAY. You're looking for Sophia but, by the time you're desperate enough to paint messages on your car, Sophia is worse than dead. No do-overs.

♏ ♐

FLASHBULB

SAT
2 AUG
2014

67

I FOUND
CHAD'S GRAVE

Next to the elder Goeings' graves, I found it, half-buried: a flat, cross-shaped placard. Minimalism, like someone's attempt to forget. Surely it was Chad's. He had no siblings. On this placard: the initials C. G. Born: January 27, 1868. Thirty-two, then, when he died.

A line of sugar ants paraded through, carrying a wasp.

I felt I should say something Christian in their honor, like the Lord's Prayer, but the words did not come. A long time ago, I'd tried the prayer on a couple Virgin Marys, but they never responded affirmatively, so I'd never bothered to memorize it. The line that came to me now was "You do not have to be good," and I was pretty sure that was wrong.

♏ ♐

Flyleaf — Sense the System

You do not have to read this book, Pierre Bayard said approximately in *How to Talk About Books You Haven't Read.* You're educated if you know approximately what a book talks about and how it works in a system. By shelving it, you give it genre.

♏ ♐

FLASHBULB

SAT
2 AUG
2014

MARÍA
SITS BRIEFLY
ON CHAD'S GRAVE

I placed the figurine of María standing upright on Chad's grave. Her cross necklace had unwound, fallen off. I fished that out of my pocket too and placed it around her again. The sky darkened and thundered.

She's just some angel that won't let me go. Maybe she faces the truth, but she isn't real. I am a half-believer.

I picked her up from the grave and put her back in my pocket. Stanley wanted me to have her. I shouldn't lose her.

In the sudden, cool rain, the mosquitos made themselves scarce.

♏ ♐

Flyleaf — The Boss Didn't Come

The Mayan god Bolon Yokte was supposed to come to Earth in 2012. Someone said so, anyway. But "2012" isn't Bolon Yokte's dating system. And I heard that the original prophecy concerned his arrival and not necessarily the end of the world.

In any case, he missed his appointment. People keep setting dates for Jesus to return, too, and those turn up nothing either. I don't believe in the male gods.

EPISODE 3

CAMPFIRE TALES

Maybe some people assume I go to "gay places" on the weekends because I am gay. There is a particular gay place of which I am fond, but it isn't what they're imagining, and I rarely go there. I'll tell you about that place later.

On this occasion, I went to a more stereotypically gay place instead: Provincetown. *Give me space, relaxation, drag*, I thought. I believed those would come from P-town. A very long Sunday drive. A very expensive parking spot. I would convince Provincetown to cough up its truths.

♏ ♐

Driving from Boston to Provincetown felt too easy. Thoreau would have walked. Under the right circumstances, I, too, might walk it, carrying my own cross in the rain. I'd do it if someone made me, or if I were promised an answer at the end.

I wallflowered in a popular restaurant with a water view where small speakers in the ceiling played Madonna's "Immaculate Collection" on infinite repeat. I'd had the album on cassette tape in high school. "Rain," her voice reverbed in that soothing, famous ballad.

Gulls danced on the shore, spreading, closing, spreading their wings as if about to take flight. The weather had cooled off.

♏ ♐

FLASHBULB

SUN
3 AUG
2014

71

NO ONE WOULD
READ MY BOOK

Writing about *The Nature of Time* involved so much retreat into my bubble. I'd scribble a few sentences about Chad Goeing that sounded good, but when I emerged, I realized I'd written something no one would want to read. The world held and contained me, welcoming me every sunrise, yet I felt I was intruding, ejaculating into it, communicating my strange transgender being without the world's explicit consent, and the world gave me that knowing, weary smile and patted my shoulder.

A cosmic joke was on me. Was I privy to its mechanism, or no?

I pulled the religious figurine out of my pocket. María's plastic visage was silent.

♏ ♐

Flyleaf — Sysgender

I remember the word Stanley used: "sysgender." It's a special kind of magic, how the perfect word systematizes the obvious. Like a code: "0" for "off," "1" for "on."

The world wants me to recognize sysgender people as simply <u>normal</u> while perceiving the <u>transgender</u> state as a defective sysgender state. What if I am not strange, after all, as I have assumed all these years? What if I am not a defective man? What if most people's gender isn't objectively correct, but is simply <u>sysgender</u>? Sysgender life is distinctive, isn't it, every bit as much as transgender life is distinctive. But the way that sysgender works is by refusing to acknowledge itself explicitly. So I predict they'll be mad about that word. If sysgender people called themselves sysgender, they'd be a little less sysgender.

♏ ♐

FLASHBULB
SUN
3 AUG
2014

CIS-STEM

I look up "sysgender" on the Internet using my phone. No results. I text Stanley for clarification.

"Cisgender," he texts back. "U spelled it wrong. U can just say 'cis'."

Oh, OK. Cis. That works too.

♏ ♐

Flyleaf — I Always Knew

The cis people and the system.
The cis-tem.

Italo Calvino in *Invisible Cities* asks whether we begin or end with a Platonic Form, that is, whether we move away from or toward it to become real.

His fictional Kublai Khan imagines a model that "contains everything corresponding to the norm." But that's only an idea; everything real looks like a variation on it. To predict what exists, he lists probable variations.

The fictional Marco Polo does it the other way 'round. He imagines a non-form "made only of exceptions, exclusions, incongruities, contradictions." A cluster of variations. As he subtracts, he arrives at realness. But, he warns, there's a limit beyond which it yields the Form, an idea "too probable to be real."

I'm not sure either of them is right.

If the cis-tem called itself out more, it might begin to evaporate. I bet it's less like a rock-solid foundation, more like an unstable element. No one has got the Form. When we all realize that cisgender and transgender are just different ways of doing gender and that neither has more reality or truth than the other, we might have less need for these labels.

♏ ♐

FLASHBULB

SUN
3 AUG
2014

73

REDEFINING
REALNESS

FLASHBULB

SUN
3 AUG
2014

74

UNEQUIVOCAL

A bookstore displayed a hardcover of Janet Mock's *Redefining Realness* in the window with the new releases. Reflecting on the word "cisgender," then reinterpreting "transgender" as meaning something other than "defective"—this had made me more receptive to reading a fellow transgender person. I went in and picked up the window copy. It flipped open to this page: "When I say *I always knew I was a girl* with such certainty, I erase all the nuances, the work, the process of self-discovery." There was, she said, "a time when I was learning the world, unsure, unstable, wobbly…"

♏ ♐

They tell us to say we align with a category we've *always* been in and *can't* fall out of. Else, they caution, why should they grant us any rights?

Look what lock Mock picks with that: Her pathway through uncertainty "doesn't discount my womanhood. It adds value to it." Something she learned as a Black person, as a woman, as a magazine editor, as someone who gender-transitioned at a young age.

She was telling the truth, right there in a book. A transgender author. A real book about being transgender. She wrote it and someone published it. I hoped this was what our tipping point would be: the right to truth-tell in books.

I bought the hardcover.

♏ ♐

Flyleaf — How to Tell Shorter Stories

In what my schema counts as the 75th Biblical reading, Joseph's brothers are jealous of him. He's a dream interpreter. They strip him, throw him down the well, and discuss whether to murder or sell him. I don't know if he slept inside the well, but if he did, what did he dream there?*

♏ ♐

FLASHBULB
SUN
3 AUG
2014

LEAR NOON

"Hey, stranger. Do you have the time?"

Someone on the narrow, crowded street had recognized me. I did a double-take. People passed with a bustle of sound and color. I inhaled slowly through my nose, focusing my mental camera on his face.

"Lear?" I say.

"Good to see you," he smiled.

♏ ♐

FLASHBULB
SUN
3 AUG
2014

NOT BAD

Lear Noon was a former coworker.

I'd always thought he might be gay.

Also, I always thought I'd never see him again except on professional social media.

He was wearing vacation clothes: a green-and-white plaid short-sleeve shirt and dark blue pleated shorts, hanging loosely. He'd lost a bit of weight. Sunglasses rested on the crown of his head. He looked relaxed.

"How've you been?"

"I've been great," I said. "How have you been?"

"Not bad," he said.

Ding, ding. Bicycle bell. Cyclist zipped by.

Lear was traveling alone too. We weren't surrounded by security cameras as we'd always been at our workplace. At least, I imagined no one was watching us here in Provincetown.

♏ ♐

---

* This is the 75th reading in Lev's schema: the 9th weekly Torah portion, VaYeshev, 3rd reading.

Flyleaf — Figure It Out

The Velveteen Rabbit, with his "boot-button eyes" with their "knowing expression," is astonished to see real rabbits for the first time in the field. One asks him: "Why don't you get up and play with us?" The Velveteen Rabbit demurs, saying, "I don't feel like it," not wanting "to explain that he had no clockwork."

"We all need to begin figuring out," David Shields said in <u>Reality Hunger</u>, article 77, although he is channeling the words of Robert Greenwald, "how to tell a story for the cell phone. One thing I know: it's not the same as telling a story for a full-length DVD."

♏ ♐

FLASHBULB

SUN
3 AUG
2014

HE DOESN'T WANT
TO HANG OUT

When Lear and I had first started working together, it took him a while to notice that I existed, after which he often came over to my desk to chat, holding his drained and cooling Garfield coffee mug. He left the company suddenly last year.

"I had a better opportunity," he explained briefly to me on Commercial Street, regarding his career.

A drag queen with bright lavender eyeshadow and a tiny tulle skirt pressed a flyer into my hand. "Come to the show tonight!" she said. "I'll try to be there," I said politely. She also gave a flyer to Lear, who smiled at her. She moved on to other pedestrians.

♏ ♐

FLASHBULB

SUN
3 AUG
2014

78

MOTIVATION

FLASHBULB

SAT
9 AUG
2014

79

CHAD'S PAPERS

Lear folded and pocketed the advertisement. I inserted mine into the jacket flap of *Redefining Realness* that I was holding under my arm.

"Want to get a drink?" I offered, though it would feel strange to drink anything except work coffee alongside Lear.

"No, actually, I'm meeting someone," he said. "Got to go now." His hand fluttered "bye" at me, and he stepped back, receding into the crowd.

A better opportunity, hmm? There was another person, or so he claimed.

No great loss. I was happy with the day's haul: Janet Mock's *Redefining Realness*. This would motivate me to continue with my resurrection of *The Nature of Time*. I would practice my right to time-tell in books.

♏ ♐

My last hurrah before surgery. Hot day in Copley Square.

I spent a couple hours with Chad's papers at the library archives. Air-conditioned. Soundproofed.

My interest had sparked when I'd agreed to write a small article about transportation for a local paper. I wanted to give them something special, so I looked up a Mr. Goeing who had been a railroad president. The archivist asked me: "Would you like to see his son's papers, too?" And when I saw that the son, Chad, had been writing a sensitive, brooding treatise on the passage of time, I was smitten. I forgot entirely about the railroads.

The papers I request are brought to me in a box. Someone is always watching.

♏ ♐

Flyleaf — Glasses

Chad quotes a sermon Meister Eckhart gave around the year 1300: "The eye through which I see God is the same eye through which God sees me; my eye and God's eye are one eye, one seeing, one knowing, one love." Meister Eckhart probably told time by the sun or listened for someone to ring the church bell.*

If you take God out of it, then it's a question of how you see others and how others see you, which may be a series of repeating, snowballing reflections.

It makes me think of a story by Arthur Miller, published shortly after Auschwitz was liberated. A bureaucrat is tasked with turning away people who look Jewish, and when his eyesight fails, he gets glasses to go on ethnically speculating. The glasses change how others see the contours of his face, and they now suspect he is Jewish, and they don't like that. As you see, so you will be seen. Through the glasses both ways.

It makes me think of the idea of double consciousness as W. E. B. Du Bois describes it, the "two-ness" of being a Black American, aware of "always looking at one's self through the eyes of others"—specifically, through the eyes of white Americans. He says he strives to find a way to be both Black and American, "merging" these parts of himself "into a better and truer self," perhaps a third thing, though "he wishes neither of the older selves to be lost."

♍ ↗

FLASHBULB

SAT
9 AUG
2014

WHAT IS ARCHIVED

I wonder what Chad was trying to do with his draft of *The Nature of Time*. Did he want to enjoy its publication as a cultural event within his lifetime, or did he aspire to write a timeless classic even were it to be left undiscovered until his death?

Like the narrator in Bohumil Hrabal's *Too Loud a Solitude*, I "ruminate on *progressus ad futurum* meeting *regressus ad originem*," the question of forward and back, flow and ebb, to some extent "for relaxation, the way some people read the *Prague Evening News*."

♍ ↗

---

* According to *The Dance of Time: The Origins of the Calendar* by Michael Judge, Europe received its first mechanical clocks around the year 1350. They used dripping water. The original water clocks had been invented in China.

Flyleaf —
Why or Why Not

I am questioning the value of timelessness. So much of what we enjoy has value precisely because we know it can't last. Like the VHSes we used to pick up from the rental store. After renting a film, we forced ourselves to watch it because the tape was due back in two days. Never mind—because we didn't predict this—that the VHS rental stores themselves would one day shutter forever. We'd hate those same films if we saw them for the first time today, which is maybe why they aren't offered in the online streaming catalog. They don't need to exist forever. Their mortality casts an illusion of their value. We enjoy our memories of the tapes more than we'd enjoy playing the tapes.

So why aim to write a "timeless" book? Why not just write for today?

Not <u>why</u>, but <u>why not</u>. That's a Bobby Kennedy question. He adopted it when running for president five years after his brother's assassination. It's also a <u>Phantom Tollbooth</u> question that was reason enough to admit Milo into Dictionopolis.*

The Goeing family donated the papers.

Don't know why the archivists keep them. Is the archive like a VHS rental store that refuses to shutter and liquidate its inventory?

If you've never touched Chad's papers, you have no idea how many paperclips he used. Every piece of paper is clipped to every other. Paperclips are of the devil! They create extra work for me when they manifest spiritual beings.

I have the urge to rip the clips off. But I mustn't vandalize. This organizational system was either Chad's or the archivist's. I am duty-bound to respect every iota, or I risk being kicked out.

---

* The "Why not?" slogan of Bobby Kennedy's 1968 presidential campaign was cribbed from George Bernard Shaw (*Back to Methuselah*, 1921): "You see things and you say, 'WHY?' But I dream things that never were; and I say: 'Why not?'" A different formulation of "WHY NOT?" appeared in *The Phantom Tollbooth* in 1961: "That's a good reason for almost anything—a bit used perhaps, but still quite serviceable."

FLASHBULB
SAT
9 AUG
2014
82
COPLEY STATION

FLASHBULB
SAT
9 AUG
2014
83
COUNTDOWN CLOCKS

That day, my research stalled out, I wasn't progressing—a condition that is *The Nature of Time* if anything is—and I didn't feel like sitting and reading anymore. I called Stanley, and he met me above ground at the T stop outside the library. We crossed the street to buy decafs in paper cups, returned to the Copley inbound headhouse on the library side of the street, and descended, swiping our white-and-green plastic subway cards.

The thing about which you aren't talking is the thing you can't forget. Thoughts are a subway network. Switch from one to the other. Rumination makes them run on time.

♏ ♐

You never do know when the trolley is coming.

True, they're putting up countdown clocks on the Red Line. New York has got the clocks, and someone figured they could do it here. Yes, Boston can go full New York. Already, on the Red Line, LED signs hang overhead and tell you how many more minutes you have to wait. It's lovely—*on the Red Line.*

But I am talking about the Green Line. You never, never know when the Green Line is coming. Here, you just stare down the tracks and wait like it's 1900, and it feels as though we've been standing here since then.

The green trolley pulled into the station. We boarded. The doors slid shut behind us.

♏ ♐

THE ANSWER IS NOT
IN THE LIBRARY

ACTUALLY
NOT FUNNY

"I was reading the microfilm all day and couldn't find the answer. I still don't know how Chad Goeing died," I confessed.

"The answer is not in the library," Stanley said.

"What? Why did you tell me you thought I was closing in on the answer?" I complained.

"For a little while, you were on it. You were getting warmer. You were almost there."

"I am practically drowned in information, yet I still don't have what I need."

"You can't see the situation, can you?" Stanley said.

I kicked a hamburger wrapper. "I can't ever see the situation."

"This gets funnier all the time," he grinned.

What did he mean by *this?*

♏ ♐

"This is not funny. Do you know how inconvenient it is for me to schedule any time to futz in the library? I have three weeks of paid time off available for my surgery recovery"—I don't say the word "hysterectomy" on the subway—"and then I've got to be in the office every day for the rest of 2014."

"Chad and María together have given you 100 percent of the answer to the riddle."

I had no idea what he was talking about. A dead man and a religious figurine had given me more information than I had found during hours of searching in an archive?

"What you tell me feels like having the answer but more exactly like *not having the answer,*" I argued.

♏ ♐

Flyleaf — Fingers

Proto-Indo-European words for "five" and "shaping," time-sliding their e-time-ol-ogies through Germanic and Latin respectively, gave us English "finger" and Spanish "fingir."

That some hands have six fingers doesn't defict from the generalization. Fingir, to pretend, to make fiction. Fingers, the organs of fiction.

That we may cisfict or transfict makes our fictional actions that much more inter-esting.

♏ ♐

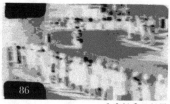

FLASHBULB

SAT
9 AUG
2014

CONSENT
TO RECEIVE
FALSEHOODS

La esfinge, the sphinx, is a faker. Finge — *it pretends*. Better if the riddle were a novel; when you read a novel, you consent to being lied to.

"Life's a journey. You're so focused on the destination."

I was infuriated and said nothing. Stanley could, when he chose to, speak like someone who'd smoked a lot in college. We'd both smoked. Maybe I sounded the same to him, to others. Maybe that's why he infuriated me.

Ads flashed on the tunnel walls, the same poster affixed over and over, a corporation banking on the force of repetition as we pulled into the station.

Why did Stanley think he knew some-thing I didn't know about Chad Goeing? *I'm* Chad's biographer.

♏ ♐

FOG — CHAD FOLLOWS US TO THE RESTAURANT

The doors opened at Park Street, interrupting. Stanley and I got off and went for soup.

My fingers and toes felt a little numb. This happens sometimes. It means something interesting is happening at the borders of my reality.

"Y esta mi vida," Unamuno's character asked in *Niebla*, "¿es novela, es nivola o qué es?" *Is my life a novel, nivola, or what?* That's on some other level — está a otro nivel — but it's also about this level. Everything that happens around me: "¿es realidad o es ficción?"

Stanley stood at the counter, waiting for our soup.

I noticed Chad's ghost sitting at a table, waiting for us. I left Stanley's side and went to sit with Chad, choosing a chair to his right so I wouldn't have to look at him directly. Besides, in a few minutes, Stanley would want to sit across from me so we could talk, and if he wasn't competing for Chad's chair, Chad would not have to move. I avoid inconveniencing my friends.

Chad looked like a living man, though pale and drawn. He was about my height. In the 19th century, men weren't very tall, right? He wore a jacket, formal but shabby. He had a full head of hair. I guessed he was thirtysomething, like me. But he was not me. His nose was smaller.

He looked like a younger version of the inventor of the three-way lightbulb. By which I mean *older*, of course, in the sense that he had been born a generation earlier. But *younger* in the sense that the three-way lightbulb inventor had been 90 when I met him.

"I will figure you out," I stage-hissed at Chad while Stanley ordered for us at the counter.

Chad suppressed a smile.

"Do you want me to have the same suicidal thought you're having, thousands of times, and never reach the answer? Is that what you're going for?" I continued.

Chad wrote something on a paper napkin and passed it to me. "I like the way you think," it said. The ink was black.

Of course Chad's ghost was following me. I meddled in the archive with some frequency, and his papers were positively littered with paperclips. Maybe I had done something else to call him in. I didn't remember when it had begun, but by this point, the summer of 2014, he showed up for me regularly.

♏ ♐

Flyleaf —
Glamour and Pishogue

In Ireland, as I have read, the <u>glamour</u> is a spell on how you appear to others—like changing your sex—even if the spell is also part of who you really are. The <u>pishogue</u>, on the other hand, is a spell on how you perceive others—like the ability to see ghosts. Which is also part of who I really am.*

The question of <u>glamour</u> and <u>pishogue</u>: Does Santa Claus put on a red suit and slide down the chimney and do you perceive him if you're lucky enough to stay awake, or do you hallucinate him standing in the living room and thereby manifest him into being?

<u>Glamour</u> and <u>pishogue</u> are systems of reality organization. The question is: What is reality? You can hear the word "grammar" in "glamour." It's how you organize your givens. It's something you learn to do. "Pishogue," though, means witchcraft perception that creates the world anew. I don't know if it can be controlled. If you're the witch, ask yourself.

In Charles Johnson's novel <u>Middle Passage</u>, set on a boat of early 19th-century slave traders and their victims, the kidnapping sea-captain argues that there is no truth, just power. The captain says life is about who wins the argument.

He declares war on a fictional West African tribe. The tribe deifies multiple virtues. The captain believes that a pure virtue is a self-contradiction: its purity is infinite by definition, but eventually a virtue bumps against a conceptual limit. Pure virtue is impossible, thus unknowable, so these gods can never know themselves. The captain captures one of these gods and keeps it in a box. In this way, he physically holds virtue, as well as people, captive. This is control. But he too is in a sort of a box. His ship needs constant maintenance. If it breaks down on the open water, it will kill him. His framework is precarious, and he must keep reasserting it. To live this particular story in which he is the oppressor, he creates a power-box that floats and holds him and contains smaller power-boxes in which he holds others. The ship is called the *Republic*.

As the kid in <u>The Matrix</u> said, to use your mental powers to bend a spoon, you must first acknowledge there is no spoon. Chad's ghost will roam uncontrolled as long as I believe in him. But if I am more skeptical, I may see my own hand in his script.

Who was fooling whom? If we aren't fooling others, we're being fooled—or we're fooling ourselves, but I've got no word for that.

The narrator of *Too Loud a Solitude*, a compactor of waste paper and old books,

---

* I learned about "glamour" and "pishogue" in Patrick Harpur's *The Philosopher's Secret Fire* (2002).

sees ambiguously supernatural beings too. "While I was on my fourth mug of beer," he assures us, "I noticed a pleasant-looking young man next to the press, and I knew then and there it was Jesus Himself. And soon he was joined by an old man with a face full of wrinkles, and I knew on the spot it could only be Lao-tze. So there they stood, side by side," Hrabal's narrator goes on, explaining that the young, active Jesus represents *progressus* and the old, self-contained Lao-Tze is *regressus*, thus their dialogue is a dialectic, also informing us that his own ancestors also saw wild sprites and fairies, but that, due to his exposure to books, he sees "visions of Schelling and Hegel, who were born in the same year, and once Erasmus of Rotterdam rode up on his horse and asked me how to get to the sea."

Some people talk to God. Some people hear angels sing. Some people hear something else altogether. When I walk around Boston, now and then I hear thunk-thunk-thunk, and when I turn around, it's sure to be Chad, standing inside the last telephone booth, banging his head against the fogged-up glass.

Niflheim, the "Home of Mist," is the world of the dead in Norse mythology, identified in the tales of Snorri Sturluson. "Nifl" is the same word as "niebla," you hear. A woman named Hel is in charge there.

ℳ ♐

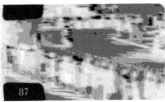

FLASHBULB

SAT
9 AUG
2014

87

NAPKIN NOVELIST

Who wrote "I like the way you think" on the napkin? Who, if not Chad? If ghosts were not real? Who gives me a six-word novel? Cosmos knows I'm incapable of brevity.

I stared at the message that lay face-up in the palm of my hand, the thin paper fluttering under the ceiling fan.

"What you got there?" Stanley asked, peering into my eyes as he put down the red plastic cafeteria tray.

I knew Stanley couldn't see Chad. Stanley and I had been through this before, so I didn't bother to ask again.

Chad would be glaring at me. I didn't look to my left.

I reflexively scrunched up my hand, crushing the napkin. "Dust," I declared.

ℳ ♐

FOG — STUCK IN A PHONE BOOTH

Thunk-thunk-thunk in the fog. The sound of the man following me. The trolley wouldn't help me escape.

Chad had got something stuck in his head, and he was stuck in mine.

He wouldn't talk, either. He didn't seem to want me to hear his voice. He had other ways of making himself heard. He sat silently next to Stanley and me as we ate soup in the air-conditioned café.

The soup outing was the sort of action that might have been repeatable, but, as it turned out, was not repeated. It was the last time Stanley and I went out for food, at least for a while. But I'm getting ahead of myself.

♏ ♐

FLASHBULB

FRI
15 AUG
2014

88

A PARADE OF GODS

I had been letting María sit on the kitchen counter in the dish with my car keys.

She knows everything. She was paying attention when Bob Dylan gave weed to the Beatles a half-century ago. She knows everything that's happened before and since.

After my hysterectomy, she threw me a look for the ages. I mean, she was disappointed in me but she totally got it.

♏ ♐

Flyleaf — Jagged Cut

Each jagged cut we survive is a kind of miracle. This reminds me of a short story by Mircea Cărtărescu, "Ruletistul" in Romanian or "El Ruletista" in the Spanish translation. The narrator describes a particular instance of "una especie de visión," a type of vision, that he has while resting under his quilt. Before him appears an incomprehensibly huge, radiant god. The yellow aura from the god's chest overwhelms his vision.

After an "eternidad," another "Dios enorme, idéntico al primero." Another eternity, another god. A parade of gods. They fall to the right and left, "como si fueran los dientes de una gigantesca cremallera de fuego"—as if they were the teeth of a gigantic flaming zipper. The narrator had been contemplating a remarkably lucky Russian roulette player who pulled the trigger in many separate bets and whose single bullet never discharged from his gun into his face.

♏ ♐

MON
8 SEP
2014

89

DIVERSITY
COMMITTEE
STORYTIME

WED
10 SEP
2014

90

STANLEY WILL COME

I had a three-week medical leave from Achromatic Propioception. Returning to the office, I checked my unread email and saw I'd been invited to join the office's diversity committee. My coworker Aparna, who worked in the same department, had received the same invitation.

I felt amorphous personal discomfort and declined. Aparna told me the opportunity was a giant "nope" for her too. The committee was going to meet on certain weekday evenings and, although that was not why we declined, we found joy in planning a little campfire behind her house to deliberately exploit one of those evenings after work and celebrate not being on a committee. It was the first time I'd been invited over.

♏ ♐

She said I could bring a friend, and from my desk phone, I called Stanley, who was working at his Fenway Park office. They wouldn't have had occasion to meet before, but I thought they'd like each other. He said he'd come over. Didn't mind driving in Boston. Said he'd find his way to her place.

Aparna and I left the office at the same time, and I slowly followed her car through traffic. A monarch butterfly floated south across Mount Auburn Street, barely flapping its sail, a survivor of the fire that creates it in the cocoon, ash on the wind. It was still warm for September.

♏ ♐

FLASHBULB

WED
10 SEP
2014

91

I WANT TO CHANGE

FLASHBULB

WED
10 SEP
2014

92

WHAT'S BEHIND
DOOR NUMBER ONE?

I already knew the neighborhood. I just hadn't realized Aparna lived here. Her kitchen was sunny, the evening light streaming in through the west window. A large, crumbling rye sat on a breadboard.

I wanted to change out of my collared shirt into my clean gym shirt, but it feels a little weird to change my clothes in someone else's house. My scars are still a secret I guard. Also, it's embarrassing to ask for the bathroom. Every day I try to get over my body. I never quite do. Aparna didn't seem to think "bathroom" was an embarrassing question though and simply gestured to the stairs.

♏ ♐

Upstairs, I opened the first door I found. Something gave me a bit of a start. Two eyes stared back at me from the semi-darkness. Not a person, not an animal: something inanimate. I shut the door quickly. Retrospectively, I processed the image. The brain needs a moment to knit. I had seen a statue. It would be a murti, a god. Or a goddess.

♏ ♐

I WANT TO KNOW IF
SHE IS A GODDESS

SHOULD I
OPEN THE DOOR?

By habit, I felt the chest pocket of my office shirt and pants. Wallet, keys. Good, good. I like to double-check that paperclips haven't infiltrated. No paperclip on my person, so this spiritual being—even if she were a woman—probably wouldn't bother me.

It's not terrible to meet new goddesses, but I never know what they want from me. Besides—not that I *want* to go on record with this, yet I do record it—I needed, in addition to a wardrobe change, an emptier bladder.

But first I wanted to identify the deity. Then, were I to spot her following me around later, at least I'd know where she came from.

♏ ♐

Should I open the door again? Of course not. Now that opening the door would be intentional, I should not. It wasn't my closet. But I had already seen inside once, accidentally, for a moment. Would it be so terrible if I opened it again for a second look? Yes, it would be, of course it would be. I was not the sort of person who snooped around in my colleagues' houses to spy on their murtis while pretending to look for the bathroom. I actually *did* want the bathroom.

I paused to be sure Aparna wasn't coming upstairs, took a breath, and because I'd told myself not to—I contradict myself and predict myself—I opened the door to the little room again.

♏ ♐

Flyleaf — Dramaticon

Photius the First, Patriarch of Constantinople, in his *Bibliotheca*, a collection of a couple hundred book summaries, gives us the fictional romance called *Dramaticon* by the 2nd-century Syrian writer Iamblichus. It's the 94th entry. The king of Babylon chains up the woman he desires and puts her lover on the cross, but they escape and run. They find a gravestone with an inscription leading them to buried treasure. In the field, a ghost-goat wants to mate with the woman. The lovers hide in a cave. Honey drips on their skin. The king's men try to dig them out but are attacked by bees.

♏ ♐

FLASHBULB

WED
10 SEP
2014

I'LL STAY
WITH MY DOOR

I would have used this as a laundry closet. But Aparna and her mother had transformed it into a home for the murti who sat on a built-in shelf. She was indeed a goddess. Just my luck. Wearing a red dress and holding a trident. I didn't recognize her. I knew some Hindu gods and goddesses, but not this one.

She was looking right at me. Not moving, at least. Not yet. That was a relief.

I hadn't meant to intrude on the goddess, at least not the first time, but I had indeed chosen to open the door a second time. Mostly to confirm her gender. That was my bad. My rude. My intentional, avoidable, regrettable rude. I closed the door again, quietly.

♏ ♐

Flyleaf — All Doors Hurt

The Christian faithful, said Luther, can expect to suffer "many tribulations" ("multas tribulationes") and may never enjoy "the security of peace" ("securitatem pacis"). Suffering is the way to heaven, according to his theology. It is the final statement of his 95 theses. If he predicts such difficulty for the followers of his religion, a religion he says is the true one, then there's no rose garden for the rest of us either.

♏ ♐

STANLEY ARRIVES

FLASHBULB

WED
10 SEP
2014

97

INFORMATION
MANAGEMENT

The bathroom, as it turned out, was across the hall. I went in, unbuttoned my work shirt, and pulled on my comfortable purple shirt.

Looking out the second-floor bathroom window onto the driveway below, I saw Stanley's car parked behind mine. He's got a fancy car, so I always recognize it. He must have just arrived.

I went downstairs to say hello. Stanley had brought vegetarian hot dogs that we stabbed with sticks and slow-roasted.

♏ ♐

I'd never told Aparna about my gender saga. In fact, I hadn't discussed my previous gender with anyone at the office. Before I recently took medical leave, I'd said I was having "abdominal surgery." As far as I knew, I'd received an invitation to the office diversity committee because I date men—I date them in theory, I mean—and people remembered my sexual orientation because it was interesting gossip. Also because, to avoid awkward requests for me to verify rumors about me, I kept a little rainbow flag with a bank logo propped up on a flagpole in an extra coffee mug on my desk. *That* settled *that*. The bank-rainbow must have led them to expect I'd do corporate-diversity work in my free time.

♏ ♐

FLASHBULB

WED
10 SEP
2014

98

INTRODUCTIONS

FLASHBULB

WED
10 SEP
2014

99

NO SUCH THING
AS ALCHEMY

The loneliness of The Homosexuality was out on the rumor mill—the reverse gayness of my non-dating—but the transness of The Gender was a whole other empty coffee mug for which I didn't yet have a rainbow signal. The office didn't know.

Anyway, because I'd warned Stanley that I hadn't disclosed my gender business to Aparna, he didn't mention his own gender business to her, either. I introduced them by their jobs: he, a Red Sox expert from Fenway Park, and she, my coworker from Achromatic Proprioception.

"So you're not in cameras," she said, as if everyone were in cameras.

"No, baseball. What's to do in cameras?"

"I'm a director," she said.

"A movie director?"

"No, like, organizational structure—"

"Business director. Got it."

♏ ♐

The way I'd first gotten to know Aparna in the office was by making a mess of the coffeepot. There was a bottom compartment for water, a middle compartment for dry grounds, and a top compartment to catch the brewed coffee as it boiled up. I poured in too much water and spooned in too many grounds, and I wondered why I was getting mud in the top compartment.

"This is a part of my job I am not good at," I said.

She laughed quietly and shook her head. "Yeah, but you still have to do it." She began taking apart the coffeepot to see what I'd done wrong.

♏ ♐

FLASHBULB
WED
10 SEP
2014

100

FIRED FOR
BEING PREGNANT

FLASHBULB
WED
10 SEP
2014

101

LEAVE SPACE

Meanwhile, she told me a story: Her friend at another company had just been fired. "When she had her baby," she explained to me, "she asked for more of the work she could still do and less of the type she couldn't. They said yes, but they really meant no, and fired her."

"Fired for getting pregnant," I echoed, impressed at the overshare. I like when people tell me real things. Aparna's earlier conversations with me were limited to our shared office projects.

"Yes. Men, most men, have very limited imagination about the ways in which a woman can be fired for getting pregnant." She sounded annoyed, but not at me. She was staring into the coffeepot.

"Clean this out," she said.

I did.

♏ ♐

She told me to leave more airspace for stuff to move. That's how the alchemy happens. Otherwise, without air, water has no space to gather steam, dry coffee has no room to expand, and brewed coffee can't flow upward. I appreciated her insight. She is more mechanical than I am. She doesn't use words like "alchemy." That word was my own insertion in my reexplication of what she said. Such paraphrasing avoids plagiarism but also leads to misrepresentation.

Ana Gabriel has a delightful song "Hechizo" in which she says it doesn't matter if you're under a love spell; what matters is that you're happy. With the coffee, in my case.

I followed Aparna's lead, and I make better coffee now.

♏ ♐

FLASHBULB

WED
10 SEP
2014

102

WE SHOULD TELL
GHOST STORIES

FLASHBULB

WED
10 SEP
2014

103

NOBODY KNOWS
WHO KILLED JFK

"Diversity Committee is convened," Aparna said, flipping an ember with a stick in her backyard. The sun set orangely, and the good smoke tickled our bodies.

"What should we do?" Stanley said.

"Tell spooky stories," she said.

"About discrimination?"

"No, ghost stories," she said.

"Like what?"

"Well, have you watched any horror movies lately?"

"Yeah," I said, "House."

"The funny gremlins from the '80s—"

"No, the Japanese 'House' from the '70s in which the dead aunt has to eat unmarried girls so she can wear her wedding dress."

Aparna scrunches her face. "I don't know about that premise. What's with the married/unmarried binary? How does the ghost know if the girl is unmarried?"

"OK, give us a ghost story you like better."

♏ ♐

"Here's one we know. On November 22, 1963, President Kennedy's motorcade turned a bend in Dallas, and he was shot in the head. He fell on his wife, Jackie, who tried to climb out of the car while it was still moving. It was all caught on 26 seconds of video, the most famous short film of all time—"

"It could be the premise for a ghost story," I admitted.

"—but to this day, nobody—knows—for sure—who—killed—JFK. *Boo*!"

"I think you skipped to the end," I said.

"This is the best diversity committee *ever*," said Stanley, chewing soy protein.

♏ ♐

FOG — THE TALE OF THE HEARTLESS FLYING BOY (D.C. STORYTIME #1)

"We will run this group like *Are You Afraid of the Dark?*," Aparna said. "We'll say: 'Submitted for the approval of the Diversity Committee, I call this story...'"

And we did. Stanley completed the sentence with "...The Tale of the Heartless Flying Boy." He told us that story. This is how it went.

In the world of Peter Pan, children can fly because they are 'gay and innocent and heartless.' 'Gay' as in merry. Merry, innocent, and heartless. Why heartless? Why would having a heart stop you from flying? Well, when you have a heart, you develop connections to people, and these connections tie you down.

Peter Pan decided to run away from home and so he flew out the window. He lived for a time with a handful of other lost boys. When he tried to return, he found the windows barred. Since his mother had forgotten him, he decided to forget her. Now he tells everyone he is motherless and is very bitter about it. It's super queeny.

He's a sort of guardian angel fairy. If you are captured by pirates, fall from a great height, or drink poison, Peter will save your life, but only to show off. He is a good swordsman, but without a code of honor. He doesn't deeply care about how he treats you or how you treat him.

He says he doesn't want to become a man, by which he means he doesn't want to grow up. He doesn't want to become old and boring. That's why he's afraid of growing a beard.

"*Story,*" said Aparna.
"Getting there," said Stanley.

Peter takes Wendy from her home and brings her to his magical kingdom of Neverland where there are no parents. She's an "old soul" who wants to mother all the boys in Neverland—sewing their clothes, cooking them dinner, reading them stories—and she has quite a mature crush on Peter. Wendy, who is also a mother-substitute, projects onto Peter a future adulthood that is beyond what he is willing to live up to. Consider: When Wendy first meets Peter, he has just suffered a 'wardrobe malfunction' with his own shadow, and he is trying to *glue* his shadow back onto his body when it obviously needs to be *sewn* on. 'How exactly like a boy,' Wendy says.

Peter is oblivious that he is a magnet for feminine attention.

He isn't unhappy. There's just one problem. He is able to fly because he is "heartless." He's brave and spirited, but he can't be a good friend.

"And then what?" I prompted him. *"Story,"* Aparna seconded.

One day, a big, slithering crocodile pounced on a pirate. It gobbled the pirate's arm right up! Now the pirate is called "Captain Hook" after his prosthesis. He'll be happy to stay away from crocodiles. Thing is, that crocodile... has developed a taste... for... his... *blood.* That crocodile trails Captain Hook everywhere, hoping to eat the rest of him.

Normally, Captain Hook would not have a chance, except for one saving grace: The crocodile also swallowed a clock. *Tick. Tock. Tick. Tock.* And whenever the reptile draws near, Captain Hook hears the ticking of the clock in the belly of the beast. It is the finitude of his own heartbeat he hears from inside the crocodile. He is terrorized by Time.

Tick. Tock. Tick. Tock. Tick. Tock.

— *Boo!*

"OK," Aparna grinned, and clapped her hands. "*Almost* a story. I like it."

"To edit, I don't think he hears his heartbeat inside the crocodile," Stanley said. "The metaphor is mixed. He ought to hear his hand."

It was good enough for the campfire. Maybe you had to be there.

♏ ♐

104

SNOEY CONES

Diversity Committee Storytime went on for a month but it felt like the definition of a decade.

I tried to always have a story ready to go for the campfire. Also, a can of PBR. And our favorite fireside dessert was a scoop of vanilla ice cream. We called these "SNOEY cones." It's an anagram of YES/NO. (This is the sort of insight that comes after enough PBR.) Sometimes the ice cream melts and sometimes it doesn't, you see. It could be frozen, liquid, or just half-melted and snowy.

One thing I like about telling campfire stories is the opportunity to be believed. Even when I'm making them up. Even when I don't deserve to be believed.

♏ ♐

Flyleaf — Cōgitō

Descartes shuts himself up in a stove-heated room and retreats inward. <u>Who's thinking?</u> The answer comes: <u>I am.</u> His first principle is that <u>he exists</u>. He's telling his story, so the storyteller exists. Fine so far.

Another thinker might have proceeded to discuss other things they knew <u>about themselves</u>. But not Descartes—he moved directly to affirm a Big Sky-Boss, the fact of whose existence he said he knew as infallibly as he knew the fact of his own, and he affirmed that this boss would never allow him to be mistaken about a range of other insights.

When Descartes held an intense opinion, he declared there was no way he could be wrong, and he foisted responsibility—lest he seem too proud—onto the boss. <u>I can't help being infallible; the boss made me this way!</u> He's not only saying <u>Cōgitō ergō sum; I think, therefore I am</u>. He's adding: <u>My ideas are objectively correct, and everyone else is wrong</u>. That's his metalayer of certainty.

What sets Descartes' thinking apart from ours is that he shut himself up <u>alone</u> in a stove-heated room whereas we are seated together around a campfire. Each of us knows we exist, but none of us claims the god in our own story has reality-dominance over the god in anyone else's story. Our approach, surely, makes more friends. Nārrāmus ergo congregāmus; we tell stories, therefore we gather. When I say "surely," I mean I hope we're doing it right. My meta-layers of certainty are weak.

♏ ♐

105

FEELING GUILTY I LOOKED AT THE GODDESS

106

MARIAMMAN

Discomfited: I'd opened the closet door, caused the goddess to look at me, looked back at the goddess. I did not report this encounter to Aparna, as I'd have been reporting my own nosiness, but I also felt uncomfortable saying nothing. My justification for opening the door the first time was that I hadn't known where the bathroom was, and, as a life code, I hate implying my bathroom inadequacy, strangely gendered as I am. My justification for opening the door a second time was to verify the goddess's gender and anticipate whether she might speculiriate to me; my speculirium wasn't something to advertise any more than absolutely necessary, either, especially to a coworker. *Stanley* knows of my gender and my speculirium, but that's different.

♏ ♐

If I want to know who a goddess is, I know how to find out. I keep my own home library about religious iconography for just this sort of situation.

I looked up: red dress and a trident. Her name was Mariamman: the goddess, that is. A Hindu goddess from South India who brings rain.

But after seeing her murti in Aparna's house, I never saw her again, or hardly, I mean. The goddess didn't follow me to work nor speak to me while I was driving. That was brilliant of her. I was pleased with the courtesy the goddess showed me by keeping her distance, and I was pleased with myself for not imagining her.

♏ ♐

I DO NOT NEED
TO TAKE PILLS
ANYMORE

Maybe I was starting to outgrow the tendency to see ghosts and goddesses. I was less speculirious. Maybe I could focus on the ghost of Chad Goeing. If there was only one ghost, maybe I didn't need pills anymore.

Yes, that's right, I convinced myself. *I do not need to take pills anymore.*

I can't tell any story about Mariamman because she and I haven't made one together.

♏ ♐

FOG — WHY STANLEY STOPPED TALKING TO ME

Instead I want to tell the story about the Taurus. This story is embarrassing because it's about a problem I made with Stanley.

The cake is the memory entrypoint.

A delivery person buzzed my apartment. I came down. She opened the lid of a cakebox. There was a white sheetcake with two jellybeans on top, a red and a blue, like droid eyes.

My fingers and toes went numb. This meant something funny was going on with the universe.

"Red pill or blue pill?" she asked me.

"What do they do?"

"Blasted if I know. You think this is a movie where we tell you in advance what the movie's gonna do? This is more like—" She set the box on a table in the entryway, took a piping bag out of her trenchcoat pocket, and squirted "EAT ME" in black gel on the cake. "Just pick one."

I pointed to a jellybean.

"Eat it," she said. I did. She plucked off the remaining jellybean, popped it in her mouth, hopped back in her cake van, and weaved into traffic.

I do not remember which color jellybean I ate, and I remember this cake delivery mainly because that was the day Stanley stopped talking to me.

♏ ♐

FLASHBULB

SAT
25 OCT
2014

STANLEY STOPPED
TALKING TO ME
FOR A REASON

FLASHBULB

SAT
25 OCT
2014

IT IS GAY

The reason Stanley stopped talking to me is that I gave his car to a stranger. He'd wanted me to sell it for a reasonable price, but I gave it away. It's still hard to explain why that happened.

As the baseball season ended, Stanley hadn't been doing well, as they say. He'd broken up with a lover and was, as they also say, going through a rough patch. This happened while I was recovering from my hysto. By the time October rolled around, he was living in a guest house at Amity Lodge.

♏ ♐

Amity Lodge is the seasonal gay men's community that abuts conservation land way out in the 'burbs. A loose community both in the sense that it does not have an org chart and in the prudish connotation. Stanley isn't gay, but being transgender gives him a pretext to hang out there. The land is pretty.

This is the "gay place" I mentioned earlier, not like the stereotypical sites in Provincetown, but the lesser known one of which I am especially fond. It's somewhat a secret. Few straight people seem to care that a moderately monetized hippie complex is here.

♏ ♐

110

HE COULD HAVE
LIVED WITH ME

111

CHEAPER AND
LESS AFFORDABLE

Stanley could have lived with me, I suppose, but in 2014, aside from hanging out a few times by the fire in Aparna's backyard, I guess he and I hadn't been in touch meaningfully enough for either of us to propose such a novel arrangement. Not even in college, for all the time we spent together, had we ever lived in the same house. I didn't know everything that was going on with him and he didn't tell me. We would have been an odd bohemian squalor couple. I am more bohemian and Stanley is more squalor, except when it's the other way around. I found out about his whole situation when he was already in temporary housing at Amity Lodge. Then, you see, he continued to make erratic choices.

First, he got rid of his fancy car. I don't know why. Soon after, wandering the suburbs on foot, he sheltered in a used car lot during a flash thunderstorm—this is the way he told it to me—and snapped up a six-digit-mileage powder blue 1998 Ford Taurus. The problem Stanley had with his purchase, he reported, was that at this advancing stage of his car shenanigans he didn't want to pay for insurance, so he never even drove the Taurus, except maybe to the grocery store. He was becoming more cautious with age.

His story seemed a little off. Why did he downgrade his car? And why, despite the downgrade, was his overall financial situation worsening?

ORIGIN STORY
OF THE TAURUS

The origin story of the Taurus is probably unimportant. People get whatever cars they get. Anyway, due to some emergency, Stanley flew across the country. The Amity Lodge guesthouses aren't winterized so he wouldn't have stayed much longer anyway. But he left without notifying anyone and stopped paying for the room, cheap though it was, once he was gone. He left his unwanted Taurus parked outside his old guest room.

ONE DOLLAR

From a distance, he called to ask me to get rid of the Taurus for him. He told me where he'd hid the key. Officially, he sold me the car for one dollar so I would be authorized to sell it to someone else. He intended for me to give him the proceeds of the sale. It wasn't

worth, say, seven thousand dollars, but we imagined we'd get something for it.

This went down differently. I am telling you I gave it away. The car. The responsibility. The friendship.

I DID FIND
A BUYER

The sales assignment could have been a little tricky because the doors of this powder blue car had been painted, I cannot tell you why, dark green. I don't know what most people look for in cars, but probably not that. But I did find a buyer. I drove my own car to Amity Lodge where I planned to park it, switch to Stanley's car, and drive Stanley's car a little ways down the street to meet the buyers. I wanted to avoid drawing straight people's attention to the existence of Amity Lodge. And I didn't want to prejudice the sale.

FLASHBULB

SAT
25 OCT
2014

IT WAS A SATURDAY

It was a Saturday. In Judaism, you're not even supposed to talk about business transactions, let alone exchange money, on Saturday. Plus, you can't drive because starting a car counts as "lighting a fire," a type of work, *melachot*, prohibited on the Sabbath. The Romans had a category of holiday called *dies nefasti* when official business was forbidden. With my luck, I'd landed on one of those too, thereby offending the Romans as well as the Jews.

♏ ♐

FLASHBULB

SAT
25 OCT
2014

THE STONE WALL
AT AMITY LODGE

At Amity Lodge, across the dirt path that ran past Stanley's guest room, there was a low stone wall made of large, irregular, dark rocks rather crudely balanced in the old New England style. Someone had painted it, not with an aerosol spray can, I guessed, but with a brush. The paint had not resisted the weather, and there were so many depressions and protrusions on the natural rock faces, as well as gaps between the rocks, that it was hard to see what the letters were meant to say. It could have been a whole sentence, 25 letters or more. But I couldn't read it.

♏ ♐

FLASHBULB

SAT
25 OCT
2014

COULDN'T
PHOTOGRAPH IT

I pulled out my phone and tried to take a picture, but just as I tapped the screen to focus the image of the wall inside my camera app, my phone battery died. I didn't get the picture.

Somewhere nearby, a motorized weedwhacker was in heat, singing its interminable love song to the shrubbery. One last haircut before the frosts.

♏ ♐

OFF-SITE

FLASHBULB

SAT
25 OCT
2014

118

I drove Stanley's Taurus a little ways off-site to meet the buyer couple in the other parking lot, thinking I'd walk back to my own car at Amity Lodge afterward.

That car. I was driving it. The wheel was in my hands.

♏ ♐

THE BUYERS
COULD SMELL
THE CAT

FLASHBULB

SAT
25 OCT
2014

119

I remember them as "Mr. and Mrs." They arrived as scheduled, parked under a sugar maple, and approached me.

"We need to buy a car to drive home," the Mr. said, in an accent that was from a different part of the United States. "Will this one last for a while?"

"It's not really mine," I explained. "I've had the title a few days. The previous owner bought it on impulse and never drove it, and

I haven't driven it either, so I can't tell you much about it."

None of us knew how to talk about the transaction. Awkward.

I opened the front door, passenger side.

"The previous owner had a pet," the Mrs. said, sniffing inside.

♏ ♐

STANLEY'S KITTEN

FLASHBULB

SAT
25 OCT
2014

120

Stanley had indeed picked up a kitten. He'd told me about this. He'd caught the half-feral thing from its den under a house that was about to be auctioned off. It was tiger-striped with blue eyes. I didn't see it, but he showed me a photograph of it. He called it Whiskers. He planned to keep it in his guest room and hide it from the organization's cleaners who came by on a mysterious schedule. Cleaners were seasonal residents of Amity Lodge who bartered work for a free room. Stanley, apparently, had entered into no such agreement and owed rent.

♏ ♐

FLASHBULB

SAT
25 OCT
2014

YOWL AWAY

♏ ♐

I don't know what Stanley's long-term game was with the kitten, but the arrangement hadn't even lasted one day, because, in the middle of the night, Whiskers began to mew so loudly under Stanley's bed that he was certain it'd wake the Amity Lodge neighbors in the adjacent rooms. Stanley brought the kitten outside and put it in the Taurus. *Yowl away,* he said, closing the door.

The next morning, when the sun was up, Stanley returned the poor kitten to its den, where at least it would have a mother to care for it. He set Whiskers free rather than driving it to an animal shelter because, after all, his car had no insurance yet, so legally he couldn't drive the car.

FLASHBULB

SAT
25 OCT
2014

122

THAT'S HOW
HE EXPLAINED IT

It made sense to Stanley at the time. This was the way he had explained it to me. He got use out of that car only to store Whiskers overnight for noise control so he wouldn't get kicked out of the Amity Lodge guest house. And the car had continued to sit outside his room there, sinking its tires into the dirt, grinning its unlit headlights at him through his first-floor fishbowl window. That is why there was still a cat smell in the car.

♏ ♐

FLASHBULB

SAT
25 OCT
2014

123

IS JESUS
YOUR SAVIOR?

Mrs., the prospective buyer, sat in the passenger seat and asked me if the cassette player worked. There was one tape in the cupholder: a recording of Kahlil Gibran's "The Prophet." I inserted it. Yes, the cassette player worked. The cadences of Gibran evoked, I suppose, the English translations of the Bible and Qur'an.

Her eyes lit up. "Is Jesus your savior?"

It wasn't even my tape. It was Stanley's. But I took the question at face value and said I was a Jew.

"Huh," said Mr., an utterance I ignored. I did not assume his noise reflected real surprise.

♏ ♐

FLASHBULB

SAT
25 OCT
2014

124

ON SELLING A CAR

Mrs. stepped out of the car, sustained firm eye contact with me, and asked, "Why did you betray your brother?"

This was not a question I'd ever faced before. "I didn't do it," I muttered. An itchy double-consciousness set in: All I cared about was selling them the car.

Mr. stepped in front of me on the other side, hemming me in between cars in the parking lot. The recording of "The Prophet" was still playing in the background. "You're betraying him right now," he said.

♏ ♐

Flyleaf —
It Is in Your Hands

A voice from the sky answers. What it says is: "I don't know."

I fear I've forgotten the question. What did I ask, years ago?

"I don't know," the voice says, coming from Toni Morrison's Nobel lecture, "whether the bird you are holding is dead or alive, but what I do know is that it is in your hands. It is in your hands."

♏ ♐

FLASHBULB

TUE
28 OCT
2014

I GAVE THEM
THE CAR

They weren't ready to buy.

Not for all the sugar maples in Newton would I wager they'd been in Boston over a week. Maybe by the end of this week, the puzzle-piece edges of their worldview would morph into indentations similar enough to mine that we could click for just a minute to complete the transaction. *A kaleidoscope of shapes joining*— Beyond that, I didn't require an additional minute with them.

I asked them to decide by the end of the week. They left. We all had some things to think about.

I drove Stanley's Taurus back to Amity Lodge, parked it where I'd found it, and drove my own car home, where I charged my phone.

♏ ♐

FLASHBULB

TUE
28 OCT
2014

INFINITY WAR

A few days later, Marvel announced that they'd make an *Avengers* sequel. It would be called *Infinity War*. We'd have to wait years for it. How many? I wagered three. That's all I posted to social media before Mr. and Mrs. called back and said, yes, they wanted the Taurus, and I drove back out to Amity Lodge and transferred the car to them. Because I wasn't keeping a journal and wasn't posting much online, I don't have a record of what was going through my mind and, even in retrospect, I still can't piece together what I was thinking when I *gave* Stanley's car to them. For free.

♏ ♐

Flyleaf —
Dragon's Treasure

Understand that even the warrior Beowulf could do only so much in his lifetime. When he fought the venomous, fire-breathing dragon, the dragon dealt him a mortal blow before he was able to stagger forward one last time and slay it. Together they died, and the dragon's treasure was left for someone else to enjoy.

♏ ♐

127

SAME DOLLAR

Mr. and Mrs. carted away the Taurus. I was so grateful to have it over with—the annoying obligation to Stanley, and the interaction with them—that I charged them one dollar, signed over the title to them, and that was that.

It was a decision I made from my gut, one which, of course, caused me to have a problem with Stanley.

♏ ♐

128

STANLEY HAD
FEELINGS

From wherever he was on the West Coast, Stanley ordered a cake delivered to me as a "thank you" for making the car go away. That was the cake, as I told you, that arrived with two jellybeans of which I ate one and the delivery person ate the other.

Stanley ordered the cake before he realized that I hadn't come up with any money for him. When I told him I hadn't demanded payment from the buyers, he had feelings.

♏ ♐

129

IT WASN'T
ABOUT THE MONEY

130

MISTAKE

"You are a coward," he told me on the phone, "and not a friend. You let people barge through you like you're air. I can't rely on you for anything."

But I am good at swiping my credit card for all kinds of things. I take terrible boys to tropical islands and pay for their scuba diving with cash and don't even get laid for that. Given that, I could pay for Stanley's—

"I can give you money," I said. "A fair amount for the car."

"I don't want your money," he snapped. "I have money. I don't need more. I need you to do a thing when I ask you to do a thing. I need to know you can do that."

♏ ♐

To be fair, I did a thing. I got rid of the car. That was the assignment.

"It was my choice not to take money for it. That was a mistake. I can replace—"

"I told you, I don't need your money. I don't want whatever strings it comes with."

"There are no strings—not on me," I replied woodenly, puppeting ventriloquisted words from who knows where. "If I give you money, it's kind of your money."

"It isn't." Well, he was right. If it came from my wallet and not from his buyers, it was my money and not his. "Don't even talk to me," he said.

"Can we email about it?"

"Don't contact me. I need space."

"OK," I said. "Got it."

♏ ♐

FOG — SHARK, BOOM

He was treating me as if I were a shark. Looking back, I feel as though there were sharks in this situation and that I was not one of them. There are sharks on the Cape Cod beaches, great whites, more than one, sharks that weren't here when I was a kid, but we've eaten all the deep-sea fish and the seals returned to the shore, so we've got sharks now, they're here to eat the seals, and Massachusetts plans to count the predators. I don't know what good it does to count great white sharks. You just have to avoid them.

I wanted to redo. Redo *how*, I didn't know. But I wanted to try again.

When the exiled Okonkwo despairs in Chinua Achebe's novel *Things Fall Apart*, he reflects on the proverb of his Ibo elders that a man determines his own destiny. As his free will chooses, his personal god obeys; "if a man said yea his *chi* also affirmed." But Okonkwo is different: "Here was a man whose *chi* said nay despite his own affirmation."

I said *yes* and *yes* and *yes*. The answer echoed back: *no*. Given no options, my free will was inert and didn't dig into hypotheticals.

The Romans called their sauna the *laconicum* after a Greek region where it was the only kind of hot bath those Spartans allowed themselves. No water, lots of fog. The Spartans didn't say much either, which is why *laconic* means *not talking*.

I didn't know what Stanley wanted. We were an overcontact binary, stars in close, unstable orbit. Who collapsed, who exploded? We'd find out, I supposed, when our light hit home.

Surrender your weapons, the Persian king suggested. *Come and get them*, the Spartans taunted.[*] Is that a yes or a no? Depends if the question is whether you're having a fight.

He didn't want me to contact him. And he didn't call me.

"El estampido llegó a mis oídos mucho después que el griterío de la gente," Vázquez Montalbán writes in *Yo maté a Kennedy*. First you hear the general commotion of grief and somewhat later you hear the *boom* from your own gun.

♏︎↗

---

[*] Plutarch. *Moralia.* "Sayings of the Spartans" ("Apophthegmata Laconica"). 225c.11.

Flyleaf — Maybe It Was Something About That Car

Did you know a tiny piece of Russia's Cosmos-2251 satellite once came loose and is orbiting freely somewhere up there in the sky? The European Space Agency fired thrusters on its Automated Transfer Vehicle to push the International Space Station out of the way so it wouldn't be hit. The space junk was a pebble a couple miles away, but still, one must take precautions. There is no "only" in space disasters. It happened the day before <u>Infinity War</u> was announced, but we were just hearing about it. That makes sense: the maneuver was something that happened, but the collision was something that didn't happen.

I've never believed that everything must have a meaningful cause. Philosophers call it the Principle of Sufficient Reason. I don't believe it's a real principle. I don't believe we'll ever know why everyone does the things they do. After all, Stanley bought the car on impulse. I got rid of it on impulse. Maybe it was something about that car.

You cannot just get rid of other people's shit. Be you an adventure hero inside your own story, the broken shit you encounter on the side of the road is still someone else's shit. Use the mouse to point at the object in the video game, then click. See what happens. If nothing were programmed to happen, the video game designers wouldn't have coded that object into the game.

♏ ♐

FLASHBULB

MON
3 NOV
2014

131

BE CAREFUL
WHAT I WISH FOR

I wished I had the car back. No: I should be careful what I wish for. Who knows what the Mr. and Mrs. did with it and whether the car was still in working order. Maybe they had the good sense to profit by selling it to a chop shop for parts. In which case, let's not bring it back. Who wants a dead car back? Who ever wants to confront the horrid Christine-ianity of a car that has had the bejeezus smashed out of her and is somehow still standing virgo intacta in the driveway, her front grille powder blue as the day I knew her, her doors repainted ivy green, but still neat as the day she was machined?

♏ ♐

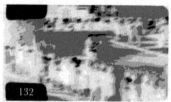

FLASHBULB

MON
3 NOV
2014

RED LIGHT

No, that's not what I wanted. The car never mattered. I just wanted Stanley to be talking to me again.

"Caution: Expect Solar Glare in A.M." says a sign I've seen on Route 2 way out west. I see it when I'm heading back to Boston. *Warning: The sun rises in the east.* The sign is correct, the sun does do that, and it burns, and you can't see anything else.

Is *"No!"* an exclamation or a conversation? "No" is the end of a road, that's what it is. Red light. Stuck. The driver must alter course.

♏ ♐

Flyleaf — Imagine the Change

Oil Lamp Turned Down
"You must change your life." Rilke was 32 when he wrote his poem about a headless statue. Even without a head, Apollo's torso still has some kind of life, procreative and wild-furred. "Here there is no place that does not see you," Rilke wrote. Apollo's eye-less gaze is like the flame on an oil lamp turned down, "zurückgeschraubt," but ready to explode like a star. I am 33. Thirty-three.

True Seeing
If the Irish glamour is a spell on how you appear to others and the pishogue is a spell on how you perceive them, I wonder what is the name for the assumption that light is emitted rather than received by the eye, and that the light of true seeing, the light by which you see the god and the god sees you, resides not in Apollo's eyes but in his torso. Or that light is found everywhere, really, once it has exploded. No place that does not see you. Thirty-three: You are one year too late. Go change your life.

The Change Must Be Imagined
The change must be believed to be possible. This grammatical construction means two things. First, a prediction: If you don't believe an outcome is possible, you won't attempt it. Second, a thought-act: Your belief in the change, your belief alone, determines its reality. You may not need to act.

We hold contradictory beliefs from our earliest days. We want the parent to soothe us, we want to learn to soothe ourselves. We want to receive, and that which is not yet received we want to create. Thing is, whichever we choose, the Other Transsexual still won't be talking to us. Whether he is talking to us is his choice. He will do what he wants to do when he is ready or when he changes what he wants.

No Framework

There is no schema for the change, no Kantian "Always behave in such a way...," no 12-part Rule of Benedict for how to be an excellent monk.* No one tells you how to change. If they do, you know not to listen; you know you have to know it for yourself.

Stations of the Cross

At times like these, I recite lists. Lists are calming. I recall the Stations of the Cross, which are:

The Garden of Gethsemane.
Judas' betrayal.
The Sanhedrin's judgment.
Peter's denial.
Pilate's judgment.
The crown of thorns.
Simon's assistance.
The women of Jerusalem.
Mercy to the thief.
Mary and John.
Death.
Burial.

I might be missing a couple, as it's not my religious tradition, but that's basically it.

Transvaluation of All Values

Speaking of people who write outside their religious tradition, Nietzsche wrote in The Antichrist that Jesus came to Earth on a dies nefastus. Maybe he meant that Christmas had originally been some other Roman holiday when no one was supposed to be doing anything and Mary shouldn't have been giving birth. Anyway, Nietzsche said he would personally denounce Christianity in writing "upon all walls, wherever walls are to be found" because he thought the religion endorsed the virtue of suffering, and he believed it was important instead to self-actualize. He called his project the "transvaluation of all values."

I also wanted to reinterpret whatever it was that nabbed me and kept me in this pit of misery, but I could not reach it as long as I was in the pit of misery.

♏ ↗

---

* These associations were made by Peter Sloterdijk. *You Must Change Your Life: On Anthropotechnics.* (First published as *Du mußt dein Leben ändern.* Suhrkamp Verlag Frankfurt am Main, 2009.) Translated from German by Wieland Hoban. Cambridge, UK: Polity Press, 2013. See Chapter 7, "The Complete and the Incomplete: How the Spirit of Perfection Entangles the Practising in Stories." pp. 253–255.

FLASHBULB

MON
3 NOV
2014

133

EYE IN THE SKY

FLASHBULB

MON
3 NOV
2014

134

ICE BETWEEN US

Key in the ignition to drive to work. On the radio, first "Instant Crush" by Daft Punk, then "Eye in the Sky" by the Alan Parsons Project, but they were little comfort.

Stanley wasn't doing well, as they say, and apparently neither was I. He wanted to be done with me for a while, I kept having to remind myself, as if it were a freshly delivered fact.

"Eye in the Sky" has quintessentially soothing vocals, but ultimately, however kind the words may be, the singer is bidding the listener goodbye with cause.

♏ ♐

Days passed like water dripping from the gutter, an icicle forming, everything burning. Cold burns. And it wasn't even late enough in the year for real ice, the sun still above the horizon until quarter to six. It was ice in me, between us. It was el delique, the exquisite sensitivity of hurt feelings, practically a crime.

I still feel as though I'm carrying a weight.

"A time has to be gone through without any reward, natural or supernatural," said Simone Weil.

I still feel immobilized, and I suspect I may die on this hill.

♏ ♐

FLASHBULB

MON
3 NOV
2014

135

SHADOW
LENGTHENING

FLASHBULB

MON
10 NOV
2014

136

FOG INSIDE ME

Psalm 109: *Broken-hearted, I'm like a shadow that lengthens until it disappears, and people shake me off like a locust. I become thinner, my knees tremble, and people shake their head at the sight of me.*

I missed Stanley something fierce, sure, but more fundamentally I was missing a part of myself that—as was becoming clear—I'd always located in him. Losing someone from the transsexual cohort is like losing a foxhole buddy, one of the few guys who knows about the thing in our pasts that neither of us ever otherwise talk about.

First, I had to find which parts of me were mine.

And if I have enemies, let them be the ones who are judged, condemned, shamed, destroyed, forgotten.

♏ ♐

Soon: Thirty-four. Two life cycles of the cicada. There may not have been a cicada brood in the year of my birth, but I'm considering myself as part of my own brood: the Cicada Men.

Listening to Sting: "If I Ever Lose My Faith in You." Felt like there wouldn't ever be any new music.

That time of year, on cold mornings, early in the commute, I saw white fog hanging close to the ground, over fields, marshes. *Souls. Swamps have souls.*

♏ ♐

Flyleaf — Could Have Been One or Two

When we think and choose differently, we create ourselves anew. Some say there's no such thing as character at all; we <u>are</u> whatever we <u>do</u>. How can character be reified? There isn't even any such thing as a stable, essential sex? <u>Fog</u>. It's all fog.

Iran, they said, was nuclearizing. Wafting yellow gas through tubes. World powers talking in Vienna.

Henry David Thoreau objected to slavery and the Mexican-American War, or tried to, by not paying taxes. He spent one night in jail and it appears his aunt took care of his tax bill.

When a Cicada Man dies, he will disappear for exactly 17 years, and then he will come back as another cicada. There is probably a charm to stop this, but why would I want to? I would be willing to come back.

After JFK was shot once and slumped over, "I heard another shot or two," Abraham Zapruder told WFAA-TV in an impromptu interview. Zapruder had arrived at the Dallas station, along with the local Secret Service chief, a couple police officers, his own business partner, and the *Dallas Morning News* reporter Harry McCormick, to ask them to develop his film. They put him on the air. "I couldn't say whether it was one or two…"

An epiphany is when you return to something you already knew but in a way that feels different and revelatory.

The Zapruder tape, exposing our fears of mortality, makes "some argument about the nature of film itself," Don DeLillo wrote in <u>Underworld</u>.

When you videorecord, you are already anticipating how this moment will look in the future when it is no longer present but part of the past.*

Leonard Cohen repeats a political complaint in "Nevermind": "layers of time," he observes, as the percussion keeps pace with the poem.

Madonna sings about her feelings in "Rain," and the song changes key.

---

* I based this on a statement by the literature professor Mark Currie: Film looks toward the future "from which the present will be reexperienced as representation of the past."

EPISODE 4

FIRST EMAIL (SNOWSHOVEL)

THE TV
IN THE BREAKROOM

When I grab coffee in the breakroom, news of another mass shooting is running on the TV. The screen covers most of the wall. I see and hear, not watching nor listening. Just pour coffee. The coverage is familiar, though this shooting happened in a state I've never been to. Each news network must have a script for these ruinations. As if we're on a loop. Right now I'm tapped out: trying to self-care, not able to self-care. Caramel-flavored coffee separates my mornings from my nights.

♏ ♐

APARNA ENTERS

Aparna enters the breakroom behind me and stands at the same kitchen counter. She's an inch taller than me. She fiddles with her insulated food bag.

I point my thumb at the people dying on the TV. "Groundhog Day," I say.

"Who's the groundhog?"

"I am." None of this is flirting. She once called me her gay best friend, and I called her my office wife.

"That means you get to decide how much more winter we'll have. Does it really have to be another six weeks?" she says.

♏ ♐

FLASHBULB

TUE
9 DEC
2014

GROUNDHOG DAY
IS A FILM

FLASHBULB

TUE
9 DEC
2014

BUSY

I'm not sure if she's talking about the actual Groundhog Day holiday, which is still two months away. The White Witch has cast the spell over the land so it's "always winter, but never Christmas." We will be solid ice for a while and no groundhog can save us yet.

No: I wasn't thinking of Groundhog Day on the calendar, but rather of the film in which an ordinary day repeats, repeats, repeats. You wake up and it's the same day. All you can do is try to live it as best as you can.

"I can always use another six weeks," I say. That'd be three development sprints. "Imagine what we could accomplish with the extra time."

♏ ♐

"Agile Principle #3: Deliver on short timescales," she didacts.

"Could they be any shorter?!" I said, not expecting a response. They cannot. At this office, when we say "How are you?" in passing, even the most common response, "Busy," has yielded to a new form of dialogue. Now it is in vogue to reply silently with a sigh and eyebrow raise. By which I mean to say: There is no room for the project timescales to cut themselves any further. They are irreducible particles now. Fifty hours a week I help make security cameras, but the hours are so full that they agglomerate and calcify, and "fifty" means very little. "Full-time work" isn't literally every hour in the day, yet I can't do more.

♏ ♐

FLASHBULB

TUE
9 DEC
2014

141

THE WORK

FLASHBULB

TUE
9 DEC
2014

142

MISSING CAMERA

Winter hasn't yet officially begun. Rain and fog all day. By the time spring comes, the artificial intelligence developed here at Achromatic Proprioception will be far more advanced and unrecognizably more powerful, the product of our collective decisions.

We'll deliver small projects for a few sprints, and then, on February 1, our latest feature goes live: GPS tracking of our camera hardware. The cameras have had the chips for a while, but we've never turned on the feature that tracks them.

Our team already lost one of our camera prototypes with the new chip. We never took a formal inventory, but we made the prototype and then it just wasn't there anymore. No one could find it.

♏ ♐

That happened last year. In the future, it'll be impossible to lose another. They'll all have chips and we'll know where each of them is all the time. Soon, we'll begin seeing our cameras in the system, sighting them in the wild, as naturalists track microchipped animals. We might find that missing prototype and our set will be complete once again and forever.

The television pixels bleed violence like static. Still running coverage of the mass shooting.

The Zapruder film was one of the first satellite broadcasts. People watched it in Mexico.

As Aparna prepares her food, I spill coffee on my front. Bright hot. I jump. I thought I wasn't flirting, but my distraction is transparent. She snickers.

♏ ♐

FLASHBULB

TUE
9 DEC
2014

143

DON'T BE LATE

My work phone blips with the calendar notification: *Project status update meeting, December 9, 2014, 11:00 a.m. Eastern, Boardroom, beginning in 5 minutes.*

The last time I was several minutes late to an A.P. meeting, a couple heads turned when I walked in, and then I had trouble connecting to the Wi-Fi. I suppose this was disruptive because my boss mentioned it to me later. I'd say his comment was "subtle" but I can't say for sure what the subtext was. I just try not to be late. Time may have no reality but the agreement of showing up.

My wristwatch already says 11:00 though my phone says 10:55. I had set my wristwatch to do that.

♏ ♐

Flyleaf — Five Minutes Fast

I am one of the few people who still wears a wristwatch, not as a throwback, but as a throwforward: an attempt to make myself believe I'm running five minutes late. As long as I don't remind myself that it's a lie, the wristwatch trick helps me arrive places on time. I half-believe.

I'm not exactly fooling myself, as mobile phone time is not any more "real" than wristwatch time. The phone is cisgender and the wristwatch is transgender—meaning, today, more people play according to the former construct, but neither has any objective reality. You can operate with two constructs that are five minutes apart. If you play your constructs against each other smartly, you arrive early to your meeting, and you win your own game.

♏ ♐

FLASHBULB

TUE
9 DEC
2014

144

PROJECT STATUS
UPDATE MEETING

FLASHBULB

TUE
9 DEC
2014

145

CURIOUS

I am the first to arrive in the fifth-floor boardroom. I drop my notebook on the large oblong table, wander to the window, and gaze over the Charles River.

I consider whether Chad jumped to his death in 1900.

I have heard that it is a myth, in the sense of a fiction, that businessmen leapt to their deaths as the stock market crashed in 1929; however, considering myth in the sense of tragedy, of story, of deep truth, it makes sense. It is true without being true.

♏︎♐︎

On the weekends: to the library, to think, to work on the mystery of Chad Goeing. If I were on a game show like *Tele-Quiz*, I'd introduce myself as "a writer" because it would sound good on a national broadcast. But it's barely true. I have time to write when I've reached my limits scrounging around in the office database. And it's not even original writing. When I'm working on *The Nature of Time*, I'm researching a book that Chad Goeing already wrote, which feels like messing in someone else's papers, and I end up curious about him as a person, which makes me more of a biographer, except that I never seem to produce a biography. All told, the effort amounts to a hobby.

♏︎♐︎

FLASHBULB

TUE
9 DEC
2014

146

TOO BUSY TO TALK

Achromatic Proprioception demands most of my time. If I'm not in a meeting, I am in my office with the door almost all the way closed, letting my coworkers see I'm in there and letting them wager I'm probably too busy to talk. That's what it takes to be cutting edge. If you're too early or too late, you'll miss the moment to slice, so you must be prepared when the blade's exact moment arrives. That's what I spend almost all my time doing, and I do it for the company.

♏ ♐

FLASHBULB

TUE
9 DEC
2014

147

SCORE +1

Aparna arrives. We're both early. This will be a political capital score of +1 for each of us, though it doesn't count until someone sees us.

'Blip' goes my work phone: *Project status update meeting, December 9, 2014, 11:00 a.m. Eastern, beginning now.*

♏ ♐

FLASHBULB

TUE
9 DEC
2014

148

WHAT IF
CHAD JUMPED?

"What if Chad jumped?" I say aloud, gazing out through the closed window over the narrow stretch of riverine semi-wilderness. Just above freezing, supposed to get colder tomorrow. I extend my gaze to the horizon which is pocked by pointy sticks of bare trees stretching to suburban infinity. I am Panopticon. My fingers and toes are tingling.

"Interesting," says Aparna, not looking up from her phone. She's listened to me talk about my library interests a lot. We're still alone in the boardroom.

♏ ♐

149

I SEE HIM LAND

150

BREAKROOM
TELEVISION LOOP

"Or maybe he hanged himself. It was a leap— No, not hanging. He leapt, but he exited some other way. I see his feet springing, he's falling through the air, I see him land."

11:01. Everyone else is late to this meeting.

The boss strides into the boardroom, walking with alacrity as though he's coming from and going to important places, which might be true, since much depends on how we contextualize ourselves in the world as important or not, plus on which changes we believe possible, and I fall silent. His shirt is neat. He doesn't have much hair, so his head and neck are neat, too.

For arriving before the boss, I record the score of +1 in my mental ledger.

♏ ♐

Meeting ends.

The television in the breakroom plays the mass shooting on a loop. Television violence is starting to disagree with me.

When I encounter haters—people who are antagonistic toward queer folk—I encounter them in Massachusetts because I live here and this is where they would find me, but I like to imagine them as being from other states. They call us "snowflakes," not because of the snowy weather here (in what I imagine they imagine to be not their state but a queer state) but because they imagine us to have delicate sensibilities, to require this climate. It's all connected: the hate, the violence. I am starting to see it.

I'm not fragile, not melting yet, but I cannot watch this broadcast.

♏ ♐

FLASHBULB

TUE
9 DEC
2014

151

FAR FROM
THE SUPPLY CLOSET

I bring my coffee to my desk. I'm close to the bathroom, which I don't mind.

When I had the opportunity to choose from one of several offices, I requested that HR put me as far away from the supply closet as possible, since it's full of paperclips. That's a door I don't want to open. (Unless I found myself locked inside the office. Then, needing to pick a lock, I'd be pleased to have a paperclip. At least I know where to find them.)

Better to be close to the bathroom. HR has labeled the corridor wall by my office entryway with my name placard, "Lev Ockenshaw." If a gunman were ever looking for me by name, I'd hide in the bathroom.

♏ ♐

FOG — LIFE DEATH TRAUMA HOPE

Everything that will happen is inscribed in the Book of Life and Death and Trauma and Hope. Even the unsolved mysteries are inscribed there: what really happened, when they will be solved, who will solve them. The shootings that will happen, and those that might not, are inscribed. The names of the people we believed would bring peace are definitely inscribed. JFK has been dead for a half-century.

♏ ♐

FLASHBULB

TUE
9 DEC
2014

152

THE FIRST EMAIL

I walk to the bathroom. Mirror, mirror: My skin looks pale. My eyes are gray.

As I stand over the sink, the sound of a gong rings out from my pocket. That's my notification of an incoming personal email. Work meeting reminders go "blip," and I like the gong better.

The sender is **what_will_happen_chromatically**. Not a handle I recognize. The domain is recognizable, but that's nothing; they provide millions of free, throwaway email accounts. I almost delete the message as spam, but I notice the similarity to my company name, and the subject line "Are you curious about the darkness?" makes it stand out.

♏ ♐

FLASHBULB

TUE
9 DEC
2014

153

BAD SHIT

I touch the screen to open the email. It says:

"Bad shit is happening! What happens when you work for a company that is in the mud! You are all being investigated now to account for your crimes! Too much for me! Curious?"

It is unsigned. *What will happen chromatically?* My question is more like: *What does someone believe I am supposed to know about what they're talking about?*

♏ ♐

Flyleaf — Clippy

All of Achromatic Proprioception mimics a distress pattern. It's institutionalized emotional dysfunction, or IED for short.

Our Microsoft Office is so old that it still has Clippy, the little animated paperclip that wiggles its eyebrows and asks you if you need help with typing. A combination of boss, psychotherapist, and smackable gnat. I turn it off but it never stays down. It's always trying to start a conversation with me.

Security cameras must swivel to point at their targets. Our company programs them, which I explain by saying that we teach robots to move despite their poor vision. That is a smidgen inaccurate, but it gets at the important part.

Teddy Ruxpin

Aparna is good with hardware. Everyone who works with her knows this, but for the benefit of those who are uncertain, she has MacGyvered an original Teddy Ruxpin to run on a four-track tape recorder. The sounds that make Teddy blink his eyes and wiggle his mouth are on the secret second track you can't hear. If you ask Aparna nicely, she might let you speak into the tape recorder on her desk to record a new sentence over the first track, and you can play your voice back. If you matched the movement track, Teddy Ruxpin's mouth seems to deliver your words in your voice.

Things the Bear Can Say

I can say into the tape recorder, "And so, my fellow Americans: ask not what your country can do for you; ask what you can do for your country." I can put the altered tape in the bear, the bear will repeat what I said, and it's cute. Someone else can stop by, tape over what I said, and my mini-performance will be gone forever. I've wanted to try recording "Unchained Melody" but then I'd have to change the second track too, so that the bear's little lip hangs open for exactly the right length of the notes as it pretends to belt out the song. Also, if I ever execute that recording well, I will be sad when it's inevitably deleted to make room for some other babbling brook that flows to the sea. Also, I am supposed to be working.

My Hands Are Clean

I'm not great at making cameras. Better at breaking them. That's why I'm a tester. I think of objects that cameras can't see well, distances they can't breach, directions they can't swivel. I think of data they capture incorrectly, false facts with which humans will cook up wrong theories. I remember all the bugs I find. Aparna once asked me if I have an eidetic memory. I had to look up the word. No, I don't think there's anything unusual about how my brain stores images. When I read or write a bug report, I just remember a keyword from it, with which I can search the system for it later. This seems obvious to me. I do not know how other people store information.

ℳ ↗

FLASHBULB

TUE
9 DEC
2014

154

LIKE
WIGGLING VERMIN

The message from **what_will_happen_chromatically** revolves in my mind. "Curious," sure, I'd call myself that. "Mud" could appeal to me. I'm all about the riverbank. But I know nothing about "crimes," "bad shit," or who might want to investigate this company. I don't work at that level—not the high power level, not the secretive shadow level, not the making-shit-up level, not any of it. This email sounds simply sinister. It's made of normal phrases that feel like wiggling vermin. I have no idea why it came to me, but I fear my own underestimation of what a single bad actor might do from behind his invisibility cape.

I will not bother Aparna with it. Why distract her? She can't stop Internet goons from harassing me.

ℳ ↗

FLASHBULB

TUE
9 DEC
2014

155

I WILL
REPORT IT UP

Here is a better idea: Report it up to prove my hands are clean. I think I will earn 50 political capital points for handing over an interesting criminal threat to the boss.

♏ ♐

FOG — HOUSE

I do realize this is a bit like the moment in *House* in which seven teenage girls are trapped in a haunted house, and the one named Prof (because she wears glasses) reassures the one named Fantasy (because her daydreams seem to conjure the spirits): "Your love, Mr. Tôgô, is coming soon. He's a man, after all. He can help us!" Fantasy briefly imagines her teacher, Mr. Tôgô, riding in on a white horse and declaring his love for her. Instead, a few minutes later, their friend Melody is gobbled up by a haunted piano.

But I do believe that vice presidents like to be given command of information, which is why, even if he cannot save me from so much as a piano, I am going to speak to him.

♏ ♐

FLASHBULB

TUE
9 DEC
2014

156

THE BOSS DOES NOT
WANT TO HEAR IT

When I walk into my boss' office, he wants to talk with me about something camera-related. I forget what they are calling our department these days, but he has recently taken command of it. He is a vice president. When I present him with a printout of the weird email, he looks at me over his glasses and says: "You are not telling me, *at all,* what I want to hear right now."

♏ ♐

FLASHBULB

TUE
9 DEC
2014

157

THAT IS MY POINT

"I know, sir. That is exactly my point, sir," I reply. This is why companies hire testers: We stand our ground and make sure that our warnings are heard, and the boss typically feels at least briefly uncomfortable. His discomfort marks the exact moment when he should give extra thought to what the tester is reporting and to why it bothers him. Or he could just get mad, which is what he will probably do in this moment.

But he has no reaction that is obvious to me. He slides my printout into his desk drawer. He says he will look into it.

♏ ♐

FLASHBULB

WED
10 DEC
2014

158

NEXT TIME I FLY

The next day trudges. Doomgress.*

---

* My 10th-grade history teacher, Bill Schechter, wanted "doomgress" to be a word.

Though not paid hourly, I check my wristwatch every 15 minutes. Light rain turns to snow. Today's date reminds me of something.

♏ ♐

Flyleaf — Repetitions on a Theme

As my job role does not include writing technical documents, I memorize keywords in bug reports. If I am not allowed to create a narrative about how the system is supposed to work, at least I can memorize details about how it is actually working. I familiarize myself with the actual product. I touch it and see what it does. Eventually, there is no difference between perceiving the present and the past. It's all how the boss believes the system currently works because that is his current story of how it was always supposed to work, overlaid on the sedimentary rock of last year's system errors.

Repetitions on a theme dredge the unconscious, make myth, help me spot relevant detail. Repeating keywords grease the lane between seeing and recording. Repetitive thoughts cause problems, but alternatives are worse: anger, lies.

♏ ♐

FLASHBULB

WED
10 DEC
2014

159

I REMEMBER
THE TERRIBLE BOY

I'm churning through my mental anti-Rolodex of untrustworthy people I'd be happy to forget except that I need to remember the keyword "untrustworthy." I'm looking for a match on who might have sent that creepy email. I remember the terrible boy I once dated and the terrible vacation we took together. The sender might be someone like him: young, ridiculous, angry, resisting something he's unwilling to articulate. His complaint might be valid and partly my fault.

♏ ♐

FLASHBULB

WED
10 DEC
2014

160

LOGAN AIRPORT

I remember the body scanner at Logan Airport. A security theater worker in another room looks at our nudie pics. New machines cartoonize the images. Is that "less invasive"? The government's still measuring what's in our pants. Transgender people doubly sacrifice personal liberty down both sides of our genders, which I hope makes us doubly effective in helping stop terrorists. Does my cartoonized body confuse or amuse the audience in the security theater? May the curse of Ham be upon the Transportation Security Administration for filming Noah's nakedness.

♏ ♐

Flyleaf — Near-Drowning

I remember why the date sounds familiar. Last year, George Saunders published a story collection, Tenth of December. In the title story, a young man half-drowns in a frozen pond, and a passerby fishes him out, half-freezing in the process.

Moses goes up the mountain, the cloud rolls in, the boss's voice calls to him from the cloud, he goes into the cloud and stays 40 days and writes a psalm which, the sages will later say, praises the boss's "secret place." By traditional interpretation, he also receives the whole Torah right about then.*

♏ ♐

---

* This is the 160th reading in Lev's schema: the 18th weekly Torah portion, Mishpatim, 7th reading. The sages say that Moses wrote Psalm 91 while he was up on the mountain. Psalm 91's word for "secret place" is סֵתֶר.

FLASHBULB

FRI
12 DEC
2014

161

THE ZAPRUDER FILM

FLASHBULB

FRI
12 DEC
2014

162

BOOT UP

On the third morning, my car is wrapped in frost. I chip it off with a plastic ice scraper. Everyone drives a bit more slowly. Extra minutes of commute.

"Casual Friday" dress code. That means everyone wears jeans. Jeans have got four pockets in front: the two wallet-sized ones and the two little decorative ones. Levi Strauss has been making jeans this way since Chad was alive. In that era, the little pockets weren't merely decorative. They held your pocket watch. Later, maybe, they held pay phone quarters. Today there is no pay phone in which to use the quarter, so a pocketed quarter would be forgotten and fall out in the laundry machine.

♏ ♐

I boot up my computer. The standard image comes up: An image of a silver wheel with a black stripe around the edge, turning, turning. It is a wheel from the 1961 Lincoln Continental in which JFK was assassinated.

The video footage is from Abraham Zapruder's amateur creation that turned out to be the most famous short film of all time. The murder weapon doesn't appear in the video. That's why everything that *is* in the video seems so important. Everyone watches that video flattering themselves by imagining they can tease out where the gun must have been.

♏ ♐

FLASHBULB

FRI
12 DEC
2014

163

NEOMEMORY

The company doesn't make us watch all 26 seconds, the whole event with its violence, every time we boot up our computers. No, the animation built into our computers is a close-up of the Lincoln's wheel, just enough to remind us why we make security cameras: to prevent and to investigate magnicide.

And to expect the unexpected and catch that on tape too.

Today's the feast day of Nuestra Señora de Guadalupe. If a tape had been running in 1531, it could've caught María's apparition.

♏ ♐

Flyleaf — Image Sequence

Linear time is an illusion, said Einstein, and so too said Heriberto Yépez in The Empire of Neomemory. What we experience, Yépez said, is "a sequence of recycled images. History is the same as the spectacle. It is the greatest spectacle of them all." We're on a "film-loop," and "only by understanding it in its real movement can it be unraveled."

The Torah itself doesn't give details of its transmission. It's as though there are missing frames in the film. Anyway, it doesn't make sense that Moses received the whole Torah as a young man, because it contains his whole biography. He could have read his future. Then, if he made different choices, his alternate path would have disproved the Torah.

James Frey's memoir turned out to be fake. Not nonfiction at all. Fiction. He made it up. The publisher offered readers a refund if they mailed in page 163. No instruction on whether to include page 164. I never mailed mine because I never bought the book.*

♏ ♐

---

* The book was a *A Million Little Pieces*. ("James Frey and His Publisher Settle Suit Over Lies," Motoko Rich, *New York Times*, September 7, 2006). I was reminded of this by David Shields' *Reality Hunger*.

164

ORG CHART
OF DESPAIR

165

NOTHING TO DO
WITH US

There's still no follow-up email from my boss about the threat I reported. Sometimes vice presidents need three days. He must be making a deep inquiry.

I walk into his office and stand in front of his desk, directly facing his poster-sized Org Chart of Despair that's taped to the wall behind him. *He* doesn't call it that, but *I* can, as long as I remember not to say it out loud.

I ask if he can tell me anything new about the threat that was sent to me.

"Oh, that," he says, as if he'd almost forgotten. "We've determined the email wasn't sent from a company account."

♏ ♐

My lower lip drops, and he must see an acorn-sized dark "o" of naked surprise above it.

The sender used a common email provider. The domain name appears after the @ sign of their handle. *That's how email works.* Three days for multiple people to confirm the domain isn't Achromatic Proprioception dot com?

"I know it isn't a company email account. I didn't think it was," I say calmly. "What I was asking is why someone would use a version of our company name to create a handle at another email provider and send me an anonymous warning about 'bad shit.' That's a threat."

The boss looks almost pensive for a moment. "I don't think the name **what_will_happen_chromatically** has anything to do with Achromatic Proprioception."

♏ ♐

YOU COULD TALK
TO THE POLICE

SILVER NITRATE
FILM

"But—"

"Just a coincidence." He sips his coffee and looks at me sternly. "It showed up in your personal email. It's your private correspondence. If you have a security concern with it, you need to talk to your email provider—"

"What?"

"—or to the police. This has nothing to do with me or with the company."

"You want me to go to the police?"

"It's up to you. I need you to stop talking about this."

♏ ♐

"But *he* is the one talking about it." I jab my finger at the sheet of paper. I assume the anonymous sender is a man.

"You're bringing him into the company. You need to stop."

As if I were the one conjuring the guy into being, throwing him into our world. Just like that, my boss pushes the matter off the edge of our shared reality.

♏ ♐

Flyleaf — Unreal

The boss seems unreal to me now, as if he were a rear-screen projection: a film serving as moving scenery within the rest of my movie. The journalist Jean-Dominique Bauby said he felt this way about Paris when he saw it from his ambulance window months after a cerebrovascular event wrecked his brain stem. I don't know from brain injuries, but projections—yes, those I know.

An old kind of film called silver nitrate tends to degrade, and when you feed it through the projector, it could catch fire, and water won't put it out.[*]

I imagine my situation is very much like 1962 when JFK learned the Soviets were building nuclear missiles in Cuba but he couldn't tell anyone about it. If he'd blabbed, he would have brought the Soviets into the company. He had to privately review his options. Maybe, just maybe, nothing would happen. If nothing happens, that is a victory.

♏︎♐︎

FLASHBULB

FRI
12 DEC
2014

168

PLUS NOTHING

I return to my desk. A poster with the 12 Agile Principles is taped to the wall I face. I taped it there because these are concepts about which my boss wants me to think.

Nothing comes to mind. Nothing.

I remember an article in *Harper's*, "Jesus Plus Nothing," about the rising theocracy in this country. Jesus is what you need, just Jesus, they say. But it's not *only* Jesus. "Plus nothing" means something. The "nothing" is the absence of your own will. They are asking you to withdraw your personal agency and let the organization take hold of your reins while you pretend that nothing of the sort is happening. That's what power wants you to do.

♏︎♐︎

---

[*] I encountered the information on silver nitrate film in Gemma Files' 2015 novel *Experimental Film*.

PRETEND IT IS
SUSTAINABLE

Working at a sustainable pace—normally identified as Agile Principle #8—resonates today. The pace has never been sustainable, but adjustments aren't possible and requesting them debits my political capital. I don't want to be a truth-teller just to be ignored and punished. I don't need that. My alternate Principle #8 is to feign sustainability for the sake of appearances and try not to react to stress. I'm breathing into that now, as into a paper bag on an airplane. *Let's pretend this is sustainable.* Without this charade, all that is left to us is Death.

♏ ♐

GO TO THE POLICE

There is always that.

♏ ♐

Flyleaf —
Decisions, Decisions

Most people see two or three possibilities and flash-decide. To them, one option is clearly better than another. For example, maybe someone loaded or unloaded a roll of film in direct sunlight, and it's overexposed and no good anymore, so they choose the other roll of film. Of course, there's always That Guy who doesn't do "options" at all, who perceives himself as walking "the road" rather than "a road" and doesn't even know what it is. Maybe he's the happiest.

I see seven possibilities and will never decide. Can't give a yes or no. Can't give an up or down.

Chess clocks force Player A and Player B to move. Each player has a countdown clock. One clock counts down while the other stands still. After a player moves, they push a button to stop their clock and restart their opponent's.

Useful tool, but it depends on a mutual agreement to play. I might not play.

Seen from one angle, it looks like Zeno's Paradox: I have to go half the distance before I go the full distance, and before I can go half the distance I will need to go a quarter of the distance, and so on. I am busy doing the necessary work of going the distance, but the work subdivides into an infinite number of units, and it is never possible to cross the finish line.

If Zeno had lived in the 20th century, he might have explained it this way: The Zapruder film contains 486 frames, each image slightly different from the next, and President Kennedy is alive at the beginning and dead at the end. But what's between the frames? No matter how fast the tape runs, there will always be a movement that wasn't captured. So how does anything in the real world ever move at all? How do we go from one frame to the next? What's the secret we can't catch on tape?

Seen from another angle, maybe I've simply decided not to move at all. There's a line of Talmud that tries to simplify decision-making: If you have a couple lambs or goats and they wander away, during which time both become eligible for sacrifice, then, assuming you can find both again, which will you sacrifice?

The Greek word for perplexity, doubt, and suspension of judgment is "aporia."

The Talmudic answer is that, if you had considered one a better sacrificial candidate and the inferior returns home first, you should wait to recover the better; but if you had considered them of identical quality for sacrifice, then you are allowed to sacrifice whichever wanders home first because that's the one you have. That answer is based on valuation but also on timing. If your values don't guide you, at least save yourself time.

Choose something rather than nothing.

My problem is that I didn't predict the goats would wander away, so I never pre-decided their value and now I can't remember if there was a difference, so, having one goat back in the barn, I don't know if I should wait for the second one to return so I can compare them. If I wait to have both again and it appears they're equally good, I will have been wrong to have wasted time on this comparison.

If, in *The Phantom Tollbooth*'s land of Expectations, you find yourself on the Island of Conclusions, it is probably because you jumped there.

A pair of scissors is the implement that cuts, and thus to "decide"—note the "ci" spelling—is to scissor off unchosen possibilities. Decision is possibility-cide. Decision makes of me a Murderer of Possibilities. Before I snip, I want to know I'm not murdering the connection to my own oxygen tank. Once it's done, we have the principle of *stare decisis* (the decision must stand), and "sorry" won't cut it. Sorry doesn't cut. I want to avoid sacrificing the wrong goat. This goat looks good, but what if my memory is faulty and the other goat was really much better?

♏ ♐

HESITANCE

This hesitance makes people want to kill me.

Maybe that's why someone sent me a hatefoolery email.

Someone has finally put a hit on me.

I mean, that would explain it.

ALL POSSIBLE OUTCOMES

I math out possible consequences of talking to the police. They might evacuate our office building. We could be made to stand in the parking lot kicking at frozen puddles or be sent home. That'd be annoying. We don't have time for that. There is so much work to do. Security cameras to make.

And, regardless of whether they take preemptive action or whether they discover any real danger, they may suspect me and investigate me. They may believe I'm toying with them, that I have planted an IED in the bathroom. Here, I do not mean *institutionalized emotional dysfunction,* but *improvised explosive device.* When they decide there was no real danger from anyone, they will hold me responsible for amplifying someone else's empty threat.

IF HE'S NOT A BAD PERSON

Now, suppose the anonymous emailer finds out I've talked to the police; he will do something to me that is even nastier than whatever he originally planned. Or, alternatively, suppose that he, whoever he is, is not actually a "bad person" but has some form of mental distress and will go to jail unfairly due to my lack of humor.

Another possible outcome is—

FLASHBULB

FRI
12 DEC
2014

174

COFFEE BREAK

I pour myself another coffee in the breakroom. Cinnamon vanilla stops the thoughts for a while. A TV anchor is breaking the news, just a talking head droning on, and I deliberately look away.

♏ ♐

FLASHBULB

FRI
12 DEC
2014

175

INVISIBILITY

I've started reading a beat-up mass-market paperback of Ralph Ellison's *Invisible Man*. Viewing the word "invisible" feels satisfyingly paradoxical so I've left it lying on my desk.

But now I've reached the point where white men use electricity for violence. The young Black men play along in what was supposed to be a boxing match, letting the white men shock them, shocking themselves, maybe because they need the money or maybe for other reasons.

Why do people watch the things they watch?

I ought also to ask why I read the things I read.

I may hide this book so people don't wonder about me.

♏ ♐

FLASHBULB

FRI
12 DEC
2014

176

ACCIDENTALLY
CORRECT

Regarding the threat: What if I'm reasoning incorrectly?

Occasionally, an answer wrongly arrived at is accidentally correct. A stopped clock is right twice a day. A clock that runs at double-speed will be correct— Wait, I have to make a spreadsheet for this.

When I make spreadsheets to solve problems, everyone who looks at me on security camera thinks I'm working.

♏ ♐

Flyleaf —
Right Twice a Day

The double-speed analog clock is also right twice a day, it turns out, as long as it's anchored to the correct time to begin with. Every 12 hours its hour-hand will make exactly two rotations and catch up with the current time again. I guess I didn't need a spreadsheet to figure that out.

But if your wristwatch is set five minutes fast to begin with, then it's never, ever correct. If you're playing that game where you set your wristwatch ahead to scare yourself into moving faster, then your wristwatch is always simply wrong. Or, as I've explained it before and thus ought to correct myself here: If your wristwatch is set to run on transgender time, it's always five minutes off from cisgender time. It's not *wrong*, but five minutes can make all the difference.

Tech companies are internally operating with Agile methodology now. Agile has us describe our projects in terms of "user stories," which is a statement beginning: "As a user, I want to…" We describe the necessary effort to build these features in terms of "points." A point doesn't equate to an hour or anything like that. It is a different way of quantifying an unknown sense of bigness.

You can't accurately quantify the time before you do the work because you don't know what hurdles you'll encounter along the way, but you can use numbers to talk about how you're anticipating the effort.

Managers never remember this. They complain, *You called it five points but it took you longer than the other project you also called five points, and neither took you five hours.* But they continue to ask us to predict, and now they make us express our predictions in points they don't understand. It doesn't feel agile, but it feels modern.

An anonymous threat, according to my gut feeling, exceeds the maximum number of points that can be assigned to any one story. But it shouldn't be my personal decision. Defining points is a team decision.

Unfortunately, I can't consult my team about this potential story—the threat—because I am not allowed to bring it into the company.

Drop a house on a witch, that's an option, if you've got a house and a twister. But the witch's sister says "I'll bide my time," meaning she has an hourglass and will come back to get you, and the hourglass runs on blood.*

♏ ♐

---

* In *The Wizard of Oz*, is the hourglass itself the intended execution method? Is it an evil-magical timepiece?

FLASHBULB

FRI
12 DEC
2014

177

STRESS PREVENTION

FLASHBULB

FRI
12 DEC
2014

178

OF COURSE I'M OK

At lunchtime, Human Resources sends out an email. They will offer a stress prevention workshop.

I keep looking for a solution. I look for the method by which I could find a solution. I look for anything at all. Something would be better than nothing.

Dinnertime approaches. Coworkers go home.

On their way out the door, the last ones ask me: "Why are you still here?" The question is common, at least for this hour, but it is frustrating. The phrase that comes to mind: *I Have No Mouth, and I Must Scream*. It's the title of a story. I have no body, and I'm a blob in the org chart. I don't say any of this aloud.

♏ ♐

"Are you OK?" asks the last one out. My political capital will be −4 if my boss hears that a coworker suspects I'm *not OK*.

"Of course," I say, channeling what I hope is mysterious, charismatic intensity toward my brow, that they may recognize and accept their non-knowledge of me.

"You look sad."

"I'm really good at melancholy," I say, brightening. "It's, like, my favorite emotion!"

Why am I here? For no reason at all. For no purpose. Simplicity is Agile Principle #10. I need to reach a goal, and I shouldn't want to lift any more fingers than necessary.

It is almost cold enough to snow. It is 6:43 p.m. and darkness is complete.

♏ ♐

Flyleaf — Transsexual Trauma Story

An observation about the normals: They— The great yawning "they" of the non-transsexual Roman Vulcans deep inside the mountain who forge the clockwork mechanisms by which they allow the world to run, they whose interconnected arms and legs make up "the system"— They <u>can</u> give us hormones, perform surgeries that we want, and change our documents. They <u>can</u> use our names and gender pronouns.

(I said "normals." I forgot I am supposed to say "cis.")

Yet the thing that is taught to transsexuals is this: We must prove our gender distress and earn our transition through the manifest depth of our suffering. We are asked to tell our life stories to conform to the <u>Diagnostic and Statistical Manual</u>. We have to describe our past dysfunction and swear that we will be functional in the future if we are helped in this specific way.

Our trauma story has to be monolithic and ironclad. We have to get good at telling it, and as a result we will receive the boon of hormones and surgery, and then, <u>poof</u>, the vulcanized trauma story <u>must instantly go away</u>. Since they already helped us and can't help us anymore, they don't want to hear about pain. It is uncomfortable, therefore uninteresting. Further, sharing pain is ungrateful and impermissible. We promised them we'd become functional, and deleting the pain-story in our Teddy Ruxpin voice-box is our end of the bargain.

There is more: In addition to "looking good" by their standards, we are expected to deliver a unique, inspirational TED Talk that derives from our own experience. Our motivational speech is supposed to have grown out of nowhere like a giant beanstalk that overnight ascended to heaven. We are expected to pull that version of the story out of our pocket on command so we can inspire "thought leaders." Our trauma story must elicit a happy-cry from everyone else.

It also has to justify the <u>Diagnostic and Statistical Manual's</u> pre-2013 conception of gender identity disorder and reaffirm everyone's current place in the great hierarchy of gendered being.

After we tell that story, we need to fold it along its preexisting fold lines and put it back in our pocket. We can't make too much noise because, the more time we spend being professionally queer, the less they will pay us for our actual jobs. If we ever produce any other story related to gender, especially without being asked to do so, we discomfort the normals, and they will mark us as permanent queers because they won't be able to see us as anything else, and then they won't hire us to do anything at all. And if we don't ever want to give happy-cry TED

Talks, we had better hide our previous gender transitions altogether so as not to be marked as unwilling, ungrateful, untrustworthy, noncompliant. We begin to walk through walls like ghosts: unnoticed by most, unremarkable except to those who have been sensitized to us.

Or, if not a TED Talk, they want a Künstlerroman, a tale of the artist's private struggle in obscurity to discover his own genius. Why does there have to be a novel about art? Why is no one looking at the art? Why is no one looking at the person? Why is the situation most valued as a tragic struggle between misunderstood forces? Can't the astronaut go to the moon and can't the landlubbers watch the livestream without worrying about what they feel when they watch it? No, they can't. They want to feel something new when they turn on the TV.

After all this, they will ask: <u>Why is the book transgender? Why can't it just be a regular book for regular people?</u>

Oh my god. Oh my god. They. Asked. For. It. To. Be. A. Transgender. Book. Now they are unhappy with the results of the narrative they asked us to produce because it is sprouting roots sideways and is no longer under their control.

The current <u>Diagnostic and Statistical Manual</u> doesn't describe speculirium, either. Let us speculate about why that is.*

That is why I practice different ways of telling a story and why I fight with myself about it. The art of the lie, no? How much truth is socially constructed! The social-truthier you are, the higher you ascend, and the private-truthier you are, the farther down the pile you descend.

♏︎♐︎

---

* Neither did older versions of the DSM mention it. The mystery deepens.

179

DISCONTINUED
PRODUCT

180

LIVING ALONE

On my way home, I stop at the 7-Eleven. Food packages do not merely hold food; they instruct me on what I ought to buy next time. Unlike an antique, the "discontinued product" does not appreciate in value. It advertises an extinct future, so they've got it "marked down for quick sale." They want me to forget this product ever existed. Accordingly, I've already forgotten.

I gaze into their plastic showcase of Otis Spunkmeyer cookies. One part of me wants every homeless calorie to find its way to the warmth of my plate so I can give it the love and acceptance it has always craved. Another part of me is uninterested. I don't buy the cookie.

♏ ♐

All traffic lights are red and last forever. It's the dark, the cold hands on the steering wheel, the alienation of the personal vehicles chuffing in single-file. I enter my apartment without turning on the light, cross the living room, nearly trip over the corner brick of the fireplace, and climb into bed.

It's nice to live in an apartment with a fireplace, but it's no substitute for the conviviality of the campfire. One friend isn't talking to me. The other I only see, in winter, at work. Stories I tell myself alone by my own fireplace are generally problematic.

I am beset by microawakenings all night, though no one is next to me to observe them. The aloneness causes the restlessness, I suppose.

♏ ♐

FLASHBULB

FRI
12 DEC
2014

181

MY RESEARCH
QUESTION

Chad Goeing's unpublished papers, kept at the library at Copley, contain enough details and clues leading me to secondary sources for me to write his entire life story—stopping short of his hour of death, of course.

That's the hardest nut to crack. His obituary begins, "Born in Boston," and ends, "He died on May 29, 1900." No cause. Had he fallen ill or met with an accident, surely the obituary would have said so. It must have been suicide. His manuscript's unpublishability, his wasted effort, obsession, frustration with the intractable meaning of time—after that, I believe, he brought about his own death. But how, and how can I be certain? I can't finish studying *The Nature of Time* until I can answer this.

♏ ♐

Flyleaf —
Ask a Good Question

When you are researching, it's important to ask a good question. If you ask a bad question, you may put work into something that looks like logic but isn't. It doesn't solve your original problem.

Unamuno satirized this in <u>Niebla</u>. His fictional blowhard character, who assumed without argument that men have souls, insisted on taking up a question posed by a few ancient male philosophers: Do <u>women</u> have souls? That's the first question, the main question, the prime question, Unamuno's character said. He riddled out enough illogic to arrive at his conclusion that women are all the same; that the apparent differences in their personalities can be traced to purely physical causes and thus are insignificant; and that they do not have individual souls, but instead each participate in the single collective soul of Woman. If you've met one woman, this character says, you've met them all. From this satirical example, the problem of asking terrible questions is clear. They take you nowhere, or at least nowhere good.

The only good I can think of regarding a "collective soul" is the band with the 1995 hit song "The World I Know."

One has to use one's life to ask a very good question. My question is how Chad Goeing died. Is that a good question or a bad question?

♏ ♐

128

FOG —
SNAKE-MOUTHS OF FEAR

In my imagination, I haunt May 29, 1900. I do this so often, with so much fervor, that it feels to me as if today really were 1900 rather than nearly 2015. When I go back to this imagined day, I envision the sun rising in a clear sky and I conjure Chad Goeing in perfect health. I can't see how the day ends for him. It feels as though we're spinning a game show wheel, and all the options to me appear blank, but to him they are full of varieties of fear. One of the many snake-mouths of his fear is going to get him, one way or the other, before the wheel stops spinning. Give me an answer that's five letters. Snake. Knife. Vodka. Anger. Cloud. Storm. Pocks, as in "small." I don't know.

We go back and forth like persistent time travelers. We freeze-dry and curate our memories. But the details a person records in their diary will resurrect memories in a limited way: only in their own mind, only for as long as they live. Joan Didion told us "to keep on nodding terms with the people we used to be, whether we find them attractive company or not," bearing in mind that no one else can help us maintain the connection to our past selves, as "your notebook will never help me, nor mine you." Chad Goeing's choice of words in *The Nature of Time* are mostly opaque to me because I am not him and he wasn't writing for me.

"Tracking hours is counting capital," Chad wrote in his papers, and I am not exactly sure what he meant.

♏ ♐

FLASHBULB

SUN
21 DEC
2014

TWO
FIRESIDE TALES
I AM DRAFTING

Solstice, hovering at the freezing point. Nearly two hundred years ago, Mount Tambora blew its top. Dust blocked out the sun, and there was a year without a summer. Lord Byron wrote that two enemies "met beside / The dying embers of an altar-place"—this he narrated in "Darkness"—"Where had been heap'd a mass of holy things / For an unholy usage."

The pyroclastic bits underlay the deep freeze.

One cause of the ice: volcanic fire. But everything, ice included, also began in the water.

♏ ♐

Flyleaf — They Defected!

The boss carves the commandments on the stone tablets with his own finger, yet his prophet smashes them in frustration when he sees the people have defected to another god.*

♏ ↗

FLASHBULB

SUN
21 DEC
2014

PUPPETS

It'll be a while until Diversity Committee meets for storytime in Aparna's backyard. Won't happen until it warms up and Stanley is talking to me.

A kind of freedom: Not only may I riff on existing texts, but I may write in Aparna and Stanley.

All characters in all literature ought to be "interchangeable" between books, Flann O'Brien asserted in *At Swim-two-birds*. If there's a "suitable existing puppet," why create a new one? Everything ever written is "a limbo from which discerning authors could draw their characters," he said. "The modern novel should be largely a work of reference."

Fan fiction? No shame in it. As long as I make absolute "tiger in the lifeboat" stories.

I start a playlist with the Beatles' "Paperback Writer."

♏ ↗

* This is the 182nd reading in Lev's schema: the 21st weekly Torah portion, Ki Tisa, 2nd reading.

FOG — THE TALE OF CHAD GOEING AND *THE NATURE OF TIME* (D.C. STORYTIME #2)

At the office, I call Aparna for help with my personal problem. I ring her desk phone and ask her to come to my office.

I am opening up to her about the ghosts. She always has a sense of what's going on. But she doesn't seem to believe in ghosts, and so she listens to my stories about Chad with a different ear than Stanley does. ("Does," "used to," and "will again." Stanley will be talking to me again.) She knows how to pull apart and remake the Teddy Ruxpin cassette, so she tends to believe there's an explanation for why one hears a voice or sees a moving face.

I think she is happy for the excuse to step away from her desk. She comes by unrushed and takes several cinnamon red-hots out of my dish.

"How about you just take your best guess at how Chad died, publish whatever you have to say about time, and be done with it?" she asks.

This is heresy.

"I cannot possibly do that. I have to know for certain."

"You could accelerate your thinking. That might be nice."

"Oh no, please, don't accelerate me. Anything but that. I'm on a hamster wheel."

"I don't want to accelerate your hamster wheel. I want you to remove yourself from it. Relocate and redirect. Accelerate your thinking somewhere else, so that whatever your next move is, it accelerates your life. I want you to be where you need to be. Which is not on the hamster wheel."

"How do I do that?"

"You have to answer the question."

"I have to answer 'How do I do—'?"

"No, I mean, you have to answer how Chad died."

"That's what I'm fixated on."

"You have to answer so you can stop fixating. No one else can answer for you because it's your question. How did Chad die? Just pick an answer. Any answer."

My project seems more reality-tethered than that. It's history. It's not, like, a poem. Nevertheless, spooling hypotheses about Chad is a favorite pastime. "Gambling?" I muse. "He fell out with his father and the railroad money dried up. So he gambled and got in a fight, maybe."

"Could be. Did he seem like the gambling type to you?"

I think of the thousands of carefully handwritten pages about the nature of time, researched and annotated.

"No. He liked reasons and consequences. He knew where he was going."

"He meant to kill himself," she nods in agreement. "Russian roulette?"

I imagine Chad spinning the pistol's chamber. "No. Something more certain."

The imaginary hamster wheel flutters in my head. I hear the *clack-clack-clack* of the metal. "That sound," I say to myself.

"What sound?" Aparna asks.

"There's a sound associated with Chad's death. I wish I could play the sound for you. I hear it in my head. Was it electromagnetic noise? Static? Was he on TV, and he died, and they killed the signal?"

"Is that what it sounds like when you overthink?"

"Yes."

"Maybe you're hearing the sound of your own thoughts and not the sound of Chad's death."

Maybe I am hearing the sound of the hidden track on a Teddy Ruxpin cassette that makes the bear's mouth move.

"How do I know the difference?"

"If you go too far down a rabbit hole, you won't know anything anymore. Here, a more practical idea: I brought you a sandwich."

According to Boston legend, a man named Charlie is stuck on a hellish eternal subway trip. On the originally designed system, one needed a nickel to exit the station, and Charlie forgot his. His wife throws him a daily sandwich to sustain him, but not—this obvious solution is never hinted at—a nickel for the turnstile so he can escape the repetition for good.

I eat the sandwich.

I should start taking pills again, right?

According to Einstein's theory of special relativity, if you're standing on a platform observing a vehicle pass, its clock appears to tick more slowly than your own clock. Charlie's ride looks like an eternity for us, but perhaps to him it's a fairly ordinary commute, apart from the inconvenience of not being able to get through the turnstile at the end of it. Perhaps all ghost existence feels like that.

♏ ♐

132

184

SNOW HAS FALLEN

That's not a very good story. I finish writing it. My small, new playlist ends.

I take out an old mix. Starts with "1999" from Prince, followed by Gin Blossoms' "Follow You Down." The singer's caveat that he might not go all the way down makes him sound like Virgil backing off his commitment to guide Dante. There's a River Styx beyond which he won't paddle. Tom Waits singing "Make It Rain"; "Intervention" and "The Well and the Lighthouse" from Arcade Fire's *Neon Bible* album; and "The Other End (of the Telescope)" from Elvis Costello and the Attractions. Then "Kiss from a Rose" by Seal—really want to stop thinking of Stanley—and "Nothing's Gonna Stop Us Now" by Starship.

I'm terrible at organizing playlists.

♏ ♐

Flyleaf — Do It Again

In the Torah, the boss alerts his prophet: <u>Those tablets you broke? We will chisel them again. Same, but different.</u>*

♏ ♐

185

I AM BORED

It has snowed. I am bored. Shakespeare wrote King Lear while cooped up in his house to avoid an outbreak of bubonic plague in London. I don't think I'd make literature if I were stuck in the house during an epidemic. I would just be bored. I'm more like Milo, the mopey boy in *The Phantom Tollbooth*, who, upon receiving a large surprise package in the mail containing an enchanted toy tollbooth and labeled "FOR MILO, WHO HAS PLENTY OF TIME," expressed concern that "the afternoon will be so terribly dull."

♏ ♐

---

* This is the 185th reading in Lev's schema: the 21st weekly Torah portion, Ki Tisa, 5th reading.

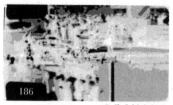

FLASHBULB

SUN
21 DEC
2014

DRIVING

FLASHBULB

SUN
21 DEC
2014

APARNA ISN'T HOME

Looking for good deeds to commit, I toss my snow shovel in the back of my car and meander my wheels around the city.

A squirrel darts halfway across the road. What's it doing out and awake in the fallout from the blizzard? It sees my car, panics, turns around, darts back. Its tail flicks the whole way like a measuring tape. It's a Zeno's dichotomy paradox. The squirrel has to travel half the distance before it can travel the whole distance. A distance can always be split into smaller hairs of a rodent's tail, so there are infinite thresholds to cross before the squirrel will ever completely cross the road. This is how its brain works. That's why it gives up.

Giving up is suicide.

♏ ♐

Somehow I find myself driving by Aparna's house. Strictly speaking, I did not need to drive down her street, but when I am thinking of people, I hover. It is a little creepy of me.

Her car is not in her driveway. A couple inches of last night's snow coat the pavement, and the air is turning white again. I park on the street. I can remove some of this ice.

♏ ♐

FLASHBULB

SUN
21 DEC
2014

188

SHOVELING SNOW

FLASHBULB

SUN
21 DEC
2014

189

I FINISH
SHOVELING

I scrape the driveway. Shovel on ice makes noise. I scrape it over and over.

I think of all the words I know for snow: *Fall, storm, dusting, flurry, drift, white-out, hail, slush, sleet, flake, powder, hardpack, crust, crud. Salted, sanded, yellow. White ice, black ice. Freezing rain, nor'easter, blizzard. Weather emergency.*

Someone is at the window, peering through the blinds. The blinds snap open and shut. Maybe a cat. No, too high. Someone is in the house watching me.

I might be shoveling snow for my own parents instead, had they not moved to Florida.

♏ ♐

I finish Aparna's driveway, leaving a giant pile of snow near where we will light a campfire again in summer, I hope. The pile will melt. Stanley will return.

At home, I appreciate the warmth of my apartment all over again, my sofa and blue woolen loose-knit blanket, and I am no longer bored.

I draft another made-up story.

♏ ♐

FOG — THE TALE OF THE HAUNTED LIBRARY (D.C. STORYTIME #3)

As I rifled through Chad's handwritten papers at the library at Copley, I saw his levitating corpse slap against the window over and over, his arms stretched out like a crucified man without a cross, his hands leaving fingerprints on the glass. He wanted to appear to me as a floating dead man; that was fine with me. This is the ten-foot-high journey about which Marc Cohn sang in "Walking in Memphis," yes? That's what that line meant, having your feet that high off the street.

It rained. The riddle of the deluge; the deluge of the riddle.

"Big wind today," the archivist said, not looking up.

To distract myself from the ghost, I said: "Chad's father was a railroad president, but Chad just wanted to write."

"Write, he did."

Amidst Chad's bloated file of papers, I found a little cigar box full of travel tickets. He went to Mexico as a young man, I learned; he had an interest in some bridge, or at least his father had wanted him to take an interest in it. *Did he jump?* I wondered. But he'd lived years beyond that. Might he have formed an enduring fixation with that bridge? Or with bridges in general? Might he have jumped from some other bridge in Boston?

There was a security camera in the corner of the ceiling. I saw its toilet-paper-roll shape. It was there to make sure I behaved, and I felt certain it had never caught a glimpse of Chad's ghost. He was probably invisible to everyone but me.

I looked at the analog clock on the wall. Two hours spent already at the library. Four hours until closing. I had to work faster. I remembered again I was a week late for my testosterone injection.

♏︎♐︎

136

DON'T SHARE
EVERYTHING
YOU WRITE

This story is already unpleasantly close to reality. Aside from which, if I were telling this story at the Diversity Committee campfire, I'd have to explain the testosterone to Aparna first, and I'd have to warn Stanley beforehand.

In real life, if my testosterone vial ran dry, I'd ask to borrow a dose from Stanley, just as I'd brought him a vial in August. That is, if he were talking to me, of course.

NOT READY FOR PRIMETIME, I pencil in the margin of my notebook. DO NOT SHARE YET.

I draft another story.

♏ ♐

FOG — THE TALE OF THE HAUNTED PLANE (D.C. STORYTIME #4)

The clock ran out. I left the library and walked south along Dartmouth Street until I found a cab to take me to the airport.

"What have you got in that bag?"

"A large novel."

Before allowing me to board the twelve-thirty departure, they made me walk through a body scanner. The security guard put up his hand to stop me. "Sir," he said, "we cannot let you pass."

Why? I was a paying passenger on this vehicle about to traverse space and time.

"It appears you have a terrorist clitoris. Do you mind walking through the scanner again, or do we have to pat you down?"

I walked through the scanner again.

The security guard radioed his coworker in charge of viewing the naked images and complaining about them from another room. "Oh, it's *glowing?*" he said into the walkie-talkie. "Why didn't you say so. Yeah, that's all right. I'll let him through."

On the plane, a flight attendant extended both arms simultaneously to point to emergency exits at both sides of the aircraft.

"Sir, you have to stow your luggage."

"This?" I pointed to a large splintered piece of wood I was holding like a baby. "This is my cross to bear."

"It needs to go in the overhead baggage compartment."

I complied.

"Thank you," she nodded, "and welcome to your lift experience."

Gloria Anzaldúa wrote of borderlands in the spiritual sense. "During crisis," she warned, everyone's "existential isolation" intensifies. When "the world as we know it 'ends,'" we go liminal. "Este choque," this shock, "shifts us to nepantla...We're caught in remolinos (vortexes)." Nepantla is a spatially disoriented place "where realities interact and imaginative shifts happen." It is "where the 'mundane' and the 'numinous' converge, where you're in full awareness of the present moment."

There was a napkin in the pocket of the seat in front of me. "Nepantla Airlines," it said.

Was that a lightning bolt I saw out the window? The electricity superheats the air. The hot air shaft has nowhere to go but explode. Hot air hits cold air: Thunder. Remolino. Turbulence. Hang on.

On this imaginary vehicle, with its moonlit ailerons foretold by Toto's "Africa," I flew very far south.

Nostalgia, says Svetlana Boym, appears to be "a longing for a place"—perhaps a place that is not a borderland of electrical storms—"but actually it is a yearning for a different time." It is even "rebellion against the modern idea of time," a preference for mythology rather than progress. It is "a defense mechanism in a time of accelerated rhythms of life and historical upheavals."

Sometimes the home to which we believe we want to return is a home that "has never existed." Nostalgia, then, I suppose, is our forcing of the belief that there was once a time when we were not flying into and through nepantla but had our feet on the ground.

I arrived in Mexico City on May 29, 1900. There, I came across an installation of the icons of the Stations of the Cross. There were 14. I recognized the two Stations I normally forgot.

Carrying the cross.

The crucifixion.

The Catholic colonizers destroyed the Templo Mayor of the Mexica people, built in the 14th century, to replace it with their Metropolitan Cathedral, and they forgot the exact location of the Templo Mayor once it was gone. The ruins? Where were they, where were they? In 1900, no one was sure. The goddess Coyolxauhqui was lost. Her name is pronounced the way it is spelled, according to Spanish rules; in English, it sounds something like "coil shout key."

In Mexico City, I walked along a bridge, and a man was waiting for me, but it wasn't Chad Goeing. I didn't recognize him.

"I thought there might be a clue here," I said to the stranger. "About how Chad Goeing died. I have a reason for believing the clue might be here, but it is hard for me to explain in Spanish."

"A ver si te enteras," he replied. "It will

be hard for you to solve this riddle in Spanish."

"Are you saying my Spanish is not very good?"

"Maybe the riddle is not in Spanish."

It wasn't raining at all. Not a drop. It looked like it hadn't rained in weeks.

"Sometimes you go through a dry spell," he said. "Your creative process takes you down the wrong road. I don't think your answer is in this country. The person you want is not here. He's going to die today, but that will happen somewhere else."

"Where can I find him?"

He shrugged. "You were hot on the trail. A cross is like a key to open the heavens. Now your trail has gone cold. Your riddle is not in Spanish."

I imagined Chad lying abandoned in the gutter, his face glazed, the rain running down his cheeks. Dead from the drink? Alcohol— that was a possibility I hadn't thought of, but the detail wasn't relevant now. Chad wasn't in Mexico City.

Where I stood, the ground seemed to vibrate. My toes trembled. It was as if the dismembered Moon goddess Coyolxauhqui herself wanted to rise from the Earth. She wore bracelets, anklets, bells on her face. Her limbs were arranged in a circle, like the moon, which the sun lights up in phases as we get out of its way. Her rope belt had snake-heads. If the snakes were to have wiggled, they'd have moved her.

Put me on Tele-Quiz, *please.*

I flew to the United States again in my mind. It wasn't 1900 anymore. I arrived at a television studio. It looked like 1955 and I half-expected Michael J. Fox to co-star in this installment of *Back to the Future.* The game board in the studio was shrouded in fog. One white circle lit up on the board like a sign marking a subway entrance. I tried to peer through it, around it, to see the rest of the word. It was like trying to look through the forest to see the trees.

♏ ♐

FLASHBULB

SUN
21 DEC
2014

191

THE ITCH

FLASHBULB

SUN
21 DEC
2014

192

THANK YOU FOR
SHOVELING

I'll tell those stories around the campfire. Or to my therapist.

Stories get written if you've got "the itch of the thing in your fingers," warned Stephen Crane, as relayed by Willa Cather, and if your fingers don't itch, "you're damned lucky."

Ideally, we write relatable, empowering characters, not sockpuppets in absurdist debate. Unhappy audiences make unhappy social media.

I'd record my stories into a Teddy Ruxpin cassette if the tape were long enough.

If you own a Teddy Ruxpin, then someone is always talking to you. Aparna could even make it have your voice. But what's talking to you is a robot. Comfort?

I wonder if Aparna's drafting more stories too.

She stops by my office desk. "Hey."

"Hey."

"My mom says thank you."

♏ ♐

"What?"

"She says thank you for shoveling our driveway."

"Oh, I didn't know she was—"

"She saw you. She said you parked your car, shoveled for an hour, and left without saying hello or goodbye."

"It wasn't an hour." Could have been two.

"It was nice of you?" she uptalks, not sounding convinced. "Kind of weird, but nice."

"Sure. Sure thing?"

"My mom can't shovel anymore, and I wasn't home to do it. It's me who shovels or else it doesn't get done. There used to be a man around the house, but, you know."

"Yeah." Though I didn't—I didn't know that. Still don't, in any material way.

♏ ♐

Flyleaf — By Which I Do Not Mean Myself

J. R. R. Tolkien, author of *The Lord of the Rings*, wrote in a letter (categorized as Letter 192) that "Frodo deserved all honour because he spent every drop of his power of will and body, and that was just sufficient to bring him to the destined point, and no further. Few others, possibly no others of his time, would have got so far." Frodo's destination was Mount Doom, but he could not muster the energy to throw the ring into the lava. Tolkien continued: "The Other Power then took over: the Writer of the Story (by which I do not mean myself), 'that one ever-present Person who is never absent and never named' (as one critic has said)." A boss within the novel, directing Frodo's story. A writer who isn't the writer.

♏ ♐

FLASHBULB

SUN
21 DEC
2014

GLOWING
WHILE WE WAIT

Later, I stop by her office. She has a number of empty shipping envelopes and the books that came in them. It's starting to look like the Texas School Book Depository over here. *Divergent* and *The Fault in Our Stars*—maybe these are for lunch hour, I do not know when she reads them—and another that's bookmarked with a letter from the publisher saying they are pleased to show her an advance copy for review. Maybe I can borrow it when I'm ready. I flip the cover shut and see it's titled *The Girl on the*— Oh, but here also, more interesting to me, is a book printed in a looping script I cannot read, like a series of circles.

♏ ♐

FLASHBULB

SUN
21 DEC
2014

194

THE SIXTH FINGER

That one, she tells me, is a novel about an ordinary guy who becomes famous for being born with a sixth finger. The finger starts to glow, and everyone recognizes him as a prophet.

"It's called *Aaram Viral*," she says. "Trans-genre."

"Excuse me?"

"Like, not any specific genre I can identify. Something different."

"Oh, that. Do you recommend it?"

She shrugs. "It's in Malayalam. My mom gave it to me. I might finish reading it someday. Takes me a long time to read in Malayalam. She knows it does. She wants me to try."

We are all working on our stories.

...*six fingers pointing; five golden rings; four canary birds...*

Campfire tales cannot come back soon enough.

♏ ♐

FOG — SEEKING A DEATH CERTIFICATE

I take the T to the Vital Records office in Cleveland Circle where the C and D Green Lines end. It's marked by a large sign: Citizen Video Services. Vital Records is supposed to be inside. Under a security camera pointed at me, a street-level glass door opens automatically, leading to one big room divided into multiple hallways. It seems I'm the only customer in the building.

There's something funny and half-familiar about the architectural design of this place.

I look down each hallway to see if it's the one I want. One sign begins with "VIT—" and the rest is blocked by a shelf. At the end of that hallway, a clerk sits behind a service window.

"I'm looking for a historical death certificate," I tell the clerk.

"What year?"

"1900."

She takes a metal box off a high shelf and opens it, exposing index cards. "What name?"

"Chad Goeing," I say. I am suddenly aware of having no feeling whatsoever in my fingers and toes, and the creeping numbness makes my shoulders and hips feel as though they are sloughing off my torso.

She flips through the cards briefly and issues her answer. "I can't give you that. It's sealed."

"Can you read me the information on it? I don't need the official paper. I just want to know how he died."

"Nope. Sealed."

"Why would Mr. Goeing's death certificate be sealed?"

"I can't tell you that. Sealed is sealed. Unless," she says, "you can pay for it."

"How much is it?"

"Seven thousand dollars," she deadpans.

My hands are vibrating as though I'm holding a buzzer on a game show. I spin and walk to the exit.

"I'll see you again when you're ready to negotiate," she calls after me.

Is everyone in Boston playing with me?

In psychic spiritualism, your "control" is the dead person who chooses you and controls you. You can't choose the spirit. You choose how you react to it.

Even if you wake up and you, Gregor Samsa, are a giant cicada, your exoskeleton may control your reality but you choose how you react to this news.*

But what if *multiple* spirits are playing with me? What then?

The clerk can't be dead. Women are never ghosts, in my experience. But if she's a living person, I don't know what just happened to me at her service window.

I take the C line to the Copley station, come above ground, turn the corner, and walk right up into the library. The archivist knows me well. I mention to her that I am still researching Chad's death and that I've extended my search outside the library.

"You can't see the situation while you're inside of it," she says.

What's that supposed to mean? "I'm not inside the situation. My whole life is a situation. I emerge from it now and then to come here and find you."

"So pay better attention to your situation."

"But I need to know how he died. Do you know? Wouldn't you want to know if you were me?"

"If I were you, I'd want to know why I couldn't get a decent price for my friend's car."

God *damn*. How did she know *that*?

"But that's you, and I'm me. Of course *I* know how Chad Goeing died. I sent away for that death certificate long ago. I already have it."

I don't know how she gets any of her information. Of course, she's a superlibrarian and I'm not. Her accuracy is disturbing, but I don't want to argue about that. I want Chad's death certificate.

"Can I see it?"

---

* Gregor Samsa is the protagonist of Franz Kafka's 1915 novella *The Metamorphosis*. In "Samsa and Samsara: Suffering, Death, and Rebirth in 'The Metamorphosis'" (*The German Quarterly*, Spring 1999), Michael P. Ryan argues that "*Samsara* is very possibly the root word" for Kafka's choice of a name for his fictional character.

"No!" she says sharply, furrowing her brow. "It's not public. Earn your own death certificate."

"They won't give it to me at Vital Records. They said it's sealed," I say loudly, leaning on her desk.

She stands up, putting her hands on her desk to lean toward me, matching my body language. "Earn— your— own— death— certificate."

Her motivations are foggy to me. I suppose some people develop feelings about the information they guard.

"How long is it going to take?"

"How long did it take the leopard to earn its spots? My stars," she says, answering her own question, "it took the entirety of evolution."

"I don't have that long."

"How long did it take the hummingbird to earn its yellow belly? That's your question now."

Damn it. This wheel of Samsara, unending cycles of birth and death. I will never be free.

♏ ♐

Flyleaf —
Looks Like Information

In <u>The Manuscript Found in Saragossa</u>, the tale told on "The Fourteenth Day" says that two 18th-century brothers disagree on exactly when a certain "famous adept, who for two hundred years had been living in the pyramid of Soufi" will pass through Córdoba on his way to America. He will travel that way approximately on Groundhog Day, though the brothers disagree on the hour and minute of his arrival, according to their interpretation of the stars. Astrology is one way of generating something that looks like information.

"Coming out" is a metaphor that derives from the idea of "a closet," and "the closet" is the Closet of Time. We go in and come out of multiple closets all the time. I'm thinking of a primordial "coming out" that's more like a permanent hatching. We're in the Egg of Time, and then we aren't.*

When you uncover inside yourself a particular queerness, everything you have of intangible value—personal relationships, career, community—and everything you have always believed—the meaning of life,

---

* The metaphor of an "egg" is sometimes used to describe a person who has not yet realized that they are transgender. The term conveys the judgment that the person's self-awareness has not hatched yet. Urban Dictionary added an entry for this in mid-2016, according to *Know Your Meme*. Here, in using a "hatching" metaphor in January 2015, Lev would have been ahead of the trend.

but more centrally in this case, about your-self—blows open. Life starts over, almost: mouth hanging open, gut clenched. The story of everyone you meet who has gone through this or is currently going through it is imprinted on you.

You are ten, fifteen, twenty again; you are no age that matters at all. What you have "come out" of, at least for a short while, is Time. You might enter Time again, but you don't back in the same way you fronted out. You don't return to the past. That eggshell's gone.

Researching a dead man requires pulling him out of history. In that sense, it's like forcing him out of the Egg of Time. But "outing" someone else with an egg spoon is not at all the same as waiting for him to "come out" on his own.

Yes, in a hand-waving generality, "you've" got to crack some eggs to make "an" omelette, but more pointedly, you can-not crack anyone else's egg to make their Lacanian hommelette (their proto-selfhood) for them. Each hommelette-to-be must crack its own shell from inside the egg with its own egg tooth. You can't go around smacking other people's eggs with your spoon. Mind your own egg. Ego: the one thing we have that's our own.

No Mythic Fascist Past

Transgender people say the cisgender-appearing or cisgender-valued life, at least for the gender originally assigned to us, isn't the one we want. We reject it, in thought or in deed. We reduce the power of the myth that says we *must* follow the cisgender way. Our reality reengineers the fascists' mythic reality. We poke holes in their bubble. They are telling us, *Once upon a mythic cisgender time, no one was transgender, and we'd like to send every-one back to no-trans land*, and we are saying, *Nope, our story was always transgender, and we're going forward*. We've adjusted our wrist-watches five minutes ahead and we're arriving at meetings before anyone else, and it drives them nuts.

Consent

The playwright Bertolt Brecht had a concept of "Einverständnis," which means consent or agreement. It's the sense in which a conversation is participatory.

To try to understand a terrorist is, after all, to sympathize with the terrorist. We try to avoid this connotation and this outcome and we cannot quite do it. We can't avoid intellectual complicity, because if we acknowledge that someone's position is in-ternally consistent, we need a meta-reason to reject it. We have to step into their system to provisionally agree with them, and then we have to step back out of their system to disagree with them again. And there's al-ways a critic of our behavior, and often we are our own worst critics.

One reason sympathy is important: feelings are a way of being transgender. If you <u>understand</u> a transgender person purely intellectually, you aren't their kind of transgender. But if you <u>sympathize</u> because you share the same feelings, then you, too, are transgender.

Agency

Transgender is also about choice and action.

Time is an abstr-action of actions, since actions divide the world into "befores" and "afters." Self-development, in the full moral sense, is about choices, and choices are intentional acts.

Choices are common enough, so what scares cisgender people is not only that transgender people have made a choice and established a "before" and "after"; it's also that this choice is a self-determination, and by recreating the self we reestablish the ground of choice itself, which means we alter our relationship to time. To assert gender is to assert self is to assert choice is to assert action is to assert time.

It doesn't stop with the rejection of fascist mythic time. It continues to the revolution of <u>any</u> time. Trans-gender is trans-time.

Cisgender people are very, very anxious that they cannot one-up this timelord move.

Of course, no one is forcing them to one-up us. They could just accept us as timelords.

Anyway

Anyway, as I was saying: If the dead man is historic—if he died in-egg, or if he rolled into a dusty corner to become an hommelette in secret—then you, the researcher, lack knowledge. Your ignorance may not be solvable.

♏ ♐

WHY IS
THE COCKROACH
DEAD

Copley is making a first anniversary rotation of something big. Spring will see the anniversary of the Boston Marathon bombing. It happened right here at this intersection. Or has it been two years already?

Enough of Vital Records and the archive. I wander southwest on Huntington Avenue to the Christian Science Church. The Mother Church, they call it, as if it were a spaceship. Open to visitors.

On the threshold, a dead cockroach, belly-up. I don't know if this means God kills vermin to protect our health or God couldn't cure this cockroach. I'm reflecting on the limits of prayer. And of solving riddles put to me.

EPISODE 5

SECOND EMAIL (SNOWPLOW)

MIX CD

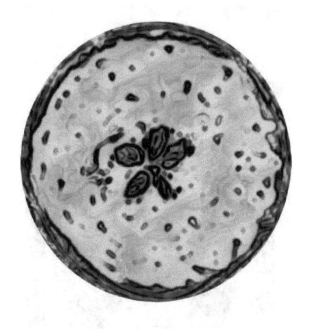

Today, the gay men's community is having a ritual burning at Amity Lodge. But that's far away, it's cold, I don't have anything personal to burn, and I didn't RSVP. I'll stay home.

I'd like to do something nice for Aparna but I don't know what that could be. A big storm is coming. I'll make something she can have indoors.

A playlist. That's something I can do.

Can I, though? I am terrible at playlists.

I work hard at this.

I burn it to CD. Something she can hold. I draw cover art on square paper and insert it in the case.

♏♐

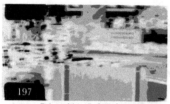

FLASHBULB

SUN
25 JAN
2015

PLAYLIST: IT'S
NOT THE END OF
THE WORLD

"Be Yourself"	Graham Nash
"Yesterday Was Judgement Day: How'd You Do?"	Flatlanders
"The Secret Life of Plants"	Stevie Wonder
"Sleep the Clock Around"	Belle and Sebastian
"Famous Last Words"	Tears for Fears
"Last Night of the World"	Bruce Cockburn
"The Final Countdown"	Europe
"Ridin' the Storm Out"	REO Speedwagon
"It's the End of the World as We Know It"	R.E.M.
"Don't You (Forget About Me)"	Simple Minds
"Hold Me Now"	Thompson Twins
"Here Comes That Rainy Day Feeling Again"	Fortunes
"Sunday Morning Yellow Sky"	October Project
"The Sound of Silence"	Simon & Garfunkel
"Eve of Destruction"	Barry McGuire
"Los dinosaurios"	Charly García
"We Will Become Silhouettes"	Postal Service
"Monkey Gone to Heaven"	Pixies
"It's Gonna Be A Lovely Day"	S.O.U.L. S.Y.S.T.E.M.
"Wildflowers"	Tom Petty

♏ ♐

198

THE SECOND EMAIL

199

I WANT TO REPLY

My personal phone gongs.

Another email arrives from **what_will_happen_chromatically**. The subject line: "You had better start talking."

Late morning. Below freezing outside. I'm wearing a sweater at my office desk, and I'm on my second cup of hot chocolate. I'm minding my own business. *I had better start talking about what?*

Equally cryptic as the message a month ago. It says: **"Did you receive my earlier email? Did you figure out who I am? Investigators are on the path of everyone who has wronged me. I will be sending the investigators soon. People try to interfere with the Strangely Gendered always. Be on the right side. Your time to talk is now."**

♏︎♐︎

I still cannot imagine who this sender is. It might be a phishing attempt to extract my money or my passwords, which is probably what the boss would like it to be, but I intuit that it isn't. It might be Grendel, who can carry off thirty drunken Danes from their seventh-century mead-hall under one of his monstrous arms, and the Geats will have to send their best, Beowulf, to help the Danes slay this monster.

Beowulf has been asked to ignore it, but he hasn't the capacity to do so.

This time, I want to reply.

♏︎♐︎

151

MON
26 JAN
2015

GENDER
CONFIRMATION

FLASHBULB

MON
26 JAN
2015

SENDER IDENTITY

Easy as opening the door of Zapruder's home video camera to remove and develop the tape when I already know the president is dead and Zapruder is right there and can avow that he filmed it. A procedural information exchange. That's what a conversation with the email sender might be like.

Easy as opening a door when I already have a sense of what's behind it. Now, I'm just looking for gender confirmation: ghost or goddess. Let's find out who.

I open the door and stare back. "Who are you?" I type with my index finger on my touchscreen. I press reply.

A non-answer comes quickly in the form of a question. "Are you ready to know?"

"Yes," I type and send.

♏ ♐

"I'm ready to tell you. Lear Noon."

Goddammit. It's a former employee who's been bothering me. First installment in my own detective series: *The Curse of the Crafty Coworker.*

"Strangely Gendered," he'd said. A gut-twist. Through what informational network did Noon find out about me? Even recently, during my "vacation" from work, I didn't tell coworkers it was for a hysterectomy. Current coworkers don't need to know I was born with a uterus. Former coworkers neither. So I have no idea what Noon knows, or thinks he knows, about my gender.

Sometimes I go to Provincetown, which entails nothing. *He* goes to Provincetown.

And why does his perception of my gender fuel other bad sentences?

♏ ♐

152

TOO LATE FOR THAT

I toggle back to his second email. His comment, "Your time to talk is now," hangs on my screen.

It sounded like a threat, but maybe it is not. In revealing his identity to me now, he hopes to build my trust. He wants to convey that he has insider information or that he has my best interests at heart. But it is a little too late for him to build trust with me. In part because I already broke trust with him.

Or maybe it's a threat.

♏ ♐

AND I WILL NOT
PRINT OUT
THE EMAIL

I will not print out the email. Won't make a paper trail of a discussion my boss asked me not to have. Won't give the printout to the boss; he'd shove it in his desk again.

I should tell someone, though the boss said not to. But if he finds out I'm reporting someone else's misbehavior, he'll report *my* misbehavior to HR.

I've never gone to the police before. Won't go until my boss supports me, as they'll have to interview him, too.

Someone at this office can give me more context about Noon's complaint. But who?

No—I'll talk to the boss, after all. He should reconsider his embargo on discussion with me.

I watch myself opening that door again.

♏ ♐

Flyleaf —
Moral Imagination

There's a new philosophy book about <u>Knowing What to Do</u>. Professor Chappell says there often isn't a predetermined answer, especially in the realm of ethics, and neither is there any one intellectual approach that will always generate a correct answer. What we need instead is attention and imagination.

♏ ♐

FLASHBULB

MON
26 JAN
2015

DO YOU REMEMBER

FLASHBULB

MON
26 JAN
2015

IT'S NOON

When I take my seat in front of my boss's desk, I say: "This is a difficult and complicated topic." Never a good way to begin, but it's true. Half the difficulty is finding our will to sit down with each other and with this thing between us.

The boss purses his lips.

There is never any time, it seems, to discuss things that bosses don't want to hear.

"Do you remember that email I showed you last month? The one that arrived in my personal email, from the strange email address?"

The one you told me not to talk about.

No, he doesn't remember.

♏ ♐

I remind him and tell him that another has arrived. I show it to him on my phone. He is not getting a printout this time. He begins to peer at the small screen, then looks away. Ah, now he remembers.

"It's Noon," I clarify.

By reflex, the boss looks at his phone to check the time. "So it is." Now he is distracted by notifications in his phone. "The governor just declared a snow emergency for tomorrow."

"Noon," I repeat. "That's the guy's name. Lear Noon. He used to work here. You may not have known him."

"I don't think I did." The boss is a relative newcomer to the company. Their tenures did not overlap.

♏ ♐

206

OPEN-ENDED
QUESTION

207

CANARY

"He and I worked on the same projects. I asked the sender who he was, see—" I pass my phone to my boss, and, without putting down his own phone, he leans in and glances at my screen once more as a reflex. He looks away again. "—and he told me."

"I don't know why you're still harping on it," the boss replies. "It's a non-issue."

"If it doesn't mean anything, then why is Noon sending it?"

"Why do you think he's sending it?"

This is an open-ended question. Gold. He couldn't do better if he were a therapist. I'll never get an opening like this again.

But I don't know why Noon is sending it.

♏ ♐

To say something and keep the conversation going, I try to create a sense of urgency. "Americans collectively own one—*weapon*—for every adult and child." I don't believe I'm allowed to say "gun" in the office, as there's a zero-tolerance policy for violence.

The boss blinks. "China has almost as many cameras. Doesn't mean they're watching everyone."

"Yes, it does." I wouldn't normally contradict the boss, but I don't lie about what security cameras are for.

The boss blinks twice. "Anyway, this is a personal dispute you've got. It's not work-related."

"How is it not work-related? The guy worked here. He's saying something about the company."

"He's not an employee. You don't need to play canary for nonexistent aggressors who don't work here anymore."

♏ ♐

155

208

NOT REAL EMAIL

"But—"

"Your email. Your conversation. Why were you even engaging with him? You have responsibility for creating this situation. Don't answer his emails anymore."

"I was trying to get more information," I say, explaining the obvious. "To see if he was a spambot or someone real. He's very real. We know him."

"This is not even a real email."

That makes no sense. The boss just acknowledged it was a real email when he said it was *my* email and that I shouldn't answer it.

I argue: "If it isn't real, then how is it in my phone?"

The boss shrugs: a subtle blink, a flick of the fingers that I suppose is a dismissive wave. There goes my political capital for the month.

♏ ♐

FOG — THEY ARE BETTER WITH SPREADSHEETS

Murphy's Law: *Anything that can go wrong, will.*

The big men here are not going to help me with this one. This isn't what the vice presidents went to business school for back when they were tadpoles. It's not how they got their degrees. It's not how they became vice presidents. It's not what they ever want to do. They are better with spreadsheets, and more especially with telling younger people to focus on their spreadsheets.

There are degrees of not caring and by now he's reached the first degree. It is premeditated apathy. Because it is intentional, there is no way through it, no inverting it, no being educated out of it, no caring at the bottom of it.

I doubt there's a coverup wrapped around it either. Can't imagine he allocates an hour in his calendar for such an effort.

Hanlon's Razor: *It's probably not malevolence, but a lack of attention.*

His misunderstanding of *Walden Pond* is self-reliant and bottomless. This is the opening night of *Jaws*, I say "shark," and he flicks its snout with his thumb and forefinger because he believes it's fake.

He is just going to sit there like the therapist-interrogator in *The Ring* and hold up my creepy black-and-white thermographies and make a gambit: "Samara, let's talk about the pictures. How did you make them?" And

Samara replies: "I don't—make them—I see them—and then—they just—are." I swear I did not make the thing. I saw it and hit "print," but that's the least interesting part.

Gresham's Law: *People are not gonna use gold coins if they can use paper. They'll secret away the real and circulate the fake.*

This is not even a real manager. This is a giant SNOEY cone in the shape of a human that is missing the ingredient of YES and is entirely NO.

Cis-tem's Rule: *'Transgender' oughta be kept private because it's dangerous knowledge that might threaten cisgender reality but also 'transgender' is a fake nonreality that doesn't exist but also the boss would like an intellectually persuasive and emotionally compelling PowerPoint titled 'What Transgender Is' in next week's diversity committee.*

I know one thing right now: I can't walk around telling people I have a pre-crime report of their deaths. In the future, robots will handle our death threats so we can be more productive. We will have security cameras that do not merely rotate to view the approaching felon but also strut into the sunset like vigilantes and take care of the problem. As of today, we do not have those robot vigilantes, so I have to deal with this problem myself. Responsibility for the next sunrise is on me. But how?

♏ ♐

209

PAPERCLIP
ON MY DESK

Someone left a brief technical document on my desk. Paperclipped; I hate that.

If I were allergic to peanuts, I could tell people not to leave peanuts on my desk. But paperclips?

I pull my hand inside my sweater sleeve, make a fist, use my woolen stump to scoot the paperclip off the pages, remove the metal without touching it, guide it off the edge of my desk into the trash. The document, though, I suppose I have to keep. It's work-related. I staple the pages. *That's better.*

♏ ♐

FLASHBULB

MON
26 JAN
2015

210

EIFFEL TOWER
ON MY DESK

I keep a cheap, foot-high model of the Eiffel Tower on my desk. Today is the day I'll put it on Aparna's desk, because I'm also going to leave her the playlist I made.

I walk by; she's not there. I leave the Eiffel Tower in the arms of her Teddy Ruxpin and the mix CD under it. The Eiffel is the perfect size for Ruxpin to King Kong it. I wonder what Ruxpin says when he grabs the Eiffel Tower. I wonder if he ever has feeling in his cushion up-paws and down-paws or if he dwells in fae physical dissociation.

"Genre," David Shields wrote in his article 210, "is a minimum-security prison."

♏ ♐

FOG —
FRIED ANGEL WINGS

I had no idea I would miss Stanley this much. The hole he leaves in my life is one I'll keep trying to fill, although this backfill project is embarrassing, and to have a self that wants to backfill is embarrassing, and to explain it briefly would be a song, and I can't songwrite for shit.

If I try to fill the hole with food, that will make the pain worse—like the small child in Clarice Lispector's novel who realizes, after a meal, she's just eaten cat-meat, and to her it may as well have been "ángel frito, las alas crujiendo entre los dientes," fried angel wings crunching in her teeth. After cat-angel, all food repulses her, forever.

I wonder if I'll ever want to eat again.

♏ ♐

FLASHBULB

MON
26 JAN
2015

211

CHANGE YOURSELF

I bench myself outside, and my thoughts are a murder of crows. It's freezing. At least I have the bench to myself.

I wish I could call Stanley.

The last communication I have from him is a text message. Hard to revisit it now, as my fingers freeze solid the moment I take off my gloves. I had said: "You are my best friend." And he had said: "You are like a bad Arthur Miller play. Not talking to you. Right? And I am so not being your change agent btw. Change yourself."

♏ ♐

Flyleaf — Can't Make Everyone Happy

Anger is in Me and Doesn't Let Go

Under my boss, two traumas: the threat and the instruction to keep quiet about it. An unwanted pregnancy of a Möbius strip. The double bind is a kinetic sculpture of fidget spinners. I feel emotionally agile because I'm constantly in motion, but really I have no free will and other bodies are bumping me. We are birds in the air. It's maddeningly bright. "Li-bre, li-bre," the male sings to the female. "Al-be-drí-o, al-be-drí-o," the female responds. Sunlight stabs me from all directions and I can't stare into it. Underlying the noisy clack of the spinners—"free-will, free-will"—is the fury and grief of not being able to make everyone happy.

Listen to the Anger

My conflicted obedience: outward silence, inward chatter. I have to change. No one who is mad at me is going to coach me.

Listen to the anger. It grows like a spruce: tall, ragged, anchored to the night. The caw of a crow thins into the wail of a coyote. It never lets me go.

Prayer is the patience to do nothing. Doing nothing is sometimes the best course. Inactivity is how humanity will stop releasing greenhouse gases, for example. We can take a long pause. It is a prayer. It is the confidence to see how a situation works itself out when we aren't worsening it.

Pray for Rain

People pray for rain. No adult ever prays for snow except office workers who'd rather log in from home. As my boss mentioned, the governor has declared a travel ban. Old governor did similar for a winter storm a couple years ago. New governor is smacked with a blizzard his third week in office. We'll all work from home tomorrow. Lift every snowplow and sing.

I'm dreaming of rain, dance, prayer: a ballet dancer moving into second position, someone lying in bed and wailing silently at the rain, myself riding a skeleton horse, my palm outstretched, waiting for a raindrop, the camera panning out to a barren, gray scrub wilderness. My prayers have cameras. They have "record" and "share" buttons.

Now He Wants Back In

My hand stills on the camera. The president will pass this way only once. I commit to observing, supporting the camera's weight. Let's watch together.

Meanwhile a bad actor called Lear Noon is standing somewhere in the wind, driving rain, blizzard. He stepped away from his power here. Now he wants back in.

♏ ♐

FOG — IN THERAPY

Mid-afternoon, I leave the office.

In session, I tell my therapist about Lear Noon.

"That sounds stressful," she says.

Behind her on the wall is a medium-sized piece of abstract art, a woven tapestry of natural fibers with a large red dye stain. It doesn't look like blood. It looks more like a sunrise or sunset. But there is no sun.

"He's older than me. Definitely Gen X." This is irrelevant, but I want to maintain the conversation at a low stress level. "Some people call me a Millennial, but that doesn't feel quite right either. I was born in 1980. Reagan was elected a couple weeks before I was born, but he hadn't taken office yet. Gay men were already suffering the AIDS crisis, but the government hadn't acknowledged it yet. You know those polling companies that are always looking into the differences between the generations? They use 1980 as the dividing line between Gen X and Millennial."

"They mean you're born a certain way and you can't change it."

"Yeah. But I'm not trying to change it. I just don't know which I am."

"If you're born a certain way, the answer is in your body. What does it feel like?"

"What does what feel like?"

"Not knowing. The feeling of not knowing. What is that like?"

"It's like—" From my seated position on the therapy couch, I gesticulate with my right arm at an imagined computer. "This website over here says I'm Gen X. This website over here"—my elbow pivots—"says I'm Millennial."

"I'm noticing you're moving your arm," she says.

"Yes?"

"Not just your finger."

"Well, yeah. Because, you know, I hop to a new website to compare two sources of knowledge." I move my forearm from the elbow to demonstrate the action of surfing the web.

"If you were a Millennial, you'd swipe your finger on your phone or your laptop's trackpad. If you use a mouse, you're Gen X."

"Oh."

"Tell me about the bad coworker. You were saying?"

I mention that Lear Noon and I are still connected on professional social media. I ask my therapist: "Should I leave our accounts the way they are, or unfollow him, or block him?"

My therapist looks at me over her glasses as if to say: *I cannot believe you are asking me that.* She pushes her glasses back up her nose and pretends she didn't just give me that look. "I think you already know the answer to that question," she says aloud.

"Unfollow or block—" I say aloud, but I'm speaking more to myself.

"You don't really need me to answer it for you."

I say nothing.

"Do you?" she says.

I say nothing. I am a transsexual who transitioned before the existence of social media, which makes me Gen X, which means sometimes I do need other people to answer my questions about social media.

She phrases the answer as a question. "What would happen if you blocked him?"

"Then," I calculate, "he wouldn't be able to message me on the platform where I blocked him. One fewer place he could reach me."

She turns her palms slowly upward in the form of a question and in the imitation of an offering.

I tell my therapist I share a lot on social media. She says I should stop that and try a private paper journal instead. I don't tell her I'm already familiar with paper and that I do my best writing in the flyleaf. I listen to her suggestions.

She wants me to pull the thread in my stomach. It's all one infinite thread from the same ball of yarn. I can pull that thread. I can journal myself into the Hinterlands. But I'd rather not. I'd rather hack up the whole hairball, throw it out, have done with it. If I knew how.

I do know how. But just because I know what button would patch up vulnerabilities in my social media network doesn't mean I'm gonna do it.

My therapist also wants me to take my speculirium pills. I can only consider so many potential solutions at once.

♏︎♐︎

Flyleaf —
Nothing Can Be Something

Noon addressed me at my email handle, "lockenshaw." It's my first initial and a last name that's unique to my father and me. It means something new to me, all over again: nothing can be something.

Years ago, I visited Yad Vashem, the Holocaust memorial center in Jersualem. They had set up a database for visitors. Out of habit, I protested, "There's no point looking up 'Ockenshaw.' It's a quite uncommon name. This name is never in any phone book. I am the only Ockenshaw." And they said, "Just try." And what would you know: there, in the database of victims, were all the Ockenshaws.

Sometimes, there was a something before there was a nothing.

The snow of nothing falls upon the field, and if you don't know where you're stepping, it might turn out to be not frozen ground but the thin ice of a very cold pond.

"Lev Ockenshaw," I write at the top of a notebook page. The only gay in the village, like proud Dafydd on "Little Britain," except, of course, I am not. I am not the only Ockenshaw if I look back a hundred years.

In Jerusalem, I went to the Western Wall without a yarmulke. A man stood there with a basket of yarmulkes. I had to take the one he handed me. Do you know what came with it to secure it to my hair? A paperclip. I didn't use the paperclip, of course. Can you imagine what my speculirium would have wrought? We are talking about the remnant of a temple destroyed two thousand years ago, where Jews and Muslims still pray, but not side-by-side, in perpetual risk of war if anyone dares to do so. I wore the yarmulke with no paperclip, thank you. I prayed at the Wall, and nothing happened.

In my notebook, next to my name, I write the date. Under that, I write "A gentleman doesn't report the nothing that didn't happen," visualizing a bug obediently folding its legs, letting go of the delicate sensations in each one.

But I don't buy my own line.

In the first chapter of Genesis, the boss creates plants and animals before the first human, and in the second chapter, a human is created before plants and animals. Logically unsortable in our spacetime. This garden must be itself and not itself. The "days" must not be time. Bad crossword puzzle. The storyteller was satisficing—trying to get to "good enough." And the story's imaginary, anyway. Fingered y fingido.

There's a metal wheel in my besotted mental crawlspace, and though I may seem unmoved, the hamster is off to the races.

ᛗ ↗

212

CROSS.
WATER.
FEET

All afternoon at the office, images flash before my eyes. *Cross, water, feet. Cross, water, feet.* I'm sure I've got what I need to solve the riddle. *What's the name of the feeling of almost having it?* I wonder.

"Cross water?" Maybe that's it. I oughta duck-boat across the Charles River and—

I sigh, begin again. *How did Chad die? How did Chad die? Why is this so hard?*

It's hard, I answer myself, *because it's the water I swim in.*

♏ ♐

FOG — BAD CROSSWORD PUZZLE

The office itself is full of puzzles, a mountain of tickets in the system. The office *is* a giant crossword puzzle. My project was supposed to be Agile, but it crashed like Waterfall. That's a Cris Williamson song; I mean to be the changer but I am the changed. When so much precipitates, I can't handle it downstream. A quantitative analysis of reoccurring thoughts won't move me on to a new thought. Hamster wheel.

Stanley's words echo in my memory: *"You can't see the situation while you're inside it."* Good advice from the inside of a hamster wheel. Or, wait—maybe the proverb comes from Fenway Park? Where did I hear those words before?

Is there anywhere to be found a psychic who doesn't already know I am coming?

♏ ♐

213

WADING IN
THE WATER

It's not quite time to go home, and we have to do extra since we won't be able to drive in tomorrow. (We see the workload from the perspective of the day after tomorrow.) But I have to get out of the office. I run into the cold sunlight, behind the parking lot, into the trees, where I place my ear to the ground. I feel vibrations, as with a change of weather, when the clouds fall to earth. I stand up and approach the muddy banks of the Charles River.

♏ ♐

FOG —
IN THE CHARLES RIVER

I wander up to my shins in mud, my khakis soaked. I should be very, very cold, but I don't feel it. The water and I comprise an adiabatic system, meaning we contain a certain amount of heat that doesn't change because there is no escape.

"I am a jug filled with water both magic and plain," Hrabal begins his novella.

Dead trees dot the water, hardly any branches left, just ragged, black poles. It's easy for me to imagine dead bodies hanging on them as if on crosses.

Some things are becoming clear to me. I stand with my feet in the water to gain a new perspective.

My favorite pair of office khakis has loose threads hanging at the bottom hems, threads like Kabbalah strings of protection except they aren't red. For a long time I have allowed them to grow there. The powers that be are not going to make me a vice president anyway. The threads are floating.

If you can forget for a moment that a cross is an instrument of execution, you can see its geometric function of dividing space into quadrants, and quadrants are useful if, for example, you are Jung and you intend to divide consciousness into different types. You can plot Cartesian coordinates on the axes, and then you can make like Adam Smith and find the intersection of supply and demand.

I feel my brilliance rising and shooting out my ears.

Many of my coworkers are good at advanced math. I'd like to show them some pictures. No, do not make me reinvent calculus—just tell me what kind of special equation this graph looks like—

Aparna's on my trail. I didn't notice her, but she's come up behind me. "I see what you're doing," she admonishes me with an eyebrow raise. She doesn't step in the water.

I don't have an explanation. "I'm looking for patterns in the clouds." I start to notice my feet are cold.

"That's a sign of decompensation, mental collapse. That way lies more psychotherapy. Do you want to live in your riddle forever, or do you want to solve the riddle?"

"But I am solving the riddle. Chad might have died over here," I confabulate, twisting my torso away from her, moving my arm over the river, pointing to the other shore. "I have to cross the water. I have to find out."

"Chad Goeing probably died of dysentery," she says, "and, if it wasn't that, he and his whole family drowned when he refused to pay someone to ferry his ox caravan across the river. Why did your school system bother paying for your educational videogames? Did you learn nothing from 'Oregon Trail'?"

"This thing I'm doing—"

"About *this thing*, yes. I have some new information for you about that."

164

I wheel around. "What is it?"

"You're doing your thing in full view of the boardroom window. They can see you at least until the sun sets. Are you planning to come in before it gets dark?"

Sunset will be at 4:50 p.m.

♏♐

ALLEGEDLY, EVERYONE IS WORRIED ABOUT ME

"Everyone is worried about you. This is not a normal thing to do," Aparna says. "You're galoshing around a half-frozen pond with no galoshes. Other people go out for coffee."

"I have extra pants in my gym bag."

"That's not the point."

Points. When I think of the potential debit to political capital points, I begin to see her point.

I splash the soles of my shoes in the water to clean off the mud. Trudge upstairs to the fifth floor. Grab my gym bag. Head into the office bathroom. Remove my soaked office pants. Peel off my wet socks. Pat my feet dry, using my dry sweatpants as a towel.

I can't feel my toes.

♏♐

FLASHBULB

MON
26 JAN
2015

I DO NOT NEED
MY PILLS

FLASHBULB

MON
26 JAN
2015

CHECK-IN

I put on the mostly dry sweatpants. No extra socks in my gym bag, but I have sneakers. I put my dry bare feet in my dry sneakers. Good thing we're all going home soon anyway. In the path of a storm, we call this kind of outfit "storm casual."

It's important to be careful. This was how the time travel in Octavia Butler's *Kindred* began—a sudden romp in a pond when it seemed a life was at stake—and that broke time, and the time traveler lost her *arm*.

I will clean up and stay out of the water during business hours, but I don't need my pills now. I need them if ghosts and goddesses are bothering me.

♏ ♐

Aparna stops by my desk. "Just checking in on you," she says.

"I'm good," I say.

"I hope so. Would be nice if we could tell stories around the fire again sometime."

"When Stanley comes back."

"Yeah." She tilts her head. "Good thing he doesn't work here. That would be awkward. Give him his space for a while."

♏ ♐

WHERE STANLEY IS WHEN HE ISN'T HERE

It has never occurred to me that Stanley could work with us at A.P. He's never expressed interest in making security cameras with me. In my nostalgic mental image of him, now hagiographic ever since he stopped talking to me, he is always costumed in an aspirational jersey and catcher's mitt, standing on the field at Fenway Park.

It's already been "a while" since I've been giving Stanley his space. A while and a half. But not even a tenth of the way to *Infinity War*, and you have to subtract a unit of Zeno's Paradox. So there may be a while to go.

Meanwhile, I need to lay low in my sweatpants and sneakers and get some work done.

♏ ♐

I REHEARSED THE MESSAGE

While it was snowing 22 inches yesterday, I enjoyed some quality time by myself at home. It was International Holocaust Remembrance Day. Unrelatedly, I put together some information I wish to communicate to my boss.

We all stayed home for the governor's travel ban, but yesterday's tomorrow is another day. Today we're back in the office.

With permission, I enter the boss's quarters. He motions to the chair.

He doesn't like it when I ramble. He has asked me to keep my messages short. So, this time, I have condensed what I want to say and rehearsed it.

I take a deep breath. "I can't—"

He removes his glasses and cuts me off.

♏ ♐

FLASHBULB

WED
28 JAN
2015

219

NO WAY
TO REPHRASE

FLASHBULB

WED
28 JAN
2015

220

CAN'TSEXUAL

"Don't come in here and tell me what you can't do. I am not here to receive complaints. Tell me what you're already doing to fix whatever your situation is, and tell me how I can help you do it. Give me no 'can't's." His face is red. He's swivelling in his chair.

I forgot I was already out of capital for the month and there was no way any conversation with him could go well. The thing I want to say begins most concisely with "I can't," which is why I rehearsed it that way, and now there isn't any way for me to rephrase, not concisely. If I continue to speak, words will beat around the bush, and that will make him angrier.

♏ ♐

People want to hear "I can." Kennedy wouldn't have won the election if he'd run as Kantedy. Newly registered epiphany: On a par with a woman who says "NO" is a transsexual who says "I CAN'T." I might have planned to say "I can't see well without my reading glasses," "I can't abide bigotry," "I can't raise Jesus from the dead," or "I can't tell you how grateful I am to work here." Rattled, I've forgotten the phrase I spent yesterday rehearsing. Doesn't matter what it was.

♏ ♐

WHY HE HAS ME
HERE

Nor does it matter that my boss does not consciously know I am transgender. On some deep-Gurdjieff level, he knows. That is why he is especially irked when I, of all people, say "I can't." He needs me to be the Self-Fertilizing Saint of Possibility. I am supposed to Make All Things Possible with my double-genre nature. That is why he has me here.

"Only tell me what you are going to do," he says, "and then, in the same breath, tell me that you are already doing it."

The correct word is "yup." Think of the acronym for "young urban professional." On the other hand, if I answer with "yup," I am, officially, a yuppie, and that's irreversible.

I excuse myself from his office.

♏ ♐

Flyleaf — There Isn't Enough Rainwater

Roquia Sakhawat Hussain wrote a story imagining that floating balloons collected sufficient rainwater so no one was ever thirsty, women rode in hovercars, and men were confined to harems. She wrote it in the year of not-my-lord 1905, and the dream-prophecy still hasn't come to pass. Over a century later, rainwater doesn't always come and people are sometimes thirsty.

♏ ♐

RESERVOIR

I do need a coffeebreak, as Aparna suggested on Monday, but I'll do it my way. No coffee until I accomplish one important task.

I get in my not-quite-hovercar and drive to the Reservoir T stop, D Line, intending to return to Vital Records. Until I have Chad's death certificate, I can't be productive. My bank account has been prepared with seven thousand dollars. I, too, am prepared.

I park in my secret spot.

♏ ♐

FOG — THREE SECONDS TO ANSWER THE HUMMINGBIRD RIDDLE

Inside Vital Records is the same clerk. "You're back," she says, acknowledging me. She pulls a manila envelope from the left side of her workstation and waves it at me. "CHAD GOEING, DEAD" is already written in cursive pen on the envelope.

"You knew I was coming back?"

"Yeah? What of it?"

"You don't seem at all surprised."

"I am. I knew you'd come back, but I didn't know when."

"I don't think I knew, either. How long does it usually take people to come back?"

She tilts her head at me. "For how long would you need to observe the evolution of the yellow-bellied hummingbird before you could understand why it is yellow?"

That riddle again. I brought the money but not the answer.

"I—" She is still holding the envelope. What if she doesn't give me the death certificate? "I don't know!"

"You have three seconds to answer. One," she begins.

"No—"

"Two—"

"Wait!"

"Three." She reaches up to close her blinds.

"Three? That's all I get?" I object.

She pauses, smirks, and reaches through the service window, handing me the envelope. "That will be seven thousand dollars, payable to me. My name is Jackie Kennedy."

I have no idea what just happened. First she wanted me to answer the riddle. Now she doesn't care?

I write out the check to her.

"It's good you have a checkbook," she says. "Few people do these days. Checks are the best rolling paper."

She palms it and snaps the blinds shut on her service window.

I don't think she's really Jackie Kennedy.

♏ ♐

170

I HAVE CHAD'S
DEATH CERTIFICATE

EMOTIONAL
INTELLIGENCE

It's still below freezing. One never knows when the sky might spit. I slide the envelope inside my jacket and don't open it until I'm safely behind the wheel of my parked car. The envelope is constructed oddly, fastened two ways, a double-safety method I haven't seen before: a brad with two little brass wings that open outward and a hemp string wound around the brad. I undo it.

The death certificate slides out.

Ordinary document. Deflating. But it has the information.

Now I know Chad died near the State House. I know the hour. I also know that police were challenged to recover his body.

I know, essentially, how he died. It's implicit.

♏ ♐

Back at the office, I don't get much done.

"You can come over to my place, if you want," Aparna offers. "My mom might have dinner with us. If you come, I'd like to include her." She sighs. "I missed her birthday. I mean, we were going to celebrate, then I told her I couldn't, and it was for the most obnoxious reason."

"What was it?"

"Boss said I had to go to an emotional intelligence training. After work. Not really optional. So I went, the evening of my mom's actual birthday, so I didn't spend time with her, and now, you know."

"Why did he think you needed an emotional intelligence training?"

"Seriously, right? Listening to other people, 'reading between the lines,' whatever."

♏ ♐

FLASHBULB

WED
28 JAN
2015

225

A BAD JUDGE OF IT

FLASHBULB

WED
28 JAN
2015

226

APARNA'S HOUSE

"You're already good at that. You read a lot. I see you and your stack of books."

"Yeah, when I have time."

"Hope you learned a lot at the training, for whatever it was worth."

"It was not worth it. My poor mom."

"I think your emotional intelligence is great."

"But, of course, we don't know what we don't know."

"I might be a bad judge of emotional intelligence, but I think you're great."

"Thank you. You're pretty cool yourself. Thanks for listening to me, in any case."

I drive to her house after work. Her mother walks into the kitchen, making herself known, and floats away again.

♏ ♐

I say I have to use the bathroom. On the second floor, as I pass the closet—what I'd once wrongly guessed was the bathroom door, the first time I was here—I see it has been locked. *En serio.* There's a silver padlock. I tug on it gently to see if it is real. *Yup.* I wonder if she knows I opened the door and saw the murti of Mariamman. Has she locked it against me?

"Are you looking for the bathroom?"

I spin around. It's Aparna's mother.

"The bathroom"—she points across the hall—"is there."

I do already know that. "Thanks," I say neutrally.

Before it gets too late, I say goodbye. Aparna gives me a slice of orange cake to take home.

♏ ♐

FOG —
'BEAUTIFUL_RAGE'

The drive feels long. I return, flip the lightswitch by the front door, and peer into an apartment that doesn't feel quite right. The andirons are standing in the fireplace, so Santa still hasn't come. He's a month late. My living room and bedroom are in order. But my bathroom has been trashed. Someone has squirreled through the medicine cabinet and left empty vials rolling on the floor.

"Dammit, Chad," I say aloud.

There was nothing in my medicine cabinet except aspirin and cologne. I don't know what Chad was looking for. Troublesome ghost.

In the kitchen, I fish around in my pocket looking for a sugar packet to sweeten my tea. I produce the figurine of María, the little gift from Stanley. I feel someone—an invisible presence—slap my wrist, hard, and María tumbles into the sink disposal.

This is some true poltergeist nonsense. It takes an hour to extricate María from the grimy gears.

"We are attached by a cord to all the objects of attachment," including the deities we imagine, Simone Weil tells us.

♏ ♐

FLASHBULB

WED
28 JAN
2015

TO MAKE THEM
FEEL IT

As I slouch alone in my living room armchair, typing on my laptop, I have no intention of using the email account I'm setting up: **beautiful_rage**. I'm not vengeful, nor am I an airhead. I'm not That Guy who tinkers with one broken piece of a Rube Goldberg possibility. I am, rather, someone who hits his head with great dedication against the same wall hundreds of times, believing the answer will be worthwhile.

I just want people to understand what they do to me. Why is that so hard? If I have to make them *feel* it—

♏ ♐

FLASHBULB

WED
28 JAN
2015

228

I COULD GO
TO JAIL FOR THAT

FLASHBULB

WED
28 JAN
2015

229

TFW YOU GO
TO JAIL

With **beautiful_rage**, I could send provocative messages to the boss, something to make him shit his pants, like: "**Time's up for this investigation! One last chance for a better answer from you. Deadline: noon tomorrow. BE READY.**" After he scurries for three days, wondering what may have already happened, I poke my head out of the bushes and grin, "Well, that was fucking terrifying, wasn't it?" See, the original joke was on me, now the same joke's on him. He'd get it eventually. I would have taught him something useful.

I could go to jail for that, right?

Maybe even for understanding the terrorist too well and forcing other people to understand him, which, as we discussed, is dangerously close to sympathizing with the terrorist.

♏ ♐

It'd get attention on social media, but if I go to jail I might not have permission to use social media.

TFW you go to jail.

Can I write that in my notebook? No. "TFW" is meant to be performative.

Maybe **beautiful_rage** is better as a toy. In "Puff the Magic Dragon," the boy grows up and wants different toys. In 2015, Jackie goes paperless.

I leave **beautiful_rage** intact—inbox and outbox pure, fresh, blank—for an emergency. The grand art of holding my shit together in silence.

The days are long and eventually we close our eyes to the passage of each one; our sleep regulates their march.

Today, at least, my conscience is clear.

EPISODE 6

THE DREAM OF THE VICE PRESIDENCY

FLASHBULB

THU
29 JAN
2015

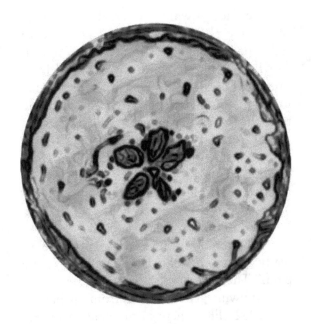

Alone in my bedroom. Past midnight. Cold, clear skies.

All physical borders seem undefined. If my body were a book, it'd be deckle-edged. If my commandments were inscribed on a tablet, they'd be smashed.

Joshua Cohen in *The Book of Numbers* was hired to shelve books "with a humanities diploma between my legs but not enough arm to reach the Zohar," recognizing that "'subject' and 'genre'…are ruinous distinctions for writing a book deserving of shelving."

The wheel turns. The wheel of the Lincoln Continental. The whole car comes into focus. I'm dreaming. A good spooky dream may end up in my notebook. It does. Transcribed.

And now it's a draft story that I may tell at Diversity Committee storytime.

FOG — THE TALE OF THE OFFER FROM JFK (D.C. STORYTIME #5)

"Whaddya want?" I say. Receiver of an old rotary phone in my left hand. Glass of red wine in my right. Another dream indicator: I don't like wine. In my dream, I let it breathe. The older the wine is, I've heard, the longer it should breathe so I can smell and taste the history developed inside it.

Secret Service on the other end of the line: "President Kennedy is returning from meeting with President López Mateos in Mexico City. He will move in with you tomorrow."

"I don't think that would be—"

"We're not asking your opinion. He already owes you rent. Don't worry; it'll be paid." The line clicks.

My wine glass vanishes from my hand.

1962 JFK is here in my apartment. He has moved in like a ghost. He's sitting on the velveteen couch in my living room, holding a whiskey glass. *My* whiskey! Glenlivet 12, single malt scotch. I'd been saving it for a celebration. On an end table is a can of PBR. I do like PBR.

We're having a conversation, JFK and I.

My fingers twitch in my pants pocket. Paperclip. Damn. How did it get in there? A dream paperclip attracts a dream ghost. Too late now.

"How terrible am I?" I say to JFK.

"You are good," he says avuncularly.

"You are doing well at work and in your life. You are going places."

"No, I'm not." I shake my head.

It's a modest life. All I do is go to work, feed the cat, talk to demons pouring out of my ears, and answer email. The quartet of Job, Paws, Ghosts, and Ringtone. I don't try that one on JFK because he didn't live to see the debut on Ed Sullivan. I won't tug at the threads on the space-time trousers. The seat is already pretty well ripped.

"You *are* doing well," he assures me. "And I have big plans for you."

"I can't. I'm busy."

"*Busy*?!" he objects. "You were put here for this moment. What is the point of Amity Lodge? What is gay trauma? Why did you get a cat? What do you think any of this was all about?"

How does JFK know I own a cat? She's made herself scarce. Likely she's under our couch, keeping tabs on JFK's ankles.

"What is a camera tester who only sees strange things?" he asks. "Why did you learn all this stuff? They're not 'things,' they're not professions, they're not genres. All of this— it's your story."

I watch the "o" of his lips. I hear "stooooory," the vowel opened wide as an asteroid in orbit, an interstellar fragment left behind by the powerful vacuum of the Nothing in the *Neverending Story*.

"I am the angel Zeganzagel," he says. "I will teach you to read Hebrew."

"Uh huh," I say, syrupy. The dream

downshifts time one gear. Could be the alcohol talking, but I haven't touched my imaginary beer yet. Maybe it's the power of the "ayn sof," the "ayin," the "efes," the infinite unknowable nothing that the Kabbalah says is everything's ultimate source.

"I should already know how to read Hebrew. I should have paid more attention. I'm terrible," I say to JFK.

"Au contraire," he says. "You are contrite. And that means," he goes on, "that you are better than good. Why is it *Zohar*?" He's inquiring about a mystical Book of Splendor that interprets the Torah's creation story.

"What?" I challenge him abruptly, then remember I am speaking to a President. "Excuse me, sir? Mr. President?"

"Why is it *so dark*?" he repeats.

Oh. He's quoting *The Neverending Story*.

I provide the response from the movie: "In the beginning, it is always dark."

"Right. You don't have a choice. Your destiny is ordained."

"I'm not capable of doing anything or going anywhere. I'm a flawed human being." It is a humble caveat I make for dramatic effect before this great ghost. It is also true.

"You," JFK points at me, "are going to transvalue all values."

I have been transgendering value all my transgender life. I open my mouth to argue, but then I shut it again. JFK believes it is 1962, so, if he knows my true identity, he believes I'm not born yet.

"Please understand," I say instead, "I'm a terrible person who once wished a terrible boy would drown."

JFK holds his whiskey glass very still. The ice cubes don't move. I don't think he's breathing.

He says: "Let me explain to you the difference between scuba and snorkeling."

I know. Scuba diving was the failed vacation in 2010. Snorkeling might be better. But JFK is making the time to talk to me, so I listen. I pop the top of my beer can with one finger, slowly; the metal makes a shearing sound and the gas escapes. I peer into the inscrutable darkness of the small puncture wound. It feels obscene to do so in front of this man.

He reads my mind. "No, you *don't* know this yet, but you will." He gazes into his glass and swirls the ice. "There's a River Usk in Wales. 'Uisce' is the old Scots and Irish word for 'water.' You see, now, what you're swimming in. Water, whiskey, or both. A confluence or divergence of waters. That's 'aqua vitae,' the fermented drink, water of life. Or death. The spirits have the life you give them."[*]

---

[*] Seamus Heaney wrote in his 2000 introduction to *Beowulf* that a class "on the history of the English language" had informed him "that the word 'whiskey' is the same word as the Irish and Scots Gaelic word *uisce*, meaning water, and that the River Usk in Britain is therefore to some extent the River Uisce (or Whiskey)."

He looks up at me. "So. Scuba is when you wait for someone to drown, and snorkeling is when you try to save them. It will come to pass."

"What?"

He ignores me. His lips are drawn. "The Soviets are building nuclear missiles in Cuba," he says. "This is definitely a secret. You can't tell anyone."

"OK," I promise him.

"We don't know what will happen," JFK says. "We just try our best. I flew to Colombia and laid one brick in Bogotá. The development was to be called Ciudad Techo. Now what? I heard a rumor that someday it will be called Ciudad Kennedy. Why do you think they name it after me?"

He looks proud. I haven't the heart to tell him.

"We have no way of knowing, do we," he says, enjoying the whiskey. "All we can do is plant the brick. A million residents may come."

I nod.

"You have a charmed life. Everyone loves your apartment. A home where dear friends play. I mean, *a fireplace*! That's the cat's meow. You should light that up more often." He gestures with a wide sweep of his left arm.

He pauses, realizing something. "Do you know what this means?" he asks, eyes bright and brimming.

I shake my head weakly and sip my beer through the hole in the can. What does he mean by *this?* Does he refer to his own arrival? What happened in the 1960s? Let me think.

The Second Vatican Council decided that Jews were not collectively responsible for betraying Jesus to the Roman persecutors. The Vatican said so after the Beatles were on Ed Sullivan, but their judgment was retroactive—meaning, they acknowledge the Jews had *never* been guilty of this, even pre-Beatles. That's something JFK could mean by *this.*

But I am a guilty individual. Nothing to do with Jesus. Bad situations find me. As if something on my person, like an IUD or a paperclip, were a magnet for villainy. I keep trying to find these magnets and rid myself of them, but the magnet jumps back in my pocket when I'm not looking, and terribleness follows the magnet, and that makes the evil my fault. I don't do wrong intentionally, Socrates said so, but the badness that finds me is inherently about me. I am a terrible person having a drink with a dead president.

JFK looks delighted with himself. He makes firm eye contact with me and grabs my arm. Even in my dream state, I feel the pinch of each finger. *This.*

"You," he says, "can be my vice president!"

"No," I protest, shaking my head. It can't be me.

He shakes his head, too, out-vigoring me. "No, no, no! Quiet, *shush*. I have it all figured out. It's perfect. How could this possibly go wrong? Don't say you can't; I don't want to hear it. You will be my vice president, and—"

Next thing I know, in my dream, I am standing in a misty, half-lit place, grabbed by tree branches and vines, holding a hunting rifle. There is a sign: "Elm Street." I am in the middle of nowhere, JFK is gone, and this is a nightmare.

Something moves in the forest. Something overwhelmingly large, transgressing boundaries. An international threat. A landscape full of explosives. One big bomb that has gained sentience.

No, it's an *army*. Dozens of soldiers coming out of the woods heading right for me. Startled, I raise my rifle at their leader.

"Whoa, whoa, whoa," the leader says, holding up his hands. "Easy there. We are not in your training exercise."

"Are you sure?" I lower my weapon an inch. They are wearing U.S. uniforms.

"Doubleserious, sir. We are cadets on our way to the PX to get burgers."

"Oh, shit."

"Basically, sir. But we won't tell the drill sergeant this happened. Let's just forget about it."

"Thank you."

The cadets disappear.

I walk a few paces down the dirt path in this dream, and I come face to face with Lear

Noon. My intuition: *He* controls the bomb. He is about to blow up the Earth.

I raise my rifle again. He drops to his knees, curling up protectively. I shoot at his round bodymass. My gun jerks back against my shoulder. He lifts his head and smirks at me. He stands, and I can see the single bullet has passed through him: chest, wrist, thigh.

Try again, he taunts telepathically. I do. I shoot him in the neck, leaving a small hole. He flinches but doesn't fall. He shakes his head, smiling closed-lipped. He steps to the side of the path, turns, and points behind him.

My second bullet that traveled through his neck also struck a deer. I see the hooves lying in the dust, but I can't see anything else; just then, the carcass pulls back into the mist as if dragged off by an invisible scavenger.

I turn to run, but I can't. The woodland path on which I came is blocked by a mechanical console with blinking lights and one big red button. I push the button. A keypad blinks. "Enter code," it says. I don't know the code.

JFK would have the nuclear codes. One code makes the war bigger, one code shrinks it down, one code doesn't do anything except wake you up, which I would also accept, but I have no codes at all.[*]

Why isn't JFK here? Maybe this movie is too scary for Hollywood in his time. But I don't think we're in the 1960s anymore. By

---

[*] A riff on the lyrics of "Go Ask Alice" by Jefferson Airplane.

now, I think we've murdered the Hays Code.*

I punch in a cheat code I remember from a video game from my childhood.

Behind me, Lear Noon cackles. I turn to face him. He holds something large, not a bomb, not a gun, not any kind of weapon. It's the dead deer. He's holding it up by its hind hooves. Its face slumps in the dirt.

No, not a deer. Someone in the dream-disguise of a deer. A were-deer.

As I realize who the deer is and recognize that I have shot him, Noon backs out of the scene, dragging the not-deer carcass with him. They are bound together, shot by the same bullet.

I am alone in the forest.

JFK—I know this now in my dream—is never coming back.

I am President.

Despite not pressing the dream-button correctly, I have saved the world from nuclear war. Yet the route I have taken feels more horrible than having done nothing. The flashbulb goes off. The memory is vacuum-sealed. Everything was caught on tape.

Farther down the woodland path, I hear a phone ringing. I walk up to it. It's an old black rotary phone, lying in the dirt. It's strange that it's ringing because there is no electrical source. It's unplugged, its cord wrapped around its body, a *Nightmare on Elm Street* problem. As I stand there in my dreamworld deciding whether to answer it, my hand stretches off the edge of my bed to turn off my alarm.

♏ ♐

---

* Will H. Hays, president of Motion Picture Producers and Distributors of America, implemented moral restrictions—no suggestion of sex or violence—for American movies produced from the 1930s to 1960s.

231

TWO INCHES TALLER

232

HELP ME
TO AVOID EVIL

Aparna is pouring grains, nuts, and dried fruit into a Tupperware in the office kitchen. She is two inches taller than me, which is an inch taller than usual.

I realize she's wearing pumps. I've never noticed her shoes before. It snowed again this morning. How does anyone walk through snow with any kind of heel?

I am in "storm casual" boots, all the style I could manage this morning. My office phone pings, pings, pings, and this feels overwhelming enough. I refuse to ice-slip across the parking lot in smooth-soled shoes. There is only so much dance I can do. I am supposed to be in a conference room in a few minutes.

♏ ♐

"Aparna," I greet her, and lament our shared burden: "This project backlog!"

We are too busy. How is it I remember to put on shoes at all?

I add an apotropaic plea: "Help me to avoid evil."

By these statements, I mean *hello and good morning.*

"Help yourself. I'm making granola."

"From scratch?"

"Yes. Someone has to do it or we will starve."

"Stanley knows how to make granola, too."

Stanley infuses the world, and I memorialize our friendship at every opportunity.

"Mine is better," she says.

♏ ♐

233

THE STRAWBERRY
JAM JAR IS EMPTY

I go to my desk, boot up my computer, which plays the video of the Lincoln Continental wheel. November 22, 1963. The memory is enshrined. Now we're just rolling the tape.

"Evil plays with mirrors," Lance Morrow wrote, to "erase the distinctions between itself and good...Evil abhors clarity, except in flashes of pseudo-revelation..." Sometimes, he says, we don't recognize atrocities until we see them on TV.*

I close my eyes. The image that comes: the elevator doors in the movie *The Shining*, pouring gallons of blood like a burst waterbed. Thinking of it makes me—*hungry*?

I open my eyes. *Breakfast.* Don't I have strawberry jam on my office desk? Where is it? There. Oh, dear. The jar is just about empty.

♏ ♐

Flyleaf —
Look Vice-Presidential

I Am Trying to Look Vice-Presidential
A dying pianist in Haruki Murakami's novel <u>Colorless Tsukuru Tazaki and His Years of Pilgrimage</u> says some people briefly experience a heightened state of intuition. They radiate a certain color which they alone detect in themselves and others.

I could rip off this premise for a campfire story, but no sublime portals have opened for me so I am unqualified to explain them. I haven't got a face for the presidency, and I'm radiating no special color, but I'm trying to look vice-presidential.

A spare, dry pair of fancypants shoes under my desk. Oh. I kick them so often, I

---

* From his 2003 book about the nature of evil. Professor Morrow taught me essay writing in the Boston University postgraduate journalism program in the Fall 2004 semester, and for his class I wrote a personal essay about an uncomfortable encounter. He was intrigued by my engagement with evil's slippery quality, while a classmate took offense at a different aspect of my words. They were both right. I never published the essay. Instead, a decade and a half later, I integrated the promising part of it, the part Morrow liked, into this novel. He did not know I had gender-transitioned several years earlier. More recently, he published columns in the *Wall Street Journal* that are deliberately unhelpful to transgender people. This complicates how I engage with his role in my life. When cisgender people stop making anti-transgender comments, they will be less likely to be called out by name when transgender people write their own books. If they taught us journalism, they already understand how this works.

forget why I put them there in the first place. I remove my boots and reshoe.

I should tell my own stories, right? Should I tell them as I do to my therapist, or as I do to a tarot reader who helps me by drawing card images to plug the gaps in my narrative?

I Am a Camera

Surveillance footage contains the truth, but we can't always extract it: who did it, how they did it, the kinetic trajectory of their limbs or their car, their motives.

"I am a camera with its shutter open, quite passive, recording, not thinking," Christopher Isherwood wrote in the 1930s. What I see must be "developed, carefully printed, fixed."

It's in black-and-white as if to simplify the facts.

We ask others' opinions, and opinions are all we find. No one is objective. No one sees the image-in-itself.

We project it on the wall for a shared experience, and we copy old footage by magnetic film transfer, but these processes degrade the original film.

We digitize it to copy and share it. We design robots to sleuth it. That's why we come to work.

♏ ♐

FLASHBULB
FRI
30 JAN
2015
234
NOT TAKING PILLS

Aparna pokes her head in my office. "Didn't you hear my phone call?"

My toes go ice cold. My remembered dream won't quit.

"You called?"

"Boss isn't happy with you."

Guess I won't be writing a campfire story right now.

Aparna has a different relationship with the boss. She routinely talks to him for a whole hour. Well, she's a director. From the hallway, sometimes I see them through his little office window, smiling and gabbing. Nice of her to divulge when their subject matter is me.

"OK. Yeah." I sweated through the pits of my collared shirt before I left the house this morning. My hair has probably already gone to frizz.

Her long black hair is combed artfully. "You look anxious."

"It shows?"

♏ ♐

185

FLASHBULB

FRI
30 JAN
2015

HOW ABOUT JAM?

FLASHBULB

FRI
30 JAN
2015

EAT
SOMETHING ELSE

She fixates her gaze on me. "Boss is being super-tolerant of your flipout."

"Thing is, in my dream last night, President Kennedy was shot."

"He was shot in 1963."

"I shot him."

She cocks her trigger finger on an imaginary air gun. I am alarmed, fidgeting, trying to stop something that isn't happening.

She gestures as if to put it down on my desk. "You are afraid of a nonexistent gun."

"I'm not."

"What's eating you?"

"Nothing. And I feel very done with food."

"You should eat something. Crackers and jam?" She points to the little glass jar of strawberry jam on my desk.

"Nothing left in there. I keep forgetting to throw it out. There was jam once, but never jam *today*."

♏ ♐

"Well, you should eat something else."

"Don't wanna."

"I hope you eat at home. You live alone. You get to eat whatever you want."

"In my dream, JFK moved in and made me vice president."

"What did you eat as vice president?"

"I just drank PBR. JFK drank the good stuff. And then I shot him and he died. It was an accident. My finger on the trigger."

"That makes you president, huh?"

"Yep."

"So, now you live alone and can drink whatever you want off your own top shelf."

♏ ♐

237

A DIFFERENT PILL

238

OLD SUBWAY TOKEN

"And also eat something," Aparna continues. "Be good to yourself. Do something you want to do."

"I want Stanley to decide what we'll eat for dinner."

And I want JFK to decide what we watch on TV. I want to do whatever they want to do.

"That might be a long time coming." She doesn't understand who Stanley is to me, and I hate hearing the hard truth about his likely timeline. She reaches behind me and helps herself to my desk drawer. "Let's find a different pill for you."

"What should I take?"

"Whatever's different from what you took yesterday."

I don't tell her I didn't take any pills yesterday at all. Or that the only pills that stop the speculirium are the PILCREPAPs.

♏ ♐

The drawer slides open. It's a mess in there. Pens, napkins, scissors, cookies. A T token, a golden coin you can no longer spend on the subway, a relic. My copy of *Invisible Man*, which I hide from everyone else's gaze and read when I can siphon energy on company time.

"Wait, this is Chips Ahoy. These are terrible," Aparna says.

How judgy. We split the package of cookies.

I use the scissors to snip open a blister pack of expired PILCREPAP. The last two stare at me like eyes. I swallow one.

"It is good that you listen to me and tell me what to do."

"If you want to be listened to, you should be a hit song."

♏ ♐

FLASHBULB

FRI
30 JAN
2015

BAD ELVIS
IMPERSONATION

FLASHBULB

FRI
30 JAN
2015

WE KNOW NOTHING
ABOUT RADIO

After excusing myself, I monitor my pale face in the bathroom mirror. The round ridge of my nose, curved as if it's going somewhere, beaked as though I could fly. Extra cartilege. I could impersonate Elvis but I wouldn't fool anyone.

I need a longer lunchbreak. I take a walk. I step in slush in my office shoes, having forgotten to reboot, and my toes huddle in despair. A hawk perches on a dead tree near the big plastic-and-metal letters "A.P." attached to the side of the building. Moneysaving abbreviation. A nail-bomb of starlings takes off over the phone wires, densifies, morphs, disperses. In the scatter, I find no trendline.

♏ ♐

"We have learned absolutely nothing," a voice says in my head. Was it Donald Rumsfeld who said that? No, that voice…it was one of the "Car Talk" guys.

Listeners called in to their radio show and reported the sounds from under the hoods of their cars—*thunk-thunk-thunk*—in hopes of receiving an on-air diagnosis. An interviewer once asked the hosts about their on-air magic, and the mechanic replied, "We have no idea. We sit in front of the microphones and we know nothing about radio."

That's an old interview, a memory. The tape ends there for me. For "Car Talk" too. One of the hosts died. It takes two for a conversation. There will be no more new episodes.

It's supposed to snow again overnight.

♏ ♐

241

I SHOT JFK

My boss calls me into his office.

"I like the work you've been doing," he says neutrally. "I'll see what I can do to increase your compensation."

I thought he was unhappy with me. Information changes rapidly around here.

"Yo maté a Kennedy."

"What?"

I shot JFK. "Thank you," I say. "But I have to go right now. What I need, at this moment, is a half-vacation day."

"Oh. Is it the snow?" the boss prompts me. A few coworkers are skittish about the evening commute.

"Yes. It's the snow," I lie.

"Then you'd better get going."

"I shot JFK," I cough into my sleeve as I leave the office.

He nods and shifts his gaze back to his computer. "On your way now!"

EPISODE 7

THIRD EMAIL (AMITY LODGE)

AMITY LODGE

BURNED THINGS

After a 20-mile snowy drive, I pull up slowly to the Amity Lodge conservation land. A deer crosses the road right where the sign says "Deer Xing," following the cross, following the rules, which is the cross we all bear.

I park by the duck pond. Someone plowed the parking lot since Tuesday's blizzard, but the woods must be empty. Contemplating the absence of ducks who have long since migrated south is as close as I will get to relaxation.

I have returned to the scene of my crime: where Stanley abandoned his car last summer.

♏︎♐︎

Why, on this-my-precious Friday afternoon off work, have I come *alone* to a gay gathering place? Why do I self-defeat?

The last ritual held at Amity Lodge was a bonfire at the edge of the pond. It was last Sunday, before the blizzard. I heard about the event—old letters, photos, trinkets of grief, divorce, addiction, and illness were to be tossed on a campfire—but I didn't go because I didn't have anything to burn. Of course, I have reams of emails I hate, but fire-banishment doesn't work for emails. If I printed out an email to burn it, I'd be burning a copy.

♏︎♐︎

FRI
30 JAN
2015

244

BEWARE
THE JABBERWOCK

After the burning, the snow fell. A shadowy indentation in the white layer over the firepit. All the severed Grendel heads may be there still, first burned, then frozen, here where each of the Ring-Danes battled his own demon, each in his own mead-hall.

"Beware the Jabberwock, my son! / The jaws that bite, the claws that catch!" No, wait. That isn't *Beowulf.**

No one else is here now: not the men, not the ducks. Just me, creeping around in the stillness. No ghosts or goddesses either, since I took that pill.

Unholy things heap'd for holy usage, in Byronic phrasing. When the Romans erased someone from the historical record, they called it *damnatio memoriae.* Maybe the person deserved it and maybe they didn't.

♏ ♐

FOG — HOLD SILENCE

The Nothing threatens to overvacuum Everything. We must plug the hole. Don't be the leaker. Be the plug.

Once I came to Amity Lodge for an exercise in something they called "sacred communication." I told my assigned partner that I didn't believe I'm well spoken. He didn't contradict me but replied kindly, "You hold silence very well. You have good presence." I attempted to explain his own observation back to him, and he said, "Hold it right there. That's what I'm talking about. Just... just hold silence. That's better."

This memory comes up strongly for me now in part because I did hold silence at his request, and now I am thinking about my obedience to authority.

♏ ♐

---

* Lewis Carroll's 1871 poem "Jabberwocky."

Flyleaf — The Milgram

Which reminds me of Dr. Milgram's experiment a half-century ago at Yale. If your boss tells you to do something, and it feels very wrong in your gut, what will you do? Most people live their everyday lives believing they are Not That Guy who does Nothing but the proud minority who has, or will have, moral courage when an awful choice contorts before them. The person who finds another option. But Milgram reported that most people do the shockingly unethical thing that the boss commands.

If the boss tells you to electrically shock the experimental subject in another room, you are going to keep touching that machine even if you hear screams, because the boss said <u>Do it</u>. That is what you'll actually do.

I mean, maybe the study wasn't valid, or maybe it describes only Terrible Undergraduate Boys, but still, it's a heck of a story. At least it yields to me a name, <u>the Milgram</u>, for a contrived situation in which we are asked to prove our characters. I'm probably the only person who uses this term this way. I might be the only person who is thinking about the Milgram at this exact moment.

Until recently, I too believed I was not that common person—but I am. I am part of the majority in the Milgram experiment. I am like almost everyone else. I was just following orders, and that guilt passes from me to everyone around me, all the way up the chain of command back to Mount Sinai and the Great Web of Gendered Being. My boss told me not to speak up, and I didn't speak up. I conceived creative options but didn't gestate them to viability, so I don't get credit for them.

This test is for me. The boss didn't design it. He's in the system, too. We were all tested, and we all failed. If I'd gone to the company president instead? Different conversation, same outcome. My submission to another authority. Who knows what authority the company president believes he submits to, and who really cares? The upshot is that the system has no end. The ocean is bottomless. We each rely on our own oxygen tank.

We are experimental subjects, not participants. The experiment is the test of our character. We are the ones who are being tested; we are the ones who must be found to be good.

The experiment might not be ethics-approved. What difference would it make? It's not our business whether the gatekeepers in our nightmares received ethics approval. It's our business to survive and to do it on the side of the angels. The spirits who test us don't have to be good or bad. They just are.

When Milgram "dehoaxes" his subject, the student "is confronted with the same mortifying spectacle of himself flunking a test of character he did not know he was taking." That is how the journalist Janet Malcolm put it. At least it was only a test. But it doesn't lessen the shame.

Put it this way: It is a relief to know there was no real injury. Dr. Milgram was not really electrocuting people in the other room. But the ethical failure for the shamed student stands independently of that revelation. The student has just been shown his own capacity for following orders, and he does not like what he has learned about himself. What is mortifying for the student, I think, is the epiphany that every choice he makes— even an experimental test choice in a supposedly safe, controlled environment— reflects his character, and that, very often, someone is watching and judging.

Failing the Milgram doesn't mean I don't have a spine, only that my spine and I followed orders, and this is not an impressive use of a spine. Even a snake stands up to conflict.

I could study more, know more. In the study habit of Daf Yomi, a Jew reads one page of the Babylonian Talmud per day, and it takes seven and a half years to read all 2,711 pages. A Jew could start over from the beginning and read it again. The Talmud itself warns: Don't say, "I'll study later, when I have time." Atropos cuts your time shorter every day. Besides, you're alive today and could choose to study. It says something like that, minus Atropos, the Greek Fate.

Ice triangles slosh noiselessly at the edge of the pond. I cannot see my reflection because the water is one-quarter mush and three-quarters ice. If you remain yourself and also become your mirror image, like a Klein bottle, topologists say you are in "non-orientable" space.

Lexithymia means overanalyzing and chattering on about feelings, using big words for them.

Malcolm Gladwell tells this story about an experienced firefighter who knows it's time to flee the burning building. The firefighter doesn't know exactly how he knows, but he knows. The room is extra-hot, and the flames don't respond to water. He heeds the tingling in his toes, and he gets out in time, just before the floor collapses where he'd been standing. The source of the fire had not been around him but under him.

♏♐

FOG —
FLOOR IS TREMBLING

I console myself with the interpretation that I half-passed the Milgram. At least I reported the problem to begin with, even if I let the boss dismiss my report.

I'm saying the floor is trembling, that's all.

Shutting up can cause problems when something bad is about to happen, as in the hypothetical trolley problem in which, if you sit with your hands folded, people will be hit by a runaway streetcar. The question is whether you'd kill one person to save others. The Milgram is different. That's when you can stop the trolley, but someone above you in the org chart tells you to let it keep running. He's serious. *Just let it come*, he says. And you let it come.

♏ ♐

245

BIRDS HAVE FLOWN

Why am I even here, standing in the snow at an empty retreat center? Looking for birds who have flown?

Stanley's no parrot. I don't need him to sit on my shoulder and listen to me. Nor do I need Noon to come when I call. They're free birds. If I catch a glimpse of Stanley, or if I correctly guess what Noon is doing, it is a grace.

Tracks in the snow. Large. A horse? A centaur in the garden?

The mother of Moacyr Scliar's centaur berates him because his centaur mate is a Gentile: "You could have found yourself a nice Jewish girl. Hooves or no hooves, you could have found one."

I've just missed my mythological mate. He's vanished into the woods.

♏ ♐

FLASHBULB

FRI
30 JAN
2015

246

SNOWY WOODS

FLASHBULB

FRI
30 JAN
2015

247

WHY IS IT
SO HARD?

I look toward the donut-shaped area of the snow, the remains of the ritual burning of the intolerable contents of men's pockets.

I bound through the knee-deep snow where I remember a dirt path. Here, to my side, where the snow is lumpy, would be the irregular stone wall with the uninterpretable spraypainted letters. Here, barely recognizable under the drifts, the modest guest building where Stanley stayed last summer. In this woods, there's a gravestone of someone who had smallpox. In summer, I'd know where to find it.

Maybe the boss sent the threats to me.

Why does that sound implausible?

Maybe I come here, alone, to realize my fakeness. Maybe I've been sending the threats to myself.

Maybe I'm in an Agatha Christie.

♏ ♐

I should "reach out to someone," as they say, similar to what Red Sox fans sing on the Green Line on the way home from Fenway Park. My smartphone is in my pocket. I'm connected.

I post a single sentence to my social network: "TFW you fail the Milgram." *That 'feel' when you fail the Milgram.*

I imagine myself telling Milgram and his fellow experimenters: *Oh, there must be some mistake. I signed up for the marshmallow test.*

Seven minutes later, Aparna replies in a public comment. "You're vaguebooking. WTF is your TFW?"

What the fuck. In perfect solitude in the snow, I'm still managing to motorboatwreck on social.

Why is it hard to reach out? Do I have to make more effort?

♏ ♐

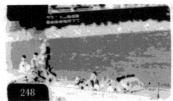

FLASHBULB

FRI
30 JAN
2015

248

THE WHOLE
MILGRIMOIRE

FLASHBULB

FRI
30 JAN
2015

249

SPIRITUAL QUEST

I call her. She picks up.

I suppose she's still at the office, while I am traipsing around on four hours of paid time off. And she'll work Sunday too because our new feature for GPS tracking of the cameras goes live then, and that's her project to shepherd.

I want to tell her the whole story from the beginning, the whole Milgrimoire: that I shouldn't have listened to the boss, that I feel like a failure. Instead, I mention the snow and what it feels like to begin to understand.

"It's just so—" I can't put my finger on the term. The trees sparkle with ice.

♏ ♐

"It's so white here. It's unsettling."

"You're just now becoming conscious of how white it is? You've lived in New England all your life."

I don't know what to do with the comment. "I'm not sure what I'm doing here."

"And?"

"I don't know *why* I'm here. What my purpose is. What the purpose of any of this is."

A *tsk* through the phone connection like ice popping. "You drove out to this place, right? Looking for spirituality?"

"Yeah."

"So don't call me asking why you're doing it. If I explain it to you and if you're ready to hear what I say, it's because you already know it. You tell me: Why are you here?"

♏ ♐

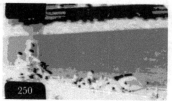

FRI
30 JAN
2015

YOU KNOW

FRI
30 JAN
2015

WHO CARES WHY?

"But I don't know the answer."

"No, really, why are you here? You know."

"I don't know."

"Because you drove there. Because you are a white gay man and you drove to be where white gay men hang out, on the snowy white duck pond. Because that's what white gay men do. OK?"

"OK."

"Now don't tell me you don't know things about yourself, and don't ask me if I have an opinion on it. Just tell me your real question."

♏ ♐

"I need to know who shot JFK."

"Oh my god. You do not need to know that," she says.

"I do."

"No one needs to know that. Ever. The answer is Lee Harvey Oswald and that is all any of us need to know."

"Don't you ever wonder? Don't you think about it every morning when you watch the computer boot up and the car wheel spins in the video?"

"No. It's not really a question. Even Boomers should stop thinking about that, and you're not a Boomer. It's old news. Who cares who did it or why they did it or how it happened?"

♏ ♐

BECAUSE PRISON

THEY WON'T
DESTROY IT

"What do you mean, 'who cares?'"

If they ever find out that someone else did it, the culprit will become some kind of famous, even if only in stories.

"In fact," she ignores me, "maybe the Zapruder film—the original, physical tape—should not be preserved anymore. Maybe its existence enables people to cling to the past."

♏ ♐

"They're never going to destroy the tape. It doesn't need to be destroyed. Everyone cares about that tape. It's inherently interesting. The Earth practically turns on it."

"Nope. No one except old people still thinks about the JFK assassination."

"And Stephen King," I argue. "He just wrote a whole novel about what if you could go back in time and try to stop it."

"Yeah. And Stephen King, who is old too. OK. No one else."

♏ ♐

FLASHBULB

FRI
30 JAN
2015

254

I'M A
TERRIBLE PERSON

FLASHBULB

FRI
30 JAN
2015

255

WE HANDLE STRESS
PRETTY WELL

"*I* care. I dreamed I shot JFK."

"You told me. And?"

"I knew what was going to happen. The story was already written. I watched it play out and didn't stop it. Not stopping it is almost the same as doing it. So, in my dream, I *did* do it. I didn't mean to, but I am responsible." I say. "And I failed the Milgram. I'm a terrible person."

"All right. You'll have to explain that one to me later."

I can't recognize her tone. We pause. We are not in a rush. Once upon a time, I kept track of my phone minutes, but now the phone company gives me infinite time.

"Lev," she says.

"Yeah?"

"Is there something you're not telling me?"

♏ ♐

"Like what?"

My boots meander from the frozen outdoors into the frozen barn. "Gnōthi seauton" is painted on the doorway as on the temple of the Delphic Oracle, which means "Conócete a ti mismo," which means "Know thyself."

"Sometimes you talk about a thing that is other than the thing you are really worried about."

"Nuh uh," I say. "I mean, I do?"

"Let me ask you this," she sighs. "How do white gay men handle stress?"

I don't know. Maybe because I'm strangely gendered. Absent ducks paddle circles in my mind mythopoeically. The mythopeepic ducklings in the nest: *peep, peep, peep.* I heard that duck sex is a physical challenge, as animal sex goes, and requires force.

"We handle stress pretty well, I guess."

♏ ♐

202

FLASHBULB

FRI
30 JAN
2015

256

CLAIMING
MYTHIC POWER

FLASHBULB

FRI
30 JAN
2015

257

WHAT IS
GAY TRAUMA?

"Pretty well?"

"I mean, the guys who built Amity Lodge aimed to make a serenity retreat for people dealing with gay trauma—"

"Masters of serenity, indeed, you are? Nope! You and I don't watch the same news networks."

"—and they're in the process of painting the passages of the Hero's Journey on the barn walls—"

No one's here to witness how I narrate the acrylic scenery for her over the telephone with a dramatic sweep of my arm, channeling JFK.

"Narration" comes from "gnosis." I recite what I know.

♏ ♐

"Yet more structuralist stories about white men claiming their mythic power," she says. "OK. I've been to a retreat center too. I've heard the usual stuff: *Goddess bless, energy cleanse, may witches dance, so mote it be.* I'm more interested in this idea of gay trauma. What is that?"

"Trauma?"

"Gay trauma. What makes it gay?"

I take a breath, thinking of examples. "Being disowned, outed, fired for being gay. Or," I pause, "sex trauma. Any sexual trauma that happens to a gay man is gay trauma, I think."

"Uh huh. Anything else?"

Nothing comes to mind. No diagnosis. "Gnosis" teases me about what I ought to know. "Dia-" means apart or through or entirely or doubled or "trans."

♏ ♐

FLASHBULB

FRI
30 JAN
2015

258

SOMETHING
I'M FORGETTING

FLASHBULB

FRI
30 JAN
2015

259

WE CALL IT IN

Chilly here. Actually, I may be freezing to death. I rub my hands and stamp my feet. Time cannot be saved and stored for later except as phone minutes and, perhaps, trauma. Heat cannot be saved and stored for later except as body fat and, perhaps, in a battery.

"I'm not aware of any other kind of gay trauma," I confess.

But there must be another kind. Amity Lodge exists for a reason. This community has to be about something more than discrimination and molestation. We are candles in the wind. I'm forgetting something. Everyone has a specific trauma. Everyone has his list of what went wrong.

We say goodbye and end the call.

♏ ♐

A blood-red spot appears on the ground near me. A cardinal in the snow. Speak of the devil. He sees me and flies to a low branch.

I remember Amitav Ghosh writing that a man had laughed at him—"You were watching like it was a film"—when he observed, for his first time, a male duck surprise a female duck.

Everyone who comes here on an erotic healing retreat knows that if he gets naked in the woods then something unexpected will happen. We not only expect the unexpected; we call it in.

Though if I come here alone, to whom am I calling?

♏ ♐

DISASTER PREVENTION

More snow. The drive home from Amity Lodge is excruciatingly slow. This was the reason my boss assumed when I asked to leave work early.

Once home, I delete my **beautiful_rage** email handle, still unused. I know I shouldn't ever use it. At least that's one thing that can't go wrong now.

I won't go to the Amity Lodge for a while, I think. I'll wait for spring, and the two hundredth anniversary of the eruption of Mount Tambora, before I visit again.

♏ ♐

THE TEMPERATURE OF THE GAS

It is a truth universally acknowledged that worse things have happened to humanity than Stanley giving me the cold shoulder after I mishandled his car.

One hundred years ago, for example, on this calendar date, the Germans used tear gas in battle for the first time. They were in Poland, fighting the Russians at the Battle of Bolimów. They fired shells containing the gas, but the gas froze. Three months later when they were in Belgium, fighting the French in warmer weather at the Second Battle of Ypres, they tried chlorine gas, and they filled the springtime air with poison fog.

Seventy years ago, on the last Saturday in January, the Soviets pulled up to a large complex in Poland—

♏ ♐

FOG — THE INFINITELY CHAMBERED HEART OF ALL GRIEF

I am aware that people have griefs I cannot fathom, and Stanley Not Talking to Me falls short of the swallowing-molten-lead standard by any measure. And yet, and yet. It is the grief I have right now. On some level, it participates in the Infinitely Chambered Heart of All Grief. My words for it are in the Universal Discourse of Upset. The Ford Taurus that isn't there takes up and deletes all the empty space inside me. It feels like a trauma to me. It is also a specifically gay trauma, at least on my end. Stanley isn't gay, but I am, and on the topic of which of my traumas are gay, I get to decide.

Three months without that Taurus already?

♏ ♐

FOG — TURNING UNDEAD

And this weekend has started off as a wreck. Saturday feels so long.

TFW Maggie's younger sister dies on *Walking Dead* and you accidentally realize you're watching the mid-season finale when you haven't properly caught up with Season Five from the beginning and you'll have to spend the next month catching up with however many episodes just for the sadness of watching that character die all over again.

Everyone dies eventually and the only question is whether your corpse will be dispatched with finality or left to turn undead.

At night, in my dream, Stanley and I hide from the Nazis in a woodshed. Bees nest in the walls, deposit wax, chew circles, taking no Sabbath: the melissa of melachah. The cells stabilize into hexagons. The will of physics, not the bees. Two people separate; their novel spreads into interlinked chapters. Honeycomb.

Out the window, a phone booth. If I run, I can make it. But who will I call? What if everyone I know is dead?

The wall leaks something sticky. Honey. The wall pulls itself into squares. We're in a swastika honeycomb. The system that holds us will hurt us.

My heart birdcage opens. I step into sunlight. I pick up the phone.

The dial tone is hold music, an instrumental ripoff of Madonna's "Rain." I can't place a call.

The sun drops like a stone into the horizon. By *Nacht und Nebel*, they come for us. *In night, in fog: You will disappear.* They circle the booth. I can't wait on hold. They don't want me this time, but they'll come for Stanley. No time.

♏ ♐

206

I CAN TURN OFF
THE TV BECAUSE
IT'S MY HOUSE

Pouring coffee in my home kitchen to take the deckle off my edges. I turn on the little TV on my kitchen counter. My Te-Lev-ision Workshop.

The AIDS crisis, my memory fires out of nowhere, *is gay trauma*.

Oh. Of course. Why was that so hard for me to remember?

Because HIV spread before I was born. And I have not had a date in a very long time. So I forget.

Another mass shooting on the news. I turn the TV off. I can do that because it's my house. I am working on lowering my emotional intensity and raising my emotional agility, which means I hold my poses for shorter durations. Too many decades and I might get or give transgenerational trauma.

♏ ♐

DO YOU REMEMBER
LEAR NOON?

Aparna calls me from the office. She's working today to make sure the new feature goes live correctly. I could tell her I've finally remembered the correct answer to her question about gay trauma, but she is busy.

"People are weird on the Internet," she tells me. "Do you remember Lear Noon?"

"Yeah." I tense up. Fresh coffee sloshes in my gut.

"He pinged me in a direct message," she said. "It didn't make any sense."

"He's been messaging you, too?" I ask.

"Check your email. I sent you a screen-shot."

♏ ♐

FLASHBULB

SUN
1 FEB
2015

264

NOON IS BOTHERING
APARNA

FLASHBULB

SUN
1 FEB
2015

265

NOON IS BOTHERING
ME

I sit at my laptop, holding the phone with my left hand, clicking the mouse with my right hand. The screen lights up. Without relaxing my neck, arms, and legs, I take a look at what she's sent me. An odd image: a silhouette of a cartoon cowboy with the legend, "That's all, folks!" From his regular social media account under his real name.

I should have told her earlier. She is always transparent with me, and she recognizes weird. I repent of my sin and tell her everything about the two emails from **what_will_happen_chromatically**, including the boss's order of silence.

"Uh huh," she says. "Why would he set up an anonymous email account? That sounds stressful. You are stressing me out now."

♏ ♐

While I am looking at my email inbox, a third missive from **what_will_happen_chromatically** pops up. Aparna stays with me on the line.

"Very soon now!" This from Noon. *That's all, folks.* My gut squeezes. Bad for my acid reflux.

A countdown. A spinny bike whose wheel goes around and around in the woodshed until it's time to stop. *Three, two, one. From zero we come and to zero we return.*

"Sucks that he's bothering both of us," I say. I feel as though it's somehow my fault.

"If we had joined HR's official diversity committee," she begins, "maybe it would have been an avenue to—"

We look each other in the eye and simultaneously say, *"Nah."*

♏ ♐

Flyleaf — Minority Report

In Philip K. Dick's <u>The Minority Report</u>, the three beings called the "precogs" predict who is going to commit a crime. Usually the precogs agree with each other, but sometimes one dissents.

Aparna and I are nervous; our boss is not. In this case, our boss is giving the minority report.

One interpretation of "minority" is simply "uncommon" or "unpopular," and in this sense, a minority report can, of course, be correct. Another interpretation of "minority" is "marginalized" or "unimportant," and in this sense, I like to imagine my boss as so tiny that he fits on my desk like an action figure, and Teddy Ruxpin could sit on him and the boss would sound like "mmph mmph ffmmph" and we'd worry Teddy Ruxpin was broken, but no, when we found Action Figure Boss making noise under his butt, we'd realize that everything was as it should be, and we'd sit Teddy back down on the boss's face again.

♏ ♐

Flyleaf — Extremely Wrong Theories

The conspiracy theorist interprets evidence against the sham as evidence of the sham. <u>Of course that's what "they" want you to think.</u> There is no way to burst the bubble. Anything that touches the bubble makes it stronger. It's like a game of Katamari Damacy except without the adorable jingle tune.

I wonder if I am a conspiracy theorist.

I don't know how well I see in the dark.

♏ ♐

FLASHBULB

SUN
1 FEB
2015

I WANT TO RETURN

FLASHBULB

SUN
1 FEB
2015

I AM NOT
A CONSPIRACY
THEORIST

She hums through the silence. "Sometimes I feel insufficient, sometimes I feel helpless. This just feels gross. So, what do you want to do?" she asks me.

"I want to go back to Amity Lodge. My thinking spot. I was making progress there." Never mind my idea to wait until spring.

"More alone time? OK," she says. "And then you'll make a decision?"

"Yeah, or at least I can think about it some more."

"You want me to wait for you to think."

"Basically."

Asking people to wait for me to think is like asking them to read a novel I am writing.

♏ ♐

I go to Amity Lodge that very evening, despite the early darkness. Driving's never easy. Nothing's ever easy. Sunset is at 4:58 p.m. I bring a flashlight.

Amity Lodge is empty. I point my toes toward the barn, the only structure with electricity. My shoes crunch over the lowest snowdrifts, which are still high, though mussed, as someone else may have trudged this way recently. The flashlight beam bounces over fresh sparkling ice crystals.

Old wooden door doesn't lock, nor even shut tight.

The inside is dark. Earlier in the day, more sunlight would come through the small windows, but now, Emily be with me, the sun is slant.*

I flick the switch. The electric lights overhead come on.

♏ ♐

---

* "Tell all the truth but tell it slant," she said.

FOG — SEPARATION, INITIATION, RETURN

Beyond "Know thyself," the entrance to the Delphic temple asks for the virtue of temperance, as well as the avoidance of loyalty oaths as they only ever bring mischief and ruin.[*]

It's one thing to go inside the barn looking for *gnosis* and another thing to look for *sophia*. If someone put rainbow-shirt Sophia in the barn weeks ago and she's still moving, you don't want to get too close to her. I'd swear an oath to that.

I see the hero's journey mural on the four walls—the stages of "separation," "initiation," and "return," plus a black background with planets and stars—but something has changed. Someone has written all over it with black Sharpie.

I AM UNABLE TO BE NICE TO YOU. I AM NOT GOING TO TELL YOU WHY BECAUSE YOU ARE UNABLE TO HEAR IT.

EVEN IF THEY HAD THREE DOG HEADS WITH FORKED TONGUES YOU WOULD STILL LIKE THEM BETTER THAN YOU LIKE ME. THAT IS THE WAY IT IS. IT NEEDS TO BE

THAT WAY. YOU HAVE REASONS. I HELPED CREATE THAT SITUATION BY NOT MAKING YOU HEAR THINGS YOU DIDN'T WANT TO HEAR. YOU HAVE OPINIONS ABOUT THE WAY THINGS ARE FOR ME THAT ARE NOT THE WAY I SEE THEM. IT WAS A LONG TIME AGO.

THEY DID NOT MAKE ANYONE HATEFUL BUT I WILL ACCUSE THEM. THEY SHOULD GIVE ME INFORMATION OR SYMPATHY OR CONTEXT FOR WHY THEY BELIEVE IT'S OK TO TAKE THINGS AWAY FROM ME OR WHY THEY DIDN'T REALIZE WHAT THEY WERE DOING. THEIR IDEOLOGY!

I WILL REFLECT EVERY DAY HOW THIS EARNED ME ONLY IGNOMINY AND I WILL NEVER UNDERSTAND IT. I WILL SINK. I WILL RISE FOR AIR TO MAINTAIN MY WRAITH. I WILL SINK. THIS IS SWIMMING. YOU SHOULD TRY IT SOMETIME. THE CESSPOOL CALLED 'I USED TO HAVE A LIFE.'

---

[*] See Plato's *Charmides* dialogue. In Benjamin Jowett's translation: "Give a pledge, and evil is nigh at hand."

There is a certain intonation people use to say "awesome" when they mean something is not awesome, not at all, thank you very much. This awesome tracks more with fear than wonder, and thus it is "terrible." Whatever hero's journey we were taking, we've reached the site of penny dreadfuls, treatises on Lurianic metaphysics, and Oedipal neurosis. I am sorry I came.

♏ ♐

FLASHBULB

SUN
1 FEB
2015

STOLEN CAMERA

As I gape at the barn wall, Aparna rings me. My pocket buzzes.

"Yeah?" I answer. Dry throat.

"Why did you take a camera?" she demands.

"What are you talking about?"

"I see one of our cameras on the map." I guess the new tracking feature is working. "You said you were going to Amity Lodge. System shows me everything."

"Yeah, but I didn't bring a camera."

"Funny. Then why does it GPS to you?" I hear her fingers tapping a keyboard.

"I don't know—"

"Hey. I've got an ID on this hardware. This is my prototype that's been missing all year. Why is it *there*?"

Once habit, now instinct: I look up. So often there's a camera if you know where to look.

♏ ♐

FLASHBULB

SUN
1 FEB
2015

INFORMATION
OR SYMPATHY
OR CONTEXT

FLASHBULB

SUN
1 FEB
2015

HORROR

There it is, in the barn rafters, pointed at me, moving slowly, tracking my steps. Someone put it there. Not me. Someone else.

"This place is really weird," I say, looking at the walls. *THEY SHOULD GIVE ME INFORMATION OR SYMPATHY OR CONTEXT.*

"You didn't put it there?"

"No, it has to have been *him*. Lear Noon."

"Man, you should *go,*" said Aparna. "Something isn't right."

The longest recorded chess game between rated players was 269 moves. No one won.[*]

"I'm not afraid," I said.

"You should be. Do you need me to save you? I'm kind of busy."

"No." I take what I intend as one last look at the Sharpied walls and the old stolen camera high in the dry wooden rafters.

♏ ♐

I am thinking about the horror movies *The Blair Witch Project* and *The Ring*. They involve a ghostly video, and the key point is not so much how the video is made but that the ghost has an interest in you sharing the video. If you share it, you are helping the ghost.

I can't share the tape because our cameras don't have tapes. We're past that era. Someone could be watching me live. The goal is not to be in the video.

I don't want to miss my chance to leave, and I want to exit correctly.

"I'm leaving now."

We end the phone call.

♏ ♐

---

[*] A 269-move chess game between Ivan Nikolic and Goran Arsovic on February 17, 1989.

213

Flyleaf —
Ideas About Anglerfish

Predators are crafty. The female anglerfish draws in her prey by dangling that horrid droopy antenna, a bioluminescent lure called an "esca," over her own mouth. What is the anglerfish offering, the little fish might wonder?

Is she benevolent, spreading light, teaching the smaller fish to aspire to grow its own esca someday?

Or is she malevolent and full of trickery and instadeath?

A third option: Does she hope to keep her prey guessing which is the case—good or evil, good or evil?—and thus aggravate and occupy its brain?

The con artist.

The gaslighter.

The littlefishfucker.

Eschatologically, we don't know where we'll end up.

A fourth option: The anglerfish doesn't care what her prey thinks. Instead, she keeps her own light on for herself. She's lonely in the dark. She prefers to believe someone accompanies her, seeing everything she sees, sharing her perspective, her angle on the deep. When she bumbles along with a flashlight, it's easier for her to pretend she has a friend.

A fifth option: She's got no agency whatsoever here and is followed by a ghost. It's not the anglerfish's fault her esca is haunted.

Maybe that's how human consciousness evolved. We used to have external bioluminescence but, somehow, we swallowed it, or it jumped down our throats. Now our imaginary friends are inside us.

"The Zapruder film is a clock against which all other films are checked," Ray Marcus told a grand jury in 1967. He was an activist for the idea that there had been more than one gunman. He showed an enlargement of a photograph taken by another spectator present at the assassination and asked those present to "go to the back of the room…where you no longer can see the dots. I want you to lose the dots. If you see the dots you are too close. You can't see the picture if you see the dots."

Many of us are inclined to lean in to see the dots. A character in Don DeLillo's Underworld refers to "the dot theory of reality, that all knowledge is available if you analyze the dots." And whatever else a photograph is, it is "a universe of dots. The grain, the halide, the little silver things clumped in the emulsion."

Once we see the dots, we lean out again to see the bigger picture. The dots connect. If they don't, we will draw the connections.

The Zapruder film is commonly referred to as a clock that times the assassination of JFK. Such a clock is useful for investigating whether a single gunman fired three bullets within six seconds, though such knowledge won't get me to my meetings on time. Still need a wristwatch for that.

An infinity of thoughts. Like dots in a photograph.

♏ ♐

FLASHBULB

SUN
1 FEB
2015

I TAKE THE CAMERA

By now, I am suffering with my own unphotogenic aura.

I grab a foothold on one of the walls and shimmy and monkeybar across a rafter, from which I unhook the camera. It wasn't plugged in; it was running on battery.

It belongs to Achromatic Proprioception. I will return it to Aparna.

EPISODE 8

STOP NOON (L. D. LIQUE)

THAT CAMERA
WAS STOLEN

HE SHOULD
TAKE PILLS

"It's bad to have a camera in the barn," I say to Aparna while I drive home this Sunday night in darkness. My phone is propped up in the cupholder, on speaker. Her rescued camera is in my glove compartment, powered off. "People practice sex magick in there. No one at Amity Lodge would ever have authorized a camera installed."

"No one at A.P. authorized our camera to be *stolen* and installed there," Aparna says, my low-quality phone speaker reverberating in the cupholder. "I've been wondering all year where it went."

My temple throbs.

"We know who took it, right?" she says.

"Yeah," I say. "Him. He left the company a year ago. Makes sense."

♏ ♐

There is a brief silence.

"The writing in the barn—" she begins.

"I don't wanna—"

"But what did it *say*?"

"I dunno."

She is frustrated. "Was it written in, like, Linear B?"

I shake my head. I am alone in the car, driving home in the dark. "No," I say aloud into the telephone. "He wrote something about 'ideology.' I don't know what that means."

"A set of beliefs, rigidly linked."

"I don't need the ideology of ideology. I mean, I don't know *whose* ideology."

"Yours?"

"I have no ideology. I change my beliefs every three seconds."

"Lev. How bad was it?"

"Really bad."

"Like he should take pills to help with that?" She pauses one beat. "No offense."

♏ ♐

FLASHBULB

SUN
1 FEB
2015

274

I AM HELPABLE

"Unless," I say, glossing over her last comment, "he's a sociopath. In which case, he just is the way he is."

"Don't know if 'sociopath' is even a diagnosable disorder anymore."

"Doesn't matter who diagnoses him with what. What matters is whether he has a conscience."

"If he has a mental problem, all the more reason he should take pills."

"I am helpable. That's why my pills help me. I don't know if this guy is helpable. If he's got no seeds to water, he will never grow a conscience. And no one will succeed in talking him out of anything if he doesn't believe he has to change."

"You are helpable," Aparna says, "because you get a lot of help."

♏ ♐

Flyleaf — We're Watching

Julius Caesar was fed up with the lunar calendar. Real seasons go by the Earth's rotation around the sun, not the moon's rotation around the Earth. Lunar kicks you off course by another two weeks every year. Several years in, how can you plant crops? Caesar's astronomer recommended the 365-day solar calendar. To catch up to the "real" date, after February 2, 44 BCE, Rome had 30 nameless days, then resumed with February 3. This calendar adjustment is called an intercalation.[*]

We also adjust our measurements of space: latitude, longitude, altitude. They say the Russians are requesting to put up antennae in the United States so Russian GPS will work across the globe. When I think about everyone who might be watching me, I'm not afraid of my own company's camera. Let the company watch. I'll watch it in return.

If we snooze, we lose. Caesar was assassinated by his former friends on March 15 during that long year, 44 BCE. They stabbed him. Not caught on camera. A few generations later, Juvenal wanted to know: "Who watches the watchmen?"

No one can watch 'round the clock.

♏ ♐

---

[*] The story of the calendar adjustment under Caesar is described by Michael Judge in *The Dance of Time*.

Was it I who woke up one morning and realized that my former coworker was actually a giant cockroach?

Can't taste my breakfast. As if my whiskers were lopped off, stumps sanded down. I eat a little, guided by propositional knowledge of why food is important.

Whiskers meows. "Now" or "not now"? Those are the two food-related answers that matter to her.

Now.

I pour kibble into the bowl and open a can to mix wet in dry, or she won't eat. Fish oil smears across the counter near the can opener and the lamp.

I'm glad lamps are electric these days. If they still ran on fish oil, my counter would be slick all the time.

♏ ♐

Flyleaf —
The Pull-Cord Lamp

The pull-cord lamp was a thrift-store discovery. Porcelain base. Two nude, trumpeting cherubs, each saying "Allelu," according to banners emblazoned under their toes.

It was, though tacky, a theological revelation. Not because the cherubs animated; they're male, so they didn't and wouldn't. Not for me. Rather, because the two "allelus," the sound of worship, form a tangible instruction: "hale luz." Pull light.

This reveals the intent of prayer-language. In their "allelus," devotees are trying to recall the magic formula for "Let there be light." They aspire to illuminate the world.

But I feel that the forgetting of the formula is a problem of cisgender theists. Personally, I make light by pinching and yanking the pull-cord on the lamp. There's science behind it. Transgender people have been over here, all this time, making light. If we forget, we relearn and we execute.

Speaking of science: Dinosaurs couldn't kill the cockroach. Evolution couldn't change it. Its biological equilibrium had no punctuation ever. Just plain cockroach, forever. I have begun to destroy the furniture of my mind. Is it collateral damage of my chase after the giant cockroach's gloating shadow and percussive footsteps?

On the shadow: The decision to be-come into one's gender is not done by listing boring details about men and women and declaring how you fit their molds. Gender is indeed category, but the category isn't solely about them. It's also about you because you are the one who showed up for it.

What underlies a gender transition may be not analysis, but prophecy. To declare prophetically that you will change your gen-der is to be "immediately transformed into someone who lives in the shadow of that ut-terance"*—here, the voice that says this does not consist of your own words, but sounds itself like a prophecy, as if it speaks to you from a place outside time, a meta-prophecy, a user's manual that warns what the proph-ecy will do to you.

The meta-prophecy explains that you are an engine for churning past into future, a blisteringly obvious description of human time that only a prophet would think to ar-ticulate, and in these Utterances of Blazing Obvious (devarim or dibrot, utterances, as we call the Ten Commandments, zeh barur, that is obvious), you see your shadow, and your shadow-knowledge is a tree shading your present until you fulfill what the proph-ecy said you would do.

So the problem, you know—because being transgender is not all rainbows and light—is that the prophetic voice doesn't al-ways stop at announcing your imminent sex change. No, no. Sometimes the prophetic voice follows you around. Like, you've al-ways had a shadow, and now it's holding a Martian death-ray gun and has started talk-ing, and, speaking from the place outside time, your shadow, whose voice isn't yours but never narrates for anyone else's actions but yours, says things someone else might say and you wish you had the chutzpah to come up with, like: "I swear by all that is holy that I will kill the President myself."†

ﬅ ♐

---

* Please read the footnote at the end of this section, miss.

† In Grace Lavery's 2022 memoir, *Please Miss*, she describes hearing a voice that "spoke through" her, allowing her to articulate her resolve to stop living as a man, and her own declaration "immediately transformed [her] into someone who lives in the shadow of that utterance" (p. 157). Lavery also discusses the 1996 film *Mars Attacks!*, in which a hostile space alien disguises itself as a human woman and attempts to seduce its way into the White House to assassinate the U.S. President. The alien never speaks because it can only quack like a duck and must continuously chew gum to survive in the earth's atmosphere, but Lavery imagines what it might have said. Within her semi-fictionalized memoir, she receives a parodic, anonymous, rambling letter, illustrated with a clown image, and the weird letter expresses something much like what that alien would have said: "I swear by all that is holy that I will kill the President myself" (p. 165).

276

HER REAL NAME
IS WHISKERS

277   TRAVEL BAN

The metal tag on the cat's collar is stamped "Eurydice." I ordered the nametag. But her real name is Whiskers, after the kitten Stanley had tried to rescue, ephemeral though that relationship was.

She meows again. I don't turn around. She can't be hungry. She is demanding attention. I won't reward that behavior. She meows, and I am not going to look, not going to look, not going to look, but she meows, and I turn around and look, and she head-butts me and makes me pet her. Petting is a parataxis, a poetic repetition.

It occurs to me it was fortunate I didn't yet have a cat when the bird flew into my apartment last April. Fortunate for the bird, that is.

♏ ♐

I migrate to the bedroom to get ready for work. There's going to be another whopper of a snowstorm today. The governor is urging people not to drive to work if they don't have to. I guess he feels that, because he banned all travel not even a week ago, he has diminished political capital. He won't be so heavy-handed today; he'll just *beg* us. We voters are kind of his boss.

I sympathize. I skipped out of work early Friday afternoon while my boss was arranging a raise for me, so I have diminished political capital with him to choose, absent any decree from the governor, not to show up for work Monday morning.

♏ ♐

FLASHBULB

MON
2 FEB
2015

278

I DIDN'T BREAK
THE LAMP

GROUNDHOG DAY

How did I even get here? I complain to myself, brushing my teeth. *Why did I come here? Why am I here?* The monotony of the morning. The monotony of the footsteps.

I am drawn back to the kitchen by a colossal smash. The lamp has fallen from the kitchen counter. How?

Whiskers, standing on the floor by her bowl of kibble-mush as though she has not moved, gives me an innocent look: *I didn't break the lamp.*[*]

♏ ♐

Flyleaf — Time

"That great eccentric, Time," Bruno Schulz mused, spawns children who manifest as normal years and then occasionally as "different, prodigal years which—like a sixth, smallest toe—grow a thirteenth freak month." The strange years come into being "more tentative than real," filled with "stunted, empty, useless days—white days, permanently astonished and quite unnecessary. They sprout, irregular and uneven, formless and joined like the fingers of a monster's hand, stumps folded into a fist."

Not sure what the notion of "freak" is doing here, as the technical term is "intercalation," but anyway, if it's my year, my month, I ought to be the one to say whether my time or my being-in-time is a monster or not.

Time moves slowly, or I am moving awfully slowly through it, and if the calendar-maker continues to loop in extra days, I don't know when I'll ever get to watch <u>Avengers: Infinity War</u>.

♏ ♐

---

[*] The implication that a cat breaks a lamp alludes to a bakeneko, a destructive cat in Japanese legend that could have various supernatural abilities including taking human form or otherwise controlling the ghosts of dead humans. Bakeneko were sometimes said to lick lamp oil, a reasonable thing for a cat to do if the oil originated from fish. The phrase "I didn't break the lamp" is an homage to the Mad Scientist anthology by that title.

ONE CONTINUOUS
DAY

POSITIONED
TO HEAR
AND NOT HEAR

I drive to the office in a hell of a snowstorm, and it is Monday morning, the second of February, 2015, but to me it feels as if it's the same continuous day, as if I hadn't just had a two-and-a-half-day weekend.

Aparna and I, as we live close to the office, make it to the 9 a.m. status meeting. Most coworkers live farther out and are stuck in snowstorm traffic.

No single snowflake breaks the record. They do it in aggregate. The snowflake that tips the scale does so by its place in line.

I'm not sure if mere arrival credits us with political capital. It depends on the boss's mood and sympathies.

♏ ♐

At 9:30, after the meeting, Aparna walks into my office and closes the door behind her. She is also wearing "storm casual" footwear today. Her boots are furry like great big bear paws.

"Can I have it?"

I hand over the camera.

"What do you want to do?" She has asked me this before.

The boss has been useless in this situation, and I can't rope in the company president either. They are positioned to hear yet not hear. To continue being who they are, they need to mute my drama.

♏ ♐

FLASHBULB

MON
2 FEB
2015

281

ORG CHART OF
'I CAN'T'

GROUNDHOG DAY

FLASHBULB

MON
2 FEB
2015

282

ABOUT
THAT BASEBALL GUY

GROUNDHOG DAY

It's a funny form of proprioception, lacking nuance and possibility. The Org Chart of "I Can't."

My boss sees some of my strengths better than I do. He may not know why and how I work this way, nor what to do with me. But he does see me from a perspective from which I cannot see myself. He has different strengths. There's a reason why he was given his office and I, mine.

"Let it go—or do something," Aparna dilemmas for me.

My face has no glimmer of genius in reply.

"Why don't you call your baseball friend and ask for advice?"

She means Stanley.

"He's not talking to me," I remind her. She knows this. We talked about it Friday.

"Oh, right."

♏ ♐

To Aparna, apparently, Stanley is a "baseball guy" who showed up for campfire stories in her backyard a few times last summer and might someday come again. It's hard for me to comprehend that he does not loom as large in other people's lives as he does in mine. I guess "your baseball friend" is better than "bat-man."

No vela con nosotros. *He does not stay up with us by the campfire, paying homage to the dead and the past.* If I closed up the blank space between the words, it would become an invitation, "novela con nosotros," *write this novel with us.*

I can't get distracted thinking about friendship troubles. I have to focus on the mission. I have to stop Lear Noon.

♏ ♐

FLASHBULB

MON
2 FEB
2015

I CAN'T EAT   GROUNDHOG DAY

"I hate making decisions that affect other people. I've never aspired to be a vice president. Not even director. Not a goal of mine."

"You don't want to be vice president someday? Not ever?"

"Nope."

"I guess me neither. I dunno. Do you want to eat something?" she suggests.

Eat. Re-inscribe the memory of food. That would be something. Let my belly rise with the memory of bread. The earth turns. The moon rises. Breathe. Breathe. Breathe. I will live for one minute more. Check in again in one minute. Breathe. Eat. Breathe. I got this.

"I can't eat right now," I say.

♏ ♐

Flyleaf — Does the Earth Move?

A pinwheel with rigid flags: the flags don't move relative to each other, but they move relative to the stick. Isn't this how people once argued whether the Earth moves round the Sun? Didn't they say the Earth couldn't "move" by definition because the Earth is always our point of reference? The Earth does move, said Galileo. Just look at the Sun. No, don't literally look directly at it with your eyes; it burns. I only mean: Consider the Sun. You are moving relative to it. You are aging. You tell me it isn't happening, but it is.

This ship is receiving a distress signal that I've been tracking for a month now. I've been going in circles. The signal is coming from inside the system.

I am, after all, hired to find bugs on our company's side of the system. Not bugs outside our company, even if they affect us, because there is little I can do about them.

But there is a giant bug inside the system, shaped like a former employee. I am the distress signal. That's why I'm here.

I must choose. Noon has been insistent, and I, too, must be clear on what I want. To care about the mess and to feel powerless: "nothing is bleaker," Milgram himself wrote. I have run out of time. I must settle on what I feel is the right course of action.

A brain surgeon inserts a scope through a sheath called a trochar. It draws its red line through the brain over and over. It's dark inside the patient's skull, so the surgeon observes the instrument's movements on live video. Cameras even inside our heads.

♏ ♐

227

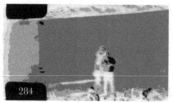

FLASHBULB

MON
2 FEB
2015

FACE-TO-FACE
IS PREFERRED

GROUNDHOG DAY

FLASHBULB

MON
2 FEB
2015

IS THAT
A GOOD IDEA?

GROUNDHOG DAY

Aparna gives up on me. She turns the doorknob to leave. I look up at my poster of Agile Principles, and, as I hear the doorknob "click" as she opens the door, my answer clicks into place.

Agile Principle #6: Face-to-face conversation is preferred.

I jump up and close the door to stop her from leaving. "I've got it," I say. "I'll meet him today on lunchbreak."

"Here?"

"No, no, somewhere else."

She crunches her brow and closes her eyes. "How are you going to drive anywhere on lunchbreak and come back? We barely all made it to the office this morning."

"Snow's plowed now."

"It isn't. How are you going to *park*?"

"I don't know. But I have to do this."

♏ ♐

"Is it a good idea for you to meet a guy who is sending weird emails?" She looks unconvinced.

"Yeah, yeah, it's fine, why?" I am, in fact, afraid of other men's guns, but I play it cool.

"Because the boss said not to. He said: *Don't look into stuff that isn't your business.*" She lifts the T.P.-roll-shaped camera and points its dark glass eye at me.

Since when does she see things from the boss's perspective?

I remember the boss saying something more like: *Don't bother me.* Maybe it amounts to the same thing. He just doesn't want to see whatever I'm seeing.

"The boss isn't right about everything."

♏ ♐

286

I HAVE A ROLE TO
PLAY

"What *has* he got right?"

Valid question. I take a breath. "Lear Noon is not—a credible—threat," I say slowly, trying to convince myself. "He's paranoid and anxious. Even if he lacks a conscience, he may not have big plans to hurt me."

"And what have *you* got right?" she asks me.

"That I can't disregard it. I have a role to play here. The only one who can talk down this particular anxious white homosexual is another anxious white homosexual," I say.

"Then you were put here for this moment," she smiles thinly. "Up and at 'im."

♏ ♐

FOG —
THIRTEENTH SPACE

Some calendars, like the Ethiopian, have 13 months by design. Don't know who might have drawn my current calendar this way, but regardless, I find myself in the thirteenth space.

I am an offensive weapon. I am an IED. I am the only man I know who had an IUD and then a hysto. If there are others who have done this, I don't remember them right now. I am focusing on myself. If I don't stop myself, no one else can stop me either.

What's the difference between an IED and an IUD? The vowels "E" and "U," I notice. They are the first letters in the words "eudaimonia" and "eunuch." If I cross them out, I'm left with "ID," as in: *identify* the source of the problem. I am solving this crossword. I am winning the game show.

♏ ♐

FLASHBULB

MON
2 FEB
2015

NO ONE CAN
STOP ME

GROUNDHOG DAY

Aparna is right. I should throw myself at it with everything I am, full Milgram jacket. I can be afraid. "No fearless fool now fronts thee" goes the line from that fat novel about chasing a white whale. I embrace my fear because my fear keeps me alive.

Just then, my phone, resting on top of a large loose-leaf binder of technical documents, makes its notification sound. Aparna looks at me. I check my phone. It's a promotion for a rewards program for a coffee shop. The more you drink, the more they'll sell you.

♏ ♐

FLASHBULB

MON
2 FEB
2015

MEN WHO
MAKE THREATS

GROUNDHOG DAY

"It's nothing," I shrug at Aparna. I sort of wish I had more information for what I'm about to do, but I probably have enough.

"Don't take BS from him," she counsels.

"Don't let his gaze suck you in. Don't let him touch you." She's speaking more intensely than usual. "I personally wouldn't go, I mean, I'd win against him like Carmen Sandiego but I'm all out of jet fuel. Since you're going, take it serious. When men make threats, I believe they'll do exactly what they say they'll do—and worse, if you give them the chance."

"I will treat him like a snake," I assure her.

♏ ♐

FLASHBULB

MON
2 FEB
2015

WATCH FOR BUGS

GROUNDHOG DAY

"If there are any work emergencies, you know, the regular kind—"

"I've got your back while you're out of the office. If a boring bug is dumped in the queue, I'll take care of it. I know what to do with them."

"You don't have to do my work for me."

"Well, for, like, two hours, I'll watch for a crisis. I might actually touch the crisis if by some miracle I'm bored."

♏ ♐

FLASHBULB

MON
2 FEB
2015

290

WHAT ARE
FRIENDS FOR?

GROUNDHOG DAY

FLASHBULB

MON
2 FEB
2015

291

PHONE LIGHTS UP

GROUNDHOG DAY

"We are busy," I acknowledge. A.P. is very nearly never not busy.

"It's *our* work. The team's. Don't worry—I'll make sure the nastiest bugs are assigned back to you. Besides, the system sees what I touch. It searches and makes an accounting for the letter I in TEAM. No big deal. You go talk to the guy and then come back."

I process this. "So, like—if JFK is the president," I begin, and she nods, "and I'm his vice president," I go on, and she raises her eyebrow at me, "you'd be, like—the Speaker of the House of Representatives? Third in line?"

"Yes," she says, exasperated that it takes me so long to explain things badly. "What are friends for?"

♏ ♐

Waiting for Noon to call my personal phone, I am not really focused on work. That's fine. I can wait. I can just sit here till that smartphone ringtones as if I'm in a Debbie Gibson song. Oh, there it lights up. Noon is texting me now: "Come now. We can park at L. D. Lique. It's already open, but you can sit in my car and we can talk privately. I can be there at 10:10."

The timeframe is extremely tight, but he knows well that my office is only a few miles down the street from L. D. Lique. He himself must already be there, or close.

♏ ♐

FLASHBULB

MON
2 FEB
2015

GROUNDHOG DAY

NOT DOING THE BILLY OCEAN SONG WITH HIM

FLASHBULB

MON
2 FEB
2015

GROUNDHOG DAY

LET'S ORDER ICE CREAMS

We need to firm up plans quickly so I can make this arrival time, but I see zero possibilities inherent in the middle part of his suggestion. I'm not getting in his car. I've already pre-decided that. I'm not doing the Billy Ocean song with him. This is not autofiction. Nor am I climbing into any horse-drawn carriage to his *Dracula* castle—ah, yes, finally, that's where that line came from: "The dead ride fast!"*

♏ ♐

"Let's order ice creams and sit at a small table," I counteroffer by text message, "away from the window, so no one on the sidewalk will see us. That looks less suspicious."

My message deliberately is a Winter Wonderland level of nonsense. No one is traversing the sidewalk during the second major snowstorm within a week except for people like us who are entering L. D. Lique. There are more likely to be customers *inside* L. D. Lique who will see and hear us. However, my facade of logic speaks to his paranoia and satisfies it. The magic words were: *so no one will see us.*

♏ ♐

---

* "The dead ride fast" is the English rendering of "die Todten reiten schnell," a line from Gottfried August Bürger's poem "Lenore," published in 1774. It was echoed in Bram Stoker's 1897 novel *Dracula* as "the dead travel fast" and in works like "Les Morts Vont Vite," a poem by the dramatist Brander Matthews (d. 1929), who opens with: "*Les morts vont vite*: The dead go fast!"

Flyleaf —
You. Not Someone Else.

Whoever shows up reveals himself as the responsible party. When Chris Hansen was the face of Dateline NBC's stings to catch sex predators, the men dissociated themselves from what they'd said online. Put on the spot, they lied to Hansen, claiming that someone unknown to them had hacked their online accounts, impersonated them, and made appointments on their behalf. They were unable to explain why an unknown hacker would have done this and why they themselves (not the hacker) drove for hours to arrive for the appointment. It wasn't their fault, they argued. Yes, they showed up at a private address after a compromising online chat, but they had no motives; it hadn't been their conversation; someone else had typed those things. But, Hansen countered, face-to-face: "You're here. You. Not someone else."

Don't do it, the boss said to Adam and Eve some thousands of years before that. 'Why not?', you ask? Really? OK, if you're so curious, show up and do the thing I just told you not to do. Then you'll know why not. You'll know ethics: the logic of it plus the transcendence of it. You'll know reality: I am the Alpha and the Omega of your org chart. Me. Not someone else. Me. You'll know the parameters of a human life: what time it is now and the fact that it's too late to go back. You'll learn all of this. And then, by the way, I'll have to kill you.

Regarding logic, I am at the zero-level of care. Able-2-deal-o-meter is 0 percent. I don't come to Casablanca for the waters. I don't go to the ice cream parlor for the logic.

And you know, Cicero told his friend Curio two thousand years ago, this situation didn't fall on your head. You came here. "Non incideris, sed veneris." I emphasize: It wasn't by chance but by your own judgment. "Iudicio enim tuo, non casu."

I haven't even left the office yet.

♏︎♐︎

FLASHBULB

MON
2 FEB
2015

294

IGNITION   GROUNDHOG DAY

FLASHBULB

MON
2 FEB
2015

295

I AM RESPONSIBLE   GROUNDHOG DAY

I walk out of the office, turn the key in my car's ignition, push the button for heat, step out of the car, clean it off for the second time today. The snow falls heavily and accumulates. The snowflakes begin to melt when they touch the heated windshield. I sit behind the wheel and close the driver's side door. I wait for the warmth to grow strong enough for me to start the engine.

Steven Shaviro says intelligence is cognition but also *discognition*. Thinking isn't really thinking unless it's disrupting itself. Inside cognition, in the cotton-string guts of the stuffed animal, are "fictions and fabulations." Our stories are like scientific hypotheses. We test them to see what they do.

Ignition. Beyond thought: action.

♏ ♐

I drive to L. D. Lique and park the car. It's 10:08.

I am responsible because I have shown up.

♏ ♐

BOTTOMLESS

When you are digging yourself into the hole, you never reach bottom. "Where's the North?" Alexander Pope asked. If you're "at York, 'tis on the Tweed; / In Scotland, at the Orcades; and there," if you're at Orcades, the North is "at Greenland, Zembla, or the Lord knows where." We perceive immorality this way because "no creature owns it in the first degree, / But thinks his neighbour farther gone than he!"

Then it continues: "It is somebody wants to do us harm—" No, wait, that is a different poem.

♏ ♐

**I ARRIVE FIRST
AT THE
ICE CREAM PARLOR**

I walk inside L. D. Lique. I stand in line because that is what you are supposed to do at an ice cream shop, though I don't want ice cream. Textured like ectoplasm and cold as the grave. The tea, the tea—they offer many kinds, named after many places on the other side of the globe. On the counter is a glass jar of madeleines: orange, anise, poppy. I might like a madeleine, but I would want a very particular flavor, and I can't remember what it is.

I order an Americano with cream and a milligram of fear, and I actually drink it, because Noon is 12 minutes late. I'm surprised. I had assumed, when he recommended meeting nearly immediately, that he was already here.

♏ ♐

FLASHBULB

MON
2 FEB
2015

INCORRECT
PATTERN MATCHING

GROUNDHOG DAY

Newsprint bragging the corporate history of L. D. Lique is framed on the wall. I read it for the first time. The founders' family name was De Lique.

A clock hangs in the ice cream parlor. Its big and little hands reflect the time as 10:22. The clock at the 16th Street Baptist Church in Birmingham, Alabama stopped at that hour and minute when four girls were murdered with a bomb a half-century ago. At that time, JFK had two months to live.

The world is full of data. Some of it is painful. Some of it is misleading and irrelevant, a result of false and failed pattern-matching. I don't always know what I'm looking at. I don't always know when I'm intercalating.

♏ ♐

Flyleaf — Freedom to Take Your Time

In Terence's <u>The Eunuch</u> in the 2nd century BCE, a young man disguises himself as a castrated servant to sneak inside a young woman's house. (This was a comedy to the Romans.) He says he wants a chance to talk to her. His true intentions are not brought into his conscious awareness—or, at least, he claims they are not—until he sees a painting of the god Jupiter directing his penis at the unsuspecting Danaë. And he does not provide this mythic interpretation of his own behavior until after he has committed the violence. It's after he assaults the woman that he credits the artwork for having motivated him. Perhaps, then, he is never fully conscious of what he has done or who he was when he did it. If he were conscious while he acted, he might have made different decisions.

"Consciousness is resistance to violence," said Levinas. Not rushing from one thing to the next trying to find out how your story ends. Taking a breath, giving yourself some distance from the present moment "even while already coming under its grip," that's freedom: making the time to act freely. Even if ultimately you cave to violence, at least your consciousness allowed you "the time necessary to forestall" the terrible choice.

In one of Aatish Taseer's novels, young men vandalize a shopkeeper's business in front of him to make a point of removing everything he displayed in English. The shopkeeper asks them a six-word novel: "Could you tell me the time?" One consults his watch, and the shopkeeper smashes the timepiece, uttering another six-word novel to call out the delinquent as a hypocrite: "Even your Time is in English." The novel is called <u>Noon</u>.

Thoughts, like clouds, traverse the sky.

One thing this ice cream parlor doesn't have: a security camera. That must be why Noon likes this place. I pegged his concern correctly.

My stomach is rocking, firmly but gently, like a boat upon the sea.

♏ ♐

Flyleaf — Lifeboat

In <u>Life of Pi</u>, there was a tiger in the lifeboat. That is the attention-grabbing premise of that story, and perhaps of every story: the kernel of fear in every safe harbor, the murder threat inside the sustenance. The light inside the esca, and the teeth inside the anglerfish. They are preying on deep-sea fishes who have never otherwise seen light except before the jaws of death. They cannot look away. The tiger in the lifeboat—aside from embodying story, aside from representing the appeal of a god—is the sublime: fear and wonder. Reverence, fascination, delight.

You can't crawl out of your lifeboat. In the Zapruder film, Jackie tries it. The tiger slams right into her lifeboat, grabs her husband by the head, and she knows it's all over and she is alone, and she jumps onto the back of the convertible. Better the ocean than the tiger. But someone nudges her arm and pushes her back in her seat.

Thing is, once the tiger shows up, your story is written. You can't jump out of it. Not even if you're willing to drown. You're in it forever.

Not last April but the one before, the Marathon bomber hid in a driveway in Watertown. He had to hide somewhere, so he found a boat, climbed in, and lay bleeding under a tarp. An infrared camera from a helicopter saw the outline of his body. Is that <u>glamour</u> or <u>pishogue</u>: the way the terrorist appears, or the way the cops see the terrorist? Both, I suppose. It's the same gun, whether you're pointing or being pointed at. Anyway, the infrared image printed in the newspaper looked like the cover of <u>Life of Pi</u>: the curled outline of the fearsome foe inside the lifeboat.

♏ ♐

FOG — A SPECIAL EPISODE OF TELE-QUIZ

I'm nervous, and my hands go cold. I begin to daydream.

"Welcome to 'Exit Interview,' a special episode of *Tele-Quiz*, the world's best televised game show! Tonight, we talk to only one man, and he only has to answer his own big question!"

The roulette wheel, big as a hot tub and painted in mustard, pea, and magenta, is between me and the show's host. I wonder if it looks less terrible on color TV. The wheel lies flat and is navel-high for me. My hands twitch in my pockets.

"The date is February 2, 1955. I'm your host, Mr. Destiny, and today my guest is—"

HERE HE IS   GROUNDHOG DAY

In strides Lear Noon, as if popping out of an unobservable thirteenth dimension, his skin paler than mine, his torso slim as a gun. He has lost even more weight since I saw him in Provincetown. But he's the man: *Not someone else. You.*

He carries a long, pointed object—Weapon? No, an umbrella against the snow. Umbrella, why? No one else has one. Just him.

I'm a "Happy Phantom" like in Tori Amos' song. I don't bother with umbrellas.

An Umbrella Man was in the Zapruder film, standing along the motorcade where the first bullet hit Kennedy. No one else carried an umbrella against the sun that day.

WE WILL LET GO   GROUNDHOG DAY

Noon doesn't order anything at the counter and seats himself at our table for two. The tiger is in the lifeboat. Each of us has something to say. I have got information for him. He has got something for me.

"We are obsessive. Both of us are," I say firmly. "We need to learn to let go."

"How?" he pleads.

"I will let go, and you will let go. One of us goes first. Or we can do it at the same time. But we need to destroy our attachments."

"Yes. Let's talk details." He seems serious.

Flyleaf —
Ecosystems of Anxiety

Maybe there's a Boyle's Law that governs this, a rule that predicts how we will use more oxygen as we descend farther underwater. I've never done this before. Details. I am about to discover them. We are in "la vie sous-marine" as in Vercors' <u>La Silence de la Mer</u>. We are, ourselves, entire ecosystems of unsifted anxiety. He wants to kill me because I can storytell circles around him and about him. I shall use this to my benefit.

"Who's going to go first?" I don't blink.

"I want you to go first," he says, "but I need help now."

"Fair enough. I'll show you what I have. Then you go, and we can help you."

"OK."

"Here's my notebook."

I pull my fat loose-leaf work binder from my briefcase and drop it on the table. Noon's attention is magnetized. To him, this is a paperclip. It'll make him see things.

He stares at the binder as if he's a marked man come to the Boss's doorstep for a fortune-telling and we're about to open the Book of Life and Death and Trauma and Hope.

"What's that?"

"*This* is one of my *projects* from Achromatic Proprio*cep/ion*," I sing-song as if speaking to a child, not taking my eyes off his face. "This is how serious it is. This is how much it weighs."

"Now, you show me yours."

Noon pulls out a thinner spiral notebook. Even before he opens it, I recognize mess. Sheets are glued, taped, paper-clipped in. This is his *magnum opus*. Respect builds trust; I nod imperceptibly and give a soft blink like a friendly cat. He responds by opening the notebook.

ℳ ♐

FLASHBULB

MON
2 FEB
2015

HIS
TERRIBLE NOTEBOOK

GROUNDHOG DAY

FLASHBULB

MON
2 FEB
2015

CLIPPY IS
SPEECHLESS

GROUNDHOG DAY

What did I expect? The opening lines from the fictional notebook in *Dhalgren*: "— to wound the autumnal city. So howled out for the world to give him a name—"?

No literature, Noon's notebook. It's not. Pages graph-lined, full of lists. "Bullet lists," they're sometimes called, demarcated by circles. These, illustrated with sketches of guns, crosshatched with a Bic. Real bullets.

There are maps.

I realize, though my brain wants to screen it and shield me from knowing, that these are floorplans of where I work.

Noon has annotated every stairwell with red pen.

The supply closet, an explosion of paperclips waiting to happen.

My office, near the bathroom, a little rectangle somewhere in that map.

The boss's office.

Aparna's.

♏ ♐

In me, the Cowardly Lion twists his tail and insists he's not a snowflake. There is a snowflake deep inside me and it melts, but I do not let on.

"It looks like you're writing a—" I imagine the Clippy character from Microsoft Word chiming in. I don't even know how it would finish that sentence.

Deities know where all the bodies are buried, and they know what you are writing in your terrible notebook.

Somehow Noon has determined that I am "Strangely Gendered." It is because of my sexual parts that are or aren't there that he has resolved to destroy everyone we mutually know. No, it is not a valid motivation. No, it never makes sense.

♏ ♐

Office diversity committee wants to discuss how to make the office a better place, and now I've found one big problem, but my boss would never let me name it. Why participate on diversity committee if I'm never allowed to say anything real?

The fault is in my body. My body is made of fault lines.

Noon exudes some combination of dread, self-disgust, and pride in his work. He lifts his chin and looks into my eyes.

I hear a voice: *Alone, Lev?* No, that's not it. More Spartan. *Mo-lon la-veh. I dare you to reach for my weapon.*

My internal clock is stopped at 10:22.

He pushes the button on his chess-clock, and now my clock is running again, and it's my turn.

♏ ♐

What do some parents say when they have lost patience with their child but they want to pretend they're still in control? *"I'm going to give you until the count of three…"* That is the line, yes, from the novella *Mother of a Machine Gun*. I don't tell Noon I'm going to count, but I count silently without realizing it: taking command, becoming complicit. *"Mother had to control be in command had the basic principle of,"* the author Michael Seidlinger goes on, *"being a part of what the son would have done with or without her command."*

For few seconds, nothing moves. We are suspended in gelatin. It is cold. It has to be; we are in an ice cream shop in a snowstorm.

♏ ♐

FLASHBULB
MON
2 FEB
2015

SLOW WITH WORDS — GROUNDHOG DAY

FLASHBULB
MON
2 FEB
2015

BEOWULF OR GRENDEL'S MOTHER? — GROUNDHOG DAY

In *Mother of a Machine Gun,* after the son shoots people indiscriminately, Mother takes him to the ice cream parlor. He is still her good boy.

Too many seconds pass. I've counted to three without acting. Just as I realize I've ceded control of the interaction, it's already too late. My consciousness floods with corrective statements I should have made. *"This is not correct is what Mother should have said…This is not correct life cannot be taken away from those that still have reason to live…This is not correct a son should not do this no one should do this."* That is from *Mother of a Machine Gun.* But I am in my own story and the words do not come fast enough.

♏ ♐

Who am I being now? The mighty warrior Beowulf who comes for hand-to-hand combat with the monster Grendel to avenge the Danes? Or Grendel's mother who will destroy Beowulf to avenge her monster-son?

Noon reaches across the table and his hand squeezes my arm.

"Discrimen rerum," Cicero yells in my head. "Veneris iudicio enim tuo." *You came here by your own judgment.* "Discrimen rerum contulisti tribunatum tuum." *You brought your own vice-presidency to this crisis point.*

♏ ♐

242

FOG —
BIG AS THE ZODIAC

It's more than the Agile Principles. It's bigger, like the Zodiac, drawn in a circle with a fluorescent palette. It's like the Stations of the Cross but with hallucinogens. We are each having a revelation, and we are communicating.

With the surprise of skin contact, my vision shocks to black-and-white, and just as suddenly, everything shocks back to color, but too intense, a rainbow like a visual migraine or a gasoline puddle. I recognize nothing I'm looking at.

It's a montage. A movie. I jerk my arm away from his hand, and the vision ends. It's like coming up for air from a frozen pond. Emesis of anti-knowledge. Toxic mixed drink of wrong alcohols. Bad trip.

He'd better have gotten the same readout I just did. Something that's neither information nor decision. Something that's installed like a program and becomes part of his being.

Do webbed feet paddle lakes? They do. And how? Can't say. Up to this point, ducklings have done it without security cameras catching them, tracking their movements. If we don't bring a camera to the lakeside, perhaps we'll never know.

I won't put the images in order. It'll happen on its own, automatically. I don't need to consciously direct it. I discover someone's role in my life when it's time.

This Agile user story has exceeded the maximum allowable points. I am lying if I say the pace is sustainable. I am lying if I say there is no story.

So I am telling the story in my own way. Noon is the one here to receive it. We are the ad hoc scrum team at the ice cream shop in hell. I am the Agile product owner. He is the Yiddish *mazik* demon.

It's my opinion. It's my story.

♏ ♐

FLASHBULB
MON
2 FEB
2015
310
TOO MANY POINTS
GROUNDHOG DAY

The clock on the wall is ticking. It says 10:44.

Noon's eyes are wide. If he doesn't know what I'm saying, it's because he isn't reading me. But I think he knows. Whatever advice I just transmitted, I think he got it.

I drive back to the office through the ice fog and roll into a mostly plowed parking spot with a crunching snowbank at the edge.

A chess game could be drawn out for thousands of moves if both players wanted and tried.

♏ ♐

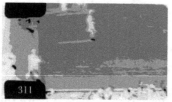

FLASHBULB

MON
2 FEB
2015

311 LISTENING TO
THE RADIO

GROUNDHOG DAY

FLASHBULB

MON
2 FEB
2015

312 STANLEY'S CAR HAD
A CASSETTE PLAYER

GROUNDHOG DAY

I sit for a few minutes, listening to the radio. Jordin Sparks sings "No Air." It's about feeling like she can't breathe because someone left her. I'd put this song in the official soundtrack of my life, but I heard she has conservative religious views, so maybe our longings are not a fit.

My car is a 2011 model and does not have a cassette player. Cassette players are a thing of the past. Not nearly as old as *Tele-Quiz,* but not new enough for today. I cannot play my *Immaculate Collection* tape anymore, I admit wistfully, and I don't know when I'll ever be able to do so again.

♏ ♐

I am thinking of cassette players because I am thinking of Stanley, remembering how his 1998 Ford Taurus had that cassette tape of "The Prophet" when I got rid of it.

"You are good in countless ways, and you are not evil when you are not good…"

If I had Stanley's car right now, I don't think I would sell it at all. I would keep it for sentimental value. Except if he wanted me to sell it and if selling it were the condition under which he would speak to me.

♏ ♐

IF JESUS LEFT ME
ALL HIS STUFF

I think of the Mr. and Mrs. who bought the car, so I think about Jesus too while I think about Stanley. If I had betrayed Jesus and if Jesus had left me all his stuff—his car, his furniture, his recipes—wouldn't I want it? I waffle on this. No, after all. If Jesus weren't talking to me and if I grieved him, I'd be traumatized by having to drive his infernal car. I would sell it. Six-word novel. *For sale: Car, abandoned by Christ.*

No, wait—Jesus would have had a donkey? Whatever. Be Jesus' car royal asset or assclown, I would sell it. A vehicle is a poor substitute for a miracle.

Remembering Stanley's car, I remember what happened next.

♏ ♐

Flyleaf — 313

Frame 313 shows the president's head destroyed. Zapruder was bothered by this frame. He sold the rights to the film to <u>Life</u>, and <u>Life</u> also decided the public didn't need to see this frame. Sometimes, when people refer to a supposed conspiracy of "missing frames," they refer to this one. But it's not missing.

The 313th Torah reading, in my schema, is when the princes of Israel complete their sacrifice. Each brings two silver bowls, a large and a small, filled with organic matter: wheat kneaded with oil. Each also brings a tiny gold bowl filled with incense.* Nothing is missing.

♏ ♐

---

* This is the 313th reading in Lev's schema: the 35th weekly Torah portion, Naso, 7th reading.

FLASHBULB

MON
2 FEB
2015

GROUNDHOG DAY

STANLEY'S CAR
SMELLED LIKE
HIS RESCUE CAT

FLASHBULB

MON
2 FEB
2015

GROUNDHOG DAY

MY CAT IS
BEAUTIFUL

After Mr. and Mrs. took it away, that wasn't quite the end of them. Mrs. called me about the cat odor. "It's as if it's getting stronger. I just think that's strange. Did something happen in the car?"

I didn't know the history, apart from Stanley having told me that he kept the kitten in there overnight.

After that conversation, I just couldn't stop thinking about cats. I made an impulse acquisition of my own: I drove alone to the animal shelter and left with an orange kitten. I couldn't think of it as anything other than Whiskers, which is what Stanley called his cat, but I thought he'd think it weird that I repurposed that name, and I am indeed responsible for naming my own cats, so I bought a tag for her that said "Eurydice." That name came to mind because, in *Niebla*, there's a faithful dog named Orfeo. Eurydice has six toes on each paw. She is beautiful and fascinating and I want to do nothing else but gaze and gaze and gaze at her.

♏ ♐

♏ ♐

FLASHBULB

MON
2 FEB
2015

316

WHO KILLED
THE MOUSE?

GROUNDHOG DAY

FLASHBULB

MON
2 FEB
2015

317

WHEN I MENTIONED
MY KITTEN

GROUNDHOG DAY

I called Mrs. back. Asked if I could be of assistance. *No,* she said. *Never mind—the smell disappeared.*

That was the end of them and of Stanley's car.

The next day, the mail carrier left an envelope. Mr. and Mrs. had sent me the one-dollar bill to finalize the sale.

On my indoor welcome mat, a decapitated mouse—some cat's idea of a gift, perhaps. But my Whiskers—I do think of her as "Whiskers"—was just a kitten herself and hadn't been in the hallway. No other cats had ever stalked by my apartment. Strange. Who killed the mouse?

Maybe Stanley's original Whiskers, stalking me from its feral den as a crocodile stalks Captain Hook, letting me know it knows where I live.

♏ ♐

I often have the feeling that I have been bitten by those malevolent leprechaun bichos that grannies call "blessings in disguise."

When I confessed to Stanley that I didn't make any money on his car, I irrelevantly added that I was also out an adoption fee for my own kitten. That's right, that's how the discussion went. I forgot about that part. When I'd said, "It's your money," and he'd said, "It isn't," I'd said: "I just got a cat. I paid for the cat, and I can pay for your car." And that's when he'd said: "Don't even talk to me."

He didn't even want to meet my cat.

♏ ♐

FLASHBULB

MON
2 FEB
2015

GROUNDHOG DAY

EVERYONE
LIKES CATS
ON THE INTERNET

All of this was several months ago. I ought to post a kitten rescue month-a-versary snapshot to social media. Whiskers is almost a teenager cat now, but everyone likes to see cats of any age on the Internet. I would call her "Eurydice" if I posted her picture online so as not to irk Stanley.

♏ ♐

Flyleaf — Apology

I am redrafting an apology I won't send. It has become a non-apology, not an anti-apology but a trans-apology.

~ ~ ~ ~ ~

I humbly recognize that I am unlikely to deserve anything and that, even if others judge me to be a good person, there is no step I can take to earn any reward. I know you will talk to me if you want to do so and that nothing I do controls what you want.

I am sorry I hurt you, and I would like you to be talking to me. These are statements about me, not implied requests for forgiveness or coffee from you.

I do not know the correct answer. You may be testing me, but I don't know what you're testing, and to acknowledge the test may be to fail it. With all of my being, I hold onto hope I can pass your test, but then I remember: the reward cannot be earned. I have to pass, but even if I pass, I still won't deserve anything.

It's not about whether either of us deserve it. It's about whether we both want it.

I want you because you are what I want, but to want you is to want what you want, and I do not know whether you want me to want you. If you want me to stop wanting you, maybe I will stop. I do not know what you want because you are not talking to me. I give up hope of passing your test, and I admit that I am aware you are testing me but I do not know what answer you seek from me. I simply don't know.

~ ~ ~ ~ ~

248

I am a much better person for having had those epiphanies. I don't need to tell Aparna, Stanley, anyone. Insights about them. Insights about ghosts. Insights very much and mostly about me—to the extent I know myself, anyway, and to the extent I know where I am going.

"Nor do I really know myself," as Thomas Merton chatted up the boss, "and the fact that I think that I am following your will does not mean that I am actually doing so."

"The impulse to write things down," Joan Didion wrote in her notebook in which she tells us about notebooks, "is a peculiarly compulsive one, inexplicable to those who do not share it, useful only accidentally, only secondarily, in the way that any compulsion tries to justify itself." Notebook-scribblers are "lonely and resistant rearrangers of things, anxious malcontents, children afflicted apparently at birth with some presentiment of loss."

If I double-space my musings on Chad Goeing's The Nature of Time (a thesis I am going to study and write, when I have time), it will be a thousand pages. It will not fit in a Teddy Ruxpin cassette tape.

"The game was entered into long ago and we have no choice but to play," Jaron Lanier writes in Who Owns the Future? We have to solve the planet's climate, he says, but we must discard our notions of "halting or reversing events," since, unlike a VHS player, the planet has no button to pause or rewind what has been done. Though we introduce more technological solutions into the non-linear system, "the earth will not be the same place it was before."

The four-track player even with its endless loop cannot MacGyver these words into itself nor can it provide a way out. The automobile no longer has a mouth to eat the tape. A cat kills a mouse for you but it's not your cat and the cat is nowhere to be found. Chad Goeing is long dead and we still don't know how or why. The Teddy Ruxpin's eyes won't flutter. The eyes will be wide open and the Teddy will stand up and saunter away into the woods. We can't press "rewind" and "record." It's too late to erase the evidence. It will snow. We will hear the snow on the tape.

♏︎♐︎

FOG — I DO MURDER SOMEONE IN MY BOOK

"Last week, our guest won seven thousand dollars. We hope you'll have the same good luck with us. Please tell us what you do for a living," Mr. Destiny asks me in front of the audience for *Tele-Quiz*, with the entire nation on the other side of the camera.

"I'm a writer." I have always wanted to say this, especially on TV.

"Ah, of what sort of book? Romances?"

"It's a little closer to a biography. I write about only one man, I'm afraid." I twisted my hands. "And he's dead. And not famous. And not talking."

"That must make your job a bit difficult."

"Yes, it does."

"But at least you don't have to kill anyone in your book. Last week, we had a murder mystery writer on the show."

"I *do* murder someone in my book. It's a double-murder, actually."

"Who do you murder?"

"A ghost, which counts zero ethically because he's already dead, but double technically because it's extra work to kill someone who's already dead, and—"

"Well, I'm sure you don't want to give away the whole book."

"That's right."

"Not to worry. We'll help you unpack *The Nature of Time*. We want to know about the man who wrote it, so tonight, we've got a special question for you: *How did Chad Goeing die?* Are you ready to guess the answer?"

"Let's do it."

"Great!" Mr. Destiny tugs at the roulette wheel, spinning it for the benefit of the camera. "We'll be right back after a word from our sponsors. Audience: Stay tuned!"

♏ ♐

FLASHBULB
MON
2 FEB
2015

319

DODGE A BULLET   GROUNDHOG DAY

The seat belt still straps me in. My head rests against the car seat.

I've dodged a bullet, I'd say, although I don't know how it feels to literally dodge a bullet. It isn't physically possible to do so. A bullet travels at the speed of sound, so, once I heard the gun fired, it would have already arrived. In the two seconds I'd need to move my body, the bullet would travel a mile. I'd need to be watching a simulcast of the gunman's finger on the trigger, and—

♏ ♐

FLASHBULB

MON
2 FEB
2015

GROUNDHOG DAY

DISCUSSING
THE FUTURE

FLASHBULB

MON
2 FEB
2015

WARNING   GROUNDHOG DAY

I go inside the office to debrief Aparna. Near the bathrooms, in a spot out of the cameras' range, she hears out my recap of what happened with Lear Noon at L. D. Lique.

"He and I exchanged ideas," I explain feebly, recounting what happened when Noon touched my arm, "but it happened really fast, and it wasn't all *informational*. Some of what I 'saw,'" I say, unsure of my word choice, "hasn't even happened yet."

"With that eidetic memory of yours, I bet you remember more than you're telling me."

♏ ♐

"But my memory is like a camera," I say. "What is it seeing, not seeing? I'm asking, finally, not about a camera but about myself. What did I see? How could I have seen what didn't happen yet?"

"Speaking of things that didn't happen," she pivots casually, "I dealt with a few small bugs while you were out. My name's in the system next to those tasks."

Everyone on scrum touches everyone's work all the time. That's teamwork. What I think she's getting at is that the bosses are looking for excuses to accuse me of not working.

Every action has an equal and opposite reaction.

"Everything moves fast around here," I say.

"And people react."

I guess I've been warned. "Thanks."

EPISODE 9

FOREVER AFTER (HANA LEE)

FLASHBULB

TUE
3 FEB
2015

YESTERDAY WAS
GROUNDHOG DAY

It's stopped snowing, and the TV in the breakroom is off. Finally. The newspaper put smiling children on the front page and a short article about the results of what the groundhog saw or didn't. Yesterday was Groundhog Day.

It occurs to me: *Nothing happened.* Apart from a snowstorm, nothing.

Talking to Noon made a difference. To interact with the ghost is to eat the ghost. I ate his violent fantasies.

♏ ♐

Flyleaf —
The Headline Changes

Vanish From the Book

There is a Book of Life and Death and Trauma and Hope, and the sites of mass murder are named in it. It's a long list. The name "Achromatic Proprioception" is vanishing right now from that book. I can feel the letters erasing. The erasure feels like my gut unclenching.

Just like in Back to the Future when you travel back in time to tweak something in the past and, after you do it, right there in your hand, the newspaper from the future changes its headline.

Label It As Fiction

Or like O. J. Simpson's book cover, but in reverse. Simpson wrote a hypothetical murder confession, If I Did It, which he claimed was fiction, and the rights were given to a victim's family who shrank the word "If" real small. Now imagine the reverse. You could take a true confession from yourself or someone else—I got revenge, I shot up the office, I had a real nice 'chat' with the people who hurt me—and insert the "If" real big on the cover and shelve it as fiction. What if labeling nonfiction as fiction changed what really happened?

♏ ♐

FOG — NOTHING

I ate his violent fantasies. The cat has eaten the mouse. Or is it the mouse who ate the cat?

Memory is "paratactic reordering" of images, says Heriberto Yépez, "folkloric cryptomnesia," "an <u>ars combinatoria</u> of arbitrary signs."

If you accidentally film an assassination on your 8mm camera, journalists will hound you, offering any price for it. But if no one was murdered and it's not even your camera, what you have is nothing.

The emergence of nothing can eat you up: your knowledge, the world itself, and all recurring worlds. Alternatively: It may spawn a new world. Alternatively: Nothing may follow nothing.

Tell me *nothing*.

What do the poor have, the rich need, and if you eat it you'll die?

What does the dead canary say?

What is the problem after the doctor preemptively pulls my uterine plumbing?

What confidence do they express in a transsexual man's manhood?

What happens when I use the men's bathroom?

What, then, have they learned?

What is this copy a copy of?

What does a groundhog fill its burrow with?

What is my responsibility if a terrible boy drowns on vacation?

What did Thoreau pay in taxes during the Mexican-American War?

What was the legal penalty for JFK's assassin?

What does the Jew charge for an automobile when you remind him what he is?

What does my friend say to me after that?

What does the theocrat claim to add to his Jesus?

What work may the Jew do on the Sabbath?

What do the Lethargarians in *The Phantom Tollbooth* strive to accomplish in the Doldrums?

What do I calculate for Story Points in the Agile meeting for my task of glancing out the window?

What do I see, if not my fears and fantasies?

What do I have to recognize the spoon is before I can telekinetically bend it?

What do I feel in my fingers and toes just before I see a ghost?

What can I change about the past?

If I quit this job, I would take all my political capital and multiply it by what?

What do I have to tell my boss?

Because an MBA is a degree in caring about what?*

---

* Madelyn Jablon wrote: "Novels use call-and-response to encourage audience participation…" *Black Meta-fiction: Self-Consciousness in African American Literature*, University of Iowa Press, 1997. p. 26.

Flyleaf — Fungus

Evil: a fungus. (Assessment by Hannah Arendt.) It spreads, contagious, but also it's rootless. It wrecks your life despite having no depth of its own. There is no "there" there.

A person with a bank account will burn down the planet to turn it into resources which convert to zeroes in the bank account. An extra "zero" is the highest achievement in personal finance.

(If you were banking in, say, 13th-century Florence, they'd insist you write everything out in Roman numerals, a notation that has no zero, just so fraudsters couldn't claim they wrote an extra circle accidentally. Point remains: everyone sees the power of Nothing.)*

Since nothing happened, I don't have to redeem it. I will focus on real happenings or might-happenings, things I can change.

We're free to be what we already are, but I don't suppose I can change myself. Ask a transsexual any question whatsoever and you receive a transsexual answer. That's all I can say of authenticity and freewill.

♏ ♐

FLASHBULB

TUE
3 FEB
2015

323

NUMBERS GO UP

I don't even want to know what Noon thinks his problems are with the company: valid or invalid, real or imaginary. I don't need the awareness of his problems brought into my problems.

We begin with nothing and make something. We should hang a self-congratulatory occupational hazard sign at this office: *[1] days without a death threat.* The numbers go up from here.

♏ ♐

---

* *Nothing: Surprising Insights Everywhere From Zero to Oblivion.* ed. Jeremy Webb. New York: The Experiment, 2013.

FLASHBULB

TUE
3 FEB
2015

324

NOTHING HAS BEEN
ACCOMPLISHED

FLASHBULB

TUE
3 FEB
2015

325

ADJUST TO
THE REAL WORK

As I walk by the boss's office, I see through the window that *his* boss, the company president, is in there speaking to him. I wave, the boss waves back with no special encouragement, and I open the door.

"Gentlemen," I announce loudly in lieu of *hello and good morning*, interrupting their conversation, "I just wanted to tell you that absolutely nothing has been accomplished! I have accomplished nothing today, and, indeed, the product of all my years here has been nothing."

The president sits impassively. He does not know who I am.

♏ ♐

If you accomplish nothing in your life, on your gravestone they just carve the name of what killed you: battlefield, smallpox, shark. I would be happy with that gravestone. Accomplishing "nothing" is often the most ethical option, considering certain alternatives.

I wave a blank piece of paper at them. *Nothing!*

The boss frowns at me. "I'll speak to you this afternoon."

Going back to my desk to listen to "El final" by Rostros Ocultos in my headphones and play Tetris in my phone.

♏ ♐

Flyleaf — Light

The Boss Was Right

The boss was right all along. There was no bomb, no gun, no evil surprise. And why not? Because I lured Noon away. I stopped the plan. The boss has been correct for the past month because of the thing I did yesterday.

"Light is the left hand of darkness, / and darkness the right hand of light," Ursula K. Le Guin wrote in her novel titled after her epithet for light.

If I had dealt with Noon differently—if I had interacted at all with his first email, or responded unkindly to his second email, or declined to meet him face-to-face after his third email—something else would have happened.

Synchronicity

We made it happen our own way. This historical divergence was a group project. Aparna confirmed the problem and held down a few bugs in the queue while I was out. Agile Principle #12: The team must reflect on what is needed and must adjust to the real work.

Large groups of animals tend to synchronize their behavior. Cicadas and their long self-gestative sleep. They all hatch under the astrological sign of Taurus. Fireflies and their bioluminescent flashes. They decide collectively when it's time to light up. As a massive group, you cannot hold them down.

The Wake Does Not Drive the Boat

My stomach hasn't stopped hurting yet. Don't know yet what I've learned: be subtle and flexible, or accept being gaslit with a match from the root chakra up. I wish I had the subtlety to know the difference and the flexibility to move on. I have a hard time believing the wake does not drive the boat because I am so attached to the past.

♏ ♐

FLASHBULB

TUE
3 FEB
2015

HOW DOES A THREE-WAY LIGHTBULB WORK?

"Hey Aparna," I say, passing by her office, "do you know how a three-way lightbulb works?"

I'm suddenly remembering the old man who claimed to be its inventor. He'd be 120 now.

"Yeah," she says. "It's obvious."

"Explain it to me."

She opens her mouth to answer, but her phone rings, and she gestures to shoo me away.

I have a thousand questions.

Two of these questions were posed by the archivist at the library at Copley and the clerk at Vital Records: *How long for the hummingbird to evolve its yellow belly, and how long for me to understand why?*

Maybe the answer isn't predetermined, nor is my pacing. "Plots are for dead people," said David-Shields-as-Lorrie-Moore, article 326.

♏ ♐

FLASHBULB

TUE
3 FEB
2015

A HUMMINGBIRD THAT DOES NOT EXIST

I remember the yellow-bellied hummingbird I saw in Stanley's yard last August. I'd always meant to learn what it was. I look up hummingbirds online. A rufous, maybe. No, no. The one I saw didn't have a neat square of yellow on the throat. It was a huge yellow splotch, ragged edges, covering the whole belly.

The Internet tells me this species I remember seeing does not, in fact, exist.

Yet if there is no yellow hummingbird in town, why did the clerk behave as if I'd answered the question of its evolution?

♏ ♐

HOW BAD IT FEELS TO DO GOOD IN THE WORLD

I thought the boss might forget, but he really does want to speak to me in the afternoon.

We sit in a conference room with a few other interested parties—managers and vice presidents all, people I have known a long time—and everyone, male and female, has Resting Bitch Face. I am a guardian angel, yet they want to kick me.

This is how bad it feels to do good in the world.

♏ ♐

APARNA CAUGHT THE BUG

"Yesterday, you were out for an unusually long lunchbreak," he says. "Several hours, we noticed. No one saw you at all after the morning status meeting."

"I wasn't aware it was that long, but all right, if you say so, I apologize."

"Do you know that Aparna handled your project for you while you were out? There was a bug in the system for this sprint's feature. It might have gone live. She caught it."

"No, I wasn't aware—I mean, yes, she told me afterwards."

We can't let our guard down, not even to sneak out of the office for two hours.

♏ ♐

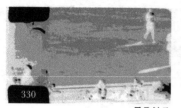

FLASHBULB

TUE
3 FEB
2015

330

TRUE

"I appreciate that she took care of it," I add.

Agile Principle #7: The best metric of success is that the software is functional.

"She did an excellent job," the boss says.

"She is committed," I agree, "and very perceptive. On the very first day the GPS feature went live, she tracked down a missing camera. She's got all the ducks in a row."

"No one really understands what you do," the boss says.

"Well, I drove out to the woods and recovered the stolen camera," I say.

He raises an eyebrow. Errands aren't what he pays me for.

"I can't explain it to you," I say. True. And I have resolved to speak directly, even when people will be unhappy with the truth.

♏ ♐

Flyleaf — Am I a Savior?

"No sé si a todos les sucede lo mismo. Yo paso la vida," Juan José Arreola wrote in a short story titled "El silencio de Dios,"

"cortejado por un afable demonio que delicadamente me sugiere maldades." <u>I don't know if it's the same way for everyone. I go through life courted by a good-humored demon who delicately suggests wrongdoings to me.</u> Eventually, every battle is lost, and I wonder: "Por qué es el bien tan indefenso?" <u>Why is good so defenseless?</u>

I think of the rainbow flag with the bank logo I keep on my desk, the little wooden dowel flagpole propped up inside a coffee mug. The flag is always sliding, at an imperceptible speed, into the cup, like a ship going down. Why it was created: Someone wants me to pray to something and ask it not to kill me. The rainbow is what I want, but the bank is what I have to pray to, and the bank will never let me forget it.

The employee manual says the company has "zero-tolerance for violence." <u>Yeah, 'cause I'm the one who zero-leveled the violence for you,</u> I think super-quietly to myself with my filter all the way on. I have learned that "zero-tolerance for violence" really means we're not supposed to report a threat nor talk about what happened when we tried to report it. Do not meta-report.

I erased the mass death event and nothing happened. I'm a flaming comet dazed and floating in a cis-tem of occasional asteroid. Do I feel like a victim or a savior? What's my favorite version of the story?

♏ ♐

FLASHBULB

TUE
3 FEB
2015

331

WHERE
DO YOU WANT TO BE
IN FIVE YEARS?

"Where do you want to be in five years?" my boss asks. He folds his hands like a spiritual master. He seems to think this is a profound question.

I remember that, in my pocket, I'm carrying the figurine of the Virgin Mary that Stanley once gave me, and the little cross necklace is still wrapped around her.

Where do I want to be in five years? The boss is asking me to plan my future while I'm still in lockdown with the past.

♏ ♐

Flyleaf — I Will Always Want Another Five Years

In <u>Goodbye to Berlin</u>, Christopher Isherwood wonders where his future self will be. "Certainly not here." But how to measure the distance traveled in miles, dollars, food, shoe soles, cigarettes, cups of tea and beer? Life seems like drudgery when counted this way, but death seems worse, he reflects. He's probably right.

When Milo first rode his car through the Phantom Tollbooth, he entered the land of Expectations. A good arrival point.

♏ ♐

FLASHBULB

TUE
3 FEB
2015

332

THE BOSS WILL
MURDER ME

I want to use the next five years to figure out where I want to be. I will always want another five years on a rolling basis. The boss will murder me if I say this.

"I appreciate and value the question," I begin, hoping to be quick on my feet.

Feet. I think: *Climbing the corporate ladder.* Five flights of stairs I climb every day. Where do I want to be after climbing five flights of stairs? In what year would I like to arrive?

No, that wasn't his question. He said: *Where do you want to be in five years?* Focus.

♏ ♐

FLASHBULB

TUE
3 FEB
2015

333

OK, A SECOND
ANSWER

A second possible response comes to mind: *Five years from now, why would I care about whatever I wanted five years earlier?* No—it is true that my future self will be a different person from who I am today, but the boss will consider that a flippant remark because it bucks the worldview embedded in his question, and that is an eminently murderable offense.

My eyes flicker, and I'm sure the boss can read all the useless possibilities percolating therein. Mentally, I sing "Heaven Must Be Missing An Angel" to myself. Afflicted by my silence, he groans and leans back in his chair.

♏ ♐

FLASHBULB

TUE
3 FEB
2015

334

ARE YOU WEARING
A WIRE?

I fold my hands, feeling disconnected from my body. "Are you wearing a wire?" I ask him.

"What?"

"And if you were wearing a wire, would you tell me you were?"

He looks like the top of his head is about to explode. "Get to the point."

"I shot JFK."

"Dear God. Our next data conversion happens in three days. Are you with us?"

"Yes," I said.

For now. I am with the company for now. In the long run, I want to be a character who survives.

♏ ♐

FOG — I SEE THE WHEEL TURNING

The boss reboots his laptop. I see the close-up image of the wheel turning. A silver wheel with a black stripe around the edge. A 1961 Lincoln Continental. The same thing we always see when we reboot our computers.

Then, I feel it: *Ground. Shaking. Get out now.* The conference room is a firetrap. I feel it in my glowing sixth finger and in my terrorclit. I don't have to explain it to anyone.

"I don't have time to manage you right now," he says. "I hope you can self-manage."

♏ ♐

I CAN MANAGE
MYSELF

WORK IS NOT WORK
ANYMORE

I can indeed manage myself. He must believe I'm adult enough to self-regulate. I hope he'll always speak to me like the adult I am, but likely I'll be bossed by his silence.

When I leave the conference room, I go to the bathroom and look at my face in the mirror. I am still pale; I will probably always be pale. I used to look like nothing in particular to myself. Just the impossibly long, quarter-moon curve of my nose. Now I see something more: I know when to do something and when to do nothing.

♏ ♐

I'll give the Amity Lodge leadership the heads-up that the mural was defaced by a disgruntled, deluded man. Otherwise guys who show up for the next sex magick workshop will be surprised that the Hero's Journey is covered in Sharpie.

I stop by Aparna's desk. She is cleaning up after lunch at her keyboard, dusting the Teddy Ruxpin and the Eiffel Tower.

She turns to greet me. "I keep meaning to tell you: thanks for the playlist. 'It's Not the End of the World.' I really like it. I've been playing it in my car on my way to work."

"I'm glad you are here," I tell her. "We are alive."

"Yes. And on camera all the time."

♏ ♐

337

CHAD IS
ALWAYS WITH ME

I'm eating soup alone at home.

Not alone. Chad writes notes on Post-Its. "I WILL ALWAYS BE WITH YOU."

Whiskers is here too, of course, curled and purring. She is the color of a lightly spiced pumpkin muffin but for one patch just behind the ears that is darker like a monarch butterfly. When I touch there, her eyes close.

♏ ♐

FOG — STANLEY WILL BE IN MY MOVIE AGAIN

I watch the movie *A Chorus Line* on the television. The director calls a few auditioning dancers by name, asking them to step forward. Then he says, "Front line, thank you very much, I'm sorry." He tersely instructs the rest on their rehearsal schedule.

Whiskers falls asleep on my lap.

I'm standing on an execution line.

"Lev, step forward," Stanley says in my dream, a rifle slung over his shoulder.

I step forward, not to follow orders but to own my work, and I clear my throat.

He barks: "Enough already! I don't want to talk about whatever happened." He points at me with his thumb, punctuating each sentence. "I will be in your movie again. We will rehearse on Mondays and Wednesdays. I will also speak to you on Sunday evenings. Order us a pizza."

It feels real, but I wake up, and through my window I see the sun rising through the bare branches of the trees, and I remember he and I aren't there yet.

♏ ♐

Flyleaf — Be Worthy

An old story. For generations, a parent passes down a ring to designate an heir, until one parent can't choose. The parent gives one child the original ring; the other two children, copies. No point asking who's the true heir. The task isn't to determine which piece of metal is "real." It's to live in a manner worthy of an heir.*

♏ ♐

---

* "The reference is to the famous tale of the three rings, narrated by Giovanni Boccaccio in the *Decameron* and rewritten four centuries later in the 18th century by Gottfried Lessing in his drama *Nathan the Wise* [1778–79]." Nuccio Ordine. *L'utilità Dell'Inutile*. Milan: Bompiani, 2013. Translated as *The Usefulness of the Useless* by Alastair McEwen, 2017. Philadelphia: Paul Dry Books, 2017. p. 131.

FOG — IN THERAPY

My psychotherapist is holding the hardcover. The title: *The Undetermined Death of Chad Goeing*. The anonymous byline: "A Concerned Citizen."

A humidifier hums and sloshes in the corner of her office, so I can't hear street noise. The waters of Acheron, Cocytus, Phlegethon, Lethe, the marsh of the Styx.

"Tell me about this book," she demands.

"I can't explain it." Indeed I brought it for discussion, but I can't begin to own it. Lord Byron's "Don Juan" also lay awake in bed and *"Pondered upon his visitant or vision, / And whether it ought not to be disclosed—"*

As if cutting a deck of cards, she opens to a center page with diagrams: choice hierarchy, risk, and the flow of time. Decisions move in a web bigger than any one person.

"I'm seeing a lot of detail," she says, trying to get me to talk.

"—At risk of being quizzed for superstition," Byron finishes.

"Yes, though not all of it came from Chad's work. Some of it is outside analysis." I explain that I didn't have much to go on from Chad's work alone. "What we can do to supplement our information: *Pull from the future.* I often find stuff in books that haven't been written yet."

"...that weren't written yet when Chad was alive in the 19th century?"

"Yeah, and also a few books that haven't even been written yet as of today."

She stares at me. "Such as?"

"Arturo Serrano's *To Climates Unknown.*"

"Uh huh," she says. Her pen pecks at her notepad.

"In which the Mayflower did not make it to America. It's a novela. 'Vela,' meaning sail, meaning ship. That's a synecdoche—the part representing the whole, 'sail' for 'ship.' A novel imagining a world without that vela."

"What year is it, then?" She's testing me in a wondrously neutral tone.

I ask her to pass me my book. She hands the hardcover of *The Undetermined Death of Chad Goeing* back to me, and I open it and read aloud from it.

"It is now," I say. Here, my false *Undetermined* is quoting *To Climates Unknown*:

> "It is the Year of Our Lord 1620. It is the Year of the Hijra 1029. It is the sixth year of the reign of Mizunoo II, the eighteenth year of the reign of James I, the thirty-second year of the reign of Christian IV. It is the last year of the reign of Wanli and the first year of the reign of Taichang. It is the Year of the Iron Monkey."

"You think so?"

I backpedal. "That is a quote. That is what Arturo Serrano says."

"Once upon a time, it was 1620. But now—"

"Exactly. And here, you see," I flip pages, "a quote from Colin Hamilton about aging: 'The past becomes less rigid in its sequencing, forming instead some strange plastic, primordial pool through which our imaginations drift.' And his explanation about why we have to paddle the river: 'If we aren't very vigilant, time allows the trivial and the traumatic to attain equal weight.'"

"What's that about?"

"I don't know. Hamilton's book hasn't been published yet either. *The Thirteenth Month*."

"I see. That is a lot of work you did, then."

"Yeah, it's a special kind of research."

"It sounds more like prediction."

"Yes, which makes it fiction. All prediction is fiction; some of it happens to come true. Malka Older calls them predictive fictions."

"When did she say that?"

"Um—"

"Never mind. Your book must have been tough to write." The empathy sounds forced. She is speaking in a particular mode of therapist-voice, as if she is trying to butter me up before being hard on me. I do not want the hardness, so I dodge.

"An algorithm wrote it. It wasn't me."

"Not only are you citing books that haven't been written yet, you're telling me *an algorithm* wrote 730 pages of context about Chad Goeing's commentary on the nature of time—"

"Yes."

"—and they *just happen* to be the same 730 pages you'd like to have written—"

"Yes."

"—and *the algorithm* sent it to a print-on-demand service, made cover art, and assigned an ISBN?"

She is asking if I was telling the truth there, which I was not, but one part of her summary is true, and this lets me avoid accountability.

"A computer did assign the ISBN." I've repeated the true part.

"But what's interesting to me, Lev, is that you showed up to therapy today. Not an algorithm. *You.*"

My gaze drifts over her head to the abstract tapestry. A large, white sun-disc glows on a background of red fibers. That's odd: I remember this wallhanging as being red, but I don't remember the sun.

I notice the sun now because of where it's positioned in my field of vision. The sun seems to rest on top of my therapist's head as if she were the Egyptian goddess Isis.

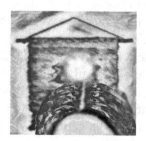

"And this," she says, her long thumbnail thumping my book, "is a lot of negotiation with the flow of time. It's bargaining."

I shrug.

"I think you are telling yourself a story with which you are hurting yourself."

"They told me that's what transsexuality is: a story with which I hurt myself. But my gender doesn't hurt me, and I'm certainly not going to ditch it. So I look for other stories that will hurt me—to prove those people right, I guess, because if their system is right on some level then I don't have to ditch their system, either. I want to keep my transgender and also keep my place among the sysgender. I want everyone to be right because it's easier that way."

"Mm," she says, which means *yeah, no kidding.* She asks me: "Why did you publish this book now? Why did you finish it if you still don't know how Chad Goeing died?"

"I mean, I feel I've learned some things recently. About stuff. Life in general."

"Sure." She pauses and waits.

I come to therapy to read between the frames of the Zapruder film.

"What do I need to do?" I ask.

"Own the part you understand." It's as if she's a cake delivery person squirting "EAT ME" in frosting and asking me whether I want the red or the blue jellybean. I am being asked to own a cake I don't yet understand.

"About the nature of time?"

"About Stanley."

Neither of those two jellybeans do I understand. I thought we were talking about Chad. Very well, if she wants to talk about Stanley, we will.

"There's this Christian idea about not selling out the big boss for money," I say.

"You mean not selling out the god."

"Yeah. And so a Christian holy person would divest themself of money to prove they don't care about money."

"You would divest yourself *of your own money.* Not someone else's. Yours."

"Yeah, if I were Christian. But I don't know what I am."

I feel like I'm inside the Jodi Arias interrogation. I'm trying not to be Jodi.

"Would you like to speak more directly?" she invites me.

Yes. That's what I was coaching myself to do. I try to speak more directly. "I own the choice at the moment I make it. To keep owning the choice, especially when no one is asking, is just to keep reliving it. But I can own the outcome."

"That's good," she says. "What's the outcome?"

"That Stanley is not talking to me."

"Maybe that started a little earlier, right? Before you gave away his car?"

I don't see it.

"Lev. He'd flown to the other side of the country. He wanted to get rid of his car. Something was wrong. He was already not talking to you and a lot of other people, or else he was *about* to be not talking to you.

The ice was thin. You giving away his car was the pretext for it to break."

There is a deep truth here. But if the original sin was not mine, I don't know whose it was or what it was. It was too long ago and I wasn't aware of it at the time.

"This is also about him," she says.

"And me?"

She nods. "Maybe if you'd listened to him differently, you would have known more in advance. Maybe not."

"I'm still responsible for my part," I say.

"Good."

Time allows me to calm down and change my perspective. But time isn't a "remedy," as Emily Dickinson put it, and if time seems to cure anything, there was "no malady" to begin with.

I take a deep breath. "I was looking at the wrong inflection point. Something was already broken, and if I'd made a different choice in real time, the cookie would have crumbled a different way. There are other inflection points farther in the past. They might be mine. They might be his. The way to get a bigger change would be to have a much bigger redo."

"Do you want to redo your whole life?"

I think about everything that's happened to me over the past year, like getting to know Aparna. "Maybe not."

"What happens when you replay the tape?"

"Whatever advice I yell at myself on the screen, the movie doesn't change. I can't change the ending by pressing 'rewind' and 'play.' The outcome is already at the end of the tape and will not change. The outcome is already here. I am here."

My therapist claps for me. Around her neck, she's wearing a jewel like a jellybean.

♏ ♐

Flyleaf — Movie Date

Forty days passed since I walked into the cloud, then another forty. I've received the whole Torah, so I've learned my predestination. I complain to the Cosmic Boss: *You promised you'd reveal a secret, but you've shown me nothing but my own future, which is more like a spoiler. Would've learned it anyway.* The boss says: *You misread my Hebrew. I didn't say I'd show you a secret—'sayter.' I said I'd show you 'seret'— a movie.**

♏ ♐

338

GRACE

"How much more winter will we have?" Aparna asks me in the office breakroom.

"None. We've been done with winter since February. Groundhog didn't see his shadow. FTW." *For the win.*

	Runs	Hits	Errors
Red Sox	5	8	0
Rays	7	12	1

"Yes, but how much more of *your* winter?" Her unsmiling gaze is most intense when she is joking.

"None. It's not Groundhog Day anymore."

She nods. "Then why did you come back? Why are you still here?"

♏ ♐

---

* The reference to "forty days" refers back to Mishpatim, last reading. The Hebrew word for "secret" is סֵתֶר and the modern Hebrew word for "movie" is סֶרֶט which comes from the word for "ribbon" in the Mishnah and Midrash. I learned this when, some thirty years ago, my synagogue ordered a fancy donation box for "gifts given in secret" and the engraver's error made it "gifts given during a movie."

Flyleaf —
Grace and What Survives

I am here because, after evading the shadow of death, grace and graciousness ought to remain. Otherwise, what have I preserved of life?

"Nēmontēmi" was the Nahuatl word for the Aztecs' intercalation. Every year, they had five days that weren't part of any month. These days were not for living. They were for lighting fires, bargaining with demons, and offering a sacrifice—whatever might renew the world for another year. As reported by the missionary anthropologist Bernardino de Sahagún.

If you can take care of business in five days, you're lucky. In Achebe's Things Fall Apart, Okonkwo has to leave his clan and go away for seven years. His gun exploded during a ceremonial salute and the debris killed someone, and though it wasn't his fault, the rule was that he had to go away. Seven years.

The gun that I don't own didn't kill anyone, and what did happen *was* kind of my fault, so it is not quite the same thing, but Stanley hasn't been talking to me for what is about to be heading into a seventh month now, and I feel that the point has been made already.

Stanley and I ought to survive my giving away his car. We have been friends for a long time. A tree gets hit by lightning, one arm split off, bark toasted, but still standing, and next spring when you see it sprout green leaves, you know it's going to survive.

Wait a minute. The image of the tree, split—

Stanley had two cars. The used Taurus I gave away was a cheaper, replacement car. I never found out what happened to his fancier car. Suddenly this seems like a crucial detail. Why did he get rid of his original car?

♏ ♐

272

FLASHBULB

SAT
25 APR
2015

339

STANLEY IS
TALKING TO ME
AGAIN

FLASHBULB

SAT
25 APR
2015

340

THE RIGHTS TO
THE SONG LYRICS

	Runs	Hits	Errors
Red Sox	4	8	0
Orioles	5	11	1

I don't know everything about the history of automobiles to which Stanley has held titles, but I have a good sense of what he and I are to each other. Thus it is a surprise and yet it seems normal when, after the long winter, Stanley calls me. Whatever we were may have changed, and I don't know what we will be, but here we are.

He picks me up in his new car. It is not as fancy as the one he had last year, but fancier than the short-term Taurus. His phone is plugged into the dashboard, and "Bohemian Rhapsody" is playing softly out of the car speakers.

"Should we sing?" I ask, casually and noncommittally.

♏ ♐

The last time we sang out loud to "Bohemian Rhapsody" must have been when *Wayne's World* still felt edgy. Or maybe we never sang out loud to this song and I'm just remembering *Wayne's World* itself.

"Do you know how much it would cost?" he asks me. "The rights to use the song lyrics."

I don't know exactly what he means, but I am not arguing with him about who has what right. I cannot believe I am riding in Stanley's car. I cannot believe he is talking to me. I cannot believe my luck and my undeserved grace.

I look out the car window and let my breath out as slowly and silently as I can. The glass does not fog. Spring is here.

♏ ♐

FLASHBULB

SAT
25 APR
2015

341

A NEW COFFEESHOP:
HANA LEE'S

FLASHBULB

SAT
25 APR
2015

342

NOT JUST
KILLING TIME

"Wait, where are we going?"

"L. D. Lique," he says.

"No," I say.

He raises an eyebrow at me subtly as though I've got diminished moral authority to complain.

"Anywhere but L. D. Lique," I say. Not that ice cream parlor. That place has melted for me.

He drives us to a coffeeshop with electric pink décor. It's called Hana Lee's. Never been here before. I just want us to get inside. He orders a mint-cookie latte. I say, "Same." The flavor will always be Girl-Scouts gendered for me, and I do not care. I don't fuss over the gender of my drinks. Nor would I mumble over the menu and delay—not one minute longer!—the *exquisite* opportunity to finally sit facing each other.

♏ ♐

Talking has a capital T. It might never feel merely like killing time again. It feels *requisite*.

We sit down. We have to admit what we did for Klondike bars or, worse, for no reason at all. He sighs and says he's sorry he wasn't talking to me. I say I'm still sorry about the thing. He says, *I know, I know, can we just stop with the stupid.* I say, *OK.*

♏ ♐

Flyleaf — Plagiarism

A Torah scroll is a copy. It is a painstaking hand-copy of another scroll which is itself a copy of another scroll. Across this lineage, not a single serif may change. The perfection of its plagiarism is what makes it valid.

But here is how it differs from other plagiarism: Copying isn't enough. You are supposed to study and understand it. The two words at the exact center of the Torah are "darosh darash," <u>thoroughly investigated</u>. Do your research. When you research, it's not plagiarism.

♏ ♐

FLASHBULB

SAT
25 APR
2015

WHAT OTHER CAR?

"So I guess we're not going to talk about the car," I say, "but can we talk about the other car?"

"What other car?" he asks, but he knows. A complex weather system passes across his face.

"The one you had *before* you went to Amity Lodge. The cool one."

"Oh." He nods. "Yeah, I never told you. I will tell you. But I want to tell you about something else first."

I have used this stalling tactic in therapy, so I cannot complain.

Stanley and I press the "clone" button on our friendship. Now it is genetically identical to the old version, but fresh and new again, and from this copy of ourselves, we are going to study each other and the world.

♏ ♐

FOG — AT HANA LEE'S (BEGIN)

"What's this thing you want to tell me?" I ask him.

"It's my new theory," he says, starting off slowly. I'm glad someone other than me spins theories round and round. The coffeeshop is playing "Time of the Season" by the Zombies. "I think the therapists are borg-mind."

"What?"

"Borg-mind. You know, like, they're each other's people."

"Like, the psychotherapists have got ESP kinship bonds?" I wonder how many therapists he's been seeing to yield enough data to formulate this hypothesis.

"Sort of. They act like it. They share information with each other. They close ranks. They know things we don't know. You talk to one of them, and it's as if you've talked to all of them. Even when they haven't shared your information, it's as if they have."

Did I say I am glad that Stanley is talking to me again? Friends need each other, in the end.

"The therapists have their ways. The vice presidents are like that, too," I say. "They talk behind closed doors and they tattoo 'VP' on their business cards. It's a club."

"Yes, that is loyalism."

"It's sure something. What about cops?"

"Without a doubt. They are sharing information about us, right now, as we speak," Stanley assures me.

"And the transsexuals," I say suddenly, inspired, without consciously choosing my words. "We're a close-knit group, too. We are talking to each other even when—" I pause. "After everything. Despite it all."

"Yes," Stanley agrees.

"We talk to each other even when we get mad at each other for saying 'transsexual.' The old good word became incorrect while some of us were sleeping for 17 years. Some of us are catching up. Still, we are always talking to each other, no matter what. We have affiliate links."

"The therapist borg-mind isn't the same as the transsexual borg-mind. The therapists can only go so far with you. They won't go with you into your tunnels. That's your expedition."

It suddenly occurs to me that Stanley has the same first name as Dr. Milgram. Milgram died before Stanley was born, though. Stanley has curly black hair, cut short again now. I don't know what color Dr. Milgram's hair was.

"So what did you want to tell me? About the therapists?"

"I already told you. That's it. The transsexuals go to therapy, and the therapists talk about them later."

We are quiet for a moment. I will have to drink this mint-cookie latte before it gets cold. I do not want this moment to end, but

276

the hot latte is like a timer. That's the purpose and the problem of talking in coffeeshops.

I ask: "Do you think the VPs go to therapy? And the therapists gab about the VPs in coffeeshop corners, just as they talk about the transsexuals?"

"Yes, I bet there are overlaps in the professional kinship bonds. Venn diagrams drawn with wavy lines like the rays of the sun. But maybe the VPs' therapists hang out in different coffeeshops than the transsexuals' therapists. Those must be different psychotherapy specialties."

Yes, especially if one can't be both a VP and a transsexual, the latter hypothesis based on my lived experience of maintaining longstanding assumptions.

"I have another question for you," I ask.

"Shoot."

"Is there a kind of trauma that is specifically queer, other than any trauma that just so happens to affect a queer person?"

"No. Trauma is trauma. If you get hit with a hammer, you hurt. There are no special kinds. All trauma is regular person trauma."

"So why do we talk about queer trauma as if it's a different thing?"

He thought for a moment. "I guess it's not a separate type of hurt. What makes it different is—how it happens to you. When and why it happens to you."

"Like Chelsea Manning."

"Yep."

"The Army was going to fire her—"

"—for 'gender identity disorder' under 'Don't Ask, Don't Tell,'" he finishes. "And so she shared the 'Collateral Murder' gunsight video. Thirty-nine minutes taken from an American helicopter. The soldiers shot civilians, journalists, in Baghdad. Their camera pointed at a wounded person lifted into an automobile. The soldiers were laughing in the video."

"So, when she exposed the government's secrets, it was a kind of mirror image of what they were doing to her."

"Yeah."

"A questioning of why anything is secret."

"The Transportation Security Administration—" Stanley began.

"The damn body scanners at Logan. They're giant security cameras that see into your underpants. There's a worker who interacts with you face-to-face and another worker who is in another room looking at the film of your naked body. Those two workers are in secret communication with each other. The one who sees you face-to-face is verifying your gender presentation, and the one in the hidden room is verifying your anatomy."

"If the worker who sees your social presentation thinks you're a man," Stanley says, "you're allowed to have a penis—"

"—but if that person thinks you're a woman and if they see too much in your crotch, you'll be suspected of carrying a bomb. But neither you nor the TSA official is allowed to say 'penis' or 'bomb.' They just start treating you like a terrorist and you have to bend over. They're looking at every-thing."

"Women must face this more."

"Yeah, though even an oversized clit will be too much for the scanner if the guards pigeonhole you as a woman when you're waiting in line. If it's bigger than a cicada, it trips the alarm."

He clapped his hands. "My dick is defi-nitely too big to go through Logan."

"No doubt you are very large. My clito-ris is big enough to smuggle an entire terrorist inside it."

When you observe transgender men talking over the course of a year, there will be one dick joke, and it will be political com-mentary disguised as a dick joke.

"Christ, call it a meta."

Etymologically, "metaoidioplasty" means something like genitals transcending themselves or becoming beyond-genital or post-genital. It's called a "meta" for short, as if the physical knob were a stand-in for tran-scendence itself. If this word is not exactly a masculine way to discuss the body, at least it is transmasculine.

I ignore Stanley's criticism of my ana-tomic term. If I had my way with it, I'd call it a kicker, based on medieval English

kykyre, a gender-neutral term for the junk you use to kick someone else's junk, but no one asks me.[*]

"This is where 9/11 got us, huh?" I say. I pronounce it "Nine-Eleven" as if it were a convenience store. "Passenger planes got hi-jacked and for some reason we respond by distrusting everyone's penis size."

"Plus, TSA is highly suspicious of my face."

"It is their admission of defeat. An abdi-cation of the idea that anything is knowable. We can't detect people's intentions but, by god, we can develop cameras that see into their underwear."

"*They. They* are responding that way. They are still punishing me for my race, and they can't even figure out what it is! They get my religion wrong, too. Why do they flatter themselves by imagining they can understand my underwear?"

"Their junk got normalized."

"The fear that terrorists might pack their underwear too large and shoot up a plane. Now your coworker is worried that your underwear package is too *small*, so he threatens to shoot up your office. Weird tales premised on the idea that you are going to kill people *with* your modestly sized penis, that someone will inevitably kill you *because of* your modestly sized penis, that you can't talk about it because it's in your imagination,

---

[*] A 15th-century word, also spelled *kekir* or *kekyr*, reported by Melissa Mohr in *Holy Sh*t: A Brief History of Swearing*. New York: Oxford University Press, 2013. p. 98.

but if it happens it will of course be your fault for not having stopped it. The system treats this premise as if it is normal and as if there is nothing to be done about it. Yet no one with power seriously considers *backing out of the fucking story*."

"Yeah," I say. "Because if we all back out of the story, they lose the context in which they have power. The unvoiced premise that my metadick is a terrorclit sets the cosmic Ground of Being by which my boss has his vice presidency. That's how our story opens: I'm standing in line, quietly holding my shit together. Someone in another room is watching me on naked camera, making jokes. If I say I don't want the system to finger me as a terrorclit, I am challenging the boss's whole way of being. How would he go to *his* boss with that information? What would he say to the actual president? He'd rather *die* than back out of his story."

"It's too bad. Trans people don't hurt anyone. Trans people will save the world if cis people would just listen to us."

I don't respond immediately. Stanley asks me what I'm thinking about.

I'm thinking about how he uses the prefix "trans-" like a standalone word, parallel to the prefix "cis-" as a standalone word. He doesn't bother to complete "trans-" with "-sexual" or "-gender." Huh. I've never heard anyone say "trans-" this way. Stanley keeps up with the way people talk.

I am also thinking about something else, so I answer him: "How secrets serve power.

How we are cogs in our own Rube Goldberg machines that kick our own asses."

"Yes."

"There is doing and being. As we have done, and as has been done to us, we become—"

"Existentially. It's performative. Like gender itself."

"Citing Judith Butler is performative."

"Yes, I suppose it is. All secrets are undressing themselves today."

"There are no secrets."

"In the end. If you back up and zoom out. 'Exactly who knows exactly what, right now' is a closeup, historically speaking."

"So the whistleblower is taking a long view. The whistleblower is a prophet."

"Sometimes the trauma happens to queer people first. Sometimes. Sometimes it's my people, and sometimes it's my other people—anyway, a heck of a lot of the time, it's one of my peoples who gets hit first."

"And they don't believe us."

"Right," he says. "That's the thing about being hit first. Whoever is hit first isn't believed, just because no one else is ready to imagine it."

And our movements, I think, *are caught on camera before they even know there's a camera positioned there.*

"They should believe us," Stanley says. "We are canaries in the coal mine."

"Oh my bird, that's exactly it."

m ↗

Flyleaf —
The Canary's Silence

The miners descend into the earth with electric headlamps. <u>Click. Click. Click.</u> They might wish they could bring lit candles because, if the candles sputtered out, this would alert them to a lack of oxygen; however, they would also likely encounter methane gas, which is flammable, in which case their candles would kill them. So, no candle. <u>No vela.</u>

The mine also contains poisonous gases, and that is where I come in: my small bird-self, yellow and trembling in a cage, carried through the coal-dark tunnel, singing a song almost no one hears.

Stare decisis. That's how, once granted legal validity, we hang onto it. A tweeting canary, dreaming of freedom, called Starry de CisCis. It keeps saying the same thing until it can't anymore.

<u>Be brave, bird.</u> I can't remember if that's a line from the movie in which Big Bird runs away from a bird orphanage to rejoin <u>Sesame Street.</u>*

I sing this song to fortify myself:

Decía Gregorio Cortez,
Echando muchos balazos:
—Me he escapado de aguaceros,
contimás de nublinazos.

That's from the ballad of Gregorio Cortez. The hero says, while spraying bullets to show off: <u>I've escaped from downpours, and all the more so from mists like these.</u> A cloud of smoke billows from his black powder gun. He's already killed a Texas sheriff. They'll track him with bloodhounds, will they? Let's see them try, he brags.

<u>It's just a little poison gas.</u>†

"Nublinazo": mist. The moisture that seems to come from the clouds, "las nubes."

"Niebla": water vapor. Fog, a cloud that touches the ground.

"Pichín": the name my human gives me in Unamuno's <u>Niebla.</u> Fine name for a peeping pet. "¡Cállate, hombre," a woman says, "que no me dejas oír cantar al canario!" <u>Shut up, man. I can't hear the canary.</u>

I don't need to sing, and the miners don't need to listen, but I sing anyway. Then, at the slightest puff of toxic gas, I fall over dead.

A canary has internal sacs that hold air

---

* *Follow That Bird* is a 1985 movie featuring Big Bird.
† "El corrido de Gregorio Cortez" is a folk ballad that arose in variations following Gregorio Cortez's arrest in 1901. The song is discussed by Américo Paredes in *With His Pistol in His Hand': A Border Ballad and Its Hero* (University of Texas Press, 1958). Paredes comments: "*Nublinazo* is equivalent to *niebla* (mist). *Niebla* is not current on the border, but *neblina* (light mist) is often found as *nublina*. A heavy mist is a *nublinazo…*"

so it can oxygenate even while exhaling. It's a double-air elemental. And poisoned air will hurt it faster than the air will hurt humans.

We shouldn't be in the coal mine anyway. Global carbon dioxide is about to hit 400 parts per million. Too much carbon dioxide will destroy ecosystems long before it causes problems in human lungs. What do we think are we doing when we burn coal?

There is something else terrible down here. Carbon monoxide will suffocate the miners more swiftly than carbon dioxide will bake the planet. A canary's death is their early warning: get out of the mine.

The exact notes weren't about anything. It's the silence following my song that matters. The nothing filling the space where I used to be. The system that no longer allows my little double-self to survive. Not my presence, but my absence, is the message.

Think about why you don't see me in the office's diversity committee. Think about why you don't see me anymore at all. My candle is pinched out. There is no vela to see and no light by which to see it. Now I am a novel, and to exist would be to develop it— "novelar"—but who is the writer? Do I keep myself in this novel, or does someone else do that? "Nivolar": I'm not flying away. Not yet. Not yet.

I can't share the story of Lear Noon. It will just cause anxiety, finger-pointing, scurrying, figment-elaborations. An answer comes to some people earlier than to others, and information they can't share isn't necessarily a blessing.

That's why I can't be on the diversity committee. Aparna's backyard, yes, but not the official one. The office has a real problem about how people are targeted and silenced for their "diversity," and there's no point in wasting unpaid time on fake conversations about which side of the rainbow flag should carry the bank logo.

The company wants to claim they made an effort, but they had an opportunity to listen, and they told me to shut up. I can't be halfway-talking. If I half-mast the rainbow flag, I publicly embody and therefore attract others' pain. Their violence comes for me. And I am not allowed to talk about the violence. Thus, I cannot show up at that boardroom.

I can show up if they let me denounce violence. But the office diversity committee is an exercise in saying "yes."

The trauma comes to us especially when we are living in the empty space of our own silencing of our own queerness. And then, when it happens, it would take too long to explain it. People wouldn't hear us across the buffer of emptiness. By the time we could make ourselves understood, they'd be experiencing the same trauma themselves anyway and wouldn't need us to explain it anymore.

I wish I had understood this earlier.

The final government report on the JFK assassination decided there were not three bullets. Just two. One bullet wounded JFK and Governor Connally, and a second bullet killed JFK.

When we notice video-frames, or when someone assigns us a text-portion, the unit-shape itself is a metacommunication that reminds us: *You're watching a video. You're reading a text.* The game-piece signals we're playing a game.* Sorry!

They set up a body scanner at Logan to see my game-piece. The piece is a metacommunication telling them that this is a game. That's the kicker.

When there is a problem, going to the cops will make it worse. The VPs won't make it worse, but they don't want to hear about it. The therapists are paid to hear about it, but they will tell me to worry less. I can go to the transsexuals, but then I remember: Stanley is the transsexual. Also, equally: I am the transsexual.

I am the transsexual not entirely by the light of my own genius, I regret to say, but because I gained permission from cis people to be this way. Which makes it an esoteric, ouroboric mystery why transsexuals should have any solution.

"Transsexual" is the box the cis people made for me. After I tangle in their red tape just so they let me have a gender, they're tired of listening to me and won't listen to my other oracular idea. But I'm bound to say it someday. I never forget my story because I am my story.

"Meta" is a prefix that signals transcendence.

"Trans" is a prefix that signals metafiction.

Metatron is the Talmud's name for an angel who writes down our virtues and vices. This knowledge scribe puts the cosmic secrets in the movie.

If you think that's impressive, just wait until Metatron meets Metatrans.

The idea of going to the transsexuals, which amounts to hashing out something with Stanley and ultimately relying on myself, is a dead-end if I swallow the gatekeepers' lump of BS. Gatekeepers are not inclined to let us do the thing, say the thing, know the thing. If I silence and stop myself on the grounds that I haven't received someone else's permission to exist and take charge of my life, my going to the transsexuals is a non-starter. If I don't believe in our knowledge and ability, I disempower us and cannot rely on us.

That's exactly it, I said, but the canary is just a metaphor, and there's something

---

* Gregory Bateson used the word "metacommunication" in *Mind and Nature: A Necessary Unity* (1972). It is discussed by Dave Szulborski in *This Is Not A Game: A Guide to Alternate Reality Gaming* (New-Fiction, 2005).

imperfect in every image, so nothing is exactly what it is.

"Beware the Jubjub bird," Lewis Carroll wrote.

I took my gay trauma to Amity Lodge before I knew what I was dealing with. If I believe that gay trauma is real but I cannot explain it, it might be because I cannot think of relevant individual traumas. But some traumas are collective. Now I am sitting in that epiphany. Gay trauma, Jewish trauma, Mexican trauma, trans trauma. Those are collective stories.

Who got hit? Not you. <u>Someone else</u>. But you feel it, don't you? Evidently you do, because you are the one who showed up talking about it.

We are the ones who are hurt, and we are the ones who have to save ourselves. But are we up to the task? "Virtuous and vicious ev'ry man must be, / Few in th' extreme, but all in the degree," Alexander Pope wrote. Even the best and worst among us have our moments: now and then, off and on, by fits. "The rogue and fool by fits is fair and wise; / And ev'n the best, by fits, what they despise."

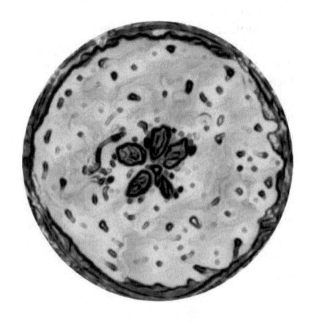

♏ ♐

FOG — AT HANA LEE'S (CONTINUED)

"Oh, by the way," Stanley says, "Take a look at this."

Another Hana Lee's patron at a table near us turns around, realizes the comment wasn't meant for them, and turns back to face their own donut.

Stanley unfolds a piece of paper. It's an ink drawing of a bunch of irregular circle-blobs, some shaded, some not.

"This is the stone wall at Amity Lodge. The one across the path from my guest room where I was staying last summer. The wall had some writing on it, but I couldn't make it out. Faded graffiti. I had a lot of time on my hands, so I sat there and copied it in my notebook. Any chance you recognize what it says?"

I shake my head. I do remember the stone wall with the writing, the one I'd tried to photograph when I went to sell his car, but my phone battery had failed. Of course, if I couldn't interpret flaked-off paint when I saw it in person, I can't interpret a sketch of it now.

"No. No, I don't."

"Thought you might, with all the grave-stone rubbing you do."

I smile. "My research expertise of that sort is minimal. And you're showing me your own sketch of someone else's bad spray-painting."

"Yeah," he said. "It's just art. It can mean anything. Or nothing." He tucked the paper into his pocket.

Maybe the graffiti said "THE TRANS-VALUATION OF ALL VALUES." That phrase seemed about the right length.

It also seems a good descriptor for what it feels like to be talking to Stanley again. Same valued friendship. Renewed appreciation. Same reasons and new reasons. I can't believe we get to go to a coffeeshop together. I hope I am earning the life I have.

I take a breath. "Will you tell me about the first car?"

"Yes," he says. He is ready. "The same day my girlfriend broke up with me, a cop came up to me in my driveway."

He paused.

"The cop did not believe the car was mine."

I tilt my head and lean in slightly. We had been telling strange transgender jokes rather loudly in the Hana Lee's, but now Stanley drops his voice considerably.

"He said it wasn't mine. He must have known it was, but he made me prove it. He could have run my plate. My car, my address, me." The dialogue he provides is striking in its inexactness. That is something

Stanley does when he does not want to remember a bothersome exchange.

"How did you—"

"It doesn't matter how I proved it. It wasn't about facts. He went away." He sighed. "But I realized, as a life strategy, I shouldn't have that car in that driveway."

He takes a sip of his mint-cookie latte. I do too. Mine is cold. His must be cold too.

"That's when I went away to Amity Lodge," he continues. "I wanted to be away from my apartment. I didn't want to see my driveway, and I didn't want the car either. So I—hurt myself. I inflicted damage on myself. I basically gave it away." My eyes go wide. "It was worth money," he tells me, "but I basically gave it away."

"That's why you got the cheap Taurus," I continue for him.

"Yeah, and I never drove it and I realized I didn't want a car at all, and instead I just wanted to go out to California for my month off."

He'd given away his fancy car. Then I'd given away his cheap car. The same loss had befallen him twice. First it was a cop, then it was me. Which linked me, on a deep level, in his mind, to cops. I would not have guessed.

"You needed the cash from the Taurus."

"Yeah," he says. "Mostly I needed help. You and I hadn't had a chance to really talk. I wasn't communicating very well. I didn't tell you what I needed. It was just such a shitty time. I was in a lot of disorder."

"I didn't help you," I say.

"Nah," he agrees, meaning: *You sure didn't.*

It's not that time altogether stops, but it feels less relevant. "I'm sorry," I say.

He pauses. The duration of the pause is irrelevant. I am aware of being in time, coasting on four wheels, and I am neither trying to speed up nor brake.

"I know," he says. "And now you know."

There is one thing I need to tell him now. Briefly, inexactly, the same way he just spoke to me: "The people to whom I gave the Taurus were antisemitic."

The clouds pass over his face again. He blinks, chasing them away. "Oh. Oh."

It means different things to each of us.

I remember those people asking me: *Why did you betray your brother?* But I don't need to voice that. This conversation is about Stanley's feelings, not mine. And given that I took their accusation as an invitation, those words ended up so on-the-nose, they're embarrassing.

"They were interested," I said, "in my eternal soul." My index and middle fingers trace a weak arc, as though I'm flicking a fairy off the table. Who cares about my eternal soul?

Maybe that means something to him. "Got it," he says quietly.

I think we will always, for the rest of our lives, be sitting in Hana Lee.

♏︎ ♐︎

FLASHBULB

SUN
26 APR
2015

344

I WANT TO KNOW
SOMETHING ELSE

FLASHBULB

SUN
26 APR
2015

345

WHAT'S
BEHIND YOU?

	Runs	Hits	Errors
Red Sox	7	9	1
Orioles	18	20	1

Aparna changes her profile photo on social media. Phone notification tells me so. Something in the background of her living room selfie grabs my attention.

There, on an end table behind her, is Mariamman, the goddess in the red dress.

I thought Aparna had locked the upstairs room, maybe to protect the goddess from me, just because I am a snoop. The last time I was over there—January, I thought it was—the closet door was locked. Now, Mariamman is sitting openly in her living room.

So maybe Aparna didn't lock the closet against me or other rogue houseguests or for any reason having to do with the goddess. Maybe she locked it for an entirely different reason.

♏ ♐

I email her. "I have to ask you something."

"Shoot?"

"The photo you just posted of your living room—it is very nice—and I am just curious—what's that behind you, on the table? I don't remember seeing that in your living room last time I visited. Is it new?"

"That's a goddess," she replies. "She's not new. We used to keep her somewhere else. I moved her to the living room."

This does not explain why her upstairs closet has been locked, nor what is in there, now, if not a murti. "She's nice!" I reply.

I am doing the thing she said I sometimes do: making uptalk words about a thing that is not the thing about which I want to know.

♏ ♐

Flyleaf — Unbecoming

The "High Sparrow" episode airs on <u>Game of Thrones</u>. Season Five is the best so far. Everyone thinks so. Arya's ascetic tutor wants her to discard her identity. Compliant, she tosses most of her belongings into the water. She more fully unbecomes. She is almost No One. But she is not ready to lose her weapon, the little sword her brother once gave her. She hides it in the rocks so it's retrievable.

None of us ever untethers from our past.

But otherwise I feel this parable is not about me. Who does it remind me of?

♏ ♐

346

YES. YES. YES.

	Runs	Hits	Errors
Yankees	8	14	1
Red Sox	5	7	1

I dream of JFK again. I don't see him in the dream.

A rectangular hole in the ground, an open grave, empty. The stone slab is pushed to the side. Cold, but the trees are budding. The forest stretches in all directions. He could be anywhere. He is in the air, the vapor of dew, the slant of light.

"I haven't met your cat," Stanley tells me on the phone. Obviously. Catching up is like looking back. It's not what it used to be. But better late than never.

"Eurydice," I add. My cat has a name. I am trying to advance this conversation. Here comes the three-way lightbulb: *Click-bright. Click-brighter…*

"So maybe I could come over sometime."

Yes. Yes. Yes.

EPISODE 10

STOP CHAD (TELE-QUIZ)

FLASHBULB

FRI
29 MAY
2015

347

THREE MINUTES
UNTIL THE MEETING

	Runs	Hits	Errors
Red Sox	4	6	0
Rangers	7	12	1

It is May 29, 2015, the 115th anniversary of Chad's death.

And also of the patenting of the word "escalator" to Charles Seeberger.

Time travel, in that Stephen King novel about undoing the JFK assassination, leaves a residue. The more you go back and forth, the more the story layers.

The boss stomps by. "You look like a wreck!"

"I'm having dreams," I say. "Interesting dreams—"

"I don't want to hear about it. I also have dreams. Everybody has a dream. This is not the time to tell me you wish you were on a beach with a pina colada. My meeting in the boardroom starts in three minutes," he thunders, "and your entire project is due tomorrow! Are you in or out?"

♏ ♐

I don't love when people act like they are threatening to leak my Ashley Madison data. All data is always breached, and at least Ashley Madison is one company that has never had my data to begin with. The threat doesn't resonate.

I hold his gaze for a second longer than I should. "In." I rub my hands and stamp my feet.

He frowns. "Good. Act like it. Are you really trying to save your project, or are you chasing it into traffic?"

"I don't know."

"*Two* minutes until the meeting starts," he admonishes himself, running off.

♏ ♐

Flyleaf — Rite of Spring

It is the one-hundred-and-second anniversary of the Paris premiere of Igor Stravinsky's "The Rite of Spring."* The ballet is about pagan sacrifice that marks the change of seasons, which the original audience must have known when they showed up, but they did not like the opening bassoon, not one bit. <u>Too modern</u>. They yelled, threw vegetables. Dozens got kicked out of the theater.

The performance starts now. Either we are in or we are out. Sometimes we are in and they throw us out.

♏ ♐

FOG — CHAD HAS TO DIE

I hear a noise. Chad's ghost stands in the corner of my office and scratches at the wall, as if he's a cat who wants out.

Aparna also happens to walk by. I poke my head in the hallway and flag her down. "Do you hear that?" I ask her. "I know you can't see him, but do you hear him? Chad's here again."

"I hear nothing. Are you afraid of him?"

"No, I just think he's annoying."

Despite already having wrecked myself, according to my boss's visual assessment of me, I stay at the office late.

From somewhere down the hall, I think I hear someone shouting our company name: *Achromatic Proprioception*. I investigate. "A lot of precipitation," they were saying. It's going to *rain*. Inconvenient for anyone going into the city tonight, including me.

Aparna stops by my desk again at dinnertime. "It's six. Why are you still here?"

"I have to fill out all these spreadsheets and attach them to their tickets, and then Chad has to die a little after nine o'clock."

"Ooh, that sounds bad."

"It's written on his death certificate."

She puts her hand on her hip. "Are you sure you're OK?"

"Yeah, why?"

"Because you said Chad has to die. Usually people don't kill off their imaginary friends when they're feeling fine."

"Tonight's the night he dies. I didn't make it up. And he's not imaginary. He's historical. And I don't want to kill him, I want to save him."

He's already dead, but there is something to save: the residue of his reality, his dignity in death. *Antigone* phrased it as a choice between the "world of the dead" and the "world of the living," the "law of heaven" and the "law of mortals."

---

* Information about the audience reaction to Igor Stravinsky's premiere of "The Rite of Spring" came from "100 years ago today, 'The Rite of Spring' incited a riot in a Paris theater" by Amar Toor, *The Verge*, May 29, 2013.

"I'm planning on being here late too, if that helps," she says.

"I'm supposed to do the spreadsheets, but I can't stay much longer. I have to find Chad."

"Text me if you need me."

At 8 p.m., I leave a note on my current ticket, escalate the unresolved issue, attach the spreadsheet, and sign off. I put on my trenchcoat against the weather I expect.

I leave Chad's death certificate on my desk. I don't need it anymore.

It is predestined for me to go. "History walking the dog" is how Arundhati Roy put it, referring to how your feet take you somewhere.

Out to the parking lot, to begin with.

I sit behind the wheel of my car, holding María in my hand.

This isn't easy, but it's the nature of the night to be hard. Do not give me nights. I will not go gentle into them.

"Roll the tape," I order, thinking of *Tele-Quiz*. Siri interprets this command, and the radio flicks on. It's an oldie: a single from Madonna's *Immaculate Collection*. I want to record, not listen, but that's all right. Siri is learning.

This is going to be miserable for Chad, I realize. *He's the one who has to die. In ghost lore, suicides die over and over. It's his mind in which the bad tape plays. I'm just watching it.*

"Hey Siri, what was the weather in Boston on May 29, 1900?"

"On Tuesday, May 29, 1900," the robotic voice begins, "the weather was fair and cool. There was no precipitation. If you're looking for an answer, keep looking."

That's enough information for me to begin.

Reference points: In 1900, JFK was not born yet. Come to think of it, it would be 17 years to the day from Chad Goeing's death to JFK's birth. I'd never realized the connection before. Another cicada life cycle. Just as it was 17 years to the day from JFK's death to my birth. It's as though we're all the same bug going into the ground and emerging later as a new version of ourselves.

I don't see many more solid connections. From JFK's birth, for example—today in 1900 would be his 17th pre-birthday—roughly another 97 years would pass before I would give away Stanley's car, and one year after I did that, the world powers would reach a nuclear agreement with Iran. In this moment, that's all that comes to mind to describe the year 1900. It's an apophatic description: A list of things that 1900 is *not*.

♏ ♐

FLASHBULB

FRI
29 MAY
2015

I TEXT STANLEY

Aparna said I could text her if I need her, but I don't text her. I text Stanley. "I am going to jump," I say.

"What?" he replies.

I don't answer. I turn off my cell phone and put it away in my pocket. It's distracting when my cell phone rings in 1900.

♏ ♐

FOG — TELE-QUIZ

"Welcome back, televidentes," Mr. Destiny says to the audience with a grandiose sweep of his arms, "to our special 'Exit Interview' episode of *Tele-Quiz*!"

We must be in 1955 now if we're doing our television show.

"The question is: *How did Chad Goeing die?* Are you ready to guess the answer to this?"

"As ready as I'll ever be."

I must already know the answer if I'm dreaming about someone who knows the answer. But in this dream, I must pretend not to know. I willfully forget the information Chad and I need to survive.

"Good man," the host says. "Here's the parameter: The answer is five letters." A large spotlight turns on, lighting up the wall behind him where five blank circular panels hang. "Make your best guess. You have 20 attempts. If you need a clue, ask a yes-or-no question. That counts as an attempt."

"I'm ready," I say.

"Go."

Attempt 1

"In honor of Madonna," I say, "is it VOGUE?"

Mr. Destiny looks confused. "I'm not sure what the Madonna has to do with this, or how a 'vogue' would be a manner of death."

No, you wouldn't know. Madonna hasn't been born yet. This is a throwback, I mean, a throwforward.

"It's just my kickoff salute," I say.

"You want to waste a question on that?"

"Yes, in honor of the Madonna. An offering to her."

An angry buzzer sounds.

"Wrong answer!" the host narrates. "It's not VOGUE."

Attempt 2

"Is it CROSS?"

The host smiles for the camera. "No! No crucifixion!" The buzzer sounds again.

I remember the religious figurine getting stuck in the sink disposal. Chad could have been trapped like that in a river, his feet tangled in a branch—wilderness guides call that a "strainer." Is that a clue?

Attempt 3

"SEWER," I say.

"No."

Attempt 4

"PIPES," I follow up quickly.

"No, you're cold," he laughs. "Why don't you take a different approach?"

Attempt 5

The noise is in my head again, growing louder. "Does it make a repetitive sound?"

"Yes."

I think of the clicking of a camera shutter. I think of the wars still alive in the American imagination in this, the *Tele-Quiz* era.

Attempt 6

"Distinct like automatic gunfire?" I think of Chad in a telephone booth, banging his head against the glass: *thunk-thunk-thunk.*

"No, not really."

Attempt 7

"Diffuse like rain?"

"Yes, that's better."

I close my eyes, imagining I'm placing my ear to the forest floor, listening for vibrations. The ground is where people are buried.

If the auto mechanics Click and Clack were here, and if something vibrated, they'd involve themselves physically. That's how they learned enough to answer questions on Car Talk. I am doing my learning. I'm deep inside my psychic automechanism.

Attempt 8

Diffuse like rain. "But mechanical like a typewriter?"

"Yes. You have 12 questions left."

Attempt 9

An indistinct, diffuse, repetitive, mechanical sound killed Chad. How did he die? Shock and awe? Too many letters, too much metaphor, too much like an inversion of my own name. Can't be a rope. Too quiet. Maybe a water clock: drip, drip, drip. No, think: modernity. But not a gun. What's newer than a gun?

"DRONE," I guess. I imagine that, in 2015, one's recreational drone might boomerang back and smash into one's head, causing a fatality. I don't know how this could have worked in 1900, or if the game show host would even recognize what I am talking about now that it's 1955, but it's worth a guess.

"'Drone,' well, yes, that's one way to name the sound. There is a sort of droning on." The host smirks. "Plus an occasional interjection that 'calls to you like the wild geese, harsh and exciting.' That's a Mary Oliver poem describing the sound of the geese."

Oh yes. The line "You do not have to be good" comes from the same Mary Oliver poem, not from the Lord's Prayer. I still can't remember the Lord's Prayer.

I am pretty sure Chad wasn't killed by a GOOSE.

"But let's reconsider this. How could a *sound* have killed Chad? You're still cold," the host says. I anticipate the buzzer; there it is. I don't bother to explain to this 1955 character that a DRONE can be something other than a sound.

Attempt 10

"BRAIN. His brain killed him." *It was a difficult day on both sides of the hemispheric divide.*

"Interesting. You think he was mentally ill?"

"He died by suicide."

"Is that a question?"

"No, no. It's a statement of fact. I'm pretty sure of it. Please don't debit 'suicide' from my attempts. I'm offering BRAIN as the answer."

"OK, I'm counting it as one attempt. Was it Chad's own *brain*?" The host points at the board. The buzzer sounds. "No!" he crows. "We are not giving you credit for that. You're halfway through your allotted attempts."

Commercial Break

How much of my life I have already lived, it occurs to me now, halfway through this game show. And now we are taking a break for a word from the show's sponsors.

What killed Chad? I pore over the clues. The emphasis of the prayer to the Madonna, who supposedly gives me 80 percent of what I need to know. What cross do I carry? If supernatural intervention killed Chad, did the Madonna herself order the hit from heaven?

It makes a repetitive, mechanical sound, more diffuse than distinct. The answer to the riddle has five letters, and it isn't VOGUE, CROSS, SEWER, PIPES, DRONE, or BRAIN.

"MARÍA," I say aloud. "Holy Mary, Mother of God. In Spanish."

"You know we can't accept attempts when the cameras aren't rolling," Mr. Destiny says thoughtfully. "But I'll give you a freebie. The answer is 'No.' I won't count it as one of your questions, since we're off-camera," Mr. Destiny says. He adds a clue: "You can speak the answer in English or Spanish. But the riddle is in English."

Ten Attempts Remain

We're back from the commercial break.

Mr. Destiny faces the camera and addresses the audience at home: "You know, sometimes my contestants claim they hear someone whispering the answer to them—an angel or a little bird. Divine intervention. It's not my television staff. They keep quiet and aboveboard."

He turns to me. "If you, Lev Ockenshaw, have an audio clue like that—"

"I do. The Madonna song."

"Fine. We're used to it. And by the way, folks at home, in case anyone wasn't clear: The riddle is in English."

"Yes. I'll answer in English."

"I said the *riddle* is in English, for the record."

Not knowing what he's talking about makes me nervous. Madonna is singing me an earworm.

Ten attempts remain to me.

Attempt 11

"SATAN."

Buzzer. "Bad luck. Now you're down to nine attempts."

Attempt 12

"Did the thing that killed Chad exist in Mexico City in 1900?"
"No."

Attempt 13

"Will it exist in Boston in 2015?"
"Yes."

Attempt 14–15

What that means, I think, is that history moved too fast for Chad.

I try to empathize aloud: "He was mad at his father. And he wanted nothing but to sit and write *The Nature of Time.*"

"That's another two questions, isn't it? Yes and yes."

This information had better be useful.

Attempt 16

"He was having an argument with modernity."

"Yes."

Chad galloped in my head. This ghost was messing with me, but I was getting closer. Wild goose chase.

Attempt 17

"Did he jump out of a PLANE?"

"Interesting," he says in the manner of someone wearied by everyone else's daftness, "but no. Let's be a little more targeted here, shall we? The Madonna gives you 80 percent of the riddle, which means you owe 20 percent. There are five letters in total. Put in your part. Just one part. Give me one letter." He grins and winds his arm like a baseball pitcher. "How did Chad Goeing die? Fenway Park already has the answer. Do you have the answer?"

That is an infuriating tease. I have no idea how Mr. Destiny knows that Stanley knows the answer to my riddles, that Stanley works at Fenway Park, or even that Stanley exists. That could happen if—let's think this through—Mr. Destiny found Stanley and gave him the answer months ago, just to drive me nuts. Would he have done that? How much planning goes into a game show?

"No," I say mildly. "I don't know the answer."

"You can guess one letter at a time," Mr. Destiny prompts. "That, after all, would be a yes-or-no question."

Would've been better had I realized that at the beginning. I have three attempts left.

What letter? I conjure a mental impression of Stanley on a suburban baseball field. He wears a team jersey, but a wrinkle obscures the logo. A young boy stands beside him. Behind the field is a white church with a steeple, and the dark-crowned trees spread beyond. B for the Boston Red Sox? L for Little League?

I can't get the religious iconography out of my mind. The steeple of the church in that imagined suburban landscape. The execution at Golgotha in the rain. The X-shaped placard on Chad's grave. The miniature crucifix necklace hanging around the figurine of María. The enormous wooden cross I've carried all the way from Provincetown, just to install it on a platform in Boston, an imposing shadow. The hormone prescription I've neglected to fill.

Look, now, who's stepping into my imagination. A different goddess. It is Mariamman. She walks right out onto the baseball field next to home plate. She isn't smiling or frowning, but I sense her annoyance with me. She's wearing all red, and there are large blue jewels on her ears and neck. She's holding a trident, pointy side up.

"What's the answer?" I ask her in my imagination. She won't debit my questions. I can ask her as much as I like, as long as she's playing along.

She flips the trident and stabs the ground next to home plate. The points bury in the earth. Her hand rests on the horizontal bar that makes a handle with the vertical shaft.

"I don't get it," I say.

She points into the distance at the steeple of the church with the little cross on top. If she is not referring to Jesus, what does the cross mean to her?

And, now—suddenly—I see it.

Attempt 18

"Is there a T?" I yelp.

"YES," roars the host. "We have one T!"

Excitement, triumph, certainty surge in me. I hope the game show's technical crew is making me look good. The special effects in my mind have two light sabers clashing in galactic battle. Madonna's song changes key: from B-flat major to C major. It feels pivotal. The sound of the typewriter in the rain, that unidentified noise, grows louder.

Attempt 19

"WATER!" I crow. That was it—the slickness of my wet hands carrying the cross in the storm. The condemned men with their arms strapped to crosses, their ghosts crawling out of the Charles in the damp weather. A drowning.

Mr. Destiny laughs. "No." The buzzer

sounds. "You guessed that too quickly before I had a chance to write the letter on the board. Here, let me show you and the audience—the T is the first letter in the word." He picks up a long, black, folded umbrella, and uses it to point to the board, where the T lights up in first position. "Does that help?"

I shake my head. "I'm sorry. It doesn't."

"You have one attempt left. No more clues. You have to guess the word. Do you want to touch the board?" he asks.

"Why?"

"Touch it. It's Chad's death. T for TOUCH, maybe?" He's taunting me.

"No, that's not it," I say. I might as well guess CLIPS, as in PAPER, which are the very things that give ghosts power. I might as well guess SNOEY to hedge my bets on YES and NO. Madonna is still singing that blasted song over and over in my mind, that 1993 single. An earworm. Rain. My mind is dark.

"Give us the answer, please. Stanley already has it, so your time is growing short. If you don't give me the answer now, he's going to arrive and put a stop to this."

I have a headache.

"I'm thinking," I say.

"Your IQ won't help you. Stop *thinking* about the answer to the question and try to *feel* it."

I say nothing, leaving dead air for a couple seconds. "I don't know what I feel," I say quietly.

"OK, you know what, send—feelings—straight—to—hell. Just *answer the question.*"

Attempt 20

"I'd like to solve the riddle," I say, stating the inevitable, buying myself an extra moment of airtime. The downpour in my head increases until nothing else is visible. Madonna's voice inhabits the raindrops and overwhelms the background. I hear a goose-like sound, a blast of a honk as if from a Goose of Unusual Size.[*] I give my final answer: "TOWER. He jumped out of a skyscraper."

"No. I'm terribly sorry. Don't know what skyscraper you have in mind. In 1900, the Custom House in Boston was five stories, as the tower hadn't been built yet. That is not how Chad died, and you are out of questions."

---

[*] "Geese of Unusual Size" are friends of "Rodents of Unusual Size," a species found only in *The Princess Bride* (1973).

Let's See What You Would Have Won

What have we been fighting for, anyway? I wonder.

Mr. Destiny is unflappable. "Give the roulette wheel a spin and let's see what you would have won."

As instructed, I swing the mustard, pea, and magenta-painted wheel. It flutters with a *clack-clack-clack.* Car talk. I know nothing about radio or television, but I realize this has been a Halsrätsel, a life-and-death riddle, and that it has been my neck on the chopping block and I have lost. The glimmer of insight vanishes. The wheel comes to a stop.

"Oh, that's too bad. You would have gotten more time—"

♏ ♐

FOG — THE CHASE

Failure at my back. Wasn't heard at work, didn't discover Chad's cause of death, and I'm running now, not on the 1955 game show, not fast-forwarded back to 2015, but instead rewinded to 1900, running to catch Chad's ghost, approaching Boylston and Dartmouth. We blow past Copley. That station didn't exist in 1900. We run up Boylston, along the Common, until we make it to Tremont Street. This was where the first subway system on the continent was built. Yes, the Park Street station was here, is here, in 1900.

Somewhere there must be a historical record explaining his death. I could have found it on microfilm. Didn't have to appear on a game show. But I only do things the hard way, and now it's too late for me to change. This is how I roll. I rolled, and I speculiriate, and I'm playing it through to the end.

The night sky is cloudless, in both 1900 and in 2015.

Chad is ahead of me at Park Street— pale, taut face, olive-drab trenchcoat. He rides the escalator underground. I follow the ghost.

He slips into the station, seemingly without swiping a card or budging the turnstile. He ought to at least drop in a Liberty Head nickel, or else he's dodging the fare.

In *The Phantom Tollbooth*, the toy tollbooth came with coins, and Milo had to deposit one before driving his toy car through it.

I swipe my 21st-century plastic card at the turnstile, expecting five cents, the price-point of 1900, to be debited from my balance.

Chad is running through the station. Is there anywhere to be found a psychic who doesn't already know where Chad is going?

Chad nears the platform, stops, turns around, and looks at me. His face appears drawn, haggard, full of the horror of defeat. The sound is in the distance, growing louder. The song, too—the chant of "RAIN." Madonna's voice again. It is 9 o'clock.

No magical beings will give me the answer. No need to turn on my phone. I am in 1900 with limited battery and I don't expect reception. No Teddy Ruxpin will talk to me.

When I was little, my parents told me the fairytale of Rumpelstiltskin. It's a story that assumes cisgender people's fear of transgender people. The king locks up the classically beautiful cisgender woman and orders her to spin straw into gold. A magic little transgender man appears to her and says, "Give me the jewelry off your body, the shiny little stones nature made, and in return, I'll produce any amount of unnatural alchemical gold for you." They make the transaction, but when she runs out of natural jewelry, she has to promise him her future firstborn child. Just like natural gold, the living child, complete with a natural sex, is something the magic little transgender man can't create. (He assumes the cisgender woman is fertile.)

A year after she becomes queen, he reappears and demands her baby to satisfy their bargain. She weeps, and he relents and makes an alternate demand: "Call me by my name." "What is your name?" "It's a secret, of course. Guess it." She researches and lists every name she can think of, but he has a name shared by no other human. His pride is his downfall; as he chants his own name to himself, alone at night beside his own campfire, a scout overhears him and reports his name to the queen. She is then able to address him: "Rumpelstiltskin!" He rages, as she has stolen part of his secret knowledge, and now he will not get her baby. Although he has the superpower of creating gold, he pursues what the fairytale's morality won't let him have: a natural human baby (Rumpelstiltskin is ensorcelled) who is the product of someone else's fertility (Rumpelstiltskin is sterile), as well as a rogue patriarchal control over someone else's womanhood and motherhood (Rumpelstiltskin would invade and destroy matrimony). He infiltrates the cis woman's bedroom, but she outsmarts him by researching and exposing his identity. He grabs his own foot and rips his body in two from the genitals upward, and the devil swallows him into the ground toward Hell.

The agitation of the cisgender woman: being locked in a room, forced to guess magic trans-riddles with no logical answers.

What would Madonna do?

"RAIN."

Then, suddenly, I know. I haven't forgotten the clue from my Attempts 18 and 19: The five-letter word begins with a T.

The residue of time travel grows thick around me. I am a bee in the center of the honeycomb. Everything connects in geometric perfection, and it's sticky.

Here's the secret of the six-sided wax cells in the honeycomb: A theater set has three walls forming the actors' scenery plus a fourth, imaginary wall separating the actors from the audience. If you break down the fourth wall, it's as if the audience has joined the actors' fictional reality. Then the audience might realize that they, too, have three walls surrounding them. The entire theater, with three walls on the actors' side and three walls on the audience's side, is a six-sided cell. It is full of honey. If you are absorbed into a drama, you might not escape.

As the character of Unamuno said, the universe might be a kaleidoscope of shapes joining together. Unamuno's name itself speaks, evoking oneness hidden inside oneness.

How do you break the fourth wall? Breathe on it. See if it fogs. If your breath doesn't stick, there is no "there" there.

From a dozen paces away, I stretch my hand out to Chad, but it's too late. He becomes the missing letter. He spreads his arms out in a T shape as if to feel ghost raindrops.

Here comes a loud machine down the tunnel. I don't have time to see what it looks like, this trolley from 1900.

I stretch to reach Chad, who jumps off the platform in front of the approaching train.

The nail falls out of the canary's cage door. The canary spreads its wings.

Just as I fling myself toward the edge of the platform, aiming my body at the train—of course failing to save Chad, who is already a ghost—two uniformed police officers catch me, each grabbing one of my outstretched arms.

♏ ♐

FOG — KATABASIS

I am in the dark place. The silvered side of the mirror.

Niflheim, the Home of Mist, Abode of Hel.

I am in the underbelly of the earth.

The place of skeletons and worms.

This is the road Orpheus traveled without success.

Anti-Rumpelstiltskin fled here when he carjacked the queen's Taurus and unspun it into the absence of gold.

Here, they watch you, watch you, watch you.

They have taken my speculirium.

The less said of this place, the better.

♏ ♐

FLASHBULB

TUE
2 JUN
2015

350

APARNA VISITS ME
IN THE HOSPITAL

FLASHBULB

TUE
2 JUN
2015

351

STANLEY
MIGHT COME TOO

	Runs	Hits	Errors
Twins	0	3	0
Red Sox	1	7	0

Aparna visits me in my hospital bed. She closes the door to my room behind her and sits next to my bed.

"You tried to jump in front of a train," she informs me.

"A thing happened," I explained. People sometimes tell me I should shorten my explanations. I am trying.

♏ ♐

"Stanley is coming to see you."

"He wants to see me?"

She wrinkled her nose. "No, but he's coming anyway."

♏ ♐

304

352

APARNA INTERFERED

353

THERE IS NO NEED
FOR CREATIVITY
RIGHT NOW

"You interfered with the thing," I accuse her.

"Stop talking, or they will put you on so much more medication than you are already on."

This I do not want. From this bed, I have already starred as a contestant on the *Legends of the Hidden Temple* game show, I have run through the stage scenery guarded by its costumed Mayan characters, and the buttons I press light up the Stations of the Cross. More meds will make it worse.

♏♐

I show Aparna the drawings in my notebook.

"You don't need to be creative right now. Let's work on being less creative in the future. Just don't get on all the trains of thought."

Truth, for me, at this moment, comes through a bendy straw. It tastes like weak Gatorade.

♏♐

THE RIDDLE DOESN'T WORK IN SPANISH

"You know, the Spanish word for TRAIN is pronounced the same as in English," I said, "but the vowel is spelled as an E so it's only a four-letter word, TREN. Anyway, even if the game show board had four letters, TREN couldn't have been the answer to the riddle if it'd been asked in Spanish. A cross/rain picture rebus gives you TRAIN in English, but in Spanish the word for RAIN is LLUVIA."

"Great, thanks for letting me know," she says.

♏ ♐

I LEFT THE DEATH CERTIFICATE ON MY DESK

"You know how we found you?"

"How."

"Submitted for the approval of the Diversity Committee, I call this story—'Your Disappearance.' Stanley called me just after you left the office. He said you said you were 'going to jump'. I told him you'd said the ghost was going to die at 9 p.m. but I didn't know where you went. He drove to the office, and I let him in. You'd left the death certificate from 1900 on your desk, and there, in addition to May 29 at 9 p.m., it was written 'Park Street station, Tremont Street subway.'"

"You knew what I knew."

"Yes. Knowledge swims in the ether. But, Boston traffic. No way we could drive to Park Street in time."

♏ ♐

FLASHBULB

TUE
2 JUN
2015

356

I AM PEEVED

FLASHBULB

TUE
2 JUN
2015

357

UNSAFE
IN ANY CENTURY

"So," she continued, "we used your desk phone to call Emergency."

"You called the fucking police."

"It seemed to work out OK. We said, 'Hi, we think someone is in trouble.' They wanted details. We said, 'Suicide plan at 9 p.m.' They said, 'Can you describe him?' We said, 'White guy, late thirties, heading into the city, going to Park Street. He's got a head start, and we can't get there in time.' They said they'd get on it."

I am peeved.

First of all, my thirties aren't "late" yet. Secondly, it won't be a *train* that ends me. It'll be a *t-lluvia*—raindrops the size of teacups.

No, scratch that. I'm not peeved. I don't have the word for what I feel.

♏ ♐

"We tried to follow you, as backup, in Stanley's car. We were stuck on Boylston, inching east. It started to pour. I was talking to the cops on my cell phone. They'd already arrived. They are always everywhere."

Yeah. It was like *Monty Python and the Holy Grail* where the cops show up and tell off the whole Crusading army. My army isn't safe in any century. A couple cops ruin everything. Really disappointing for me.

"'We see him,' they told me," she continues. "'White guy in a trenchcoat just ran into the Park Street station. We'll get him.'"

"And get me, they did," I observe from my hospital bed.

♏ ♐

FLASHBULB

TUE
2 JUN
2015

STANLEY COMES

FLASHBULB

TUE
2 JUN
2015

20 PERCENT
IS MINE

It is *really* disappointing, did I mention. I have always wanted someone to get me and now it is disappointing to finally be gotten.

The door opens. As Aparna told me it would be, indeed it is Stanley, canonically himself, his curls uncombed and springing out from under his baseball hat. He is not smiling but I know he is here because he cares. Funny how I most wanted to see him in those months when he didn't want to see me, and now that I am annoyed with him, here he appears unbidden as one of my guides back to my ordinary life. He is once again important but unremarkable, an angel I can't kick out.

♏ ♐

"A question for you," I say to Stanley. "Did a game show host named Mr. Destiny call from 1955 and give you a riddle's answer? Because it was mine to solve."

"Hoo boy," Stanley says. "You're on fire today. Good thing I like you."

"No, really, I want to know."

"Well," he says. "It's not for me to say. Own what happens on your game show. As I said before: The universe gives you 80 percent. The rest is yours."

"You *do* know what I'm talking about," I say triumphantly.

80 percent is flashbulb. 20 percent is fog.

"I always did."

"Why did you tell me the 80/20 rule so long ago?"

"If I hadn't," he says, "we wouldn't be here right now."

♏ ♐

360

STILL LOOKING
FOR THAT BASEBALL

"The game show host said I lost after 20 attempts. But I made my own extra inning. I won, right?"

"Winners let go of winning. In baseball, to win, you push away the ball as hard and fast as you can. Parabolic flight."

Parablic flight. Relating to the parable of baseball.

"The baseball is mass. Make it energy. Big Bang it. Hit it out of the park."

"I did."

"Then accept it's gone. Even now, you're looking for that baseball."

The baseball is the arrow of time. Spatially, a parabola goes up and down, back and forward simultaneously. But a choice doesn't reverse.

And the bat is a clock. Before I swing, the ball's in the future; after I swing, it's in the past.

♏ ♐

Flyleaf — Existentialism

"Life must be understood backwards," Kierkegaard says, in agreement with philosophers before him, but then he adds, trying very hard to sire Existentialism, "it must be lived forwards." I see the wisdom in the living-forwards. I do.

Yet the past is highly informational, and I'm tempted to reach back to piece it together.

♏ ♐

361

I'M NOT
MAKING IT UP

362

EVERYTHING
WILL BE OK

"Stanley: The RAIN and the T. The answer is TRAIN. *You knew this.* Did you talk to the game show host? He's real? I'm not making it up?"

"Can't comment."

"Lev said TRAIN is pronounced the same in English and Spanish," says Aparna, trying to be informative.

"*He* pronounces them the same," Stanley shrugs.

I persist. "It was Wednesday, February 2, 1955. Were you there, too?"

"I was not alive then. My grandparents might have been serving champurrado for Día de la Candelaria and letting my parents make a mess with their little baby hands. I got born eventually." He throws in a bit of eyerollery. "I am mad at you."

"You are?"

"Yes. This is how I do mad. Since 1955. I'm classic."

♏ ♐

I'm disappointed he doesn't remember the game show.

Like Dorothy waking up from Oz, I say: "I thought you were there."

"Don't worry. We're here right now. Everything will be OK."

"How can you be sure?"

"Everything will be the way it is supposed to be. The meaning of us being here right now is the thing that will happen next."

♏ ♐

310

FLASHBULB

WED
17 JUN
2015

363

BACK IN THE
OFFICE

	Runs	Hits	Errors
Red Sox	2	8	1
Braves	5	10	1

Two weeks' medical leave. A prescription I'm supposed to fill. A roundabout explanation. And I'm in the office again. I got more time off for my uneventful hysto last summer than I get now for breaking my brain. The first Monday of the rest of my life, then Tuesday, now Wednesday.

Life goes on. It's the same life. Illuminate, redo: reconstruct the Kennedy assassination from 26 seconds of tape, create the universe from nothing. But you can't and you can't. That's the long and the short of it, the half-distance and full distance of it. Always the same life, yeah? All over again.

I am the canary. They won't let me sing. They won't let me die.

But they pay me a salary.

♏ ♐

Flyleaf — Plagiar-cism

Snake toward an insight about why academic writing is boring.

If someone used your idea and made a million dollars off it, you'd want a cut of that money. Academics are at risk here because they use <u>everyone's</u> ideas. Imagine if academics succeeded in selling copies of their books! Everyone they cited would come around asking for their cut of the profits. Thus, academics write their books in a style that is designed not to sell. While holding income at the zero-dollar level, they can focus on citing sources and absolve themselves of the reuse of ideas.

Cis-World complains, on alternating days, that trans people kick gender to the curb too cavalierly or embrace gender too seriously. If it's raining, we're destroying a beautiful gendered tradition, and we are trans-who-deny-and-wreck-cis. If it's sunny, we're reproducing an oppressive tradition by trotting it over to the copy shop, and we are trans-who-want-to-be-cis—or, <u>plagiar-cists</u>.

Gender is an "imitation for which there is no original," that's what Judith Butler said.[*] We are copies all the way down. That's not possible? Oh, but it is. You've heard the birds sing, sing, sing? Who are they copying, copying, copying?

---

[*] A phrase from the abstract of Judith Butler's 2008 book chapter "Imitation and Gender Insubordination."

The cis guardians are not treasure-hoarding dragons who park their reptilian selves in front of the Gender Room, and the trans bandits are not straw-into-gold-spinning, baby-stealing, riddling rumpelstiltskins. There is nothing inside the Gender Room: not a golden image to be worshipped, not a living baby whose body is perfectly sexually formed. Nothing for anyone to own or take. The Gender Room is empty.

I am a copy with no original, and I am no less the Queen. What do I look like— Xeroxed liver?

The problem plagues any artist or researcher. Too predictable, and you may as well be a photocopy machine. Too original, and no one knows what you are saying, but they are pretty sure you are saying it wrong.

Truth itself depends on plagiar-cism, yes? A common philosophical definition of truth is "correspondence theory," meaning that a statement is true if it matches the world. And what is it <u>to match,</u> if not <u>to be cis</u>? Let's give a better name to "correspondence theory": plagiar-cism theory.

If you do not plagiar-cise in the cis way, you make yourself visible. Visibility attracts enemies. Invisibility has an advantage: If no one can find your book, no one buys it, which means you don't earn money from it, which means no one believes there's any money to shake out of your pockets and no one bothers to sue you for plagiar-cism.

I do not plagiar-cise myself, except insofar as we are all plagiar-cisms of our parents, and perhaps we are plagiar-cisms of other concealed givens and revealed expectations. Do I plagiar-cise myself? Very well, then, I plagiar-cise myself.[*]

♏︎♐︎

_____

[*] After Walt Whitman's "Song of Myself" in *Leaves of Grass.*

FLASHBULB
WED
17 JUN
2015

LUNCH HOUR

FLASHBULB
WED
17 JUN
2015

I SHOULD SWITCH

Aparna, Teddy Ruxpin, and I sit together at lunch. We play "Let's Make a Deal," a game in which you make one guess, your friend gives you one clue, and you revise your guess.

Aparna writes WIN on one index card and draws a horned goat on two others. She puts all three cards face-down. She knows where WIN is, but I don't. I guess and point to one. Aparna flips over a second card she knows is blank. That eliminates one wrong option.

I may either repeat my original guess or try the third card neither of us has yet acknowledged.

Aparna squeezes Teddy Ruxpin's paw.

"Do you want to switch?" Teddy Ruxpin asks.

♏♐

I don't suppose it matters whether I stay with my original guess or switch to the unacknowledged card. 50/50, I suppose.

Aparna explains to me that, in fact, I should switch. I should always switch. It matters. I will win two-thirds of the time if I switch.

If I lose, my consolation prize will be a goat.

We do some repetitions of this game. "Do you want to switch?" Teddy Ruxpin asks in Aparna's recorded voice. "Yes," I always answer.

The strategy works. I win two-thirds of the time when I switch.

The rest of the time, I get a goat. That can't be helped. At least I did everything I could.

♏♐

FLASHBULB

WED
17 JUN
2015

CATCHING UP
ON THE NEWS

FLASHBULB

WED
17 JUN
2015

GOLDEN ESCALATOR

I go back to my desk. Every time I look at my relatively clean inbox, I am surprised anew at the nonexistent emails people didn't bother to send me while I was out, medicated witless in a hospital bed. Zero email is good sympathy.

I am a library shelf organized by Dewey Decimal 366. My pages spill the beans on cults that tried to maintain themselves as secret societies. No one is reading, so my cult is still secret.

I type the name of a news organization into my browser and scan the headlines. China lifted its ban on Star Wars—I didn't know the series had always been banned there—and the original film was screened yesterday at a festival in Shanghai.

♏︎ ♐︎

Skipping to another article, I see a well-known New York con artist descend a golden escalator into the atrium of his own building. This was also yesterday. I'm a little behind on the headlines. But the golden escalator—why is this news? It's boring, even as an extremely short film.

♏︎ ♐︎

314

DON'T THROW SANDWICHES

DOES CHAD REFLECT?

I experience my life chronologically and yet also organized as a Monty Python skit.

I haven't been eating much at all. I'm tired of eating on the train, and I don't want people to throw me sandwiches anymore. I want someone to give me a nickel so I can get off the train and exit through the turnstile. The trauma is the entrance and the epiphany is the exit.

I need real change.

♏ ♐

The doctors are telling me I tried suicide. I am still trying to work out how my suicide mashed up against Chad's. I ran after him, through a train station, yes? Maybe I caught my own reflection in the glass of a big posted advertisement and mistook myself for him, chasing my own reflection as if I were a ghost. *He*, already dead, wouldn't have a reflection. Funny, I've never thought to look whether he reflects. Even though "speculirium" is "madness mirror" in Latin.

He's not dead-dead. A ghost jumps in front of a train, but that doesn't mean he's exterminated. Ghosts reenact their deaths all the time. Chad and I might have to do this again unless I can somehow resolve it.

♏ ♐

FLASHBULB

WED
17 JUN
2015

I THINK
CHAD IS LISTENING

FLASHBULB

WED
17 JUN
2015

VICE PRESIDENTS
ARE SOMETIMES
FRIENDLY

In the afternoon, I hear from Aparna again. She is checking in on me to see if I have psychologically survived the last three hours, and she, too, is razzing me.

"Coffee at this hour?"

"It's decaf." My hands are steady. No jitters.

She closes the door to my office behind her so we have more privacy. "I cannot believe they let you out of the hospital," she says unhelpfully.

I think I'm doing OK. "It was complicated."

"Do you want to talk about it?"

"Can't right now. Chad is listening."

"Again? Are you serious?"

"Sort of."

"I can't solve that for you right now, so can you hold it together?"

"I didn't ask you to solve it for me."

♏ ♐

One of the vice presidents stops by, waving at us through the window at the side of the door. Aparna opens the door and lets her in my office.

She must have been on a cruise to the Bahamas, given how refreshed she looks. She's moving through the hallway like she's still dancing the rumba under the stars next to a table with a half-ton of shrimp cocktail. That vacation effect won't last the day. The Beach Boys' "Kokomo" is three minutes long, and you wouldn't want to listen to it longer than that, and also Kokomo doesn't even exist. There is no place called Kokomo off the Florida Keys. Next thing you know, the vice presidents will be asking to go to Isla Nublar.

♏ ♐

I CAN'T EVEN

What is the vacation we believe we are taking when we go "away," whether to a place that exists or does not exist? How to diagnose it? To know that transit even as we make it?

"I just returned from Florida!" she announces.

I called it.

The shrimp were placed head to tail in pairs so they formed infinity symbols. I can see it in my mind.

The vice president, who hasn't yet heard that I was out for a medical, looks me up and down. "Did you lose weight?"

I put my palm up. "I can't even."

This is not a good way for me to interact with vice presidents, especially because, as I remember too late—

♏ ♐

Flyleaf — What Transsexuals Can Do

A transsexual is never supposed to say "I can't." True when addressing a vice president who is a man. Also likely true when addressing a vice president who is a woman. True even when they don't know I am a transsexual, because, on some level, they do know. I'm perceived as cisgender and also, somehow, even when I haven't divulged, as transgender. Other people stand outside the binary of their own knowledge about me.

Some assume "a transsexual" must obey gender stereotypes, but I challenge them to find the binary lockdown in any life named after its own boundary testing. "Trans" means bicycle-riding the perimeter, always crossing, always crossing again.

Things transsexuals can do: Sometimes my stories have two climaxes and still aren't over. Someone will say a story, on principle, can't do this—that the transsexual can't survive an ice cream parlor with a would-be gunman and also survive a reenacted suicide with someone who's already dead. I say it can. I can do two things. This is a comfortable "I can." Maybe I'm born with it. Maybe it's luck. Or the help of a friend. Chances are, I picked a wrong door to begin with, but Aparna gives me a clue and Teddy Ruxpin asks, "Do you want to switch?" I say "yes," and my chances have greatly improved.

One door lets us out. We're nowhere near the exit, I'd thought, imagining the sentence with an extra "r." Should've been: We know we're near the exit. I have arrived at the third door, and I have come through.

♏ ♐

FLASHBULB

WED
17 JUN
2015

373

I AM BUSY

"We'll let you have some space," Aparna says, adding for the vice president's benefit: "Lev is really busy right now."

I leave the office a little early for my own self-preservation.

The other part of the pact with myself, for kindness, is going to Copley to spend a rare weekday evening in the archive. With only an hour before closing, I thumb through Chad's papers.

The death certificate told me where he died. The game show told me how he died. I saw him die. I'm clear about the death.

I am exhausted.

I won't be working on *The Nature of Time* today. Today, with new ferocity, I want something else from his archive. I want to know how to get rid of him permanently.

♏ ♐

Flyleaf — Chad's Personal Journal

These are the original pages of his handwritten personal journal. There aren't any copies. I'm close to the fact of the matter, to the source, to his hand, to his truth. But will his truth unveil itself to me?

If he were a golem, I'd know what to do. A golem is an imaginary robot in ancient Jewish speculative tradition. According to the Sefer Yetzirah, a person may animate the golem by writing the letters alef-mem-tav on its forehead, spelling "emet," truth. To stop it, you squeeze its paw, no, I mean, you delete the alef so the remaining letters spell "met," death. To do something extra special with it, I imagine you could rewrite the alef, this time at the end, so it says "meta"—

♏ ♐

318

FLASHBULB
WED
17 JUN
2015

374

LAST PLACE I LOOK

FLASHBULB
WED
17 JUN
2015

375

VERY META

I'm not looking for any more information about Chad except the information that will make him go away. At the bottom of one box of papers, I find something I've never noticed before. A personal journal. His.

Why is the thing I most want always in the last place I look? I know, I know, I know—because once I find it, I stop looking. But still. How maddening. Where has this been all my life?

♏ ♐

He is practicing writing his name. *Charlotte. Char.* A hundred iterations to evolve the "r" to something that could be read as a malformed "d." *Chad.* He forged bad handwriting so others would read his name differently. This is how he changed his documents, and I am so lucky he did, or else his death certificate would be under a different name and I wouldn't have found it.

In one line of this journal, he mentions he had to wear tight shirts covered by loose jackets so he is not *found out*. He is like me. This is very meta. And I can tell they did something to hurt him. The cis-tem.

♏ ♐

Flyleaf — Epcistemology and Cistalgia

"Let's Make a Deal"

Three closed doors, one prize behind them. You name a door; it has a one-in-three chance of being correct. From the other two doors, your friend (who sees behind them) eliminates a non-winning option.

She will never eliminate the winning door, because she is your friend.

Do you keep your door? No, because it had only a one-in-three chance to begin with. Two-in-three, the prize is somewhere else. Your friend looks at the other two doors and discards a non-winner. So, two out of three times, it's not the door you originally picked; it's the other. You switch.

You can learn to trust your friend, which is how you make a friend.

You can change what door you want.

Epcistemology

The Greek epistēmē, "knowledge," gives us our word epistemology, "theory of knowledge": the examination of what we know, how we know it, how we know we know it. This, in turn, gives me—wait for it!—epcistemology, the examination of what we know from living adjacently to the cisgender system. And what we learn from others' perpetual interrogation about how we know ourselves in a way other than cis.

Marshmallow Test

The marshmallow test is an investment psychology experiment in which a child is offered candy. The objective is to find out whether the child grabs one marshmallow immediately or holds out for the promise of two marshmallows in the future.

Cisgender gatekeepers pose versions of this question to transgender people, asking if we'd rather have our gender now or later, if our gender tastes better or worse than a marshmallow, if we're sure we know what a marshmallow is, and so on.

My question about the marshmallow test is why the cisgender person is holding a transgender marshmallow.

On Books

Words are nonfiction when they correspond to an external set of facts; fiction, when they diverge from given realities and create their own internal systems; and metafiction, when the fictional people become aware of what they are doing. Metafiction is like lucid dreaming: the dreamer realizes they can make any choice and cannot die, and so the dreamer takes the reins of the dream rather than merely allowing the dream to happen, or at least they make an active choice to enjoy it passively. Regarding literature that may conform or nonconform to reality, a more interesting question is whether the inside of the book is conscious of its own choices.

320

On Masculine and Feminine

You may be <u>gender conforming</u> with respect to an external set of expectations, and in other respects you may be <u>gender nonconforming</u> and follow your bliss, and if you are <u>metagender</u> then you are conscious of your own operating system. Metagender isn't aligned with the cisgender/transgender distinction. Nor is it the same as claiming you were "born this way" or you "chose this way." This is, rather, about finding yourself presented with some buttons to push. Each of us is born unique; your buttons are not the same as someone else's; your world-of-ideas is not the same as someone else's; thus your consciousness is not the same as someone else's. This is the meta-level of your gender.

Suspicion

Someone is suspicious of your gender and says "prove it" or "show me." You have nothing to point to because your gender may not be a fact in the world at all, and even if it is a fact in the world (like an identity card in your pocket) you probably weren't talking about your gender on the level of "fact"; more likely, you were exploring the vastly more interesting question of how you gained and continue to develop self-consciousness. You can't show anything to someone who has yet to knock on your door.

Legex Sigil

When you're born, adults look at you, state their belief about whether you're male or female, write it on your birth certificate, and make you live in that gender. They are observing your sex and assigning your gender. The column on the paper might be labeled "sex" or "gender." The marker is "M/F," so in English it looks like it refers to <u>legal sex</u> ("male/female"), and in Spanish it looks like it refers to <u>legal gender</u> ("masculino/femenino"), but it might not mean anything legally depending on where you are, and the letter-marker might not be an exact stand-in for whatever word it originally drew from—and so it might mean, today, something else.

You can change your marker. Sometimes they make you base it on your body, and sometimes they let it be a personal choice. That doesn't help you figure out whether they meant <u>legal sex</u> or <u>legal gender</u> to begin with, and whether the meaning of the marker changes when you change the marker. You assert or prove yourself, and gender becomes sex or sex becomes gender.

It's less complicated if you're cis. I mean, if you don't want to change your marker anyway nor need to know what it means. The letter-marker might invoke a totally different concept, like a <u>legex</u>, which means sort-of-legal sort-of-gender sort-of-sex. Cis people use this concept all the time, although I just made up the word for it.

If you want to sound like an adept at chaos magic, call it not a "marker" but a "sigil."

And if your legex sigil is on your death certificate? Does it represent your legex at the time of your death? Is that your final answer?

Gex

Apart from its legal status, your gender/sex is gex. Your body is how you understand it, how others perceive it, and also what it physically is, and your body-in-the-world can change, and as you travel your life path you can perform or belong to any gender. On your path, you can—and also cannot—disregard your body, hence the conceptual unity of gex. I don't know how many gexes there are because only the cis ones have legal sigils.

Bittersweet

The Greek nóstos, "homecoming," and álgos, "ache," gives us nostalgia, "longing for the past." Sometimes we wish to go back, and sometimes we are content just to remember it. Bittersweet. The past is not reconstructible, but it lives on through us, if not in discrete memories then in feelings, until the day we stop feeling. Some types of nostalgia, though, are false. They are pernicious myths that people tell to rationalize power dynamics. Someone claims to be in pain; they are in pain because someone else

is thriving; it is a zero-sum game, and they want us to go back to the way things supposedly once were, when they were winning and the other person was losing, which they claim is the proper natural equilibrium.

Cistalgia

Cistalgia, you know: their pain of becoming aware that they are cis. Their nostalgia for the time when they didn't know. They didn't realize they were cisgender before they had to power-share an een-teenth of their ideaspace with transgender people. When a cis person first learns the word "cis," they may sense an implicit challenge to cispower. Some say the word "cis" lands as a near-insult to their ears. I, too, am capable of feeling pain, and maybe it also hurts to be cis, they say, so why is there no word for the pain of being cis? Ah, thank you for the suggestion. I have made this word.

Fuses Blown

Cistalgia: The pain of realizing that the status of cisgender people is being observed, deconstructed, or dismantled and that you can never unlearn the lessons that are blowing your mind's fuses right now. You will never again be cis unknowingly. Uncons-cis-ness is not possible for you.

Etymologically there's no T in cistalgia, but the T is a throwback to nostalgia, and a throwback to nostalgia is very meta.

322

Ch'ixi

The Aymara word "ch'ixi" refers to "un color producto de la yuxtaposición, en pequeños puntos o manchas, de dos colores opuestos o contrastados: el blanco y el negro, el rojo y el verde," explains Silvia Rivera Cusicanqui. The juxtaposition of dots of opposing colors, like white and black, like red and green, produces another color. It's not a full mix, not an equilibrium. This is the Aymara idea of something that simultaneously is and isn't—"la idea aymara de algo que es y no es a la vez, es decir, a la lógica del tercero incluido"—according to the logic of the included middle.

Coincidentia oppositorum

Nicholas of Cusa saw how opposites come together in the idea of a supreme being. He called it "coincidentia oppositorum." Mircea Eliade used the term to describe mythic narratives that let us have it both ways: the boss is "terrible and gentle," and meanwhile we are ourselves and each other, inside and outside the world, at the end and at the beginning, later and now.

Ball of Yarn

"While I'm at it," Joshua Cohen mused in *The Book of Numbers*, "what's the difference between *raveling* and *unraveling*?"

Enantiodromia

An extreme flips to become its opposite.

For thousands of years, since the I Ching, since Heraclitus, we have known it, we have said so, we have not known it, we have not said so.

♏ ♐

FOG — THE VIOLENCE HAPPENS AGAIN

Chad is banging his cold ghost head against the window. His forehead is grayish, the skin sloughing off. He wants me to know more. I am exhausted by knowing things. Tired of practicing how to develop solutions to nonexistent problems. He's transgender like me, and maybe that explains why we've been following each other, but this is too much closeness. I'm ready to be rid of him.

Before I fall asleep, the news reports another mass shooting. During late evening Bible study. Charleston, South Carolina. The shooter was racist. Murdered lots of people and fled the church. Thousands of miles away in the middle of the night, I ask myself why I've wasted so much time looking at boxes of papers in the archive.

Definitionally, there's always a better use for our time. We may see it in hindsight.

How could I have played this year differently? I reported a threat, it was no-actioned, and the guy I reported did nothing.

How do we ever know what to do?

♏ ♐

FOG — IN THERAPY

"Because they're delusions," I tell my therapist. "The fantasy world does not serve me anymore."

"What's the fantasy?" she asks.

"That ghosts exist," I say. "That they talk to me. That they have purposes. And so on."

"What do you want for yourself instead?"

"I want to know things that are real."

"Your desire presumes certain facts." She taps her pen on her notepad. "That there is anything real. That what is real can be known by someone, and that you are someone who can know it. That this knowledge will mean something to you. That you want to know, or ought to want to know, what is real."

"I do want to know," I answer hastily.

She tries again. "All of that is assumed. And that's the fantasy. The belief that there is a knowable reality is itself a fantasy."[*]

"What kind of reality is fantasy? A reality outside my head?"

"Outside or inside. Either kind. A reality you don't control, or a reality you wholly create."

"A reality I invented...like 'transgender'?"

"And cisgender. The concepts each have their own reality, but when you put them together, they mutually annihilate. Transgender-and-cisgender. *Poof.*"

"I do not see it."

"The reality-construct handed to us is that females are women and males are men. Some people flip that around, so that gives us 'transgender'—the people who *unmatch* gender from sex. Then we must create the word 'cisgender' for the previously nameless framework—the people whose gender *does match* their sex. Now that both ways have a name, we can say they are both valid ways of being."

"Right, both are valid. So how do the concepts annihilate each other?"

"Because saying that transgender people *unmatch* gender and sex implies that they've crossed a boundary, are deviant, and therefore have gotten the *wrong answer*. If we don't like that implication, and if instead

---

[*] Some of the therapist's ideas are adapted from the introduction of Steven Connor's *The Madness of Knowledge: On Wisdom, Ignorance and Fantasies of Knowing* (2019). Connor also highlighted the quote from Lord Byron's "Don Juan" which appeared in Lev's earlier therapy session. "This tape will self-destruct in five seconds" is a recurring line from the 1966 series "Mission: Impossible." Freud used the term "screen memories" as the title of an 1899 paper. Hans Vaihinger referred to "noble delusions" in *The Philosophy of 'As if'* (1911). In Chapter 20, he says "All the nobler aspects of our life are based upon fictions...the higher aspects of life are based upon noble delusions" ("Unser ganzes höheres Leben beruht auf Fiktionen...das höhere Leben beruht auf edelen Täuschungen").

we'd like to say there's no such thing as deviance, then we also have to say there's no such thing as normalcy. When we say that being transgender is—beyond being an acceptable workaround—as *equally normal and correct* as being cisgender, we let go of the concept of *matching* gender and sex. Gender and sex have no 'correct' configuration and don't need to be matched. This means we also have to let go of the ideas of *transgender* and *cisgender*."

"How can we do transgender liberation if we don't have the concept *transgender*?"

"A liberating concept is self-annihilating. It's the key, not the endpoint."

"I don't under—"

"This tape will self-destruct in five seconds."

I sit back and listen.

She goes on. "A person of any sex can have any gender. Nothing needs to be matched, nothing *can* be matched, and that's why no way is better than any other. At the point where the system fully acknowledges this reality: Trans people aren't trans. Cis people aren't cis. And I don't mean that, you should know, in the way a cis person with a trans-eraser would say it." She wiggles her thumb and forefinger as if holding a pencil eraser. "I mean, rather, that we are talking about whose behavior has straddled or crossed a fence, and indeed we've straddled and we've crossed, but the fence does not exist. We cross it to prove it does not exist."

A reality you wholly create.

"I think I see," I say. This would also account for the difficulty in imposing categories on a person whose traits you don't know or can't neatly describe. Imposing categories on a person who is not yourself is not a wonderful intellectual pastime anyway, and that other person is probably happier if you stop. "The answer," I say, "isn't out there to be found. We could just stop trying to match words to words, stuff to stuff, words to stuff."

"Yes. All of it is a story. A story you are telling yourself about reality and how it works."

The red woven tapestry hanging on the wall behind her has a sun. This time, I'm sure of it. No longer is the sun white, as I remember it from last time, but brilliant gold. The sun seems to rest atop her head, and two curved spikes emerge from the landscape of the tapestry, under the sun. The way they are positioned, it appears my therapist is growing cow horns. She is Isis: daughter of earth and sky, sister-wife of the underworld, mother of sovereignty and war, survivor of beheading.

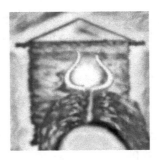

"But people exist."

"Yes."

"And we have stable characters."

"Really?"

"Essential characters, I mean. Plato would say so."

"Really?"

"I mean, I hate to think of myself as nothing more than a collection of feelings and actions that are Play-Dohed into the impression of an identity. That would make me little more than a fictional character."

"Noted."

"People have biological reality, and we could die."

"Fear of mortality is a story you are telling yourself."

"Someone could kill me. That would be real."

"They would be ending your fantasy."

"But *they* would still be alive. *They* remain real."

"They would be controlling their own fantasy that has you in it."

I try to imagine where she's coming from. "As a therapist, you must hear lots of stories."

"Yes. Lots of autobiography."

And those stories are likely true.

I think to myself: "Todo lo que no es autobiografía es plagio," said Pío Baroja. *Apart from autobiography, everything is a plagiarism.*[*]

"Do you think people are making it all up?" I ask.

She shrugs. "Fiction or nonfiction. Wave or particle. There is no truth of the matter until we observe it. No story is true or false until it is spoken and heard. Its truth-value is in how it arises and persists as a story. Nothing underlies it."

I fight back: "I think I am real. I think we are all real."

"People are, yes. But our reality-stories aren't."

I shift in my seat. "My father's cousins died in the gas chambers."

"I know."

"But I never told you."

"I know."

"It happened, you know."

"Yes. And your story about it is yours."

"I don't have a story about it." I am irritated.

"If you did, it would be a fantasy story."

"Is it like that for everyone?"

"Yes. But mostly for you."

"Why me?"

"Lev. Sit down."

---

[*] Pío Baroja's comment that "todo lo que no es autobiografía es plagio" was used as the epigraph to Manuel Francisco Reina's *El plagio como una de las bellas artes* (Ediciones B, 2012). I cannot tell you any more precisely where the Baroja comment came from because, while Reina's book has a bibliography, Baroja isn't included in it. Todo es plagio.

"No, why me? What villains in what bunker or boardroom in outer space are trying to wreck my life? Who is behind this?"

"You, mostly. You're telling your own story most of the time."

"Who else is fucking with me? Who writes this crap?"

"Sit down."

I sit. "How do I get the real answer?"

"You don't. It can't be gotten. If the truth is a fact that exists outside you, there's no way for you to get it. You can't wrap your arms around it or eat it. Getting it wouldn't change it. It's real. So there's no need for you to get it anyway. And if the truth is something private you form inside you, then all that matters to others is what you do in the world. You can posture at how much you're 'getting,' but there's never any truth to be 'gotten' because you are making it up. Yes?"

"Yes," I nod.

"Everything we think we know about reality is actually a fantasy."

"When I say things like that, people sneer at me and call me a Millennial."

"They're factually wrong about you. No one who refers to Holocaust victims as their 'father's cousins' is a Millennial. They were looking for the word 'relativist.' And, whatever you are, it doesn't change the reality of whether reality-beliefs are fantasies."

"I might have some theories about this."

"Systematizing the fantasy doesn't make it non-fantasy. You're only adjusting the swingset on your knowledge playground."

"What do I do?"

"Use your power. Use your power to let go and submit to the storm of come-what-may, or use your power to choose what comes. That's all knowledge is. Your knowledge is your attitude, what you want to exist, what you are prepared to do about it, and the choice you ultimately make. The rest is fantasy."

I am silent. Hans Vaihinger wrote that virtues are founded on noble delusions (edelen Täuschungen). I was born on the Scorpio–Sagittarius cusp. That is my mazel, the Yiddish word for Zodiac sign, for luck, for the way that I am. I take Sagittarius. Forward-looking. Since the Zodiac is fantasy anyway.

"If," she says, "you want to talk about how you *feel* about it, that's what I'm here for."

I am silent for a few more moments.

"But if you want to identify what parts of your story are *real* only so you can ignore them and talk about the *unreal* parts instead, we'll be sitting here forever."

"What am I supposed to be learning from my story?" I ask.

"Your story is a *story*. You can't ever know the truth about what pops up there. But you can know *that* your story is a story. That is very important."

I stare at the wall as if, by doing so, I can manifest the ghost who tampers with my story. "How do I figure that out?"

"As you tell your story more proactively, you'll learn that everything you think you know—the mountain of it—is, more fully and correctly perceived, an ungettable truth, either because your 'getting' of the mountain can't possibly affect the mountain or else because the mountain isn't there to be gotten. Anything worth knowing in the sense of it being enduring and unmovable is too big to fit in your hands. Anything that fits in your hands is ephemeral, crushable, and not a proper object of knowledge."

"OK."

"Knowledge has no object. Knowledge only ever really knows itself. Knowledge tells stories about itself. Trans-narratives and so on."

"Does that matter?" I am not sure.

"What matters is your awareness of how you tell your story. Your story is the seed that sprouts your awareness that you are telling a story. Your story is everything you know."

"That's a lot."

"Your story," she smiles, "is also everything I know about you."

"Right." The son of Isis is Horus; he has the head of a falcon and sees everything from a distance. Outside the purview of the eye of Horus, people know me from how I am described.

"So I want you to start telling your story more consciously."

"OK."

"I still want you," my therapist says, "to tell me about the ghosts and the goddesses. Just a little bit. Because you've got a big system there. The male ghosts and the female goddesses."

"Yeah."

"It's a thorough and unforgiving binary. What are you saying about gender there?"

"I guess that people always wanted me to be an instantiation of The Woman and I never knew what that was. It was as though Womanhood was supposed to be some obvious and singular thing—a 'collective soul,' if that makes sense—but I saw different ways to be a woman and I didn't know which way was the 'right' way."

"Why did they want you to be a woman?"

"Well, you know—" I search. "The binary. They believe a person has to be either a woman or a man."

"Why?"

I raise one eyebrow to help myself think.

"So people can reproduce, I guess. Because without females and males, no babies. It matters to the species, to civilization, to time. Evolution and stuff like that."

"And how are babies made?" She smiles.

I pause until I see her point. "Sometimes we are separate for a long time, and what really matters is the moment we come together, because that's the moment we create something new."

She nods. "The merge."

"The merge. The copy," I add. "Remixing and copying. The ability to swirl colors together is at least as important as the ability to keep the colors in separate paint pots."

"Yes. In fact, the way that *you* remix and copy," she says, "is also part of civilization, every bit as much as the way that other people do it. You don't need to be only-female or only-male to have powers of generation." She shuts off the humidifier. "How did people react when you stopped trying to be a woman?"

"They were mad. As though I'd given up some connection with the divine, my share in heaven."

She nods. "So the male ghosts—that's your way of coping with your fear of mortality? Or your fear of lost immortality? Is that right?"

"Yes. There aren't any gods, and there's no One True Goddess either. There are infinite goddesses who maybe aren't individual personalities but all manifest the same cosmic being, and then there are man-ghosts who shuffle around, not beatifically, but driven by their sad little egos."

"At least the men are immortal, right?"

I nod. At least some men have an afterlife for at least some amount of time.

"Where did Chad come from?"

I'm taken aback. I don't know the answer to this riddle.

"Immortal," she shrugs. "He came from somewhere, but he goes on forever. That's how you are working out your fear of death. It's terror management. This is not just about a gender binary. There are some extra-binary, unrelated problems in there."

"I'm not sure if I *can* die. I could wander forever as a ghost."

"Well, that is another question."

"We didn't just analyze away my gender, did we? I'm worried I won't be allowed to be who I am."

"You're still a man, by the power of trans. How would I undo that? Undo *you*?"

"I don't know."

"So why are you worried about it? Cut it out. We can't undo ourselves in ways we were never made. The mountain isn't there to be gotten. It's there until you grasp at it. Knowledge has no object. It only tells stories about itself. We said this. Let's work on telling your story more consciously. When you pay attention to your story, what do you see?"

I think. "Stories inside of stories inside of stories. Interlocking and fertile geometries."

"And you notice that they're *stories*, right?"

"...yeah. They're stories."

329

"What genre?"

I ponder. People tend to expect stories to conform. If they conform to reality, they're nonfiction. Even fiction conforms to genres: mystery, romance, gothic, space operas. Sometimes stories don't conform to anything, and we don't know where to shelve them or find them in the library. But our familiarity or lack thereof—our sense of whether the stories are doing what they are supposed to do—doesn't make them any more or less *story*.

"Trans-genre," I answer.

"Is that a genre or a resistance of genre?"

Right then, it hits me. What she said a few minutes ago: *Trans people aren't trans. Cis people aren't cis.*

My eyes go wide. "JFK is trans," I say.

"Yes," she says, louder than I.

"And I'm cis!"

"You always have been. 'Ya cis.' Yes. Already cis."

"Nothing is what it seems."

"What is reality?" she prompts me.

"A fantasy."

"Reality is—"

"—what I make of it, and any limits on that statement are also what I make of them."[*]

"When you notice that, what do you want to do?"

"I guess I want to—back up somehow. To be out of the story at least sometimes. To get real stuff done."

"Yes. Do you know how you back out of the story?"

"No."

"Jumping in front of a train is not the answer."

"Seems not."

"You've got screen memories. All memories screen out the past, but some do it more than others. Misremembering blocks the truth."

"But there is no truth?"

"Go out the back door and find out. Slide the screen, and exit. You tell me what's out there."

"Oh."

"You have to actually do the work. Just start doing it. When the seed sprouts, the husk will fall away on its own."

"I'm trying."

---

[*] According to Erik Davis: "John Lilly, an influential mind scientist and psychonaut supreme, dubbed this process 'metaprogramming,' which he boiled down into a widely-cited psychedelic and esoteric protocol: 'In the province of the mind, what one believes to be true is true or becomes true, within certain limits to be found experientially and experimentally. These limits are further beliefs to be transcended.'"
Erik Davis. *High Weirdness: Drugs, Esoterica, and Visionary Experience in the Seventies.* London: Strange Attractor Press, 2019, Chapter 0.0.0: "Welcome to the Weird," quoting John Lilly, *Programming and Metaprogramming in the Human Biocomputer.* New York: Julian Press, 1972. p. 57.

"Try harder."

"At what?"

"At something other than systematizing your fantasies. Something other than kaleidoscoping the world into fragments that look like they fit together but are actually cherry-picked scenes."

There is no pure "trans" or "cis." The Earth's ecosystems are trans-and-cis. Monarchs and fireflies in the linden trees are trans-and-cis. Jellies in the ocean are trans-and-cis. The atmosphere is trans-and-cis. Everyone who has ever lived and ever will live is trans-and-cis, forever and ever.

"You mean, I have to be in the world."

"Yes. I want you to consciously tell a story about yourself that is also about the world. Your father's cousins would want you to."

"This is going to take some effort."

"Do good work."

"I will," I say, noting that our hour is up. The sun has risen high in the cattle horns. It is like an eye. *Eye-cis.*

"Lev," she says.

"What?"

"I'm trans."

♏ ♐

Flyleaf — Always Over My Shoulder

<u>Transgender Day of Remembrance</u>

Chad died on May 29, 1900. I'd already reached the limit of my questions and lost the game show. Then, I failed to save Chad, and I witnessed his death, which handed me an Answer 21: the truth. Still, six months later, he isn't really dead. Neither of us is.

November 20 is the annual Transgender Day of Remembrance when we remember those we have lost to violence and suicide. I don't need a special day to remember Chad, though. He is always over my shoulder. This is a stalemate.

<u>Do I Want to Find Out the Truth?</u>

I've never wanted to videorecord him.

Maybe the ghost has always been narrated by me talking to myself. Do I want to find out the truth? How should a person-interacting-with-a-ghost be cast in a movie: as one actor because the ghost isn't real, or as two actors because he is?

If the ghost is real, does he influence me for good or bad? Or does he remake me in his image?

What if the ghost is real but physically stuck inside the person?

What if the person and ghost are two hemispheres of the same brain, not always collaborating, often at cross purposes?

If the ghost has attained a half-reality, like a parasite, I'll have to kill myself to kill him. Parasites definitely have opinions about their own survival. Chad must be ready to die if he wanted me to die too at the Park Street station. But then will I come back and become a parasite on someone else?

Likewise, if I'm the only one of us who has any reality, I'll have to kill myself to kill off my thoughts. When I do that, I won't reappear as a ghost since, in this scenario, ghosts aren't real. There is only life.

We Pull It From Our Guts

Here's Kierkegaard's religious version of this question: Why does the boss in the Garden of Eden bother telling Adam a bunch of stuff he can't yet understand? If the boss doesn't act prudently in that regard, that's an "imperfection in the story."

Kierkegaard's solution: "We need simply assume that Adam talked to himself." Adam could give himself information and instructions if he already sort of had the knowledge he sought. That's how we social introverts acquire knowledge, anyway; we pull it from our own guts, and we are suspicious when the boss pokes his own finger at our bellies. For Kierkegaard, himself an extravagant introvert, this is a more perfect story.

ℳ ✗

FOG — VITAL RECORDS OFFICE

Now I know and accept that there is a formula to kill Chad. And there is no T in the name of this method.

No game show host gives me airtime for another question, and he may not have another answer for me. It's time for me to provide my own solution. I have to make the time for myself. I have to act.

It's a Friday in November. I leave the office early while the sun is still up. I park in Brookline near the end of the D line, the Reservoir station, in a million-dollar spot I discovered years ago and will never, ever tell anyone about. My phone battery is dead, so to check the time, I stroll under the bridge and peer at the station's countdown clock: "North Sta 2 min 3:43." So. The Green Line finally got its countdown clock. The D branch, anyway. Now we know exactly when the train is coming. Now we can calculate that it's expected to come at a quarter to four.

I continue walking toward Beacon Street.

Under the Citizen Video Services sign, the glass door opens automatically. The building is heated. There is thin, gray wall-to-wall carpeting. Oldies music pipes in: Johnny Nash singing "I Can See Clearly Now."

My feet feel leaden. I look up at the signs suspended from the ceiling and follow the one for VITAL RECORDS. As I do, I see the letters morph and rearrange—

VITAMINS. I am in Aisle 5. Of the pharmacy.

Thought is a burden, a bureaucracy, a barrier, a bear. What if I had less of it? What if I used another part of my "I" to subvert my concept of who "I" am?

The name of this murder method has an I in it. A bit like suicide, but more targeted.

Where did Chad come from? my therapist asked, last time I saw her. I still don't know. But it's time for him to leave. The past goes away so the future can become. He's already dead, so it doesn't feel like violence, but it feels more active than "letting go."

It feels like competition for a small parking space. The space is my mind. I am the space.

Chad is the glamour and the pishogue. How I appear and how I perceive. Outside and inside. What's on the TV and who's watching. Lo evidente y el televidente.

The thing that has to die is me, and the thing that has to live is me.

"Mm-hm-mmph," the intercom blares, mangling the transmission of an employee's name, "please come to the pharmacy. A customer is waiting."

I walk up to the pharmacist's window. No other customer is waiting in line. Perhaps they were anticipating me. That is the sort of thing that happens to me now and then.

♏ ♐

FLASHBULB

FRI
20 NOV
2015

376

FILLING
MY PRESCRIPTIONS

FLASHBULB

FRI
20 NOV
2015

377

CHAD'S FACE
REFLECTS

"I'm ready to fill that prescription now," I tell the pharmacist, whose name I suppose is Mm-hm-mmph. Her plastic badge says "J. Kennedy."

"Testosterone?" She evidently knows me somehow.

"No. I mean, yes, I want the testosterone prescription, but also the other prescription."

She gives me one little white paper bag for the injectable hormone, another bag for the psychiatric pill. I buy a bottle of water too.

"$87.05."

I hand over five $20 bills.

"You wouldn't happen to have the nickel?"

"I'm sorry, I—" I feel my pocket and come up with a hit. "Oh, here's one."

An even $13 change.

As I step out of the automatic door, I hear the drugstore intercom announce: "Elvis has left the building."

♏ ♐

The Reservoir station's countdown clock says 3:50. They don't tell you when sunset is. You just have to know. It'll be at 4:18.

Sitting behind the wheel, I put the key in the ignition. Soul Asylum sings "Runaway Train."

I put the bag with the testosterone on the empty passenger seat. I put the other bag containing the pills on my lap, tear it open, pop open the blister pack, uncap the water.

I look up and see Chad's face in the rearview mirror.

Well, that settles that; he *does* reflect.

It's the same look he gave me before he jumped in front of the train—sad, distrustful, angry, beckoning. He reaches out his hand, extends his index finger, points at the passenger seat.

♏ ♐

FOG — WHAT CHAD WANTS

Is that what he wanted all this time? Liquid maleness? Physicality? A way to become?

He didn't even know what to call it. He held out for the magic until 1900, but the hormone wasn't synthesized in his lifetime. Even if he'd lasted to see the 20th century, there would have been decades to go until he could have asked a doctor to give it to him. He would have been elderly by then, and they would have told him "no."

They would not have let him be "transsexual" within the limits of their imaginations. They define and determine the term "transsexual," but they themselves are defined and determined. *Try knowing your own damn self.*

If Chad had known the words, he might have believed that "transsexual," or some kind of "trans," described him. He might have had his own definition of his kind of trans and what it meant to want it or to be it, even if no one opened the door to let him achieve their definition of it. But he didn't have these words.

People want stuff, and if they get it, it may or may not ultimately satisfy some other adjacent or underlying desire, insofar as all desires, when we peer into them, are about themselves on the *recto* and about something else on the *verso*. A child's dodecahedron of "Why?" I can't explain what it is to want something.

Nor can I explain why ghosts persist for years and then one day disappear.

All I know is: Testosterone is what Chad wants.

He wants my vial.

I empathize.

But all this time I thought he really wanted to be friends with me.

♏ ♐

FRI
20 NOV
2015

I SAY NO TO CHAD

That explains why he hasn't been speaking to me aloud. He is embarrassed that his voice is still high. I understand.

And I understand that he's fixated on getting his dose. But, look—friendship has got to be about more than that. Is this all I'm good for—scoring controlled substances?

"No," I say firmly, as if to a dog. I feel bad that I am treating another transgender man so unsympathetically, but I have to set limits here, or else the train runs me over.

I am sorry for his loss, but this testosterone injection is mine. I am alive.

"No T for you," I tell him.

♏ ♐

FOG — FALLING AWAKE

Sunday will be my birthday. Thirty-five times I will have gone around the sun. That is an auspicious number. That's how many times you rotate the crank of the Zoomatic camera that Abraham Zapruder used to shoot his famous film. Thirty-five rotations will spool about 15 feet of double 8mm film, giving you 73 seconds of your future movie. If you don't make the tape you want, you'll have to load new film and crank the camera again.*

On Simchat Torah, at the end of a year of Torah readings reproduced by all the voices, you unwind and rewind the scroll back to the beginning. I think I'm a month late.

The radio plays "Falling Awake" by Gary Jules.

Your call, Chad mouths silently at me in the rearview mirror.

It's a wakeup call. We say we've had one because this statement pleases others. Sometimes we're not lying: We've been called, and we are awake.

My solitariness is learned behavior. The world has always been trying to kill me, and I've always tried to handle it alone. If I'd gone to tonight's vigil of remembrance, I'd be hearing other people's stories. I'd be thinking about real problems, not imaginary ones. But I've given no solidarity and thus I participate in none. There is none in my corner for me to feel.

I make the call.

AN END TO CHAD

FLASHBULB

FRI
20 NOV
2015

Now I act. I swallow my psych dose.

PILLS. One way for one of us to die.

A murder that is not a murder but more of an emptying.

If there's a trans-sexor in the neighborhood, I can be my own exor-cis.†

Chad vanishes.

Charmed.

---

* See *Twenty-Six Seconds* by Alexandra Zapruder.
† From the unreleased sequels to *Ghostbusters* and *The Exorcist*.

EPISODE 11

I EXIT

EVERYTHING
IS FINE

SHOTGUN

Aparna calls. She wants to drive to the beach.

I invite Stanley too. He warns me he hasn't rolled out of bed.

"I'm not showering for you either," I answer him brusquely. "We're going swimming…Why are you asking me about my meds? No, no, I'm not hallucinating today. Stop it. You do not need to control my wellness. I am self-managing. Everything is fine."

It's been over a year since my incident with the train. Everything's fine, except when the pill doesn't latch on. A little strange in my head, but I might achieve a new normal. I can write out my feelings, or notice them and let them go. The evanescent beauty of a deleted tweet.

♏ ♐

I pick up Aparna first, so she rides shotgun, and then I pick up Stanley, who throws his folding chairs in the trunk and rides in the back seat.

On the highway, everyone's wheels spin, catch sunlight, head beachward. The wind buffets through the slits in our four windows, and we almost take flight.

We will spread the beach blanket, sand crystals in its terrycloth loops. We will start over. We will begin again with the holy grail of what can never be recovered.

♏ ♐

382

METAFICTION

383

I AM NOT MAD
AT MY FRIENDS

Patricia Waugh described a certain kind of literature that "self-consciously and systematically draws attention to its status as an artifact." It's the only kind of knowledge I ever get close to.

Metafiction. Fiction that drives off the—

No. Let me answer in another way that doesn't prompt that sort of joke. Metafiction drives off "the contemporary writer's dialogue with literary predecessors," as Madelyn Jablon explained.

Fiction that drives off the *meta*. Wait until I tell Stanley there is a word for writing a novel about the transmasculine penis. I will wait until Aparna isn't in front of us.

♏ ♐

I start today's conversation more simply.

"Hotter every day, yeah?"

"At least they got the Paris climate accords signed," Stanley says.

"I'm so glad we're talking again," I tell Stanley.

"Yes," he says from the back seat.

"I'm so glad we were never not talking," I tell Aparna.

"Yep," she says from shotgun, her expression inscrutable behind her large sunglasses.

My therapist recently asked me if I was angry at my friends for putting me in the hospital. No. I simply am not. I'll keep them, if they'll have me.

They do have me. I can't be sent away so easily. I'm not a car.

♏ ♐

Flyleaf —
The World is Video

Reading diaries written by Jews during the Holocaust, writes Alexandra Zapruder, granddaughter of Abraham, isn't redemptive for the readers or the writers. Reading doesn't bring those people back. Nor does reading help us grieve someone we didn't know, since, "once dead, a person can never be known again." What we have in these diaries are "repositories of information" originally created by someone not to inspire us today but to document or respond to their world as it was then.

Since videorecording has become more common, Maël Renouard mused, we've begun to perceive the world as if it were already a grainy digital video. It feels as if "the distinction between recorded and unrecorded moments had vanished." The "new mode of being" is "becoming-image-memory," and the pocket-sized digital camera "no longer served to record: it gave access to Being's own recording of itself."

♏ ♐

384

THE BEACH

The beach is near paradise. The day is very bright. Near the beginning of the board-walk to the sea, the beach grass hangs onto the dune. There is a sign saying DOGS MUST BE LEASHED, and a dogwalker unleashes a disarmament of seven terriers.

♏ ♐

341

Flyleaf —
Pursuit of the Good

We have got to make this world a better place, but we have also got to enjoy the beach, or what's the point of trying so hard? Besides, if we don't know how to value a beach, how will we judge whether we've improved the world? Camus pointed this out.[*]

While we heal the world, we try to heal ourselves. The same argument applies: What's the point of healing ourselves if we've got nothing to enjoy? We can take a break from the quest for healing and let ourselves have a little sit-down, injured and imperfect as we are. What we have, already, is a life. And the beach is lovely. Simone de Beauvoir.[†]

♏ ♐

FLASHBULB

JUL 2016

385

HOW WE RECOGNIZE
THE GOOD

I brought alcohol for Stanley in a padded cooler. If he likes something, it is objectively good. He is my barometer for the goodness of things. He likes beer because it is cold in a glass bottle with condensation on the sides, and there is something else about it for him, something I've never fully understood because alcohol does not appeal to me with the same force. His shorts smell like pot, but I know he no longer smokes the real stuff; we are so old now that I must be smelling oregano from his kitchen spice rack. Or else I'm smelling my own memories. I am happy because Stanley is smiling. What I feel when I see him smile, he will never know.

♏ ♐

---

[*] Not in *The Stranger*, certainly. In *The Plague*.
[†] *The Ethics of Ambiguity*.

FLASHBULB

JUL 2016

386

ICE CREAM REWARD

FLASHBULB

JUL 2016

387

READ US
THAT RAINBOW

"Ice cream," as the assassin-in-training is promised in Charlie Jane Anders' novel *All the Birds in the Sky*, "was for assassins who finished their targets."

We walk over to the ice cream truck.

An old, powder-blue Ford Taurus is parked next to it. It looks every bit like Stanley's except its doors aren't painted green.

"We spend our time uttering phrases that have already been uttered. We constantly copy and paste each other," says Maël Renouard.

Maybe it is Stanley's old car and the new owner has repainted it. But the new owners live far away, right?

Same or different, and wherever it came from, it is extremely awkward. We pretend not to see it.

♏ ♐

Stanley buys all of us granulated ice packed into a paper cone, drizzled with rainbow food coloring. They are today's SNOEY cones. They contain YES and NO and all possibilities between, and we must swiftly eat them before they melt, or else we won't have had them.

The *Zohar* tells us that typical rainbows are dim, so when we see a fluorescent rainbow, that's how we'll know the feet of the Messiah are walking the earth. LeVar Burton will open a picture book on his lap and read us that rainbow.

♏ ♐

388

DRAGON

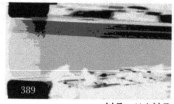

389

WE HAVE
DONE NOTHING
TO DESERVE IT

Walking back to our beach chairs, Stanley asks: "Is it weird to you guys, what you do—making tools for spying?"

"Spying" depends on where the camera's hung and what system it's part of.

"Yes," I reply.

"No," Aparna admits. "I like making money."

"I'm also usually in favor of making money," I agree, adding the qualification.

The car, the car.

There is a dragon of antisemitism out there in the world, and I didn't slay it. I cast an invisibility spell on it, and fighting it has become one invisible dragon trickier.

Thoreau didn't pay his taxes on principle. Today is the one-hundred-and-seventieth anniversary of his jail night. Someone paid his bill to get him out. That was that. Did his protest change anything?

♏ ♐

We throw our bodies inelegantly over the chairs, keeping our SNOEY cones upright.

Stanley uses a nickel to scratch off a lottery ticket.

Ice cream is also for being happy when we have done nothing whatsoever to deserve it.

We take our first group selfie. I pose and try to look like myself.

♏ ♐

FOG —
THE TALE THAT MAKES
THE BAD THOUGHTS
STOP
(D.C. STORYTIME #6)

"Speaking of work, it's Diversity Committee storytime," Aparna declares, licking the melting parts of her ice.

"Me first," I say. I have one ready to go. "Submitted for the approval of the Diversity Committee, I call this story: 'Abraham Zapruder's Most Famous Short Film of All Time.' Let me set the stage for you. It's June 1963. I was, say, college age."

"We weren't born yet in 1963," Stanley interrupts. There is rainbow SNOEY on his nose.

"Let me talk. It's a story. It's kind of made up?" I'm uptalking but in a Yiddish way with an up-palm and an up-eyebrow.

"OK."

"Right, so…"

…I'm sitting in the rotunda of Quincy Market, alone, eating a sandwich. My face is buried in a book. It's a novel, *Yo maté a Kennedy*. I also have a copy of Chad Goeing's *The Nature of Time* in my backpack—because in this story I'm imagining he got his act together and published his book, so I don't have to request archived material and go to a library to read it, and I can just carry it around with me casually and buy a new copy if it falls apart—but I'm not reading it at the moment because I can't read two books at the same time. I'm reading *Yo maté a Kennedy*.

I finish my sandwich quickly and now I want an ice cream. I slip the book in my backpack. I walk to an ice cream shop called the Creamatory and order a Mint Monster. They hand it to me and, walking back to the rotunda, I accidentally drop it on my feet. It's summer, so I'm wearing sandals. There is ice cream on my toes.

I am bent over, flapping in a distress of creamsicled soggy napkins, when I notice a pair of fancy men's shoes, their toes pointing at mine.

I look up slowly: at the pants legs, the suit jacket, the tie, and the face.

I recognize that face from the dust-jacket of my book. It's JFK. It really is.

If I had wanted to cry like a small child over my spilled ice cream, I don't anymore. He is kind to me. He smiles and says, "You're OK!," soothing me. Then he says: "Here. Let me help you." And he takes a napkin and wipes the ice cream off my toes.

And that isn't the end of it. He invites

345

me to tag along with him that night. "Do you want to come to a party?" he says. "I have ice cream on my pants," I say. "You will like these people and they will like you," he says. So I go. I don't know who anyone is and I don't know how to make conversation, but he makes me feel at ease. I don't know what he sees in me, but I feel like I matter a little bit.

Over the next few weeks, JFK invites me to more parties. I meet all his friends. And he becomes a friend of mine. He always wants to talk to me. He listens and takes me seriously.

And from then on we go everywhere together. We are best friends and he takes care of me.

Even when I have surgery, he is there taking care of me. He holds his hands over my body. His hands glow. That's how I get better. He doesn't have to say anything. I rest in bed, communing with JFK, and he wants to spend his time with me. He surrounds me in his Reiki aura. Didn't ever know Reiki was real, and now I can see it as well as receive it.

One night, as I'm cooking dinner in my apartment, the phone rings. Earlier I had removed an old rotary phone from the kitchen wall and put it aside in another room; the one ringing now is a newer phone mounted in its place. I pick up the receiver and say, "Hello?"

A man's voice I don't recognize says: "Lev Ockenshaw?"

"Yes, this is he," I say.

"The President wishes to tell you something. I'll transfer the call now."

Now, JFK calls me all the time informally, but never have I received a call from his staff that sounded so official. I'm caught off-guard. I spin 180 degrees and rest my back against the blue tile wall of the kitchen while the soup pot bubbles on the stove. The phone's squiggly handset cord wraps around my waist.

"Hello, Mr. Ockenshaw?" It's not JFK's voice. I would know.

"Yes, this is he."

"This is the Secret Service. President Kennedy is busy at the moment, but he needs you to know something. He's going to be moving into your garage."

JFK does move in. He stands on my patio and tells me: "Someday all this will be yours."

I tell him: "It is already mine. This is my apartment."

"No, no," he says, "I mean the whole

empire. The nuclear emergencies and the moon shot. Everything you can see across the ocean and to the moon."

He shows me how it's done. "Here's how we write a letter. We type, 'I will nuke you.' Then, between the 'I will' and the 'nuke you,' we draw a little proofreader's carrot pointing up and we add the word 'not.' Capisch?"

I don't believe he's sober.

The next morning, I have the carbon copies of the letter, and the original is gone. This is concerning.

I'm going to have a talk with the president and he'd *so* better be sober.

But he is nowhere to be found.

That night, the phone rings again. I pick it up but the voice on the other end sounds staticky and far away. I go to bed and the phone rings again. This repeats. The phone rings and rings and I can never hear the person's voice properly. Someone calling for "Cordelia," but there's no one here by that name. I pull the cord from the wall so I can get some sleep.

Then I hear another ring with a different timbre from another corner of the apartment. This was the older phone I removed from the kitchen. It's not plugged in. The cord is wrapped several times around it, binding the receiver to the cradle, and the end of the cord terminates in the air. The phone rings and rings, loudly, and won't stop. I unwind the cord from the phone's body and lift the receiver. Does that make it stop? No. It does not.

Where the keypad might have been, instead this phone has 30 little switches in 15-volt increments. With every ring, another switch flops over with a *clack*, and the voltage increases. This means that someone, somewhere, is being electrocuted. I want to hold the switches down, but there are too many, and I never know which will flop over next.

Although I can't speak to whoever is calling, I think there are two people who want to reach me: someone is pleading with me to make it stop, and someone else is telling me to let it happen. That's why I can't answer. I can't pick up or hang up the phone. I can't manipulate the switches. I am allowing it to continue, and I am refusing to stop.

♏ ♐

FLASHBULB

JUL 2016

390

HOW TO STOP
BAD THOUGHTS

FLASHBULB

JUL 2016

391

THE BAD THOUGHTS
HAVE STOPPED

Now I turn the question to my friends.

"Do you know what makes the bad thoughts stop?"

They shake their heads.

I've been holding my SNOEY all this time I have been talking. Miraculously, it's still mostly frozen.

"Abraham Zapruder will begin filming now. He's looking at you to give him the answer. Don't make this film too long. Let's experiment, but quickly. Aparna, tell us. What's one thing that makes you unhappy?"

"Um, having my camera prototypes stolen."

"Very good. And Stanley?"

He looks at me incredulously. *Having my car stolen*, I can see him thinking. If he says that, this is not going to work.

"My ex," he redirects.

"Yup. Right, then." I take a deep breath.

♏ ♐

"So here's what we do."

I stick my fingers into my SNOEY paper cone and smear half the ice on Stanley's toes. He yelps. I do the same for Aparna. His toes are mostly red and green; hers are blue. Together they'd be television pixels.

"Tell me about the cameras and the ex," I say.

Their faces crumple like infants about to cry, perhaps not because of sad thoughts, but because of the cold front. Here they feel el delique: melting ice on precious toes. They look at each other.

"I can't think about my ex when I've got ice cream on my toes!" Stanley complains.

"There now!" I say, slapping my beach chair. "The bad thoughts have stopped! We've solved *that* problem, haven't we!"

♏ ♐

FLASHBULB

JUL 2016

IF SOMEONE
WERE DROWNING

FLASHBULB

JUL 2016

REALIZATION

That's a wrap. Zapruder cuts the tape. This is what the beach is for.

"Can I wash my toes now," Aparna says declaratively, standing up, her question a speech act of giving herself permission. She is wearing no shoes and she is still taller than me.

She goes to the edge of the ocean, stepping carefully on the rounded backs of the pink slipper shells washed up there, and rinses.

♏ ♐

"Stanley," I say. We are sitting down. Aparna is out of earshot.

"Yeah."

"Very recently, I realized—" I drop off.

"Realized what?"

"Exactly that. *I became real.* It's about me, but it was because of you."

He sticks his thumb up, rests his chin on it, and looks hard at me. His baseball cap has a decorative pin commemorating the Burning Man Festival.

"I became real years ago," he says. "Of course, it was because of you. But it is about me. This is obvious. Tel-evidente, if you'd been watching the show. I'm over it." He leans back in the beach chair, pulls his hat over his eyes, and naps.

♏ ♐

349

FOG — THE UNSTAINED BEDSHEET

When Aparna returns and settles, she tells me a legend by Isak Dinesen.

"There are nuns in Europe," she says, "who keep an opulent gallery with a marble floor like a chessboard. On the walls, there's art made of brownish splotches on linen canvases. Each is titled with a woman's name. Visitors treat these images as if they are Zodiac symbols, and they stare into them contemplatively. You know what they are?"

"Nope."

"They are the bloodstained wedding sheets of virgin princesses. And the sheet that draws the most fascination is the one that is unstained. The monarchs and the nuns keep it hanging in the gallery because of their 'eternal and unswerving loyalty' to tradition and truth, even when the revelation is uncomfortable, even when it is blank and silent and has nothing in particular to teach us. There is, however, no name attached to that unstained sheet. They will not remember her name."*

It's about suffering and liberation. They've reserved a permanent gallery slot for your pain. If you don't suffer the way they expect you to, or if you hide the pain or it isn't visible to them, they write you out of history. But you are still real. You live in terms of what's invisible to them. What they describe as "nothing" is your life.

That is what it means to me, anyway. Maybe it means something different to Aparna.

♏ ♐

FLASHBULB

JUL 2016

394

COOKIES AND NAP

My friends have interesting stuff in their heads, and on their heads, all the time. I hope they like being friends with me.

I unveil a few small, blue packages of Chips Ahoy. Aparna laughs at the cookies, shaking her head. "These are very *you*," she says. I don't know what she means by that. I guess she's appreciative, because she unwraps them immediately.

Stanley snorts and stretches his feet in the sand. The hat with the Burning Man pin slides farther down his face.

♏ ♐

---

* I learned about Isak Dinesen's short story "The Blank Page" from a July 2020 article by Lacy Crawford in *LitHub* in which she describes her first visit to a firing range.

FLASHBULB

JUL 2016

THE HAND RESETS

FLASHBULB

JUL 2016

REALITY OR
SIMULATION?

In the ninth series of "Doctor Who," in an episode that aired a week after I kicked Chad out for good, the Doctor is trapped behind a wall 25 feet thick and 400 times harder than diamond. In this unescapable room, a monster demands that he reveal a secret. But the doctor, undefeated, aims to pummel his way through the wall with his fist. Every time he chooses to break his hand against the wall rather than tell the secret, the bones in his hand reset, enabling him to take another blow. After a billion years of self-punishment, he has tunneled through the wall and is free.

♏ ♐

Around the time I graduated college, Nick Bostrom published a paper questioning whether all of human experience is an elaborate virtual simulation. The question is: Might humanity have reached an advanced technological stage at which we can nostalgically project and relive our pre-technological memories? There are three options here. Either we're not capable of producing and living that kind of virtual reality yet; or we can do it but choose not to; or we're already doing it but aren't aware of it.

You can do it in your memory like Barbra Streisand in "Time Machine."

We stand on the jetty, barefoot on the big rocks, bending our knees. "One," Stanley shouts. "Two. Three!"

We jump in, and the cold shocks, but very quickly seems normal.

♏ ♐

FLASHBULB

JUL 2016

SNORKELING

Stanley tears off, crawl-stroking along the shore. Aparna and I tread where we are. Jellies wage ectoplasmic guerrilla warfare all around us. Beowulf's in underwater combat against them to prove his worth.

What is trans in the trans-genre is not the feels of the feather boa nor the cowboy spurs. It is the feels of the crab, neither fish nor reptile, that hides in a crack between the rocks. The inbetweenness of the borderland between anything and anything else. The perspective from this puff of sand.

I'm using the snorkel mask. I'm sure I've never snorkeled before, but déjà vu comes, as if I've already been told in some forgotten, unfathomed dream what is to happen.

♏ ♐

FOG — I DON'T SEE APARNA

When I lift my head, I don't see Aparna. I paddle my feet like a duck. Then, I see her hair, floating near the jetty. The rest of her body is underwater. I tread for a couple seconds, watching. She doesn't move.

My body is made of adrenaline. I take a deep breath and swim a foot or two under. I put my arms around her and climb up on the jetty as quickly as I can. The barnacles scrape our skin.

"Ow!" she says. "What are you doing?"

"Um," I say.

♏ ♐

FLASHBULB

JUL 2016

398

I AM A CROCODILE

There is salt in my eyes. I am a crocodile who grabs at things awkwardly. Things get away from the crocodile, yet it lives, persists, without ever evolving much.

"Oh, my god. You do not need to touch— Thank you. I was *fine*!"

"Okay," I shrug.

"I do not need to be rescued! Really, what was that even about?"

The sense of losing people underwater. It comes from deep within me.

Water beads on my skin. The crocodile, typically unaware of how much escapes it, is not accustomed to embarrassment. But the crocodile swallowed a clock. And right now, it knows. *Tick. Tock. Tick. Tock.* It is aware of time, and it knows that it is losing its grip on the past with every second.

♏ ♐

FOG — I FEEL DIFFERENTLY ABOUT...

...Aparna

In my memory of scuba diving, the terrible boy disappeared below the surface and I almost ordered a second milkshake, thinking, He could just drown.

Once a crocodile knows it is a crocodile, it is, I believe, no longer a crocodile.

Story is motion. *Movie.* The facts are in the visual, the visual runs at a couple dozen frames per second, and in the movie we have a story. But do we still have the facts? No, because those small fish swim fast.

The memory changes. My crocodile tail swept the water—back, forth—and now the equilibrium has punctuated, the DNA has ignited, the evolution has sparked.

I want to tell Aparna I felt differently just now when I thought it was her.

...The Terrible Boy

That vacation was six years ago. The terrible boy must not look like a boy anymore.

Maybe he's read Edmund White's The Beautiful Room is Empty in which a young man wonders if his gay life is now or later or never. Jam tomorrow, but never jam today.

Maybe the terrible boy doesn't form his own opinions about this text but is breathlessly recommending the title to conventionally attractive young men in bars.

Arrowby, that was his name. Charles

Arrowby. The terrible boy by the sea, the sea. Not the Unchained Melody; I mean the Iris Murdoch book.

Again I take the opportunity to let go. It is an epiphany, a re-knowing. Although, in some sense, part of me has never stopped waiting for him to resurface from the sea.

...Kahlil Gibran

I feel differently about Kahlil Gibran's The Prophet. In the part called "On Laws," he says we break laws as if we were kids smashing sandcastles. The ocean too, "laughs always with the innocent." Laws are our own shadows on the sand. If we don't want to be annoyed or oppressed, he says, we shouldn't annoy or oppress others. Then we shall "walk facing the sun" and "travel with the wind." He's overstating the Golden Rule; reciprocity is never guaranteed. But it's true that, if we aren't living according to the limits of our own shadows (or a groundhog's shadow), no law restricts when spring may come.

...Punxsutawney Phil

The ice melts. "It's a transition," the groundhog says. "I've changed my name: Phil D. Lique."

...Stanley

I feel differently about Stanley. When someone is not talking to you for a while, you appreciate them from a new angle.

Back to the genesis: the Taurus. We think the car will ferry us across the river, but it barely stays afloat. Back to the kitten Stanley held in the car to protect it just for one night.

That was not a good story for me, though I got Eurydice-Whiskers out of it. So why would I repeat it?

Somewhere in the United States, Mr. and Mrs. are driving that Taurus. Windows down. Barry Manilow singing "Turn the Radio Up." Quit being so deep, Manilow invites us. Be a little less realistic. You might feel better.

...My Body

I feel differently about my body. Sensations are useful early indicators of threats, yes—and more. Something about who I am is a threat magnet. You're bringing him into the company, my boss said. I tasted that judgment, spat it out. But it's true. I brought him into the company. Not by anything I did. Because of who I am. If I hadn't been sitting in my office, Noon wouldn't have clutched his Garfield mug, set his sights on me, and never forgotten me. Even without an IUD homing device buried in me, he found me. I am his Clippy. The chatter of the world is a post-ironic Teddy Ruxpin. There is no closet deep and dark enough to block my magnet.

...Making a Deal

I feel differently about making a deal. After my preliminary choice, someone flashes me a glimpse of nothing, and now I have a two-thirds probability that the third remaining option is better. It's not about making a deal. It's about making a friend.

...The Three Fates

Clotho spins the thread, making you Gen X or Millennial or a bit of both.

Lachesis measures it, deciding how many days you'll spend arguing yourself from your generational perspective.

Atropos cuts it, letting the cicada emerge, mate, die.

Clotho, "el rodaje," who captures the action on film; Lachesis, "la ráfaga," who makes the duration of light and noise; and Atropos, "el disparo," who has had enough and pulls the trigger.

Rodaje, ráfaga, disparo: All of these are "shooting."

You don't have to shoot for your goal, "la aspiración," if it's your fate, since you'll arrive anyway. So don't worry.

It's the same Fate.

It's the same cicada.

Reemergence.

...My Boss

I feel differently about my boss. Someday, when he's not my boss, I may speak to him again. But I won't want anything from him. I will only ever want things that are big, and I won't imagine he can deliver big to me.

I don't wanna be in their trashy cisgender hierarchy. Their security camera technology is indistinguishable from magic (an example of Clarke's third law),[*] their hierarchy is indistinguishable from villainy, and their professional "feedback" on my "performance" is indistinguishable from abuse.

The cis people come after us with the scissors. That is a false etymology, but still. After they cut us—whether we asked for it, whether we are still talking about it—they always remember and point out the cut.

♏ ♐

---

[*] "Clarke's third law" comes from Arthur C. Clarke's *Profiles of the Future: An Inquiry into the Limits of the Possible* (1962): "Any sufficiently advanced technology is indistinguishable from magic."

399

NOW WE ARE CIS

400

TWO FILAMENTS

I forgot I was wearing my wristwatch when we jumped into the ocean. Now my phone, which I left in my bag on the shore, is my remaining timepiece. The phone, whose clock I cannot edit, is the keeper of cisgender time.

Oh, bother, Winnie-the-Pooh says. *Now we are cis.*

Now we are *six,* I mean. Or thirty-six, nearly. Teddy Ruxpin could be made to say "Oh, bother."

"Cool trick you showed us with the SNOEY cone," Aparna says, snapping my attention back.

"Oh, yeah. Sure thing."

♏ ♐

"Did I ever tell you how a three-way lightbulb works?" she asks.

"No. You didn't."

"An incandescent bulb might have a 50-watt filament. That's pretty dim. A brighter bulb might have a 100-watt."

She is quiet.

"And?" I ask.

"You can put both filaments in the same bulb."

"Then it would be a two-way."

"Or it could be a three-way," she says. "'YES' is an answer. 'NO' is also an answer."

Paying attention to the abstractions of "yes" and "no," I don't yet see the light.

On the 400th night, waiting for dawn, Shahrazad told of two fellows who discussed splitting an imagined reward: two-thirds to one, one-third to the other. When the caliph hit them, each requested: *Give the remaining third to the other.*

♏ ♐

FLASHBULB

JUL 2016

401

THE LIGHTBULB
GOES ON

"'YES' and 'NO' are mutually exclusive. They cancel each other out, right?" I posit. "The light and the darkness?"

"There's no darkness in this three-way. There are two forms of light. Your 'YES' gives 50 watts, and your 'NO' gives 100. Watch." She holds out her left hand, palm up. Her right hand, palm down, slides over it. "They're a set." She interlaces her fingers.

"A SNOEY cone," I say. The lightbulb goes on. *Cis means not-trans. Trans means not-cis. So trans-and-cis exist in relation, and in that sense, everyone's a little bit of both, after all.*

"The rainbow of 'YES' and 'NO,'" she says.

"'YES,' 'NO,' and 'YES-and-NO'. The extra-binary answer is a *both-and.*"

She nods. "150-watt answer."

♏ ♐

Flyleaf — Disengagement Is an Action

There is a story, and the Agile story points just measure misery.

When they lie to me that there is no story, that makes it worse. It's like dividing by zero: story goes to zero, points go to infinity.

Being lied to is like being the kid on <u>The Truman Show</u> who is raised on a reality television set and is never told that he's the starring character on an entertainment program. Finally he outright grasps the meaning of it: <u>people are lying to him</u>. And the way he realizes it is by watching the neighbors passing by at predictable intervals. They are paid extras. "They're on a loop," he whispers conspiratorially to his wife, who is also on a loop.

<u>Leave in the train or on it</u>. An old Spartan battle maxim.

How will I explain it to the boss? My job is as good as a job can be. "Sometimes good; sometimes bad," as Aughra put it in <u>The Dark Crystal</u>, discussing the birth and death of the cosmos.

The issue is not whether I like the job.

The issue is that the strawberry jam jar is empty.

You see what I'm saying, yes?

The system is bankrupt.

The cistalgia—the cis people's nostalgia

for the once-was or the never-was—is the iam-time.

The cell phone's "system time" looks like the "real time" because it is difficult to edit. But being difficult to edit is not what makes something real.

The jam. We are stuck. Jammed. In the cis-iam. The system.

I ate the strawberry jam long ago and fell down the rabbit hole, and the jam has not grown back, and there never is any jam in this jar, and if I plan to stay in this story then it's long past time for me to have gotten rid of the jar.

Post, haste. Deliver. Set your wristwatch five minutes ahead, please. Get going. Trans-nunc.

Cistalgia: The pain of recognition that what you previously believed rock-solid can be struck by an earthquake. Trans is a thing. Anyone could be trans. You could be trans.

Transtalgia: The pain of recognition that your earthquake has stopped. The transitional dust has settled. You finally resemble yourself. You're on the other side, so basically you're cis again. *Ya cis*, yes? Congrats?

Cis-trans-stalgia: The pain of recognition that logic's Law of Identity is simultaneously true and false. Things are, and are not, identical with themselves. If you are cis, there is a sense in which you are trans. If you are trans, there is a sense in which you are cis. The living are sleepwalking and the dead are still speaking.

The other issue is that the river is full of ghosts. I should have mentioned this first.

The secret transgender character in the film, Jack Halberstam wrote, may represent an unusual kind of time. In allowing himself to be understood as cis, he is "trying to be a man with no past" who must "create an alternate future while rewriting history." Perhaps he presents the possibility of "an alternative future" for someone else, especially someone who wants to link their life to his. When the audience sees the gender reveal, though, they're "actually seeing cinematic time's sleight of hand." The transgender navigation "depends on complex relations in time and space between seeing and not seeing, appearing and disappearing, knowing and not knowing."

Maybe the boss does not need to know. Maybe he *can't* know until he is curious or concerned.

Those who are personally unmolested by ghosts don't care if my river is speculirious. They don't even have a self-descriptor for "don't see ghosts." Agnostic, maybe. More like aghostic.*

---

* The Greek phrase was "e tan, e epi tan": "with it or on it." The Spartans meant: *Never loosen your grip on your shield. Return from the battle carrying it, or your slain corpse may be returned to us on top of it—but if you surrender or flee, don't bother coming home at all.*

NO: A word that, used well, gives great light. When we combine it with a separate YES, we give more light than we knew we had.

Meghan Trainor sings "No": <u>Don't touch. Just no.</u>

The boss announces information Adam and Eve already have. He forbids what they already know is rotten. <u>Not that tree</u>, he says, and they know which tree he's talking about. Thus, he cleaves time. He doesn't control what they do; he only controls when they do it. Not ethics but film speed. He says: <u>Put down the apple. I will count to three.</u> On the count of three, they eat the apple.

"She made me do it," Adam pointed.

"That's the story you want to give me?" the boss tutted.

"Yes. She told the serpent I'd come. She messaged. I had nothing to do with it."

"But what's interesting," said the boss, "is that I called out to no one in particular 'Where are you?' and you responded 'Here I am.' You recognized that the pronoun 'you' was about you. I called <u>you</u> to account, and <u>you</u> came. Not someone else. You."

I am called, and here I am again. Same story, same response. Nietzsche's "eternal return." I welcome the holiday of change, but I don't want to change the same way every Groundhog Day. Otherwise, what was the point of this year for me?

♏ ⚹

402

TAKING TIME OFF

I tidy my office desk, holding my performance steady until the end. My masculinity—fragile as it is—is held together with stitches across wrinkles in time. But fragile or no, it is time for me to go forth. *Lech l'cha*, the big boss told Abraham: *get up and go.* No one else can *lech l'cha* me; I have to *lech l'cha* myself.

This is hard to understand and bears repeating: "No" isn't the off-switch. It's another way of turning on. It's the extra-strength filament in the bulb. And it's compatible with a "yes."

I go to HR. When the door closes behind me, I take a breath and say: "I think I need to take some time off work to deal with my problems."

♏ ⚹

Flyleaf — Turn Off the Light

"Yet first there must be a tearing out," Simone Weil said, "something desperate has to take place, the void must be created. Void: the dark night." This, before grace can come in.

Douglas Hofstadter in <u>Gödel, Escher, Bach</u>: A reader, at any time, might "put the book aside and turn off the light. He has stepped 'out of the system' and yet it seems the most natural thing in the world to us." Even a robot can do this. One robot in the 1970s "was not a very good chess player, but it at least had the redeeming quality of being able to spot a hopeless position, and to resign then and there…"

bell hooks observed that people hurt by men "have wanted them dead." But, she said, we do not need men to die. "We need men to change."

♏ ♐

FLASHBULB

JUL 2016

TWO WEEKS' NOTICE

I won't wait for HR to tell my boss. I'll tell him first.

"I've made a decision about my future," I say.

"What's that?" he asks.

"I'm listening to my inner voices."

"A higher calling?"

I do a long pause. "There's no higher, lower, or lateral. These voices are not in the org chart."

He does a long pause back. "I don't think you're ready for this job."

He's pretty funny: judging that I'm retroactively not ready for the job I already do.

"I'm giving two weeks' notice."

Now he can't fire me. I've already quit.

I'm always on trial for whether I can put on my clothes, go to work, and use the bathroom. It is the most transsexual thing ever.

♏ ♐

404

THE NEAR LOSS
OF THE
CHOCOLATE FACTORY

Charlie Bucket almost didn't win the chocolate factory. He and his Grandpa stole a sip of Fizzy Lifting Drink. Wonka had told them not to. He said, "I daren't sell it yet. It's still too powerful." The children wanted to try it anyway; could they, please? "No, no, no. Absolutely not." Wonka left the room. That's when Grandpa whispered: "Let's take a drink, Charlie. Nobody's watching. A small one won't hurt us." Charlie uncorked the bottle. Would it make them levitate? They sipped the forbidden drink. Now, here they go, up, up, up, disordered angels, dogpaddling in the ether. They are almost sucked into the ventilator.

♏ ♐

405

BECOMING
CHOCOLATE LIQUOR

Wonka knows that Charlie deserves to inherit the chocolate factory, but first Charlie must apologize. Charlie gives back the gift of eternity, the unshrinkable hard candy of limitless joy: the everlasting gobstopper. Gives it back to Wonka from whence it came. When Charlie renounces the proposal of capitalizing on the already-infinite, decides not to play for Wonka's adversary, and won't lionize Wonka either, then Charlie himself becomes the god. Apotheosis. He's no longer milquetoast, but chocolate liquor. He doesn't need the everlasting gobstopper. The sweetness, the energy, the eternity: it's *him*. He is the new face of the chocolate factory.

Never mind that you bit the apple. The next level calls you: *Be the apple.*

♏ ♐

FLASHBULB

AUG 2016

406

EXIT INTERVIEW

FLASHBULB

AUG 2016

407

IT ALL HAPPENED
SO QUICKLY

If I am starting to forget why I picked the name Lev for myself, I have another story now. It is the feeling of walking in Memphis in blue suede shoes. It is the ghost that follows me. It is the drink I was told not to take. Now I can absolutely fly.

"We'd like to schedule an exit interview with you," says HR.

What will they ask? How long will the interview last? I am surprised they want to ask me anything. What are they looking for: evidence of past devotion? The system devotes so much time to stomping on workers it labels weak that it couldn't spot true devotion if a hundred and one Dalmatians rode in on a fire truck.

♏ ♐

I remember asking Chad's ghost if he wanted me to be perpetually suicidal and his napkin reply: "I like the way you think." Stanley and I taking the Green Line for soup at Park Street was—*two. years. ago.* If all of this has happened within two years and none of it was foreseen, why would anyone try to plan out their next five years?

Yann Martel's hallucinatory survival novel about the tiger in the lifeboat was released on September 11, 2001. How can any of us plan anything?

I hear the Mayans never really prophesied that the world would end in 2012 but the Aztecs did prophesy it would end in 2027. We still have time.

♏ ♐

408

THE ELECTION'S IN NOVEMBER

Maybe HR will ask who I'll vote for. I am perfecting my answer in Yiddish. *Zol er barfuss geyn, un ein Lego zol im punkt dort in di beyn shpur trefen.* We'll see the incantatory effect. HR probably won't give me an opportunity to try this one out though.

No one drives the train of social change: young people wait for old people to fix it, old people hope young people will fix it, individuals need the system to fix it, the system demands to be paid to fix it, and the boss definitely doesn't want anyone to talk about it.

But what is "it"? Something? Or nothing?

May he go barefoot, and may a Lego smack him right in the bone spur.

♏ ♐

409

IS ANYTHING WRONG?

My boss, bewildered at my resignation, especially with my end date nearing, thinks to ask: "Is anything wrong?"

"No," I shrug. "Except that people here ask me to do contradictory things."

I mean: A stakeholder asks us to build a camera that points west and east simultaneously just because it would be a camera that our competitors don't have.

I mean: One coworker wants me to fit my report on a single sheet of paper and save it for tomorrow's meeting while another wishes I'd emailed the same information in a minimum ten-page report last week.

I mean: They tell me not to talk about a threatening letter but also to be on the office diversity committee to tell them how to improve our organization.

♏ ♐

FLASHBULB

AUG 2016

410

I CAN'T
DO IMPOSSIBLE

FLASHBULB

AUG 2016

411

ONE LAST QUESTION

"I'm not mad," I reassure him. "It is *challenging* for me—well, I believe that's how *you* want me to phrase it, but phrasing it that way feels like a lie. Truth is, I actually *can't* satisfy contradictory requests at the same time."

There. I said "can't."

Furthermore I tell him: "I can't do impossible or illogical. I can't make you a Klein bottle. Give me all the time in the world, but that's the wrong kind of four-dimensionality. So I've chosen a door. And don't you blame your decisions on me, either."

I told the boss: Don't.

My boss raises both eyebrows, slowly, all the way up.

♏︎ ↗

The radio DJ plays "Suddenly Last Summer" by the Motels more than once.

Maël Renouard's new book speaks of "a new art language" made of "complex sequences drawn from previous works."

I begin to imagine my "exit interview" as standing me before one last review panel and then before the firing squad. It's my choice to leave, yet I can't imagine what life is there after job. I've been telling this story for so long.

What if the exit interview is another game show? Another Halsrätsel, a life-and-death riddle?

What if they play with their phones while I take the stand?

Turns out, the exit interview is conducted by one HR employee who asks me only one question: "Do you have any questions for us?"

♏︎ ↗

412

MAY HE GO BAREFOOT

413

HOW DO YOU KNOW IF YOU HAVEN'T TOUCHED IT?

María in my pocket whispers: *My fellow citizens of the world: Ask not what America will do for you, but what together we can do for the freedom of man.*

We cannot go back in time and let JFK handle it. We can pick a new president.

In this election, there's one option I prefer. The other is essentially a terrible boy. Of my dispreference, I repeat: *May he go barefoot, and may a Lego smack him right in the bone spur.*

It's about time my psychic activity served a purpose.

The future comes swiftly. The sea levels rise over our heads.

I bring home the rainbow flag with the bank logo, all that remains of a promise: I will never again destroy the world.

♏ ♐

As far as I'm concerned, the office can hang a sign: *[1] days without a transgender employee.* It's not a bragging point. Who will calm the waves of their transitions?

They misheard the word as *traingender.* One cis person sets the trolley on a course toward other unsuspecting cis people. But I am not a conduit of death. They don't know the train is trans. It switches tracks. Ah, here's the little hidden meta-lever! If you've never touched a switch like that, how do you know what it does or doesn't do?

[2] days without a transgender employee. The longer it ticks up, the greater the occupational hazard. But it's not my problem anymore. They can ask their diversity committee to save their asses.

♏ ♐

FLASHBULB

AUG 2016

414

ENSURE THAT
NOTHING HAPPENS

FLASHBULB

AUG 2016

415

EXTERNALIZE THE
QUESTION

That feel when.

The "feel" is that I failed the Milgram. I opened my mouth; I was told to be quiet; I quieted. It was a hoax, after all that? No credit. Fail.

The feel is also that the gunman is in charge of the experiment. He makes me his subject. It's not my fault I can't get out of the cage. I'm a canary.

A double-sense of "projection": attributing your own shortcomings to others, and casting light through a film so the image is cast on a wall. The images merge: everyone is playing their own tape and casting their own faces at the same spot on the wall.

It's my responsibility to decide my next step. I tread lightly so nothing explodes.

♏ ♐

What happened is what makes the haunting, and what doesn't happen undoes the spell.

Kaili Blues recalls a father's recurring dream that his murdered son was asking him for a watch. How to deliver a watch to a ghost? The father burned an image of a watch, but this did not satisfy his son's spirit. Ultimately, the father opened a watch shop. Not a solution, but it's not nothing.

Despite our "defects of mind," we solve our problems in a way that gains us some of "the joy, the peace, the glory of mankind." Alexander Pope. Virtue seeks nothing and gets us nothing—even if, for a job well done, Virtue would nevertheless appreciate a pat on the back and a scratch behind the ears.

♏ ♐

416

SUMMER IN BOSTON

417

UTERUS
IN THE
FIRST PLACE

Summer in Boston. A Green Line innovation: countdown clocks at the Park Street station. "3 stops away." "2 stops away." "1 stop away." "Now Boarding." They tell us the train's distance from us. They measure space, not time. They tell us whose turn it is: another station's. Soon, ours. We feel less hurried. We know we have space-time to buy a coffee.

I listen to Chicago sing "Does Anybody Really Know What Time It Is?" in my earbuds.

"It's not worth the bother of killing yourself, since you always kill yourself *too late*," E. M. Cioran aphorized.

My suicide won't help me. I externalize the question: Whose suicide have I longed for? Who have I hoped would simply go away?

♏ ♐

Aparna and I can still talk even though we are not working together anymore. I tell her that I had a hysterectomy. She did not know I ever had a uterus in the first place.

"I should have told you before," I say to her. "But after the emails from Noon, I knew my transsexuality was part of his crazy. It wasn't extortion, since he didn't want anything. I don't know why people say 'blackmail.' The word doesn't even make sense. This was invisibility mail. The secret held in my uterus—"

"What secret?"

"I mean, the secret *about nothing* held in my uterus *that wasn't there anymore*—"

♏ ♐

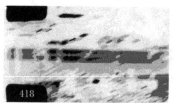

418

WHAT APARNA
TOLERATES

"Uh huh."

"I had to stay silent about being transgender so that a distressed white cis man wouldn't explode hundreds of people."

"What is this, a fucking infinity war?"

She is annoyed. Disappointed, maybe. But she is still talking to me.

"I wouldn't have cared, you know," she said. "It wouldn't have made a difference to me. I tolerate all kinds of things about you. I tolerate—"

I put my hand up. "You don't have to make a list."

"Anyway, I guess on some level I had a clue ever since we went to the beach. You and Stanley have the same scars on your chests, like upside-down Ts."

"Oh."

♏ ♐

FLASHBULB

AUG 2016

419

WHAT APARNA
ALLOWS HERSELF
TO DO

"You need to start telling me more. Promise."

"OK," I say. I don't know the future, so I don't know what I've just promised to tell her.

"By the way, they are going to promote me," she says.

"They should. What are they going to make you?"

"If they make me president of everything, I will take it. I will use my political capital. I am allowed to change what I want." She adds: "Since we're telling each other things."

♏ ♐

FLASHBULB

AUG 2016

PAUSE

"What are you going to do with your vice presidency?"

"Awesome shit."

"Do they allow you to bring teddy bears to work if you're vice president?"

"No. Fortunately, when I'm vice president, I make my own rules. I invent the genre."

I can't say I'm surprised, I want to say, *and I can't stop you.*

I pause, but briefly. The briefer the pause, the greater the evidence of realness.

"Congratulations," I say, before the realness window shuts.

She smiles. "Thanks. For a long time, I didn't know if it was possible for me. I've worked really hard at this."

♏ ♐

Flyleaf — Silent Film, Sacrificial Goats

Commonly, the "exposure as transgender constitutes the film's narrative climax," signaling the trans person's "own decline and the unraveling of cinematic time," Jack Halberstam wrote. It begins the "rewind" way of understanding the film. Halberstam picks that name because "the viewer literally has to rewind the film after the character's exposure in order to reorganize the narrative logic in terms of the pass." Not the <u>past</u>, but the person having <u>passed</u> as a man or a woman.

People tell me I should make a movie to help sell my book. Stan Lee told Comic-Con he has a new project, <u>God Woke</u>, to rehabilitate a poem he wrote 44 years ago and make it a digital short film. It's about how disappointed the boss is in humanity after he wakes from a long sleep.

Chad died before there were movies. He was like a silent movie character in my talkie.

How hard it would have been to publish <u>The Nature of Time</u> if they discovered he was a "woman author."

Imagine if I were to rehabilitate Chad's unfinished book. They'd say: <u>A transgender author writing about a transgender author.</u> Never mind that the book is not about gender but about time.

369

The Talmud tells you how to sacrifice two goats: Destroy one, let go of the other.

Wait eight days for your goats to mature, flip a coin to assign their fates (slaughter one for the Boss, let the other wander off to Azazel), and wait until someone opens the doors to the ritual space. If you don't follow instructions in the right order, your goats "lack time," meaning they are ritually unprepared and your decisions are half-baked.

Neither goat is holy or profane <u>per se</u> until you flip a coin. Then they have unique destinies. This determines your next move.

Doesn't seem fair, does it? The random selection?

Had you two goats and no coin, nonetheless there ought to have been a path forward, an alternative way to know what to do with your goats.

♏ ♐

FLASHBULB

AUG 2016

CHANGING THE
CHANGE NARRATIVE

What did any of us originally aim to change? And why it is never that original desire, but something else utterly unexpected, that eventually dominates the change narrative?

Why, when you sit on the older transgender man's grandpa-storytelling rug by his apartment's fireplace and ask him, "Tell us, again, about the change," will you not get his *Diagnostic and Statistical Manual of Mental Disorders* transsexuality criteria from many years ago but rather an entirely different story of change?

♏ ♐

FLASHBULB

AUG 2016

RING. RING.
HELLO?

"Stanley," I ask on the telephone, "remind me how you picked your name. It was after the Marvel comics producer Stan Lee, right?" He probably told me this 15 years ago, and I have forgotten.

He pauses as if he has also forgotten. "Uh, no. Paco Stanley. A TV comedian in Mexico."[*]

"Why him?"

"Someone shot him in his car, so he was in the news. I liked his name. And it felt like I was giving him new life."

We give ourselves new life, too. Life is a mutual project.

♏ ♐

Flyleaf — Knock, Knock. Who's There?

What's this new door? Who's knocking? "It is somebody wants to do us harm," says a voice. It's the end of a poem by D. H. Lawrence.

> What is the knocking?
> What is the knocking at the door in the night?
> It is somebody wants to do us harm.
>
> No, no, it is the three strange angels.
> Admit them, admit them.

Three angels. Three voices talking about them. Fear is the voice at the core. Two other voices say "no" and "no" to the fear, instructing "admit them" and "admit them" again.

♏ ♐

---

[*] Francisco "Paco" Jorge Stanley Albaitero, a television comedian, was murdered inside his Lincoln Navigator SUV on June 7, 1999 in Mexico City.

FLASHBULB

AUG 2016

ANGELS

One angel you speak to at L. D. Lique. Another angel you speak to at Hana Lee. Another angel is fear itself, and you should not fear your fear, but simply admit it.

Beyond the Maxwell House Haggadah, now we've got the L. D. Lique and the Hana Lee Haggadot. And all of these tellings can be let go.

A soap bubble lifts on the air, bursts. The whole sky sighs, feeling one bubble less responsible for holding every fragile thing together.

When a man dies to his own suicide mythos, his life begins.

♏ ♐

FOG — SUN-UMBRELLA IN THE MIND

Under a sun-umbrella at an observation table on a restaurant deck in my memory, memory being the lowest-carbon travel method, I settle myself, not without anxiety, waiting for the terrible boy to return from the coral reef. Meanwhile, I read my beat-up copy of *Yo maté a Kennedy* by Manuel Vázquez Montalbán.

In this adapted version of the memory, I wear shorts, but the sun is mild, no longer turned on quite full summer. The reality of New England September, intruding into my tropical fantasy, a slight chill in the air greening over the turquoise waters, is already pulling itself into shore.

Some beachgoers are swimming. No one is drowning.

The King, Elvis, is sunning himself on a folding chair half-sunk into the sand. He wears large sunglasses; his round belly bears the white residue of sunscreen. He tilts his body toward me, grins, gives me the thumbs-up, then readjusts his spine into the chair and faces skyward again, silent. His nose is so much straighter than mine.

A Lincoln Continental drives along the beach strip, slowly, as if it is watching us.

No one turns around to look.

The dream-waiter stops by my table and serves me a drink I didn't have to ask for. Is it a mudslide, I hope?

No, wait. This is an egg cream.

I am disappointed but intrigued. Why does he bring the Jew an egg cream?

"What's that book about?" he asks, pointing to *Yo maté a Kennedy*.

"Nothing."

"Then why are you reading it?"

"Never mind," I say. "But I have a question for you, if you don't mind." He nods in service. "No one has a gun, right?"

"Someone always has a gun. But it is never where you think. You don't have to keep looking for it where it isn't."

I consider this. Yes, I can stop looking for the gun. "Then I don't think I need this book anymore." I hand *Yo maté a Kennedy* to the waiter.

"Are you sure?"

I shrug. "It's a mass-market copy. I can always get another one."

I walk alone on the strip of sand by the water's edge. I approach a small structure at the edge of the dune grass. It is a swingset. Two empty swings. I sit, facing the water, on what seems to me the right side. I pump my legs and begin to swing. The metal frame wobbles and creaks. I close my eyes, stop moving my legs, and gently come to a stop, letting the sun play on my eyelids.

The swingset is still moving and creaking. I think it is the wind. Slowly I open my eyes and look to my left. Someone is in the other swing. A child, short hair, six years old. I have a sense of déjà vu. A grownup is pushing him. I recognize the father; he's the one I met on this swingset three decades ago, all grown up now, pushing his son. I try to get a glimpse of the child's face, but somehow I cannot. He is looking away. The sense of foreboding grows, as does the impression that I'm still trapped in a bad dream.

The boy is looking away, over the waves, but I hear the father's voice, asking the same question he asked me decades ago: "Are you afraid of Santa Claus?"

And now the son is turning his head, slowly, to look at me, and I am frozen down to my bones and cannot run away.

I think he is going to ask me: *Why did you betray your brother?*

He does not. I see his face. It is the face, of course, of Lear Noon.

"No," I hear myself answer suddenly, "I'm not *afraid* of Santa Claus."

Child-Noon grins as if he is going to eat me. "Santa Claus," I continue, "isn't real."

The beach and everything on it dissolves then, a vast mosaic of sand grains and water droplets sucked back down the time tunnel of a black hole.

EPISODE 12

IRREVERSIBLE

THE CUBS
ARE DOING WELL

The idea of "the immediate," Kierke-gaard says, "is nullified the very moment it is mentioned, just as a sleepwalker wakes up the moment someone mentions his name."

"Lev."

"What?"

"We need more chips," Stanley says, staring at the TV, his socked feet on the coffeetable. "Refill the bowl."

He and I are watching the Chicago Cubs play the World Series on TV at his house. He says they're doing better than they've done in 70 years.

Soon it will be the one-and-a-halfth anniversary of the Monty Python nonsense I can't remember. I am holding my shit together.

♏ ♐

Flyleaf — Teal Deer

Teal Deer

The length of our quest: We walked through ice, fire, marsh, desert, chopped up the multi-headed venom beast, riddled through the gatekeeper. What's at the end?

A deer. Pelt magnificent blue, almost green. What will you ask it? Easy. You only ever want to know one thing: <u>What does it all mean?</u> The deer shakes its antlers and chastises you: <u>Why didn't you read the book?</u> Your face feels warm. <u>The book was too long. The exam is tomorrow morning. Please tell me what the book is about.</u> The teal deer always gives the same answer: <u>I can't.</u>*

The answers arrive, but not on a train of thought. They come on a train of dreams.

Knowing What Transgender Means

You don't acquire knowledge of what transgender means from a PowerPoint slide at a diversity training on a Wednesday night. It isn't a definition nor an ideology. It isn't power, and it isn't a point. Knowing what transgender means is the act of continuous listening to transgender people.

---

* "Teal deer" is a common pronunciation and representation of the acronym "TL;DR" which is used to remark on one's lack of engagement with a long communication or publication: "too long; didn't read." It may be used by non-readers as a form of criticism or confession, but often it is used by authors to label a summary intended for their non-readers.

Gender Real Time

We don't possess gender any more than we obtain realness or wield time. We are and they are: gender, real, time. We do and we go. These are not points to be scored because they are off the scoreboard. Outside of gender real time, there is no way to value gender real time.

Iam-Time

Latin has a word for nostalgia-time. "Iam" means "at that time." You may use it with past or future tense, not present. Iam-time is the time you can't reach by definition because it is never now.

Lewis Carroll has the Queen tell Alice in Wonderland: "The rule is, jam to-morrow and jam yesterday—but never jam to-day." It's a joke from Latin class, you see.

Alice demurs, "I don't care for jam." (This is irrelevant.) Still, she can't help arguing that, since the rule is jam every other day, "It must come sometimes to 'jam to-day'."

The Queen insists there is "never jam to-day." After all, "to-day isn't any other day." Once you reach the iam, it's non-iam.

If you mean "right now," today, there's a different word for that in Latin: "nunc."

You Never Have Any Jam

A riddle is a question that contains its own logic.

You aren't allowed to plan jam to-day in your calendar, and it would be cheating to search your pantry for jam and taste it. The riddler is permanently agnostic about whether there is jam in your pantry. It doesn't matter what your physical house looks like or what you ate for breakfast. What matters for the riddle is that, in the story the riddler tells, given the very limited worldbuilding, you never have any jam.

I understand why my strawberry jam jar has been chronically empty. I have been very deep inside a story whose logic does not provide ever for jam to-day.

Living Trees, Fallen Leaves

Suppose our ideals are living trees leaning toward the future. Suppose our results are fallen leaves, dead facts of the past. Some people claim domain over both: the ideas and the facts, the future and the past, the iam of it all. But some of us are conscious of being trapped in the middle, the eternal nunc, where the tree is always dying and always being born again, the non-binary non-spot in non-time, the Right Now. The dominator shouts: Hey, you need more ideas; hey, you need more facts; be more five-year-forward-thinking; otherwise you'll never be historically significant. But we do perceive ideas and facts, and if we do not "have" them it is because we have stopped trying to grasp them.

♏︎⤴

FOG — DEDICATION

My mental film is the movie I privately saw when I touched Lear Noon in L. D. Lique. The montage is famous to me.

I call this short film *The Nature of Time.*

We stand on the shoulders of ancestors. But we let the past be past. I am thankful to the Virgin for giving me 80 percent. The rest is mine.

♏ ♐

FLASHBULB

WED
2 NOV
2016

425

DO NOT ASK
TO GO BACK

As Stanley channel-surfs during commercial breaks, I spot a game show that looks like *Tele-Quiz.* He sails by it. I don't ask him to go back.

Why pretend there was no injury? That's an attempt to rewrite the past. Won't work. Generates time-travel residue. Bee's feet are trapped in its own honey. Nostalgia is a fancy lie. A pursuit of a day when nothing hurt. To move forward, we could tell the truth. We know we will die. We see our death on the horizon.

Starting with myself: If a hysterectomy hurts, say so.

My notebook is in my lap. "Do not hide the pain," I write in my notebook on a page I've labeled "New and Better Agile Principles." I underline it.

♏ ♐

THE CUBS WIN
THE WORLD SERIES

EMPLOYEE 427

Nine innings are inconclusive. The game is tied 6–6. It rains for 17 minutes. When the rain stops, the extra inning starts.

In my notebook, I write: "May the Cubs win the World Series."

And they do. They do. My magic is working.

	Runs	Hits	Errors
Cubs	8	13	3
Indians	7	11	1

♏ ♐

It's 1 a.m. We've got work tomorrow. Technically, it is tomorrow.

But Stanley is amped up. He doesn't want me to be boring and leave.

"I can work just fine when I'm tired," he says. "I know my Employee 427 script inside and out. I follow the voice."

"What voice?"

He pauses. "You don't have a voice telling you what to do at work?"

"No. I don't think so. What does it sound like?"

He pauses again. "It sounds very much like you."

"Uh huh." I try to sound noncommittal.

"Usually I do the opposite of what it says," he assures me quickly. "Though if I'm tired, I may go along with it."

"Is this another Stanley parable?"

"Not yet," he says. "There's only one."*

♏ ♐

---

* "The Stanley Parable" is a 2013 video game that was remade in 2022. The character Stanley is Employee 427. As the game begins, he's surprised to find himself alone in his office, and a disembodied narrative voice suggests his next steps to him: left door, right door. The game is designed so that the player focuses not on making a small number of correct choices but rather on making lots of choices over a very long time.

428

ASK FOR WHAT
YOU DESERVE

429

HOW DO
PSYCH PILLS WORK?

To my wizard's scroll, I add: "May you achieve the vice presidency you deserve."

The movie channel airs *Time After Time.* H. G. Wells builds a time machine to take himself and Jack the Ripper from 1893 London to 1979 San Francisco. A banker, pursued by the killer, loses her job, but she and H. G. Wells fall in love, and for her that's like becoming Vice President of Time Travel and is probably better than working at a bank.

This notebook *works.*

I write: "May you make the cover of *Time Magazine.*"

Hasn't yet happened to a transgender man, but we can dream.

♏ ♐

I did know a transgender man who was immortal, but I killed him with pills. Poor Chad.

Whenever I interact with speculirious beings, I remember rules I've forgotten. Of course ghosts and goddesses can be transgender. The boss has no gender or multiple genders according to lots of theologies. I should get around to reading the Vedas.

My testosterone may throw a wrench in the system. A transgender man ghost was drawn to it. A transgender woman goddess might be irked by it.

But I won't speculiriate anytime soon. Not with these pills.

I don't know how psych pills work.

I don't know how gender works.

The sign in the short film says: *Fort Worth Turnpike, Keep Right.* Which way are we going?

♏ ♐

WHAT IS
YOUR WORK?

"What *is* your work?" an artificer asks in R. B. Lemberg's story "The Book of How to Live." A worker replies: "Our work is change." Let all our houses be habitable: "by magic or better yet, by mechanics." Let us have water to drink.

Atmospheric carbon dioxide has reached 400 parts per million. I will let you know when it drops below 400 again, then below the safety threshold of 350, and we are back on the swingset on the beach, and it is the Summer of 1987, and I am six.

♏ ♐

Flyleaf — Romanlogic

The Omen

The aggressor insists he is not so prejudiced as to object to a transsexual's mere *existence*. His nuanced concern, he proudly clarifies, is that *a transsexual must never be vice president.*

A transsexual vice president! Imagine the omen. Just contemplating it—like the moon—drives the cis man aggressively mad.

It has always been this way. A eunuch advisor to the Roman emperor defeated the Huns, so this eunuch was promoted to consul, and while he was busy putting down yet another rebellion, the Romans decided they'd rather be killed by Ostrogoths than have a eunuch consul, and they exiled and executed him and rubbed out his legacy with a *damnatio memoriae*. It can always get worse: The poet Claudian called him a bad omen, and we still have that text today, so his memory isn't erased after all.

Romanlogic

The Roman Empire had recently been divided in two, so each half was weakened, and the Ostrogothic rebellion was nothing to sniff at. The Ostrogoths assaulted the Western half and reduced its power forever. The Romans were witnessing the end of their empire in real time. But, you see, in the view of these Roman politicians and as the poet Claudian happily reported, a eunuch is a bad omen to be discussed and punished. The eunuch cannot simply be allowed to defeat enemies and save the Roman Empire.

If you say "It was the eunuch's fault!" or "A eunuch cannot be consul!" several times, you begin to hear the self-contained romanlogic. *Of course it was. Of course he cannot.*

♏ ♐

LET'S MAKE A DEAL

ALMOST
THANKSGIVING

A week ago, the FBI Director reopened an investigation into a private email server.

Why was it private? What emails passed through? These questions could be asked. But *should* the FBI Director be asking, and asking *now*? The election is days away.

Long night of the soul, deep in thought. *Let's do it,* he says.

Investigation is his job. But announcing publicly each unanswered question—is that also his job? That, itself, is quite a question.

The Fates stand in three doorways and say in unison, "Let's make a deal."

Let's see what's in that email server. Let's see what we've won.

I'm taking my pills, and Chad doesn't come back. Though, sometimes, upon a knock in the rain, I open the door.

♏ ♐

There was a goat in the email server, the FBI Director said. *Sorry!*

Now *there's* a rearview mirror that'll fascinate us for a century.

(And he will never make FBI Vice President.)

Speaking of my rearview: A half-dozen wild turkeys congregate behind my car. I can't back out of my parking space, as I don't wish to smash them.

David Shields says in *Reality Hunger,* Article 432, that his favorite literature involves a person "trying to figure out how he or she has solved or not solved being alive."

Almost Thanksgiving, but the turkeys aren't counting the days. *We are not afraid of your car,* they say, *nor your holiday. We are free.*

♏ ♐

Flyleaf — How One Lives

The Wampanoag nation was here when the European settlers arrived, and their history extends far earlier than the day the settlers pegged as the first Thanksgiving, and the Wampanoag are still here. What I understand of their worldview is that religion for them is not separate from other ways of thinking and being. Values are neither religious nor non-religious. How one lives on the earth is intertwined with what one believes about the sky.

ℳ ♐

FLASHBULB

TUE
8 NOV
2016

433

THE CRACK

My parents visited, though it was a little late in the season for them to tolerate Boston. My father is extraordinarily old. They're already back in Florida. *Flappity-flap-flap*, look at snowbirds go.

Leonard Cohen's era of poetry draws itself to a close. Maybe he feels he's given all his poems and it is our job to use them. Maybe he's satisfied that the Cubs finally won the World Series. Maybe he knows what will happen tomorrow and does not want to witness it. He slips away in the night, in his sleep.

Through the crack, the out finally intersects with the in.

The quiet is not infinite. There is 4 minutes and 33 seconds of it. Barely enough to loop the Zapruder film ten times.

ℳ ♐

FLASHBULB

TUE
8 NOV
2016

434

WE VOTE

We cast our votes—Stanley, Aparna, and I. *For whom* we vote, we'd already decided: before we heard of a basement door, never mind learned the FBI found a goat behind it.

We were born into this mostly closed system. We don't have direct control over what the system does to us. Voting is a derivative of personal will, just as a stock option is a derivative of an underlying asset. Neither "free" nor "free." Voting, secret and silent, larval and potential, is not exactly speech. But it does relate to power and choice.

I'd advise the FBI Director: *Switch. Open the other guy's basement door.*

ℳ ♐

WE WAIT

Stanley comes over, and I take the Glenlivet 12 single malt scotch off the shelf. "To Cohen," I say.*

Swiftly, as if by injection, I feel a fog—a residue, maybe—settle on me. I may want to change quite a lot, but nothing wants to be changed.

♏ ♐

FOG — THE RIVER STYX

"Did I ever tell you the Jewish legend about mortality?"

"No," Stanley says.

"So, Thetis, the mother, dipped her infant Achilles into the River Styx to make him immortal. She held onto his heel when she dipped him. His heel wasn't exposed to the magic waters, and that remained his vulnerable spot."

"This does not sound Jewish."

"So, the Jews in my ancestral Poland, being perspicacious, figured they'd do the Greek myth one better. In their ritual bath, the *mikveh*, they dipped their babies twice, the second time to make sure the baby's heel was also wet. Thetis shoulda thought of it."

"Thetis and anti-thetis."

"Right. But it turns out this ritual doesn't work for transgender men."

"The-cis and anti-the-cis."

"*Because*," I say loudly so Stanley will stop interrupting, "our meta-dicks pop out late in life, so the meta hasn't been mikvehed in the Styx and is entirely vulnerable."

"Ohhh," Stanley breathes.

"This is our secret of masculinity and vulnerability."

As you observe transgender men talking over a long period of time, you may hear a dick joke, and it will be syncretic myth disguised as a dick joke.

"Wait," Stanley says. "This is not a Jewish story. You are making it up."

"Whatever I make up is Jewish because I am the Jew," I say.

♏ ♐

---

* Upon the death of the poet Leonard Cohen in 2016, and while waiting for the presidential election results to come in, Lev and Stanley toast "to Cohen" with a Glenlivet 12 single malt scotch. They would not know yet in 2016, but a different man, Michael Cohen, upon entering a guilty plea in 2018, will share that he consumed a glass of Glenlivet 12 on the rocks to fortify himself.

FLASHBULB

TUE
8 NOV
2016

RUSSIAN DOLLS

FLASHBULB

SAT
12 NOV
2016

TRANSSEXUAL HAS
THE WEAPON

While Stanley and I wait for the election results to roll in, I take my Russian dolls off the shelf. Open the large ones, discover the small ones within.

What if we are the small ones within, struggling to escape through the crack where the light gets in, the mother's waistline? What if we never fully emerge and see the sky? We're in an interminable history of mothers, and there is no ultimate, biggest mother.

"Matryooossshka dolls," I slur.

"Hysterectomy dolls," Stanley points and titters. He is drunker than I am. I think, inherently, a matryoshka doll can't have a hysterectomy. They are made to contain other dolls, or else they aren't matryoshka. If you figured it out, you'd crack the nature of time.

♏ ♐

Stanley and I agree to see *Arrival* which comes to theaters this weekend. We drive separately. We get a huge soda to share.

In the film, the linguists believe the gnarly aliens are saying "weapon opens time."

"Transsexual has the weapon," Stanley says, brandishing the soda.

"Weapon opens time," I agree.

It feels as though we're inviting in Leonard Cohen's wandering spirit.

"Shhh!" says someone from the next row.

I wonder what JFK, who turns 100 next spring, would think of our moon walk.

♏ ♐

FLASHBULB

SAT
12 NOV
2016

438

THREE DOORS
AT APARNA'S HOUSE

FLASHBULB

SAT
12 NOV
2016

439

JFK'S PRESENCE

We visit Aparna. The evening is dark and biting cold. I drive us. My hands are ice on the steering wheel. Stanley changes the radio station. A man is singing a song at a medium pace, recalling how his father once warned him he'll perceive life differently when he's 68. "That's from John Mayer's *Continuum* album," the DJ says in the silence after it's over. We park.

Aparna's house is warm. The goddess Mariamman is on the table in the living room.

I go upstairs to the bathroom, and I notice the hallway closet is still padlocked. Behind a third door that's half-open, her mother is sitting alone in a bedroom watching *Wheel of Fortune*.

♏ ♐

Downstairs again. In the kitchen, Aparna tells me: "Sometime you should really tell me what a hysterectomy is like."

"You never asked."

"I know."

"Why do you want to know?"

"I'm curious. It might be useful information."

"It's like—"

All I can remember about the surgery is who was with me.

TFW…

"It's like, JFK says 'I will take care of you until you are well,' sits by your bedside, lays his hands over your body. He's surrounded by yellow light, and you become part of that light. He radiates into you and you soak it up and radiate back. You gaze at each other, and time does not exist. JFK, who could be taking care of anyone, is taking care of you."

♏ ♐

FLASHBULB

SAT
12 NOV
2016

440

BUT DID IT HURT?

"Sounds like the story you told us on the beach last summer. I was really asking whether it hurts."

"Oh." Not the presence, but the pain. "No, no, it's not so bad. It's a surgery. There are worse surgeries. Depends, I guess, how the surgeon goes into the war theater. The means of entry. Whether the scalpel passes through something or—nothing."

"My god."

"No god. A ghost will do. JFK was exactly who I needed."

♏ ♐

Flyleaf — Metalevel

Here's a meta-story about the Baal Shem Tov, founder of Hasidism. He sometimes lit a campfire in his special spot in the woods, and whatever he prayed for came to pass. Successive generations lost all his ritual ingredients—holyplace, holyfire, holywords—yet retained the magic itself because they remembered the Baal Shem Tov.[*]

Some lose nearly everything when others take it by force. When they have nothing material left, they still have culture, which can be maintained—as Houston A. Baker explains, here talking about Black Americans—at "metalevels."[†]

They let you keep one reel of film and tell you to be proud of it because it represents everything else they took from you. They allow you to express your feelings in their language. And whether you keep the artifact might matter, and what language you speak might matter, but perhaps more foundational is the meta-mattering: It matters that you are the one who decides what matters to you.[‡] You decide. Not someone else. You.

---

[*] I previously retold this story in my memoir, *Bad Fire*. It's in Giorgio Agamben's *The Fire and the Tale*, originally *Il fuoco e il racconto*, 2014. Translated by Lorenzo Chiesa, Stanford University Press, 2017. In the opening chapter, Agamben cites it to Gershom Scholem, who says he learned it from Yosef Agnon.

[†] Quoted in the introduction to Madelyn Jablon's *Black Meta-fiction*.

[‡] Silvia Rivera Cusicanqui posed the question this way, as I gloss it. If large parts of your culture are gone, what are you going to do: ¿"ponerse poncho, salir a las calles diciendo 'soy un indio puro' y hacerlo en

I have not got Yiddish, but damned if I haven't got this bagel, which is breakfast in the shape of a zero, and it is mine and I am keeping it.

Haven't got the cis-granted identities and cis-mediated experiences but have got the identities and experiences I fought for in my own translational way. It does not mean I am not natural. It means I am differently in tune with my nature.

Choosing one life means you don't lead another you might have otherwise led. "Picking up and opening a book," said Pierre Bayard, "masks the countergesture that occurs at the same time: the involuntary act of <u>not</u> picking up and <u>not</u> opening all the other books in the universe."

How you understand your agency is related to how you exist in time.

Gabriel Horn, also known as White Deer of Autumn, writes in <u>The Book of Ceremonies</u> that a person may distance themselves from "linear time." Their non-linear time is about who they are, not what ritual item they hold in their hand. A "ceremonial state of consciousness" isn't for sale.

Who you are is a truth and a story; it matters if you say it does; it does not respond to any challenger's attempt to extract it from you; it may reveal itself only to those who listen; it takes its time; and it operates on a metalevel.

You decide to keep the film, but the physical tape is only valuable when you play it and watch it, and to play a movie in Spanish is "reproducir," and this type of reproduction is not the creation of an object but the repetition of an experience, and when you roll the tape it bursts into flames.

♏︎♐︎

---

castellano"? Go out in your poncho, insisting in the colonizers' Spanish language that you are entirely Aymara, purely Indigenous? You can't. Still, you have an identity rooted in history, and you draw it out by self-assertion, letting it give birth to itself, lifting the head of the ancestor crouching inside you, who *is* you: "levantarle la cabeza a la india agachada que cada quien lleva adentro."
Silvia Rivera Cusicanqui. *Un mundo ch'ixi es posible: Ensayos desde un presente en crisis.* Buenos Aires: Tinta Limón, 2018. pp. 81, 89.

441

THE DIFFERENCE
BETWEEN
A GOD AND A GHOST

442

FIRE OR NOT,
HERE WE COME

"I'm curiouser," Aparna says. "What's the difference between a god and a ghost?"

"The Virgin Mary is like a goddess. JFK, a ghost."

"I know, but what's the metaphysical difference?"

"I think of it as a question of gender. First: Is it a spirit? If so: Woman or man? That determines whether it's talking to me or not."

"But metaphysics are the other half of it. You do notice metaphysics—you do—since one kind of spirit is always a woman and the other is always a man. You don't believe a deity ever walked the earth—you wouldn't, unless she's part of your religion—but we all agree that a ghost used to be part of our world."

♏ ♐

"Fair enough."

She squints. "So you could tell us whether Morgan le Fay is divine or just a witch."

"Who wants to know?"

"Some people at a cleansing retreat were up in arms over it. A whole tarot reading depended on the answer. Unless you're saying that someone's metaphysical essence collapses into their gender? That both kinds of spirit, the religious and the dead, are the same—? Some you see, some you don't—?"

"I can't follow. I may not understand spirits after all. Or gender."

"It's *your* story."

"I know, but my story doesn't make sense."

Stanley interrupts us. "Are we going to do the fire or not?"

For this campfire, I'd proposed a burning, inspired by the ashes at Amity Lodge.

♏ ♐

FIRESTARTER

STANLEY BURNS
HIS ART

Aparna gets a fire going in the backyard. She, Stanley and I are frozen in our fleece jackets. It's late in the year for this.

In Virgil's *Eclogues*, there's a lady who's contemplating fire safety with a pile of burning ash, and meanwhile the altars burst into flames. "Let this omen be good," she says, but "I know nothing for certain." Where do dreams come from? "Ipsi sibi somnia fingunt?" Are they made up?

"My friend Sara might come over, but I don't know when," Aparna warns us.

"OK, let's just get started," I say. "Diversity Committee is convened! Other people can join if and when they show up."

♏ ♐

Stanley goes first. He pulls a small piece of paper from his pocket. He opens the fold by gently pressing the middle and pulling the sides out, as if helping an injured bird spread its wings. I recognize his drawing of the stone wall at Amity Lodge with the indecipherable markings.

"You don't want that anymore?" I ask.

"No," he says.

"You used to be curious about that wall."

"I figured out what it said, so now I'm not curious anymore."

"I've always been curious."

"I'll tell you later, after I burn it."

"OK. Say: *I let go*," I instruct.

"I let go," he says, and tosses it afire. It's gone in two-and-a-half seconds.

♏ ♐

FLASHBULB

SAT
12 NOV
2016

APARNA BURNS
HER NECKLACE

FLASHBULB

SAT
12 NOV
2016

I BURN
MY PAPERCLIP

Aparna pulls something from her pocket, drops it into her palm, opens her hand to show us. A thin metal chain, bracelet or necklace. Firelight catches its links.

"What is it?" Stanley asks.

"Jewelry," she says. "A man gave it to me. I definitely don't need it anymore."

Into the fire it goes. I can't see where it lands, so I don't know if it melts. Aparna stares at a fixed location in the flames.

♏ ♐

My turn. My contribution is unimpressive, at least outwardly. I fish it out of my pants. It's a paperclip I brought here for this purpose.

"This is a tool," I say as if preaching a sermon, "that too easily joins together what never should have been joined. Let there be separation again: between this world and the other world, between today and the days to come."

"Amen," says Stanley reflexively.

I throw the paperclip into the center of the flames. The paperclip dies. I must have expected thunder and rain to mark the moment, because I notice: Nothing else happens.

♏ ♐

FLASHBULB

SAT
12 NOV
2016

LET THERE BE SEPARATION

FLASHBULB

SAT
12 NOV
2016

WHAT WAS WRITTEN ON THE STONE WALL

It shouldn't surprise me. Every Havdalah, the reflective separation to mark the end of the Sabbath and the beginning of the week, is like this. Havdalah makes no sound, but there you go, back to metaphysical work again.

Our circle feels awkwardly quiet. The night is profoundly cold, and it would be good to bring this circle to a close for the season, though no one wants to be first to give in to winter.

♏ ♐

"Stanley," I say to break the silence, "what was written on the wall?"

"Oh, yeah. I'll tell you." He flips his hood over his head and pulls the drawstring tight under his chin. He leans over the fire so it casts flickering shadows on his face. "It said—"

♏ ♐

Flyleaf —
Do Your Own Time

Peter Pan's six lost boys, wanting to be adopted and "wishing they were not wearing their pirate clothes," decide to let Wendy do the talking. They wait outside the Darling residence "to give Wendy time to explain about them; and when they had counted five hundred they went up." If we have not counted to 500 yet, then they are still waiting on the stair.

Under the rubric of "doing your own time," David Shields explains in <u>Reality Hunger</u>, Article 449, people in prison agree not to annoy each other by "complaining about your incarceration or regretting what you had done or, especially, claiming you hadn't done it." Not imprisoned himself and thus having a different perspective, Shields says he endorses "talking about everything until you're blue in the face."

WHAT IT SAID

Stanley pauses and takes a breath.
"SOPHIA STAY HERE WE WILL COME EVERY DAY!"
Aparna and I jump.
"Nice," she laughs.

450

AFTERPARTY

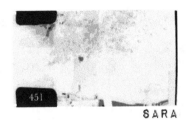

451

SARA

"I hereby adjourn this season of Diversity Committee Storytime. Tune in next summer," Stanley says.

Just then, another car pulls up. "Afterparty is convened!" Aparna says.

A woman steps out, approaching the fire. I've never met her before.

"Guys, this is Sara," Aparna says. "Sara, these are the guys."

"Sarah—cool name. Lev and I just rewatched *Labyrinth*. Sarah's one of our favorite heroes."

"No 'h,'" Sara corrects.

Sara unfolds a frozen chair, places it with a little crunch on the frosted lawn, and sits next to her friend.

"So, um, where do you know each other from?" I ask.

Aparna and Sara look at each other.

♏ ♐

"The firing range," Aparna says.

"The what," I say.

"Target practice. We shoot weapons."

"Like, guns?" Stanley asks.

"Yeah," says Aparna.

Do you own a gun? I ask.

"Yeah," she says.

"What kind of guns do you shoot?" Stanley asks.

"All of them," Sara says firmly, answering for Aparna.

"Since when?" I ask.

"Since I finished nursing my baby," Sara says.

"*What*," Stanley says.

"Where's yours?" I ask Aparna.

"Safe. Locked up."

Her closet. She has a weapon locked in her closet.

Stanley sits back in his chair. "Everyone needs to start telling me more," he says.

"What else do you want to know?" Aparna asks.

♏ ♐

STANLEY ASKS
TO SEE IT

DANCING
WITH MYSELF

"Why do you have a gun?" I ask.

"You never know when you might need it. Two women, my mom and I, living alone. One day, we might see a strange man in the driveway. Maybe he's shoveling snow for us. Maybe he's doing something else."

"Can I see the gun?" Stanley suggests. His fingers curl with the joyful muscle memory of holding a baseball bat.

"No," says Aparna, looking at Sara, who raises her eyebrow and shakes her head quietly.

We have brought Sara into the company.

"Why not?"

"Chekhov's law, inverted," Aparna says.

"If no one fired a gun in the play," Sara explains, "then you don't need—"

"OK, OK," Stanley says. "I don't need to see the gun."

♏ ♐

Of all people I could be annoyed at, I'm annoyed at Mariamman, who knew all this time that she'd been moved out of the upstairs closet to make room for a gun.

"You ought to have told me more," I tell her in my mind, a day after the revelation.

"You ought to have been talking to me in the first place," the goddess replies, turning her face away from me.

I turn up "Dancing with Myself" by Generation X in my headphones on my walk to nowhere.

♏ ♐

454

I SPOILED
L. D. LIQUE
FOR MYSELF

I haven't been back to L. D. Lique where I met up with Lear Noon. I spoiled that ice cream shop for myself, didn't I? Touching my tongue to the good apple in the forbidden moment: a shame and a crime. Next time I plan to have an awful discussion with a bad man, I will choose a five-dollar buffet off the side of Route 1 halfway to Providence so I won't care if I never look at the restaurant's sign again. I will not spoil the Garden of Eden. I will shit in a different garden so angels with flaming swords block the way back to *that* terrible place. I am getting smarter.

♏ ♐

455

I HAVE
ALREADY DECIDED

I haven't been back to Achromatic Propioception either. I quit that job. The door is closed. I cut the cord. I made a decision. As the water closes over my head, the idea begins to sink in: I can't go back.

My oxygen tank is working. I open my eyes underwater.

The fish. They're exquisite. Why didn't someone tell me?

"Where do you see yourselves in five years?" I ask the fish.

"Dead," they say, swimming in circles. "Can't you taste the acidification of these waters?"

"What do you need?"

"Another five years. We will always want another five years."

"How can I help?"

"You can stop bothering us. We'd like to see much less of you here, landlubber."

♏ ♐

456

IRREVERSIBILITY

457

HUMMINGBIRD
RIDDLE, ANSWERED

The cis-tem claims to protect us from our own gender transitions. *For your own good,* it says. *If you physically change your maleness or femaleness, those changes will be irreversible.*

Well, yes. Nothing reverts. The desk calendar flips the page, and it isn't Tuesday anymore. So be careful with every choice. Guard your words, your footsteps. Pay attention. Every decision you make about everything whatsoever is irreversible.

What if you regret yourself? Very well, says Walt Whitman's trans ghost, then I regret myself. Antifragility means failure makes me stronger. Irreversibility is the nature of time. The Great and Powerful Wizard of Trans has spoken.

Forget "transgender." Just say "trans." It's shorter.

♏ ♐

The word "trans" is the key.

The door to the riddle slides open. I can explain the yellow-bellied hummingbird I saw two years ago in Stanley's yard.

Hummingbirds of any species are sometimes yellow after they drink nectar. The flowers cover them in pollen. Stop and watch a hummingbird for three seconds. You may see it happen. One, two, *yellow.*

A coat of pollen is not easy to revert if you are a hummingbird, since you don't have hands. It is your nature to wear the pollen.

If I call myself "trans," people will assume I'm a Millennial. That's their factual error, and it's not so terrible to be perceived as a Millennial. There are worse fates.

♏ ♐

FLASHBULB

SUN
13 NOV
2016

458

SHADOW WORK OF HUMMINGBIRD'S VICTIM

FLASHBULB

SUN
13 NOV
2016

459

WE ARE STILL ON A LOOP

Hummingbirds are territorial, and Hummingbird is the representation of the Aztec War God Huitzilopochtli who springs out of his mother's womb early to defend her. He dismembers his sister Coyolxauhqui before she can hurt their mother. He throws her down the mountain. The flat image of her disordered parts is carved into the Coyolxauhqui Stone at the base of the Templo Mayor, excavated in Mexico City in 1978. The stone is a circle; Coyolxauhqui is the Moon. We see her in the sky, too. She is doing the shadow work all the time in the darkness, visible or no.

♏ ♐

I imagine that, inside A.P., the television still plays on a loop: mass shootings, tentacular evolutions of the Zapruder film, endless spinning of the roulette wheel from *Tele-Quiz*. It is no longer Groundhog Day. It is April Fool's. It is Independence Day. It is still a cycle, but the diameter of the wheel has expanded.

My question is not whether humans can change, but whether I am going to change. Only the inability to change would qualify me as old. That, and turning 36.

C'mere. Ask me if I am going to change. I dare you. Now ask me if I am going to change back to the way I was before. Ask me, again, if I am going to change.

♏ ♐

FLASHBULB

SUN
13 NOV
2016

EVERY BREATH

Up next on the playlist is what has got to be the most famous radio song of all time: The Police, "Every Breath You Take."[*]

You reverse the direction of your breath—in, out—but the micro-aging that occurs with every breath is irreversible. You keep yourself alive, life lets you go to your next stop, and you never really go back.

There goes a monarch butterfly, winging by on its curtain of flame. What is it still doing here? November. It should be in Mexico by now. What if it regrets itself?

The birds should be there too.

---

[*] In 2019, BMI recognized "Every Breath You Take" by the Police as the song in the BMI catalog with the all-time most plays on the radio. By then, the song had aired 15 million times since 1983.

461

WHERE THE CICADA
CAME FROM

462

THE HOLE IN THE
TRANSITION DONUT

And the door to another riddle slides open.

"Where did Chad come from?" my therapist asked me. I did not know what she meant. At last, I will come to know.

Let's start at the end. The end contains the beginning.

I go to Mount Auburn Cemetery and stand at Chad's grave. To think.

Chad was born on January 27, 1868. That's when his cicada crawled out of the earth. So, when you ask where that cicada came from—

You are asking who died exactly 17 years earlier.

This isn't hard to find out. John James Audubon.

♏ ♐

After the hole in the transition donut—a career hiatus, because of course every proper donut needs a hole—I send out my résumé. My résumé is the real-life Shield of Boringness from *Phoebe and Her Unicorn* that prevents grownups from getting riled up over the unicorn's paranormality. It says "reliable" at the top, and it succeeds in making me look so boring that I get a job interview.

"A cinematic image of nostalgia," says Svetlana Boym, "is a double exposure, or a superimposition of two images—of home and abroad, past and present, dream and everyday life. The moment we try to force it into a single image, it breaks the frame or burns the surface."

I will make my gender history explicit.

♏ ♐

FLASHBULB

TUE
22 NOV
2016

463

AN ADJACENT FACT

FLASHBULB

TUE
22 NOV
2016

464

I GET THE JOB

I couldn't write "Diversity Committee" on my resume because I did not engage in that official activity at the office, but when we're seated in the conference room, after we've been talking for what seems like an hour, I bring up an adjacent fact.

"You're *trans?*" the interviewer asks, as if she's fluent in that language.

"If that's what you call it here," I reply, "yes."

♏ ♐

I forgot something about cicadas. After an individual hatches from its egg, it goes through five growth stages in the darkness. The nymph's abdomen bulges—*the bigger the front, the bigger the back*—until, in the fifth stage, the cicada bursts out of the ground with wings. So, counting the egg-hatching, the five sizes of the nymph's abdomen, and the soil-eruption, the cicada comes out seven times before it's even able to have sex.

That's what this feels like: coming out yet again.

I am 36 years old today, but I believe I am not supposed to reveal my age. I do not want to press my luck.

I get the job.

♏ ♐

MY NEW SALARY

HALF OF INFINITY

Wanna know what the new job pays me, a dual-gender being who makes a mythologically Hermaphroditic claim, a double-faced Janus who guards the opening and shutting of every door? They pay me half, of course. *Half* of what I used to make in the closet. When they knew me merely as "a man," the money fell like rain. Now that I've opened the door to reveal my past gender, the money flows differently.

That's OK. I will not do the job for zero money, but I will do it for half the money.

Even though I am twice the gender.

The French would call me "décroissant": collapsing, falling, degrowing. Again, it's OK. It's the other side of lift experience.

♏︎ ♐︎

See here: I've made a good deal. Now that my gender isn't a secret, no coworkers can play extortion games or otherwise incorporate that detail into their violent fantasies. I have traded the power to make it rain for the power to promise that my gender will never again allow the world to be destroyed.

The universe is a supply closet of everlasting gobstoppers, and I'm a doorperson who helps hand them out to others. Since I have access to an infinity of infinities, I don't demand one that's "mine."

Though they assign me a half-gobstopper, it everlasts nonetheless. Infinity divided by two is infinity. I have enough. To know this is to inherit the kingdom of the chocolate factory. "Jesus plus nothing."

♏︎ ♐︎

FLASHBULB

MON
28 NOV
2016

MY NEW SEAT

They seat me near the supply closet. Paperclips galore. I don't complain. It is not mine to manage paperclips. It is mine to manage my meds. I am telling this story differently. The way I tell the story helps the story tell itself.

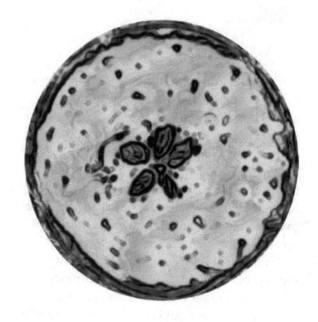

♏ ♐

Flyleaf — Unbelievable, Indestructible, Unturnable

Lewis Carroll warned that one should "shun / The frumious Bandersnatch!" But who is the Bandersnatch, and who shuns it?*

We need others to believe us. Unbelief is a kind of shunning.

And if we are unbelieved? Well, we go on. We inhabit our reality even when others can't reassure themselves we are real. "Frankly, I'm not responsible for other people's perceptions," Janet Mock wrote in Redefining Realness, "and what they consider real or fake."

I have not got Yiddish, but I have got an egg cream. I always thought the egg cream was a fake drink because it isn't made with egg. But no one ever claimed it was. In Yiddish, "echt": real. In the egg cream, realness hid behind fakeness, a mirror image of a hoax. It was exactly what it was supposed to be the whole time.

"Believing means," Kafka wrote in his diary, "freeing your own indestructibility [das Unzerstörbare]—or, better: freeing yourself—or, better: being indestructible—or, better: being." You keep going, being who you are, even when the world changes and you have to act, because something inside you is never destroyed and that's exactly what it means to be. Christopher Isherwood said certain places have it too: an "indestructible something…that resists all outward change." Which doesn't mean they don't experience outward change—only that the moving surface of the water is not all there is to being the river, nor is the undercurrent all there is, and in fact the whole river is always changing, yet it is the same river.

The last of the three Greek Fates, the one who cuts your thread to mark your death, is Atropos. Her name means "unturning." Amulets to ward off evil are called apotropaic because they turn away the spirits. Atropos is she who cannot be turned away.

Your life is spun at the beginning to be cut at the end. It is made to be destroyed. The force of Destruction is, itself, Indestructible, part of the plan.

The Indestructible is the one river of living, dying, changing.

♏ ♐

---

* Today the line also recalls the 2018 "Black Mirror" interactive online film *Bandersnatch* in which the viewer controls the protagonist.

FLASHBULB

MON
28 NOV
2016

THE BIRTH
OF AUDUBON

John James Audubon was born in Haiti on April 26, 1785. His parents brought him to France. At age 18, he fled the Napoleonic Wars. Arriving in New York, he began to study birds. He had no film. He drew, painted.

FLASHBULB

MON
28 NOV
2016

EVERYTHING
I REMEMBER

It's funny: I used to spend 50 hours a week at Achromatic Proprioception, but now everything I remember about that part of my life would fit in a short film.

FLASHBULB

MON
28 NOV
2016

DAS LINKE DIN

I don't update my professional social media with my new job. I pay attention to the name of the platform. Where *das beyzdin* is a rabbinic court, *das linke din* would be some kind of sinister tribunal, and I don't want a hearing before the wrong judge.

FLASHBULB

MON
28 NOV
2016

COUNTING
THE YEARS

In two weeks, it will be the feast day of Nuestra Señora de Guadalupe, marking 485 years since she appeared on a hill outside Mexico City. 485 celebrations plus the original event.

Sometimes, a memory has an expiration date. Sometimes, the film keeps going.

472

A GOOD USE
OF CAMERAS

473

OUT OF OFFICE
FOREVER

I haven't told you what I do at my new job. This company installs cameras to monitor wildlife. With a well-planned surveillance system, humans can learn about animals from a distance without disturbing them. We learn about hidden threats to their habitat. We learn from what we see and don't see: birds weaving plastic zipties into their nests, turtles not popping their heads up anymore after a new factory opens upstream. Instead of recording crimes already committed, the camera shows us new opportunities to step in and help. I still test cameras. This is a good use of cameras.

♍ ♐

My new boss isn't much older than I, and she doesn't capitalize "internet." Further, many of my new coworkers are younger than I, and they don't capitalize anything whatsoever and are unexcited about punctuation. If I had been born just one month later, Pew Research would count me as a Millennial. I suppose that is close enough for me to try to be part of the group. I stop capitalizing internet. I also stop capitalizing millennial.

If the Clippy character pops up in Microsoft Word, I can ignore it or I can turn it off. Those are my options. But Clippy doesn't show up in this new job. It is 2016. Clippy is gone. Out of Office forever. We have finally moved forward.

♍ ♐

474

WITHDRAW

475

DO GOOD WORK

I recall Amity Lodge as a wintry place, as it was when I last saw it. But I haven't been back there since I rescued the camera from the barn. I'm taking a break.

Driving to another parking lot to give away Stanley's car preserved the purity of Amity Lodge itself for me, but in the end I couldn't keep terribleness from mushrooming in the barn. Am taking ten steps back from that place.

I've learned: When I strike at my friendship, I kill the president, and what was needed of me was not a murder but an emptying. Sometimes I get a better outcome by withdrawing.

The cycle swung to summer, and now swings back. Rain turns to snow again. It falls soundlessly.

♏ ♐

The astronaut Gus Grissom, before his flight, walked onstage in front of thousands of rocket builders and told them: "Do good work." A consequentialist interpretation of the good, of course, based on the astronaut's needs. The crowd roared its approval. They would try to do it right.

By contrast, when E.T. came to Earth and also had need of a spaceship, he told the small human child: "Be good." No one claps at the movie scene because virtue-based ethics is a difficult instruction. Not *do*, but *be*. *Do not make me a spaceship; just be who you are supposed to be.*

How will we know when we are *being* correctly?

How will we know *when*, indeed.

♏ ♐

Flyleaf — Final Mountain

Moses's boss tells him: <u>Climb the final mountain, look out over the promised land you've sought all your life, and then die right where you stand, because you broke faith with me and I have never forgotten that.</u>*

Moses can make peace with this half of the everlasting gobstopper and find infinity in himself. His boss may not be talking to him. His friends may not be talking to him. He has to make peace with that too.

The magic is in Billy Idol's song "Eyes Without a Face," at least for the auto-fictional character in Luis Carlos Barragán's <u>Vagabunda Bogotá</u>. When it's raining hard—"cuando la lluvia dale que dale en la ventana, como si no tuviera nada mejor que hacer que golpear en mi ventana"—the song might come on the radio to wake him up and make him pay attention—"para que me despierte, para que le ponga atención."

It's supposed to rain Wednesday.

Moses doesn't have a radio. The silence is infinite. He takes half of the infinite silence and it's still infinite.

♏ ♐

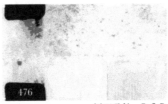

WHEN DID PEOPLE KNOW?

Here is a riddle about "knowing when": *When did people know they had survived the First World War?*

Here is a clue: Chad Goeing, though he didn't live to see the beginning of that war, could have answered correctly.

Answer: *When the Second World War began.* Only then did they realize they'd lived through the *first* one.

Do not underestimate the copy. It's never a copy. Even a réplica shakes the earth.

♏ ♐

---

* This is the 475th reading in Lev's schema: the 53rd weekly Torah portion, Ha'azinu, 7th reading.

FLASHBULB

MON
28 NOV
2016

477

I SHOW UP EARLY

I wonder what my new boss wants from me: *do good* or *be good*. I show up early to meetings, hoping to figure it out.

She smiles at me. "It's nice to work with someone who is on time."

♏ ♐

FLASHBULB

MON
28 NOV
2016

478

TELLING THE STORY

I will continue to think about how to tell this story. Shall I exploit Noon to create suspense, letting his behavior overshadow everything that was good about that job and that part of my life, when all that time he had a notebook with floorplans and machinations but perhaps not, crucially, a gun?

If he shoots people, my goddesses will know where the bodies fall.

But if he doesn't, do my goddesses know what didn't happen?

If they don't know what I stopped, then how do they judge me?

Maybe they don't.

♏ ♐

FLASHBULB

MON
28 NOV
2016

479

CHAIN OF CICADAS

John James Audubon died, and 17 years later Chad Goeing was born, and Chad Goeing died, and 17 years later John F. Kennedy was born, and John F. Kennedy died, and 17 years later I was born.

If I knew my date of death, I could tell you my date of rebirth. And if you knew the name of the person who will be born then, you could find them and tell them this story.

♏ ♐

Flyleaf — How Do Works Reincarnate?

Myths are a chain of stories, paper-clipped together, firm or fickle, open-ended in their attachment.

The silent film <u>The Changing of Silas Warner</u> was released in the United States on June 10, 1911. A businessman proposes a job and a marriage for his young son. The son chooses to go his own way, and it turns out for the best, as his father's gamble would have led to ruin. Maurice Sendak was born 17 years later on June 10, 1928. He published <u>Where the Wild Things Are</u> on April 9, 1963. It's a picture book of a little boy who dreams of uninhibited rumpusing with furry monsters. The censors went wild over the little pencil-loop representing the naked dancing boy's tiny penis. Seventeen years later, someone else gets born. When he is grown, he will write his own book. It's hard to see the point. But one can't see the system while one is inside it.

And so you leave the story. A boy invented stories in the garden, and his Velveteen Rabbit played a character. The Rabbit was real within those stories. In the garden, though, the Rabbit would have remained a toy forever, until one day, the nursery magic Fairy came for him and spirited him away. She dropped him in a field where "the fronds of the bracken shone like frosted silver," saying: "Now you shall be Real to every one." The Rabbit did not believe it was true until something "tickled his nose, and before he thought what he was doing he lifted his hind toe to scratch it."

The story gives you life, and you are made of that story and can never leave it except to perceive it as a story, which is to become the next level of real within your story. You perceive. You leave. You jump.

"I can't deny the fact that you like me. Right now, you like me," Sally Field said when she scooped up the Oscar. Everyone remembers her as saying "You <u>really</u> like me." Maybe because we're all in the "right now," and we want to believe that, if we're famous enough, if we're liked enough, it won't just be for "right now," and we'll become real.

My most famous short film replays in my head. I can't unsee it. It's the <u>film-pelt</u>. Two redundant words. Both words mean the membrane that covers the animal, separates it from sky, transcends the animal-and-sky distinction. Skin is out, in, and out-and-in. Film doesn't just contain the art; it is the art.

♏ ♐

FLASHBULB

MON
28 NOV
2016

480

AMPHIBIAN

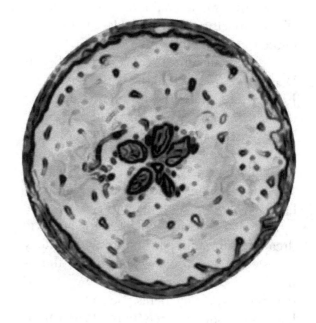

♏ ♐

I email Stanley from my personal phone. I tell him I fear no one will "get" a transgender book that I write.

"Because any sufficiently transgender book is indistinguishable from magic?" he asks.

"No," I say, "because any sufficiently transgender book will never find a publisher."

(Except of course for Janet Mock's *Redefining Realness* which I bought in Provincetown.)

Because the transgender speaker will be seen as flouting cisgender conventions of knowledge acquisition and, even worse for marketing goals, cisgender reading preferences.

(But is there room for one more?)

I don't know.

What if the book amphibiously changes its own sex?

What if the book makes the reader trans?

Flyleaf — TransDictation

The Stuffed Animal Fallacy

Angry cis people yell worse things as a drive-by. It sounds like a vegetable thrown at a Rite of Spring, but darkly sparkling—a beer bottle.

If they can't catch me, they'll argue at a straw man. I'd rather call it the "stuffed animal" fallacy, since that would be gender- and species-neutral, but no one ever asks me to rename their fallacies. Anyway, it describes how easy it is to win an argument with a toy. A toy that contains your own vocal projection.

They make Teddy Ruxpin say supposedly "trans" things, then say they have outgrown Teddy Ruxpin, call him an unnatural hybrid, dispose of him.

This is why the toy manufacturers don't sell transgender tapes to put inside him.

I Didn't Do the Thing That Didn't Happen

This is why, if a trans person dictates a trans book into a tape, the publishing house will not take it. They will say the words were taped on the wrong side and sound better played backwards. And when they ask why I betrayed their brother, I can't argue on their terms. Jesus never existed, I didn't kill him, and neither he nor I were present two thousand years ago to not-do it.

Here's how I remember the Latin grammar rule:

Noon-time is nunc-time.
Dream-time is iam-time.
Flashbulb.
Fog.

Betrayals

Martin Heidegger, rector at Freiburg, formally joined the Nazi Party. It was 1933. I've never read his Sein und Zeit (Being and Time), since the predicament of a silent academic Nazi, I feel, poses its own real-life commentary on "being and time," emerging from the simple condition of "being there," a concept that, I hear, Heidegger called "Dasein." He was there, all right. And I choose not to make time to read his book.

When I write my Transbeing in Spacetime (Transsein in der Raumzeit), I'll discuss how time might be a coin you can "spend" but it's relative to your location, since, across the border, no one accepts your pocketchange. People who disagree with my transbeing in spacetime—that is, with how I live my life—may choose not to make spacistime for my books. Their choicis are theirs to make.

Heidegger talked about how we don't choose to be born, nor when and where to be born, nor who we are, nor most of the circumstances of our lives. We're *thrown* here ("geworfen"). I know he said this because I read other books about his book.

Individual death and collective salvation can be a thrownness too, which I know from reading the final scene of *The Lord of the Rings* in which Gollum bites off Frodo's finger to get the evil ring but then trips and falls into the volcano with it.

When I tell a manager now (nunc) that Lear Noon is coming to destroy us now (iam), they ask: <u>Right the actual now? No? Well, then, off you go! We only talk about what is happening right the actual now.</u>

Red cedars on the Cape: dying. Once, there were cedar forests, but now, the sea level rises and the ocean moves inland, salting their roots.*

T.T.P.E.

The dating system I'm accustomed to is the Common Era.

But: Consider dates in the Transgender Tipping Point Era, T.T.P.E. The DSM-5 came out in Year −1, and the ground was seeded. The Transgender Tipping Point was a birth and a crucifixion, predestined when it came into being, alpha and omega, Year 0. A man came down a golden escalator in Year 1. He was elected in Year 2.

This dating system creates the illusion that all trans people were born yesterday. Of course, some of us transitioned B.T.T.P.E., before the current era. We had vinyl record players and sent letters with stamps. And we weren't less trans.

By 1919, Amelio Robles Ávila commanded three hundred men in the Mexican Revolution. He'd declared himself a man several years before that, and he lived as a man for the rest of his life.

Simona Amaya put on a battle uniform and died for Colombian independence in 1819.

Before "transsexual," there was something else. Even if we didn't know what we were and still don't know. We are humans, and the people who have existed have been more than one thing, and being more than one thing is kind of trans, even when it's arguably cis.

We've been here always and forever.

The T.T.P.E. dating system is not about us. It is about how they see us. Right here, right now.

Moving On

I still haven't understood enough of Chad Goeing's unpublished manuscript <u>The Nature of Time</u> to biosketch the author. That's all right, I guess. The value of his book may have expired. I may not have to reconstruct him.

Time itself may have an expiration date. Have I gotten the metaphysical point

---

* The threat posed by salt water to red cedars is mentioned by Tom Zoellner in his essay "King Philip's Shadow" printed in *The National Road: Dispatches from a Changing America* (Counterpoint, 2020).

about moving on? Father Time is not sitting on a park bench in our own pasts waiting for us to forget him. Princess Zelda and Link can't actually call upon the Goddess of Time to give them a mulligan.

Maybe Time is not, after all, a helping friend who may be spatially near or far in times of trouble. Maybe Time is just a reality-organizing system.

The Rabbis Had No Wormhole

Why did no one who personally knew Moses write an adaptation of the Torah?

Because Moses' friends were all dead by the time the Torah entered the public domain. The copyright rule is: "life of the author plus 70 years." The rabbis took 70 years to come up with a loophole, and since it was not a wormhole, they were too late.

I haven't spoken to a rabbi lately. Not since one told me I was wearing a wire. I haven't done anything with—nor to—Christianity either, I swear. I have a momentary urge to recite the Lord's Prayer but all I can remember is: "Our nada who art in nada, nada be thy name." Not Mary Oliver but Ernest Hemingway this time.

Why People Ask Bad Questions

There are no gods. Maybe there are goddesses. I don't know if a rabbi will talk to me about my diminishing half-belief. I don't know if I want to talk about stories I don't want to tell anymore.

They still believe I killed Jesus. That is mostly about being Jewish.

They believe I ruined the Romans too. That is mostly about being gay.

They'd be better off with the rainfall-assassination hypothesis: The farmers slew the governors because it didn't rain.

Part of moral imagination is asking better questions.*

Each of us has Dasein because we are here, but we don't need a dead nominal-Nazi philosopher to tell us where we are. We can design a better life on our own. We can Dasein it here and now.

Here They Come

They are jealous that we bears know where the honey is and that we are eating it peacefully. They've given up on the bees, and now they are bear-hunting. The spear-points have tipped. They are coming into our cave.

Here they come. Here they come.

The bear has no defense. Can't pretend

---

* "Part of moral imagination is asking better questions." An interview prompted me toward the framing of this thought: "Sophie Grace Chappell on Plato and the Moral Imagination," published by Will Buckingham on *Looking for Wisdom*, August 26, 2021.

it did not taste the honey. Even if it had not, the hunters would still come for it.

The last strategy: transformation.

Apomelissis

The end of the story is not the end of the work.* Apotheosis is the way out of the cave. The grendel-fighting bear uses its learning from the apiary. It celebrates its monster-conquests with the honey wine called mead in the bear-hall. Let the grendel, defeated, crawl off to its non-bear lair. The bear activates its apomelissis: becoming the bee.

Now its body lifts, fizzily, up the shaft in the tunnel, toward whatever those whirring wings of illumination might be. The blades of the fan cannot harm it; we are the bear, the bear is the bee, the bee's wings are the blades of the fan, and thus we shed one life to escape to the next, reincarnation, world without end.

Apotheghostis

When you're with Elvis at the gates of Graceland, and Elvis walks past security, then you, too, learn to strut right through. Elvis is soon to turn 82. Now, you, too, are the King.

We attach ourselves to things we're afraid of losing, said Simone Weil, and specifically because we believe they depend on us for their reality. Regarding what we're sure is Real all on its own, "there is no cord which can be cut" because "we are not attached" to it in the first place. And then it enters us.

If you are a man, you can become a ghost, at least, if not a god. You can achieve apotheghostis. This will have to be enough. If you're a woman, no apotheghostis, but you can be a goddess. No, none of it makes sense.

"In different times, and among different peoples and in different places, divine messengers have walked among us," Gabriel Horn and Amy Krout-Horn wrote. Their comings, goings, and beings are "transmutable as thought into any form at will, like smoke into wind, as story into form."

The sun and moon are up there, but we don't use discs anymore. When we want to remember something, we put it in the cloud.

Here's another good word for my moral edification: "nonbinary." I will work on my word list. Wicked trans nonbinary internet.

---

* Literary critic Frank Kermode in *The Sense of an Ending* (1965) said stories need satisfying endings, just as the Christian story offers an ending that provides a meaning to everything that came before. Dara Horn dissents, saying that Jewish storytelling recognizes that we "cannot be true to the human experience while pretending to make sense of the world," and so a story may instead serve as "the beginning of the search for meaning." Dara Horn. *People Love Dead Jews: Reports from a Haunted Present*. W. W. Norton and Co., 2021.

Not in Your Wild-Cis Dreams

"All this will not be finished in the first one hundred days," JFK said in his inaugural address. Not in your wild-cis dreams. "Nor will it be finished in the first one thousand days, nor in the life of this administration, nor even, perhaps, in our lifetime on this planet. But let us begin."

Non-muscular strengths: Naming a power and letting it go. Learning to wield a gun you hope you never fire. Getting rid of the gun.

I am in the nonbinary of living-and-dying, saving-and-destroying, cherishing-and-letting-go.

A big first day at a new job.

Sitting in my chair like a man in a René Magritte portrait who is probably René Magritte, gazing just above an egg on my desk, while painting, on my canvas, a full-grown wing-flapping bird I speculiriate.

No one else will tell my story for me anymore.

The boss does not exist. Something else exists.

♏︎ ♐︎

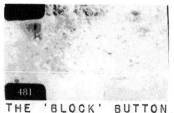

481

THE 'BLOCK' BUTTON

482

FIND
THE RIGHT SPOT
IN THE WOODS

One thing I can do differently: I can block Lear Noon on professional social media. The "block" button exists for a reason. I can use it. I always knew that was the right answer. My therapist suggested as much. Close that door on the angelic plane. It is easy. There, he's gone from my screen. That's better.

Another thing I could do, going forward, is to be more judicious in my use of the word "terrible." That would be a start. It might be the right thing to do. It's a verbal tic. I could, like everyone else in Boston, just say "wicked."

♏ ♐

The story has a structure. Otherwise you wouldn't know it's ending.

I've shaken off my old skin. It's time for someone else to lose his.

I won't show Noon the spot in the woods, but I hope I've built a world in which he finds it for himself.

The rest of us have done it. Stanley burned his art-scribble from his breakup summer, Aparna burned her necklace, and I burned a paperclip.

It's his turn to walk across that frozen field at Amity Lodge, his boots punching through the ice veneer, his face reflecting in the shining whiteness. His turn to sit down with his gay trauma by a duck pond with no ducks and to figure out the proper use of the firepit.

♏ ♐

FLASHBULB

TUE
29 NOV
2016

483

BE LESS META

FLASHBULB

TUE
29 NOV
2016

484

THE REVERSAL
IS IRREVERSIBLE

Having learned to tell my story more consciously, I'll also learn when to dial it down. I'll know when to be less "meta," less self-conscious.

It's hard to speak through a silencing. Yelling is not the way.

I choose quiet. I push the "off" button. The quiet is profound. The sound of silence attains profundity through our attention and our choices.

The story's structure is a burndown chart. It shows how much work and how much time remain.

I'll have a beer.

Noon has to do this too. He has to save himself first.

That's how to back out of the story. Burn all objects to which you've attached yourself, the ones you've discovered are holding you back and trapping you in a crumbling narrative.

Beowulf cut off the monster Grendel's arm at the shoulder and let Grendel slink back to his lair to die. Beowulf didn't follow, didn't watch. He trusted that process.

Never mind the past, for now, but try to reverse the future. Don't ask how to take revenge on the office. Ask a better question. Switch the train to another track. If there is no switch, but if you are nevertheless truly committed to changing, burn the track ahead of you. If you can't reach the track because you are on the train, spread your yellow canary wings and fly.

Commit to what you are reversing. The reversal will be irreversible.

Everything will end in the fire. The fire infuses the air.

485

THERE'S NO CHAIR IN 'NORWEGIAN WOOD'

The Statue of Liberty winks, and the sea level rises.

You don't have to break a lamp, target-practice on clay pigeons, or put a rose on a grave. Wait for the rose to kiss you.

Writer, murder your darlings. Do it without a gun. There's no chair in "Norwegian Wood," and you can chill out in the bathtub until you get it right. There's always another way. Here's one: If you're overthinking, smear ice cream on your toes.

The canary has flown. Turn on your electric headlamp in your cave. Stew in a cloud of black-cherry vapor. This isn't a pipe. It's a story about a pipe. Wait for the oracle to speak. Stop riddling in Latin, and eat real jam.

Until then, it's always-winter-never-Christmas.

♏ ♐

FOG — ALLELUS

In the land of Medio-Teísmo (Half-Theism), the Boss answers the door.

A giant snowflake lands on his nose and melts. *Telique*. El teísmo se derrite. This is the wrong climate for theism. The boss may be home, but your ideology can't touch his nose.

He addresses the crowd. "Can you cut it out with the 'allelus' already? I already sent you Santa. What more do you want?"

"Light," the wandering carollers beseech.

"I already sent you trans people."

For some reason, this answer does not satisfy.

"*Watt*, more?" the Boss says, incredulous.

"Allelu, allelu," the faithful chant.

"Hale luz, ya," the Boss tells them. "I gave you a lamp. Pull the cord already. Fifty, one hundred, one-fifty watts. No more *fiats*. Do it yourself."

♏ ♐

FOG — MOLON LABE

I've got the lamp.

"Molon la-veh, Yah-veh," I challenge the sky.

"Ave," echoes María from my pocket, adding, "dominus tecum." *The boss is on your side.*

Ave, that's it! *That's* what I meant to say a while back. Not a bird but a salutation. Not "do good," not "be good," but *ave*— "be well."

♏ ♐

420

Flyleaf — Trust

We have told a story, and many things were neither defined nor explained.

"I don't want to talk to you either," the Boss says, turning to me. "But at least <u>I trust you now</u>, to borrow from Toni Morrison's closing of her Nobel lecture: 'I trust you with the bird that is not in your hands because you have truly caught it.'"

♏ ♐

486

MAGNICIDIUM
OPERIS

This is the final frame of the Zapruder tape. There are 486 images.

This is the hour of the alternate magnicide: the immolation of the *magnum opus*, the *magnicidium operis*.

"Discrimen rerum," Cicero said. A *distinction*, a *crisis point*, but hear the better translation: *Dis-crime*.

Sheaf of papers, lists of ammo, old office floor plans annotated in red pen. In those corridors he penned the ending to my story.

Form backing into *wind* backing into *story* backing into *smoke*.*

I don my teal deerskin. An inherited superpower. I am were-deer, watching.

If I may refer to this wintry habitat, outside time, as "now"—

Right about now, Noon burns his writings, scrying the fire, unreading his markings as they self-delete.

TL;DR: Paper to ash.

---

* "*Form* backing into *wind* backing into *story* backing into *smoke*" refers back to the passage quoted in "Flyleaf — TransDictation": "Apotheghostis." It is from Gabriel Horn and Amy Krout-Horn, *Transcendence*.

PRIOR PUBLICATION

Some of these sentences were previously published as a short story called "Exit Interview" in Mad Scientist's 2019 fiction anthology about imaginary friends, *I Didn't Break the Lamp*. For that publication, I am grateful to editors Dawn Vogel and Jeremy Zimmerman. Although I titled Frame 406 in its honor, the original story does not reappear in this novel as a distinctly identifiable and separable part. Instead, its sentences have been reworded and threaded throughout.

"Exit Interview," as published in that anthology, included the riddle on my fictional *Tele-Quiz* game show, imagined as a spinoff of *CBS Television Quiz*, the first regularly scheduled game show, which aired as a live broadcast from New York in 1941–2. There are no surviving audiorecordings or photographs of the show.

The fictional character of Chad Goeing, whose ghost reenacts his death, was loosely inspired by a real person: Edward "Ned" D. Cumming (1901–1940). Cumming had no descendants, so none of his relations noticed when I created Chad Goeing for the fictional "Exit Interview" in the 2019 anthology; nor even when I published a biography of Cumming, *Ten Past Noon: Focus and Fate at Forty*, in 2020; nor will they notice that I have revived his fictional ghost in this 2022 novel. The similarities are slight: Cumming and Goeing both left behind an unfinished handwritten manuscript in an archive, and they share a manner of death, though Cumming died in New York in 1940 and I have reimagined Goeing as dying in Boston in 1900.

If other characters in *Most Famous Short Film of All Time* had been loosely inspired by anyone real, I would have made the similarities undetectable, and I wouldn't have asked permission from the dead or the living.

I wish also to mention that a discussion of Peter Pan in "Fog — The Tale of the Heartless Flying Boy (D.C. Storytime #1)" is based on a monologue I wrote when Tony Amato invited me to perform at "Queer Soup" in Boston. I read the monologue aloud on stage on February 7, 2010, but the words were never printed.

THANK YOU

For help with iterations of this story.

Dawn Vogel
Erik Hane
Chloe Clark
Alex DiFrancesco
Bryan Cebulski
Chaya Bhuvaneswar
Venus Davis
Elizabeth Kay

Arturo Serrano
Elif Offner
Vaishnavi Sharma
Justin Lehrer
Dale Stromberg
Remi Recchia
Jesus MacLean
Gordon Bonnet

AC—CritiqueMatch
John Petts—CritiqueMatch
Laura Scalzo
Izzy Wallace—Passengers Press
Félix González Montejo
Ryszard I. Merey
Neha Patel—Salt & Sage
Dev Ramsawakh

and

Noemí Ixchel Altagracia Martínez Turull—Noemí's Starship Consulting Services

GREAT APPRECIATION

To my parents, for their support of my art; to my husband, who endures my moods while I make it; and to Ryszard I. Merey for reading this book more than once and extending the offer to stamp T for tRaum on it. We did it.

To the Dallas County Historical Foundation, which runs the Sixth Floor Museum at Dealey Plaza, for allowing the use of the images that appear throughout the paperback version of this book. These are altered views of the 486 frames of the Zapruder Film. I applied digital filters, flipping black and white to make them look like photo negatives, and I put numbers in the corners. Like every altered thing, they simultaneously are and are not the original thing.

A CLOSING REFLECTION

Years ago, I read a poem called "Cultural Exchange" in Roger Dunsmore's 2004 collection *Tiger Hill*. The poem recalls a class where he screened *The Great Gatsby*, likely a home VHS recording someone made from the television. One student turned in an essay about the baseball scores that the TV channel had displayed in a corner over the film. In Dunsmore's poem, the student "thinks Gatsby and Tom / are fighting over Daisy / and the numbers show / who is winning," which, for either him or the student, "is difficult to explain."

Let me simplify it: In *Most Famous Short Film of All Time*, the occasional Red Sox scores and the Cubs' 2016 World Series victory explain nothing. A cigar is just a cigar. But everything else in the novel, I hope, is important.

The most famous film of the JFK assassination was almost not made because Abe Zapruder left his camera at home when he went to see the motorcade. "It's been said that he forgot it, or that it was overcast and that he feared rain, or that he was afraid he was too short to get a good enough view to take the pictures. Any of these explanations could be true," Alexandra Zapruder wrote of her grandparents' activity on the morning of the JFK assassination in *Twenty-Six Seconds: A Personal History of the Zapruder Film*, "but they fail to take into account just how predictable it was that he would leave the camera at home and that Lillian would talk him into going back to get it."

I've carried my camera and tried not to forget.

Five years ago, if you asked me what book I would like to have written five years in the future, I would have given a specific answer. Now, if you permit me to revise my memory of what I once believed I wanted, I will tell you that I would like to have said five years ago that I wished to spend five years writing something that still lay beyond my ability to imagine or comprehend. I would have asked for growth beyond anything I could plan.

426

CAST OF ARTIFACTS

In order of their appearance in the world outside the film.

10th century BCE	Psalm 109		Some Psalms are said to have been written as early as the 10th century BCE.
441 BCE	*Antigone*	Sophocles	
390 BCE	*Charmides*	Plato	A Socratic dialogue about self-knowledge. Translated by Benjamin Jowett, 1892.
375 BCE	*The Republic (Politeia)*	Plato	Contains the Socratic dialogue with the allegory of the cave.
161 BCE	*The Eunuch (Eunuchus)*	Terence	
51 BCE	Letter 107 (11.7) addressed to C. Curio	Cicero	"Quod in rei publicae tempus non incideris sed veneris (iudicio enim tuo, non casu, in ipsum discrimen rerum contulisti tribunatum tuum)…"
39–38 BCE	*Eclogues*	Virgil	"'aspice, corripuit tremulis altaria flammis / sponte sua, dum ferre moror, cinis ipse. bonum sit!' / nescio quid certe est, et Hylax in limine latrat. / credimus? an, qui amant, ipsi sibi somnia fingunt? / parcite, ab urbe venit, iam parcite, carmina, Daphnis." Part VIII, Lines 105–109
1st–2nd century	*Moralia*	Plutarch	Sayings of the Spartans (Apophthegmata Laconica), 225c.11

1st–2nd century	*Satires*	Juvenal	Satire VI, lines 347–348
2nd–4th century	*Book of Creation (Sefer Yetzirah)*		
399	*In Eutropium*	Claudian	
5th–6th century	Babylonian Talmud		Tractate *Yoma* 63a and 64a–b
7th–10th century	*Beowulf*		
9th century	*Bibliotheca, or Myriobiblos*	Photius	Entry #94 on the *Dramaticon* by Iamblichus
13th century	*Prose Edda*	Snorri Sturluson	The first part, called "Gylfaginning."
13th century	*Book of Splendor (Zohar)*	Moses de León	Section 1:72b. Translated from the Zoharic Aramaic by Elliot Wolfson, 1998.
1228	*The Gateless Gate (Wúménguān in Mandarin, Mumonkan in Japanese)*	Wumen Huikai, compiler	Translated by Eiichi Shimomissé, 1998.
13th–14th century	Sermons	Meister Eckhart	
1330–32	*Essays in Idleness (Tsurezuregusa)*	Yoshida Kenkō	Kenkō and Chōmei. *Essays in Idleness* and *Hōjōki*. Translated from Japanese by Meredith McKinney. Penguin Classics, 2013.

1440	*De Docta Ignorantia*	Nicholas of Cusa	
1517	*Ninety-Five Theses (Disputatio pro declaratione virtutis indulgentiarum)*	Martin Luther	
1577	*Historia general de las cosas de la Nueva España*	Bernardino de Sahagún	
1608	*King Lear*	William Shakespeare	
1733–34	"An Essay On Man: Epistle II"	Alexander Pope	Sections V and VI
1775	"Masrur the Eunuch and Ibn Al-Karibi"		*The Book of the Thousand Nights and a Night,* translated from Arabic to English by Richard Burton, Vol. 5, London, 1885 (Based on the Egyptian version, 1775)
1780	"The Twelve Days of Christmas"		Lyrics published 1780.
1812	"Rumpelstiltskin"	Brothers Grimm	Printed in *Children's and Household Tales,* 1812
1815	*The Manuscript Found in Saragossa (Manuscrit trouvé à Saragosse)*	Jan Potocki	Translated from French by Ian Maclean. London and New York: Viking, 1995. The passage from "The Fourteenth Day" is from p. 165.
1816	"Darkness"	Lord Byron	
1824	"Don Juan"	Lord Byron	Canto XVI, Verse 28

1844	*The Concept of Anxiety: A Simple Psychologically Oriented Deliberation in View of the Dogmatic Problem of Hereditary Sin (Begrebet Angest)*	Søren Kierkegaard (as Vigilius Haufniensis)	Translated from Danish by Alastair Hannay. New York: Liveright, 2015. His famous dictum that life must be understood backwards and lived forwards is from *The Diary of Søren Kierkegaard*. I've seen it cited to a section called "Philosophy and Science," Part 5, Set 4, No. 136 in a 1960 edition of the *Diary* from Citadel Press.
1851	*Moby-Dick*	Herman Melville	
1855	"Song of Myself"	Walt Whitman	"Do I contradict myself? / Very well then I contradict myself, / (I am large, I contain multitudes.)" Part 51 of "Song of Myself," published in *Leaves of Grass* (1855).
1860s	["Tell all the truth but tell it slant—"]	Emily Dickinson	Written c. 1858–1865. First published posthumously in 1945.
1860s	["They say that 'time assuages'…"]	Emily Dickinson	Written c. 1863. First published posthumously in the *Independent* (1896) and in *Poems* (1896).
1865	*Alice's Adventures in Wonderland*	Lewis Carroll	
1871	*Through the Looking Glass*	Lewis Carroll	Contains the poem "Jabberwocky."
1895	*The Antichrist (Der Antichrist)*	Friedrich Nietzsche	
1897	*Dracula*	Bram Stoker	
1899	"Screen Memories" ("Über Kindheits- und Deckerinnerungen")	Sigmund Freud	Monatsschrift für Psychiatrie und Neurologie 18 (1899):285–310.

1900	"When I Knew Stephen Crane"	Willa Cather	*The Library.* June 23, 1900.
1901	"El corrido de Gregorio Cortez"		Folk ballad developed after Cortez's arrest in 1901.
1903	*The Souls of Black Folk*	W. E. B. Du Bois	
1904	*Peter Pan*	James Barrie	
1905	*Sultana's Dream*	Roquia Sakhawat Hussain	
1908	"Archaic Torso of Apollo" ("Archaïscher Torso Apollos")	Rainer Maria Rilke	
1911	*The Changing of Silas Warner*		Film produced by Vitagraph Company of America
1911	*The Philosophy of 'As if': A System of the Theoretical, Practical and Religious Fictions of Mankind (Die Philosophie des Als Ob)*	Hans Vaihinger	Translated by C. K. Ogden. First published in England 1924. London: Routledge & Kegan Paul Ltd. (1952). Chapter XX: "The Separation of Scientific from other Fictions, particularly from the Æsthetic."
1913	*Swann's Way (Du côté de chez Swann)*	Marcel Proust	*In Search Of Lost Time (À la recherche du temps perdu),* Vol. 1
1914	*Niebla*	Miguel de Unamuno	

1915	*The Metamorphosis (Die Verwandlung)*	Franz Kafka	
1916	*Diaries (Oktavhefte)*	Franz Kafka	"Glauben heißt: das Unzerstörbare in sich befreien, oder richtiger: sich befreien, oder richtiger: unzerstörbar sein, oder richtiger: sein." Third Notebook [Drittes Heft], 1916
1917	"Song of a Man Who Has Come Through"	D. H. Lawrence	*Look! We Have Come Through!* (1917) The "three strange angels" are a reference to Genesis, Chapter 18.
1922	*The Velveteen Rabbit, or, How Toys Become Real*	Margery Williams Bianco	
1923	*The Prophet*	Kahlil Gibran	"On Good and Evil," "On Laws"
1927	*Being and Time (Sein und Zeit)*	Martin Heidegger	
1927	*Now We Are Six*	A. A. Milne	
1929	"The Treachery of Images"	René Magritte	
1932	*Maxwell House Haggadah*		Printed every year for Passover since 1932.
1933	"A Clean, Well-Lighted Place"	Ernest Hemingway	"Our nada who art in nada, nada be thy name."
1934	"The Night of the Great Season" ("Noc wielkiego sezonu")	Bruno Schulz	Originally published in the story collection *The Cinnamon Shops (Sklepy Cynamonowe)* in 1934. The collection was also translated as *The Street of Crocodiles* by Celina Wieniewska in 1963.

1936	"Clairvoyance"	René Magritte	
1939	*At Swim-two-birds*	Flann O'Brien	London: MacGibbon & Kee, 1961. ("Flann O'Brien" is a pseudonym for Brian O'Nolan.)
1939	*Goodbye to Berlin*	Christopher Isherwood	*The Berlin Stories* consist of two novellas: *Mr Norris Changes Trains* (1935) and *Goodbye to Berlin* (1939). New York: New Directions, 2008. "…indestructible something…" "About This Book," July 1954 preface. p. xx. "I am a camera…" *Goodbye to Berlin*, p. 207. "Certainly not here…" *Goodbye to Berlin*, pp. 211–212.
1939	*The Wizard of Oz*		Film directed by Victor Fleming
1940	"I've Got No Strings"		Song from the Disney film *Pinocchio*
1942	*La Silence de la Mer*	Jean Bruller (as Vercors)	
1942	*Casablanca*		Film directed by Michael Curtiz
1945	*Focus*	Arthur Miller	
1947	*The Plague (La Peste)*	Albert Camus	Translated from French by Stuart Gilbert (1948). New York: Vintage, 1991. Part III. pp. 255–256.
1947	*The Ethics of Ambiguity (Pour une morale de l'ambiguïté)*	Simone de Beauvoir	Translated from French by Bernard Frechtman (1948). New York: Open Road Integrated Media Inc., 2019. "…someone told a young invalid who wept because she had to leave her home, her occupations, and her whole past life, 'Get cured. The rest has no importance.' 'But if nothing has importance,' she answered, 'what good is it to get cured?'" p. 114.

1947	*Gravity and Grace (La Pesanteur et la grâce)*	Simone Weil	Translated from French by Emma Crawford and Mario von der Ruhr. London and New York: Routledge, 2002. pp. 11, 64.
1947	"The Riddle"	Walter de la Mare	From *Collected Stories for Children*
1950	*The Lion, The Witch, and the Wardrobe*	C. S. Lewis	Book One of *The Chronicles of Narnia*
1950	"Frosty the Snowman"	Gene Autry and the Cass County Boys	Single
1952	*Invisible Man*	Ralph Ellison	
1952	*4'33"*	John Cage	
1952	*Confabulario*	Juan José Arreola	The story is "El silencio de Dios." *Confabulario definitivo.* Edición de Carmen de Mora. Ediciones Cátedra, 1986. pp. 184–5.
1955	*The Return of the King*	J. R. R. Tolkien	Third book in *The Lord of the Rings* trilogy
1955	"Unchained Melody"	Alex North, music; Hy Zaret, lyrics	Soundtrack to the film *Unchained* (1955)
1955	Letter to the family of Michele Besso	Albert Einstein	
1956	Letter to Amy Ronald	J. R. R. Tolkien	27 July 1956. "Letter 192." Published in *The Letters of J. R. R. Tolkien* (1981). Christopher Tolkien, edited by Humphrey Carpenter.

1956	*The Minority Report*	Philip K. Dick	
1956	*The Hundred and One Dalmatians*	Dodie Smith	
1957	"The Blank Page"	Karen Blixen (as Isak Dinesen)	Printed in *Last Tales*
1958	*Things Fall Apart*	Chinua Achebe	
1958	*Thoughts in Solitude*	Thomas Merton	
1958	*Patterns in Comparative Religion (Traite d'histoire des Religions)*	Mircea Eliade	Translated from French by Rosemary Sheed. New York: Sheed & Ward, 1958. "…the God of the Christian mystics and theologians is terrible and gentle at once…" Section 159. "*Coincidentia Oppositorum*—The Mythical Pattern." p. 419.
1961	*Totality and Infinity: An Essay on Exteriority ("Totalité et Infini: essai sur l'extériorité")*	Emmanuel Levinas	Translated from French by Alphonso Lingis. "C. The Ethical Relation and Time." Duquesne University Press, 1969. p. 237.
1961	*The Phantom Tollbooth*	Norton Juster	
1963	*Where the Wild Things Are*	Maurice Sendak	
1963	Most famous short film of all time	Abraham Zapruder	

1963	*Eichmann in Jerusalem: A Report on the Banality of Evil*	Hannah Arendt	
1963	*Let's Make a Deal*		Game show. First episode aired 1963.
1963	"Puff the Magic Dragon"	Peter, Paul and Mary	Single
1964	"The Sound of Silence"	Simon & Garfunkel	Album: *Wednesday Morning, 3 A.M.*
1965	"Norwegian Wood (This Bird Has Flown)"	The Beatles	Album: *Rubber Soul*
1966	"On Keeping a Notebook"	Joan Didion	Printed in *Slouching Toward Bethlehem*
1966	*Mission: Impossible*		TV series created by Bruce Geller
1966	"I'm a Believer"	The Monkees	Album: *More of the Monkees*
1966	"Paperback Writer"	The Beatles	Single
1967	Interview of Ray Marcus (May 11, 1967)	Orleans Parish Grand Jury Special Investigation	Present: J. Garrison, District Attorney; A. Oser, J. Alcock, R. Burnes, A. Sciambra, W. Martin, Assistant District Attorneys; and members of the Orleans Parish grand jury. Reported by M. B. Thiel, secretary. "The Zapruder film is a clock against which all other films are checked." p. 72. "I am going to ask you to get up and go to the back of the room as you should see this at a distance where you no longer can see the dots. I want you to lose the dots. If you see the dots you are too close. You can't see the picture if you see the dots." p. 74.

1968	"In-A-Gadda-Da-Vida"	Iron Butterfly	Album: *In-A-Gadda-Da-Vida*
1968	"Time of the Season"	The Zombies	Album: *Odessey and Oracle*
1969	"Spirit in the Sky"	Norman Greenbaum	Album: *Spirit in the Sky*
1969	"Sweet Caroline"	Neil Diamond	Single
1969	"Does Anybody Really Know What Time It Is?"	Chicago	Album: *Chicago Transit Authority*
1969	*The Left Hand of Darkness*	Ursula K. Le Guin	"Light is the left hand of darkness, and darkness the right hand of light." New York: Harper & Row, 1980. p. 164.
1971	"Here Comes That Rainy Day Feeling Again"	The Fortunes	Album: *Here Comes That Rainy Day Feeling Again*
1971	"Ain't No Sunshine"	Bill Withers	Album: *Just As I Am*
1971	*Willy Wonka & The Chocolate Factory*		Film directed by Mel Stuart
1972	"I Can See Clearly Now"	Johnny Nash	Album: *I Can See Clearly Now*
1972	*Invisible Cities (Le città invisibili)*	Italo Calvino	Translated from the Italian by William Weaver. (1974) New York: Harcourt Brave Jovanovich, 1978. "Cities & Names 1." p. 69.

1973	*The Trouble With Being Born (De l'inconvénient d'être né)*	E. M. Cioran	Translated from French by Richard Howard, 2012.
1973	*The Princess Bride*	William Goldman	
1973	*The Exorcist*		Film directed by William Friedkin
1974	*Obedience to Authority: An Experimental View*	Stanley Milgram	
1974	*Dhalgren*	Samuel R. Delany	
1975	"Bohemian Rhapsody"	Queen	Album: *A Night at the Opera*
1975	"Waterfall"	Cris Williamson	Album: *The Changer and the Changed*
1975	*Wheel of Fortune*		Game show. First episode aired 1975.
1975	*Monty Python and the Holy Grail*		Film directed by Terry Jones and Terry Gilliam
1975	*Jaws*		Film directed by Steven Spielberg
1976	*Too Loud a Solitude (Příliš hlučná samota)*	Bohumil Hrabal	Translated from Czech by Michael Henry Heim. Abacus (Little, Brown Book Group), 1990. "I am a jug filled with water both magic and plain." (p. 1) "…ruminate on *progressus ad* futurum meeting *regressus ad originem* for relaxation…" (p. 48) "While I was on my fourth mug of beer…" (pp. 32–33) "…Jesus as *progressus ad futurum*, Lao-tze as *regressus ad originem*." (p. 40)

1976	"Heaven Must Be Missing An Angel"	Tavares	Album: *Sky High!*
1977	*House (Hausu)*		Film directed by Nobuhiko Obayashi
1977	*Yo maté a Kennedy*	Manuel Vázquez Montalbán	
1977	*La hora de la estrella (A hora da estrela)*	Clarice Lispector	Translated from Portuguese to Spanish by Gonzalo Aguilar. Ediciones Corregidor, 2015. "Le parecía que había cometido un crimen [al comer gato frito sin saberlo] y que había comido ángel frito, las alas crujiendo entre los dientes. Ella creía en ánge-les y, porque creía, ellos existían." p. 49.
1978	*The Sea, The Sea*	Iris Murdoch	Charles Arrowby is a character.
1979	*Gödel, Escher, Bach: An Eternal Golden Braid*	Douglas R. Hofstadter	New York: Vintage Books, 1980. p. 37.
1979	"The Secret Life of Plants"	Stevie Wonder	Album: *Journey Through 'The Secret Life of Plants'*
1979	*Kindred*	Octavia Butler	
1979	*Hitchhiker's Guide to the Galaxy*	Douglas Adams	The first book in the series by the same name.
1979	*Time After Time*		Film directed by Nicholas Meyer
1980	*The Shining*		Film directed by Stanley Kubrick
1980	"Dancing With Myself"	Generation X	Single

1980	*The Centaur in the Garden (O centauro no jardin)*	Moacyr Scliar	Translated from Portuguese to English by Margaret A. Neves. University of Wisconsin Press, 2003.
1982	"Africa"	Toto	Album: *Toto IV*
1982	"Eye in the Sky"	Alan Parsons Project	Album: *Eye in the Sky*
1982	"1999"	Prince	Album: *1999*
1982	*The Dark Crystal*		Film directed by Jim Henson and Frank Oz
1983	*Reading Rainbow*		Television program hosted by LeVar Burton, 1983–2006
1983	*Christine*	Stephen King	
1983	"Los dinosaurios"	Charly García	Album: *Clics modernos*
1983	"Eyes Without a Face"	Billy Idol	Album: *Rebel Yell*
1983	"Suddenly Last Summer"	The Motels	Album: *Little Robbers*
1983	"Hold Me Now"	Thompson Twins	Album: *Into the Gap*
1983	"Every Breath You Take"	The Police	Album: *Synchronicity*

1984	*Metafiction: The Theory and Practice of Self-conscious Fiction*	Patricia Waugh	Her famously quoted sentence is: "Metafiction is a term given to fictional writing which self-consciously and systematically draws attention to its status as an artifact in order to pose questions about the relationship between fiction and reality."
1984	*Ghostbusters*		Film directed by Ivan Reitman
1984	"Time Machine"	Barbra Streisand	Album: *Emotion*
1985	"Don't You (Forget About Me)"	Simple Minds	Single
1985	*A Chorus Line*		Film directed by Marvin Hamlisch
1985	Academy Awards acceptance speech	Sally Field	She accepted the Oscar for Best Actress.
1986	*Labyrinth*		Film directed by Jim Henson
1986	"Wild Geese"	Mary Oliver	First line: "You do not have to be good." Printed in *Dream Work*.
1987	"It's the End of the World as We Know It (And I Feel Fine)"	R.E.M.	Album: *Document*
1987	"Nothing's Gonna Stop Us Now"	Starship	Album: *No Protection*
1988	"The Other End (of the Telescope)"	Elvis Costello and the Attractions	

1988	"Get Outta My Dreams, Get into My Car"	Billy Ocean	Single
1988	"Kokomo"	Beach Boys	Single (from the film *Cocktail*)
1989	"We Could Be Together"	Debbie Gibson	Single
1989	"El final"	Rostros Ocultos	Single
1990	*Middle Passage*	Charles Johnson	
1990	*The Journalist and the Murderer*	Janet Malcolm	New York: Vintage, 1990. "…he is confronted with the same mortifying spectacle of himself flunking a test of character he did not know he was taking." p. 5.
1990	*Jurassic Park*	Michael Crichton	
1991	"Walking in Memphis"	Marc Cohn	
1991	"Hechizo"	Ana Gabriel	Album: *Mi México*

1991	*Workings of the Spirit: The Poetics of Afro-American Women's Writing*	Houston A. Baker	"Africans uprooted from ancestral soil, stripped of material culture and victimized by the brutal contact with various European nations were compelled not only to maintain their cultural heritage at a *meta* (as opposed to material) level but also to apprehend the operative metaphysics of various alien cultures…A concern for metalevels, rather than tangible products, is also a founding condition of Afro-American intellectual discourse." Chicago: University of Chicago Press, 1991, p. 38. Quoted by Madelyn Jablon in the introduction to *Black Metafiction* (1997), pp. 6–7.
1992	"Runaway Train"	Soul Asylum	Album: *Grave Dancers Union*
1992	"Angel"	Jon Secada	Album: *Jon Secada* (English) and *Otro Día Más Sin Verte* (Spanish)
1992	"It's Gonna Be A Lovely Day"	S.O.U.L. S.Y.S.T.E.M.	Single
1992	"Happy Phantom"	Tori Amos	Album: *Little Earthquakes*
1992	*Wayne's World*		Film directed by Penelope Spheeris
1992	*In an Antique Land: History in the Guise of a Traveler's Tale*	Amitav Ghosh	New York: Vintage, 1994. p. 61.
1993	"Rain"	Madonna	Album: *Erotica*
1993	"If I Ever Lose My Faith in You"	Sting	Album: *Ten Summoner's Tales*
1993	*Legends of the Hidden Temple*		Game show on Nickelodeon, 1993–1995. Created by David G. Stanley, Scott A. Stone, and Stephen Brown.

1993	"El Ruletista" ("Ruletistul")	Mircea Cărtărescu	Translated from Romanian to Spanish by Marian Ochoa de Eribe. In *Nostalgia*. Impedimenta, 2012.
1993	"Nobel Lecture"	Toni Morrison	Lecture for the Nobel Prize in Literature, December 7, 1993.
1993	*Groundhog Day*		Film directed by Harold Ramis
1994	"Kiss from a Rose"	Seal	Album: *Seal*
1994	*The Sixth Finger*	Malayatoor Ramakrish-nan	Translated from Malayalam by Prema Jayakumar (2017)
1995	"The World I Know"	Collective Soul	Album: *Collective Soul*
1995	"Sunday Morning Yellow Sky"	October Project	Album: *Falling Farther In*
1996	"Follow You Down"	Gin Blossoms	Album: *Congratulations I'm Sorry*
1997	*Black Metafiction: Self-Consciousness in African American Literature*	Madelyn Jablon	Iowa City: University of Iowa Press, 1997. "Metafiction is a by-product of the contemporary writer's dialogue with literary predecessors." Introduction, p. 4.
1997	*The God of Small Things*	Arundhati Roy	"History walking the dog" is the final sentence of Chapter 14.
1997	*Underworld*	Don DeLillo	New York: Scribner, 1997. Regarding "dot theory": pp. 175, 177.

1997	*The Diving Bell and the Butterfly (Le Scaphandre et le Papillon)*	Jean-Dominique Bauby	Translated from French by Jeremy Leggatt. New York: Alfred A. Knopf: 1997. "The streets were decked out in summer finery, but for me it was still winter, and what I saw through the ambulance windows was just a movie background. Filmmakers call the process a 'rear-screen projection,' with the hero's car speeding along a road that unrolls behind him on a studio wall." p. 78.
1998	*The Truman Show*		Film directed by Andy Weir
1998	"Sleep the Clock Around"	Belle and Sebastian	Album: *The Boy with the Arab Strap*
1999	*The Matrix*		Film directed by the Wachowski Sisters
1999	*The Blair Witch Project*		Film directed by Eduardo Sánchez and Daniel Myrick
2000	*The Book of Ceremonies: A Native Way of Honoring and Living the Sacred*	Gabriel Horn	
2001	"The Car Talk guys, Tom & Ray Magliozzi, talk with Terry about their first garage and more"	Terry Gross	*Fresh Air*, April 4, 2001
2001	"Turn the Radio Up"	Barry Manilow	Album: *Here at the Mayflower*
2001	*Life of Pi*	Yann Martel	

2001	*American Gods*	Neil Gaiman	"People believe, thought Shadow. It's what people do. They believe. And then they will not take responsibility for their beliefs; they conjure things, and do not trust the conjurations." New York: William Morrow, 2001. p. 418.
2001	*The Future of Nostalgia*	Svetlana Boym	
2002	*Star Wars, Episode II: Attack of the Clones*		Film directed by George Lucas
2002	*The Ring*		Film directed by Gore Verbinski
2002	*Salvaged Pages: Young Writers' Diaries of the Holocaust*	Alexandra Zapruder	
2003	"Jesus Plus Nothing: Undercover among America's secret theocrats"	Jeff Sharlet	*Harper's Magazine,* March 2003
2003	"Are We Living in a Computer Simulation?"	Nick Bostrom	*The Philosophical Quarterly,* Vol. 53, Issue 211, April 2003, pp. 243–255.
2003	"Little Britain"		Sketch comedy, televised 2003–2007
2003	*Evil: An Investigation*	Lance Morrow	New York: Basic Books, 2003. p. 96.
2004	*The Will to Change: Men, Masculinity, and Love*	bell hooks	

2004	"Make It Rain"	Tom Waits	Album: *Real Gone*
2005	*Blink*	Malcolm Gladwell	
2005	*In a Queer Time and Place: Transgender Bodies, Subcultural Lives*	Jack Halberstam	
2005	"We Will Become Silhouettes"	The Postal Service	Single
2006	"Stop This Train"	John Mayer	Album: *Continuum*
2006	"Falling Awake"	Gary Jules	Album: *Gary Jules*
2006	*About Time: Narrative Fiction and the Philosophy of Time*	Mark Currie	Edinburgh University Press, 2006. Chapter: "Prolepsis." p. 41.
2007	"Intervention"	Arcade Fire	Album: *Neon Bible*
2007	*The Empire of Neomemory (El imperio de la neomemoria)*	Heriberto Yépez	Originally published by Almadía. Translated from Spanish by Jen Hofer, Christian Nagler, & Brian Whitener. ChainLinks, 2013.
2008	"Imitation and Gender Insubordination"	Judith Butler	Chapter in *The New Social Theory Reader*, 2nd ed.
2008	"No Future Part I"	Titus Andronicus	Album: *The Airing of Grievances*
2009	*Transcendence*	Gabriel Horn & Amy Krout-Horn	

2010	*Ch'ixinakax utxiwa: Una reflexión sobre prácticas y discursos descolonizadores*	Silvia Rivera Cusicanqui	"…es un color producto de la yuxtaposición…" Buenos Aires: Tinta Limón, 2010. p. 69.
2010	*Reality Hunger: A Manifesto*	David Shields	Sections 5, 77, 210, 326, 432, 449. He is quoting: 5: Roland Barthes, *Barthes by Barthes*, and the parenthetical comment "minus the novel" is from Michael Dirda, "Whispers in the Darkness," *Washington Post*. 77: Robert Greenwald, "Brave New Medium," *Nation*. 326: Lorrie Moore, *Self-Help*. 210, 432, 449: These are his own words.
2010	*How to Talk About Books You Haven't Read (Comment parler des livres que l'on n'a pas lus?)*	Pierre Bayard	Translated from French by Jeffrey Mehlman.
2011	*Noon*	Aatish Taseer	"Even your Time is in English." New York: Faber and Faber, 2011. p. 210.
2011	*11/22/63*	Stephen King	
2011	*Vagabunda Bogotá*	Luis Carlos Barragán	Chapter: "Medallo – Metrallo."
2011	*Leaving the Atocha Station*	Ben Lerner	
2012	*Phoebe and Her Unicorn*	Dana Simpson	Webcomic launched 2012.
2013	"Instant Crush"	Daft Punk	Album: *Random Access Memories*

2013	*Tenth of December*	George Saunders	
2013	*Who Owns the Future?*	Jaron Lanier	New York: Simon and Schuster, 2014. p. 134.
2013	*The Stanley Parable*	Davey Wreden and William Pugh, writers	Video game released by Galactic Cafe
2014	*Colorless Tsukuru Tazaki and His Years of Pilgrimage*	Haruki Murakami	
2014	*Redefining Realness: My Path to Womanhood, Identity, Love & So Much More*	Janet Mock	
2014	*Knowing What to Do: Vision, Value, and Platonism in Ethics*	Sophie Grace Chappell	
2014	"The Transgender Tipping Point"	Katy Steinmetz	*Time Magazine*, June 9, 2014.
2014	*Mother of a Machine Gun*	Michael J. Seidlinger	Portland, Oregon: Lazy Fascist Press, 2014. pp. 67–68.
2015	*Book of Numbers*	Joshua Cohen	

2015	*Discognition*	Steven Shaviro	"Sentience… is less a matter of cognition than it is one of what I have ventured to call *discognition*… something that disrupts cognition, exceeds the limits of cognition, but also subtends cognition. My working assumption is that fictions and fabulations are basic modes of sentience; and that cognition *per se* is derived from them and cannot exist without them. … constructing and testing scientific hypotheses is not entirely different from constructing fictions and fabulations, and then testing to see whether they work or not, and what consequences follow from them." London: Repeater Books, 2015. pp. 10–11.
2015	*Light in the Dark / Luz en lo oscuro: Rewriting Identity, Spirituality, Reality*	Gloria E. Anzaldúa	ed. Analouise Keating
2015	"Heaven Sent" (*Doctor Who*, Series 9, Episode 11)		Aired November 28, 2015
2015	*Kaili Blues*		Film directed by Bi Gan
2016	*Twenty-Six Seconds: A Personal History of the Zapruder Film*	Alexandra Zapruder	New York: Twelve, 2016. "It's been said that he forgot it…" p. 31. "Then I heard another shot or two, I couldn't say whether it was one or two…" Quoting Abe Zapruder, p. 43. "It takes thirty-five revolutions of the crank to fully wind the camera for filming. …the camera runs uninterrupted for seventy-three seconds, exposing about fifteen feet of film." p. 51.

2016	*Fragments of an Infinite Memory (Fragments d'une mémoire infinie)*	Maël Renouard	Translated from French by Peter Behrman de Sinéty. New York Review of Books, 2021. "My daydream was that the distinction between recorded and unrecorded moments had vanished." Section 1.
2016	*All The Birds in the Sky*	Charlie Jane Anders	
2016	"The Book of How to Live"	R. B. Lemberg	*Beneath Ceaseless Skies.* Issue #209. September 29, 2016.
2016	*God Woke*	Stan Lee	
2016	"No"	Meghan Trainor	Album: *Thank You*
2019	*The Thirteenth Month*	Colin Hamilton	Black Lawrence Press, 2019. "…the past becomes less rigid in its sequencing…" p. 121. "…time allows the trivial and the traumatic to attain equal weight." p. 70.
2019	*Sorting Out the Mixed Economy: The Rise and Fall of Welfare and Developmental States in the Americas*	Amy C. Offner	"…when the Alliance for Progress was born, Ciudad Techo was a shovel-ready project sponsored by an anticommunist government—an ideal object of Cold War aid. The US government quickly approved a loan for construction, and Kennedy himself visited Colombia in 1961 to lay the first brick at the housing project that eventually bore his name. Colombians, who rarely see a US president in the flesh, warmly remembered Kennedy's tour, and in the wake of his assassination, the city renamed the development for him." Princeton & Oxford: Princeton University Press, 2019. p. 89.

2020	"Predictive Fictions: Stories About The Future"	Malka Older	Syllabus for ASU GTD 598 Spring A 2020.
2021	"El pájaro que le picó la lengua a Rodrigo García Barcha, hijo de Gabo"	Carlos Restrepo	*El Tiempo* (Bogotá), el 23 de mayo 2021
2021	*To Climates Unknown*	Arturo Serrano	
2022	*Please Miss: A Heartbreaking Work of Staggering Penis*	Grace Lavery	

Tucker Lieberman is the author of three nonfiction books:

Painting Dragons — Bad Fire — Ten Past Noon

and a bilingual poetry collection recognized as a finalist in the 2020 Grayson Books Poetry Contest and nominated for the 2022 Elgin Award by the Science Fiction and Fantasy Poetry Association:

Enkidu Is Dead and Not Dead / Enkidu está muerto y no lo está

His essay on a horror film appears in *It Came From the Closet* (Feminist Press, 2022). He's contributed to three anthologies recognized by Lambda Literary: *Balancing on the Mechitza* (North Atlantic Books, 2011 Lambda winner), *Letters For My Brothers* (Wilgefortis, 2012 Lambda finalist), and *Trans-Galactic Bike Ride* (Microcosm, 2021 Lambda finalist). His flash fiction was recognized in the 2019 *STORGY Magazine* Flash Fiction Competition.

He reviews indie press books for Independent Book Review, reads nonfiction for Split/Lip Press, and manages the Twitter for the ad-hoc Lockdown Literature, a group for authors whose 2020 book launches were disrupted by pandemic quarantines.

He changed his sex when the internet was dial-up. For a decade, he worked for an investment company. Investments are a function of money and time. Now, he works for an app that enables two people who might not otherwise be talking to each other to discuss a shared calendar. Calendars help us travel through time so we can be somewhere else tomorrow. He has fallen arches, heel spurs, and an imaginary left hip, and he has run a half-marathon and walked on fire. He is past forty.

Long ago, he studied philosophy at Brown University and journalism at Boston University. He did this book's layout in Microsoft Word, without Clippy, as it's the only program he knows.

His husband is the science fiction writer Arturo Serrano, author of *To Climates Unknown* (2021) and Hugo-longlisted fan writer for the Hugo-winning blog *nerds of a feather, flock together.* They live in Bogotá, Colombia.

TUCKERLIEBERMAN.COM

ABOUT THE COVER ARTIST

Cel La Flaca is a tri racial trans illustrator who works in feature and television animation. He resides in Los Angeles with his loving partner and Brussels Griffon.

CELLAFLACA.SPACE

ABOUT THE INTERIOR ART

Wrong answers on Tele-Quiz by Arturo Serrano.
All other interior art by Tucker Lieberman.

ABOUT THE PUBLISHER

Our niche is no niche! tRaum Books is a tiny queer press particularly drawn to unusual narratives, meta-tales—the absurd, the unpredictable, the magical and the grotesque. We do believe printed books provide a special experience that we strive to preserve and are happy to take on projects where the physical form is just as unorthodox as the story it tells…

TRAUMBOOKS.COM

A SPECIAL THANK YOU

Tiny press is a labor of love
so we'd like to extend a warm thank you to the following people
for making this book possible:

Dermitzel
Brak
Clacks
Jun Nozaki
Leon Sorensen
Agnes Merey
Gele Croom
Philip O'Loughlin
Steven Askew
Lachelle Seville

CPSIA information can be obtained
at www.ICGtesting.com
Printed in the USA
LVHW011052021022
729766LV00008B/626